AFTER *the* SIREN

Darcy Green has been writing and reading queer stories since their LiveJournal days. They lived in Adelaide, Sydney, Canberra and Oxford before settling in Melbourne with their wife and two very spoiled rabbits. When they are not working or writing, Darcy can be found playing ice hockey, gaming, or planning elaborate sewing projects.

AFTER

the

SIREN

Darcy Green

PENGUIN BOOKS

UK | USA | Canada | Ireland | Australia
India | New Zealand | South Africa | China

Penguin Books is part of the Penguin Random House group of companies
whose addresses can be found at global.penguinrandomhouse.com

First published by Penguin Books, 2025

Copyright © Darcy Green, 2025

The moral right of the author has been asserted.

All rights reserved. No part of this publication may be reproduced, published, performed
in public or communicated to the public in any form or by any means without prior written
permission from Penguin Random House Australia Pty Ltd or its authorised licensees.

Penguin Random House values and supports copyright. Copyright fuels creativity,
encourages diverse voices, promotes free speech and creates a vibrant culture. Thank you
for buying an authorised edition of this book and for complying with copyright laws by
not reproducing, scanning or distributing any parts of it in any form without permission.
You are supporting writers and allowing Penguin Random House to continue to publish
books for every reader. Please note that no part of this book may be used or reproduced
in any manner for the purpose of training artificial intelligence technologies or systems.

Cover image and design by Jessica Cruickshank © Penguin Random House Australia Pty Ltd
Typeset in Sabon by Midland Typesetters, Australia

Printed and bound in Australia by Griffin Press, an accredited
ISO AS/NZS 14001 Environmental Management Systems printer

A catalogue record for this
book is available from the
National Library of Australia

ISBN 978 1 76135 525 7

penguin.com.au

*We at Penguin Random House Australia acknowledge that Aboriginal and Torres Strait
Islander peoples are the Traditional Custodians and the first storytellers of the lands on
which we live and work. We honour Aboriginal and Torres Strait Islander peoples'
continuous connection to Country, waters, skies and communities. We celebrate
Aboriginal and Torres Strait Islander stories, traditions and living cultures,
and we pay our respects to Elders past and present.*

*This book is for all the queer stories I found a home in,
before I knew I was looking for one.*

Content Warning

One of the characters in this book experiences symptoms of anxiety and depression, including panic attacks, and there are references to a previous incident of self-harm. Another character is dealing with a parent being treated for a potentially terminal illness with an uncertain prognosis. There are infrequent instances of homophobic language.

Chapter One

'That's not *Spirited Away*.'

Theo jumped and banged the space bar. He'd been so focused on the video that he hadn't heard Priya's footsteps in the hall. On the screen, his own pixellated face froze in an expression of intense anxiety. Things were about to get much worse, but video Theo didn't know that. Lucky him.

Theo shoved his laptop back onto the coffee table and turned towards the door. Priya was leaning against the doorframe with a bowl of guacamole under one arm and a quizzical look on her face.

She tipped her head towards the screen. 'What are you watching?'

He tried for a winning smile. 'Would you believe it was an ad?'

'That smile doesn't work on me.'

She crossed the room and leaned over the back of the couch to rest her chin on his shoulder, imperilling the guacamole.

'Top Five AFL Fails,' she read off the screen.

'I'm number one.' Theo rescued the bowl and deposited it on the coffee table next to the knafeh. 'It's nice to be on top.'

Priya pressed a friendly kiss to his cheek and hurdled the back of the couch to thump down beside him.

'Talk to me.'

She shoved a couple of cushions against the arm of the couch and curled up, tucking her bare feet against Theo's thigh. Her toenails were bright pink. So were Theo's – one of the day's activities had been pedicures. God knows what his new teammates were going to think about that.

They'd both been pretending that Priya was visiting with no ulterior motive; a casual trip from Sydney to Melbourne to see how Theo was settling in. She'd curated three days of activities that she'd characterised as celebratory ('It's not every day you sign a new contract!'), but that, in fact, had been a precautionary measure to keep him from brooding. It had worked quite well until he'd been left unsupervised with his laptop and burgeoning existential dread.

She nudged his thigh with her foot. 'Talk.'

'You've suffered enough in this cause.'

'Don't be silly.' She nudged him again. 'If we don't talk about it, I'll know you're thinking about it, and I won't be able to enjoy my Miyazaki. I'll suffer *more*.'

Priya had decided that Sunday would culminate in Ghibli movies – a tradition carried over from their school days. She was a couple of years older than Theo, but their friendship had been forged in the fires of high-school debating, and tempered by a shared appreciation of niche pop culture and frustration with white boys from Vaucluse. Now she was a barrister, and he was . . . well . . . a footballer. Just.

Theo ran a hand through his hair. 'It's stupid.'

'I doubt it.' She fixed him with a look that meant evasion was futile.

'I feel like . . . if I watch it enough, and if I learn from it, I can stop it from happening again.' He heard his own voice catch, and he swallowed. 'It just – it can't happen again.'

Priya looked away and reached for a tortilla chip. 'You've

never really talked to me about it.' He could tell that she was picking her words carefully. 'About what it was like on the day.'

Theo gathered his thoughts while she coaxed an alarming amount of guacamole onto the chip. He'd spent a lot of time trying not to think about what it had been like. But Priya was unlikely to be deterred. And perhaps he did need to talk about it.

They'd talked about a lot of things, after. What he wanted to do. What he was going to do. What his parents thought he should do. Where he should live. Whether a Law degree was the right choice. But he'd never talked to her about those few minutes; the few minutes that floated to the front of his mind every time he had an idle moment.

He sighed, letting his eyes rest on his own face on the screen. 'You know why it was a big moment, yeah?'

Priya nodded, crunching the corn chip. She was absolutely uninterested in sport of any kind, except insofar as it directly affected Theo's wellbeing. 'Big game, scores level, you needed a win to progress.'

Theo took a steadying breath. It was stupid that it still bothered him this much. That his heart rate picked up just thinking about it: the roar of the crowd, the feel of the ball in his hands, the coppery rasp of his breath in the back of his throat.

He closed his eyes for a moment. 'I couldn't . . . I couldn't catch my breath. I don't know. It's hard to describe. I took the mark and then when I got up, I couldn't breathe. All I could hear was my heart beating. I kept thinking *breathe*, but I couldn't get enough air. And the crowd – you have no idea how loud it was – I couldn't shut it out like I usually can.' Priya's shoulder was solid and reassuring against his. 'I'd been running really hard, but it wasn't that. And my hands were shaking. That'd never happened before either. I think . . . I think I had a panic attack.'

He'd talked about that part with a psychologist, because Priya had basically dragged him bodily to see one. He hadn't had the energy to fight back, so he'd stared at a potted plant in a beige room while a woman with a kind face and knowing dark eyes had gently coaxed him towards phrases like *panic attack* and *burnout* and *generalised anxiety disorder with low mood*. She'd talked about tools and management, but he hadn't booked another appointment. No amount of guided meditation was going to un-fuck his career.

Priya made a thoughtful noise. 'Shall I play it?'

He nodded.

She leaned forward and tapped the space bar. The clip sprang back to life.

Round 23, Sharks versus Falcons. The game to decide who would make the eight. Scores level. Twenty seconds to go. A mark thirty metres out from goal. It had happened so fast, he hadn't realised the ball was in his hands until he'd hit the ground. No time to play on, no time to do anything but go back and line up the shot. He could have recited the commentary off by heart.

What a moment for this young man.

Twenty seconds. Mouthguard. Laces. Walk back.

Thirty metres out and almost directly in front. The atmosphere down here is electric.

Siren.

A shot after the siren for Bestavros. And this could really be a moment of redemption, couldn't it?

Breathe. Spin the ball. Breathe. Look up. Breathe.

It could be – all is forgiven if he gets this through. And he'd have to try pretty hard to miss from here. All they need is a point. You'd want a goal, in his position, but a point would do it.

One step back. Three steps. Five steps. Ten steps. Fifteen seconds gone already.

He's taking his time. Trying to find that composure. What a chance to make up for a disappointing season and repay the Sharks for taking a chance on him.

Breathe. Spin the ball. Breathe.

You could hear a pin drop.

He'd known before the ball left his boot that it was wrong. All wrong. He watched it and felt it at the same time: the awkward connection between his laces and the leather, the thud as the ball cannoned into the chest of the defender. The incredulous roar of the crowd.

And he's kicked it straight into the man on the mark! Absolutely extraordinary. He'll be taking a good hard look at himself in the mirror tonight. What a cracking victory for the Falcons – and a real shocker from Bestavros. You'd think his days are numbered now.

Yeah, it's a pity. Sometimes these players who dominate at the State level just don't have what it takes. A gamble for the Sharks that didn't pay off.

Theo let his breath go as the footage cut to the Falcons celebrating. Video Theo was still in the same place, other players eddying around him. He shied away from remembering the rest of it – his own nails digging rusty divots into his palms as he tried to stop his hands from shaking, the cold sweat in his eyes, the nausea creeping up his throat as he walked back to the race. A thump on the back or a squeeze on the shoulder from a teammate.

He and Priya continued watching as Jake Cunningham, Falcons fan-favourite and pest-in-chief, bounded up to Theo and held up his hand for a high five. Theo shook his head. Jake said something, then shrugged and jogged backwards, blowing Theo a kiss.

Theo realised he'd clenched his fists in his lap. *What a dick.* Even Aleksandar Yelich, the Falcons captain, had thought Jake's antics had been a bit much – he'd said, 'Sorry about him,' as he'd clasped Theo's hand. And then, 'Bad luck, happens to everyone,' with a tilt of his head towards the goals.

'Who's that?' One of Priya's glossy mauve fingernails tapped Jake's face on the screen.

'Jake Cunningham.' His new *teammate*. Oh *joy*.

'What did he say to you?'

'"Thanks for that, mate, couldn't have done it without you."' Theo tried to unclench his jaw.

'So . . . he's not going to be your new best friend?' There was a note of laughter in Priya's voice that almost made him smile in return. But it was probably going to be another couple of decades before he found the whole thing funny.

'Probably not.'

'Seems like a dick.'

'Google him.'

Priya snatched up her phone. On the laptop screen, the countdown to the next video had started. Theo closed the tab before Priya could see what it was. He hadn't shown any of his friends the *Full Forward* skit that had aired a couple of days after that game. Priya would have blown her top, and he hadn't had the energy for that. He still didn't.

There'd been a time when Theo thought *The Footy Show* was the peak of poor taste in football media. He'd been wrong. *Full Forward* was the Gen-Z version, just with even fewer boundaries and in even poorer taste because it was on YouTube rather than broadcast television. The hosts were all men, all white and all douchebags. They had a segment called 'Woke Wednesday', where they heaped scorn on things like women who played professional football being paid a liveable income. But because it was footy, a bit of garden-variety misogyny, racism and homophobia hadn't stopped them from being accepted as part of the discourse.

Occasionally, when they were punching up, they were quite funny. Unfortunately, they preferred to punch down.

Theo had watched the skit innumerable times, like pressing down on a bruise to see which angle hurt the most. They hadn't put the host who played him in brownface – nice to know that there were some limits – but they'd also turned the fact they couldn't do that into a joke. He'd thought the ache of it would fade with time, but it hadn't, not really. The feeling had just become familiar.

The other feature of that episode of *Full Forward* had been an interview with none other than Jake Cunningham, sprawled on a couch in the studio with a baseball cap on backwards, drinking a vibrant purple bubble tea through a straw so large it looked a bit obscene.

The host had asked him about kicking goals under high stress and he'd said, looking into the camera with those shockingly blue eyes, 'It's a lot of pressure. Some people just aren't cut out for it.' Then they'd showed a compilation of all the times Cunningham had managed to handle the pressure: quick snaps, game-changing set shots. Celebrations before the ball had even gone through.

Theo was not a violent person, but he had occasionally contemplated what it would feel like to 'accidentally' elbow Jake Cunningham in his stupid fucking face.

Theo knew exactly when Priya hit the bewildering array of content that emerged if you googled Jake Cunningham and scrolled a bit, because she whistled softly between her teeth. Not that he'd ever indulged in an orgy of rage-fuelled internet stalking.

'Okay, Instagram first,' she said. Her eyebrows shot up. 'His overall aesthetic is very . . . *Home and Away*, but if it was directed by Lil Nas X.'

That took a moment to parse. 'You're not wrong.'

Priya, now wholly consumed by Jake's Insta, turned the phone to show Theo a post. 'I find this very confusing. Sexually.'

Priya's taste ran to butch women with sleeve tattoos but, as she often reminded him, you could appreciate art without wanting to touch it.

The caption on the post announced: *Thx @nakedmelbourne this was fun.*

The first photo was of a mud-splattered and dishevelled Jake sitting on a bench wearing nothing but socks and a pair of sneakers in a melange of pastel colours. The football in his right hand was preserving what remained of his modesty. He was looking straight at the camera, his tousled hair falling into his eyes. Just to remove any shred of doubt that this was a sexy product for sexy people, he was biting his left thumb, his lips quirked in a half smile.

Theo hoped he'd gotten dirt in his mouth.

'He's . . . very attractive.' Priya's eyes were still glued to the screen. 'What is Naked Melbourne? Is it an exhibition? Can we go and see it?'

'It's a brand of sneakers. You'll see the creative team took the flying leap from "naked" to "naked".'

Priya swiped through the photos. 'I do see.' She flipped the phone towards him again. 'I think this violates community standards.'

Jake was sprawled in the mud in only socks and footy boots. A sneaker adorning a toned leg was planted in the middle of his chest. The camera angle ensured that the image didn't break any rules. The text emblazoned across the photo read: **for every play.**

'It has certainly violated my eyes,' Theo agreed.

Priya gave him a look. And okay, yes, he had to concede that Jake Cunningham was hot. There were definitely circumstances – the sort of circumstances where Theo wasn't a footballer and Jake Cunningham wasn't an arrogant little toerag – where Theo wouldn't have minded seeing those abs. And those thighs. And that look.

'Are the sneakers any good?' Priya asked.

'Oh, they're great, I have several pairs. Wear them daily.'

Priya stuck her tongue out at him.

Theo held out his hand for the phone. 'If you're going to look at his TikTok as well, we won't have time for any Miyazaki.'

'I'll save that for later.'

Priya unfolded herself from the couch and occupied herself with the HDMI cord. She handed the phone to Theo and he flicked through Jake's Instagram, only half concentrating. It wasn't the type of content that required many active brain cells.

But the chat had shaken something loose in his chest.

'Do you think I've made a mistake?'

The words were out before he could stop them.

Asking Priya that sort of question was always a risk. She knew him too well and was much too honest. He'd signed the contract with the Falcons before he'd talked to her about it. Well, before he'd talked to anyone about it. Eva – his older sister, current housemate and unofficial legal advisor – had given him an absolute shellacking for signing a contract she hadn't subjected to meticulous review. But he hadn't wanted pragmatism or common sense from either of them.

It had been Priya, though, who'd answered the phone at 11 pm and driven him to the ER six weeks after his last match with the Sharks. It had been Priya who, when he'd croaked out, 'I did something stupid,' had immediately said, 'Where are you?' Priya who'd had the spare key to his parents' house and had come in to get him when he hadn't come out. Priya who'd sat with him all night under the fluorescent lights, breathing in antiseptic and listening to podcasts with one AirPod each, even though she'd hated hospitals since she was twelve. Who'd only left him twice: once to go and scour the vending machines for a Twix and once to find a 7-Eleven to get them terrible, scalding coffee and a handful of sachets of brown sugar. Priya who, when he'd been discharged at 5 am, had driven him to Bronte Beach and walked beside him in the freezing surf under the rose-gold spring sky while the salt water soaked her rolled-up pyjama bottoms.

She looked up.

'No, I don't think you've made a mistake.'

'Why? Why was *this* the right call?'

She regarded him steadily. 'You should know the answer to that.'

'Humour me.'

'You didn't tell anyone about the offer because you thought we'd try to talk you out of it. That means you wanted it.'

It had been more than that. It had felt like it might vanish if he'd told anyone, dissolve in his hands. That didn't feel like a *why*, though. The offer had come almost out of the blue. He'd been waiting to be delisted, ready to enrol full-time at uni. Then there'd been Kat Lloyd's soft, matter-of-fact voice over the phone. Sure, he was steak knives, but a second chance was a second chance.

Priya abandoned whatever it was she was doing with the HDMI cable but stayed kneeling next to the table.

'You remember that game I came to watch?'

'Your first and last.'

It had been a high-school game: a preliminary final. She'd been roped into coming as part of a gaggle of Theo's debating friends. They'd won the granny the week after; he'd kicked five goals and felt like he'd never come down from the high.

'It was funny seeing you out there. I mean, I knew you very well, but it was like seeing a different person. Or . . .' She paused. 'Not a different person. It was like seeing you be yourself in a way I'd never seen before.' She busied herself rearranging the snacks. 'It was weird, too – you're the furthest from a bossy person, but you were just so in command. You know how I feel about sports. I had no idea what was going on. But any time the ball came near you, you were gesturing and shouting, and the other players just did what you said. You snapped your fingers and all of these lads who would never have spoken to us in a hundred years at school were falling over themselves to get the ball to you.' She grinned at him. 'The significance of you having the ball was mostly lost on me, but it was impressive. And then you won and I think it was the first time I'd ever seen you look *joyful*.'

He hadn't thought about those junior games for a long time. They'd been swallowed up by week after week of stats and schedules and the creeping realisation that he was fucking it up.

'But I *failed*, Priy.' He hadn't said that to anyone before. Not even on the way to the hospital while she'd laughed at his jokes and kept one hand resting on his. 'I wasn't good enough.'

'Bullshit. If that were true, you wouldn't be here.'

'Single, in a new city, with no friends, living in my sister's guestroom so I can be kept under surveillance?'

He didn't mind living with Eva, even if it did sometimes feel like living with a stranger. Of all his siblings, she was the closest to him in age, but she'd moved out of their parents' house when he was ten. His two eldest siblings, Simon and Alisa, were more like an uncle and an aunt. He loved Eva, but they weren't close. Still, when he'd told her he was moving to Melbourne, she'd offered him the spare room in her two-storey terrace. Right after she'd finished telling him off for signing a legal document she hadn't read.

He'd sworn Eva to secrecy and told her about 'the incident' (as he called it in his mind), because Priya would worry if he hadn't told anyone in Melbourne. Maybe softened some of the details a little. 'I'm on medication now, it's much better.' (It wasn't a *lie*.)

Priya clicked her tongue, disapproving. 'Always chasing something.' She sighed and rocked back on her heels. 'You know I hate being earnest, so just be quiet and let me finish, and then we can go back to being glib and dismissive.'

He nodded obediently.

'Football was the only thing I ever saw you do for yourself. And you cared about it enough to pursue it even when lots of people in your life told you it was stupid. Including me.' Her grin was rueful. 'I know the last two years have been shit. But you wouldn't be getting a second chance if people at the Hawks —'

'Falcons,' he corrected.

'Whatever, they're all scary birds – if the Falcons hadn't seen something in you that they liked. So, you haven't failed.'

'I might, though.'

'Yeah, but at least you haven't just given it up to become a moderately successful lawyer who bores all the grads with stories about how you' – she puffed out her chest and assumed a tortured expression – 'could have been a football star if only you'd taken that deal.'

'Excuse me, I would be a very successful lawyer.'

'Not if you're tormented by thoughts of what might have been. Aren't there some motivational sports quotes about the courage to risk failure that we could stick to your mirror? Being in the arena or some shit?'

'Eva is way ahead of you there. She keeps pointedly leaving books about stress and perfectionism on the coffee table.' He leaned forward to close the YouTube tab. 'Thanks, Priy.'

She reached up and ruffled his hair. 'That's all the earnest you're getting for the year.'

'Noted.'

'And we're watching *Princess Mononoke* first. I've changed my mind.'

'Done.'

'Also, I expect daily updates on your budding bromance with Jake Cunningham.'

'Of course.'

They settled back on the couch. Theo let his breath go as the familiar music chimed.

Priya raised her glass of kombucha as the first scene rippled onto the screen. 'To old friends, and new beginnings.'

'Cheers.'

NOVEMBER / DECEMBER

PRE-SEASON

Fly or flop? Second chance for Bestavros at Brunswick Falcons

After a dismal end to a patchy 18 months at the Sydney Sharks, 24-year-old forward Theodore Bestavros is getting a second chance at the Brunswick Falcons.

Sources inside the club say that new development coach Kat Lloyd (former star Geelong AFLW defender and Hawthorn assistant coach) led the push to recruit Bestavros as part of the deal that saw veteran Falcons defender Jamie Collins move to the Sharks. Bestavros was drafted at age 22 after stand-out performances at the State level but never delivered on that early promise for the Sharks, playing ten uninspiring games at the AFL level before the memorable Round 23 mishap that sealed his fate.

'A distraction': Falcons CEO weighs in on Pride Round debate

Brunswick Falcons CEO Randolph Jones has weighed in on the debate about an AFL Pride Round. LGBTQIA+ supporter groups have been calling for a competition-wide Pride Round, following its success in AFLW. Several players have spoken out in support of the idea, including Falcons captain Aleksandar Yelich and vice-captain Morgan Reyes. Jones was less enthusiastic. 'I worry that these things are becoming a distraction,' he told *Ferret Footy*'s Briony Gallagher. 'The focus needs to be on the footy.'

Five Falcons players to watch (who aren't Jake Cunningham)

Aleksandar Yelich (#3)

Falcons captain Aleksandar 'Yelks' Yelich spent the first six weeks of the 2023 season on the sidelines after a pre-season knee injury. Some people speculated that the All-Australian fullback would hang up his boots – he turned 35 in August – but he's not showing any signs of that. We're betting on a big season for Yelks: after all, he probably doesn't have a heap of them left.

Morgan Reyes (#7)

Morgan 'Raze' Reyes's 2020 move from the Currawongs to the Falcons drew plenty of skepticism. He's proved the doubters wrong, though, quickly establishing himself as exactly the hard-at-it, up-and-under inside midfielder the Falcons needed. Having got on top of his conditioning, we're predicting a huge year in the middle for Raze, who's also joined the Falcons leadership group.

Padraic Riley (#25)

You'd never know from watching Padraic Riley that he only picked up a Sherrin for the first time in 2019. The star Gaelic footballer was recruited by the Falcons from Kilkenny. He's more than repaid the investment: after a bit of a shaky start, Paddy is a dominant force on the halfback flank – and if you're really lucky you'll see him forget where he is for a moment and kick it like he's still playing Gaelic.

Tommy Ryan (#14)

A proud Gunditjmara man, Tommy is the second Ryan to play for the Falcons. His father, Jimmy Ryan, was an integral part of the Falcons in the late 80s and early 90s, and he's now back at the club working on their new inclusion framework. The younger Ryan has the forward craft to match his famous father. He had a rocky start to his AFL career, plagued by a sequence of niggling injuries, but he came good in 2023. He and Cunningham are going to be hard to contain.

Jonathon Xenos (#30)

Johnny 'Xen' Xenos will always have his detractors; some people just can't wrap their head around the idea that a guy who's 5'7" can play at the highest level. But we love an underdog, so we're going to back Xen in for a big year. The ultimate one per-cent player, the stats sheet doesn't reflect the real impact he can have on a game.

aflthirst my body is ready for the @brunswickfalcons pre-season camp. keep the content coming @jcjk9 @jxenos @paddyriley25 @tryan2002

brunswickfalcons The younger players in our squad are gearing up for their pre-season camp. Keep your eyes open for all the latest on our socials. 👀

falconfortnightly we're back baby! tune in for the tea on the collins exit, jake cunningham's saucy off-season antics, and the choice to pick up bestavros from the sharks. beers are cold and the takes are hot. 🍺 🍺

falcons754 replying to @falconfortnightly @katlloyd's first move is bestavros? guess she wont be here for long

matty357 replying to @falcons754 reckon he's learned to kick over the summer?

gofalcons77 replying to @matty357 like @jcjk9 said on @fullforward some ppl just don't have what it takes

Chapter Two

Jake Cunningham was not a punctual person. But he hadn't been late to a footy commitment since under-12s, when his coach had benched him for missing the team bus. Shivering in the rain through four grim quarters had made an impression. As had the 45-minute lecture his mum had delivered in their car on the way to the ground. If it had been anything else, Debbie Cunningham would have refused to give him a lift to teach him a lesson. But football came first.

He'd left himself plenty of time to get to the pre-season camp bus: time to go back for the charger he knew he'd forget, time for the traffic, time to get coffees. Just not time to get rear-ended at the lights by some dickwad in a Porsche Cayenne who was too busy texting to brake.

It wasn't a bad ding, but the dickwad had taken one look at Jake and decided that he could be bullied. So Jake had to waste time while an asshole in an expensive suit (probably? Who fucking knew, all suits looked the same) tried to convince Jake that the accident had been Jake's fault. As though Jake hadn't been stationary at the lights, minding his own business.

On any other day, he would have been pissed about his ute. He *was* pissed about his ute, but he was mainly pissed that he was going to be late. And because he'd already picked up the coffees, he was going to look like an asshole who'd stopped for coffee even when he was late. At least it wasn't his first season. If it had been, he might have had to ditch the coffees.

These last three weeks, the prospect of development camp had been the sunshine at the end of a really shitty tunnel, but this was not a good start.

Because the universe was against him, the radio was also playing a morning interview with Randy Jones, the Falcons CEO, about the topic of the week: Pride Round. That would have been bad enough, but then they'd gotten onto why there weren't any out AFL players.

'Statistically, there must be queer players,' the host was saying. 'So that begs the question, why haven't they come out?'

'Well, Theresa,' Randy said, 'people are entitled to keep their private lives private. Speaking about the Falcons specifically, we pride ourselves on being a welcoming club. I'm sure if we had any gay players, they'd know they could come out if they wanted to.' Jake forced himself to relax his hands on the steering wheel. It wasn't like he hadn't heard it before.

Theresa made a sceptical noise. 'A lot of the queer players in the ALFW have spoken about the homophobic abuse they've received, especially online. Isn't it likely that AFL players would be concerned about the reception?'

Randy chuckled. 'Everyone always has a lot to say online, but our players are used to that type of chatter. No, Theresa, if they wanted to be out, they'd be out.'

Jake's phone started to ring, cutting out the radio so Siri could say 'Johnny heart-emoji drip-emoji leaf-emoji Xenos'.

He hit the bluetooth answer button. 'Yeah?'

'Where are you?' Xen had never been late to anything. First in the rooms, first on the field, usually the last to leave. Xen would have left enough time to get coffee *and* have a minor car accident.

'Some asshole rear-ended me at the lights, I'm ten away.'

'Shit, you good?'

'Yeah.'

'Car okay?'

'Bit banged up, but drivable.'

'I'll tell Kat what happened.' Kat Lloyd was the Falcons' new development coach, and the person who had the authority to tell the bus driver to leave without Jake. She'd also known Jake since he was a toddler, but that just made her less likely to show mercy.

The Falcons senior coach, Jarrod Davies (Davo since his playing days), would come down for a couple of days of camp, but he liked to let the junior coaching staff handle development camp and all the chaos that came with it.

'Xen thought maybe you'd gotten . . . distracted on the way out the door.' Padraic Riley's Irish accent was unmistakable. Jake could imagine him sitting next to Xen on the bus, jostling Xen out of the way to talk into his phone.

'I fucking wish, Paddy.'

Jake and Kyle had been planning to spend the week before camp in Melbourne, before Kyle went back to Canberra. They were going to chill in parks, go for walks, drink coffee. Book a fancy hotel. Be boyfriends. Probably see some pretentious play that Jake wouldn't understand. Have a lot of sex on sheets Jake wouldn't need to worry about washing.

It would have been nice.

'We'll let you drive,' Xen said. 'See you soon.'

'Thanks, bro.'

Jake ended the call and flexed his fingers on the steering wheel. He was going to have to tell Xen and Paddy about the break-up. Soon. He should rip that band-aid off, but he'd always been more of a soak-it-in-water kind of guy.

They'd both been delighted when he and Kyle had started dating. Jake had known Kyle for years – initially as his friend Olly's cool older brother, then as the subject of a crippling crush, then as someone who'd started to pay Jake a lot more attention than he'd expected. Olly and Kyle had lived in a big house in Woolamai with their immaculately dressed parents and the kind of couches you weren't actually supposed to sit on.

Jake caught every possible red light, but managed to swing into his parking space only seven minutes late. He hauled his stuff out of the back seat and headed for the team bus. It wasn't possible to run with two duffel bags, a tray of coffees and a surfboard, but he managed to get up a fast waddle. Kat was leaning against the side as he approached. She pointedly checked her watch, but then she came over to help him with the board.

'Car trouble,' he told her.

'Xenos said. You need to get checked out?'

'Nah, it's all good. He barely hit me.'

'Last time you said that you had three broken ribs.'

Sometimes Kat liked to remind Jake that she'd been there when he first picked up an AFL ball. Sometimes Jake liked to remind her that she'd been his English teacher and coach when he was playing under-14s, so she was old now.

Kat had gone from teaching – where she'd met and hit it off with Jake's mum – to the AFLW's Hawthorn Harriers. The Falcons had poached her from her assistant coaching role there.

'I was fifteen. I was an idiot.'

'And that's changed?' Kat slammed shut the door of the under-bus storage compartment. 'Glad you're alright.' She gave him a friendly bump with her hip. 'Don't want to lose one this early. Bad form. Now get on the bus.'

'Yes, Miss.' Jack snapped a salute and did as he was told.

Xen and Paddy were on the back seat. Jake had met them for

the first time in the same seats on an almost identical bus three years earlier.

'Cutting it fine,' Xen told him, making a swipe for Jake's coffee. He was looking good, his olive skin tanned a couple of shades darker than at the end of the last season and his curly black hair cropped shorter than usual.

Jake jerked the coffee away. 'I got one for you, bro, leave mine alone.' He handed Xen one of the KeepCups.

'Sure you're okay?' Xen was looking at him like he might be concealing a gaping wound.

'I'm good.'

Paddy pulled Jake down onto his lap and wrapped his arms around Jake's waist. 'Missed you.'

Paddy had spent the two months of off-season downtime with his parents and siblings in Kilkenny. He was one of seven children and, as far as Jake could tell, family time consisted of jumping naked into freezing cold water then drinking pints of beer.

The bus driver made a pointed comment over the speaker about seatbelts and Jake slid sideways into a seat of his own. The engine vibrated into life and the bus lurched out into Victoria Street, heading for Sydney Road. Right past the billboard that was going to cause Jake grief all year.

If Jake had gotten his way, Naked Melbourne would not have put up the advertisement featuring him within half a kilometre of the Falcons' training facility. He hadn't, though. He'd gotten a fat cheque, but not his way.

'Like I need to see *that* on my way to work,' Paddy said, pointing. His Irish accent always sounded stronger when he'd been home to see his family.

'You're the one who made me do it.' Jake had been three shots beyond sensible when he'd made the bet, but he'd followed through.

'Can't believe they photoshopped abs onto you. False advertising.'

'Fuck off!'

'Where are they now, then?' Jake squawked as Paddy shoved a hand – a cold hand – up the front of his singlet.

'That's harassment!'

'You love it.'

'Behave, children,' Xen said.

'They put, like, ab make-up on me,' Jake admitted.

Unlike Paddy, who could have been used on advertisements for protein powder or weird supplements, Jake didn't put a whole lot of effort into maintaining a sixpack. His body got the job done, and that was all that mattered.

He did hope that Kyle had to drive past the billboards in Canberra. Often. Just to remind him that he didn't get to come on those abs anymore.

'They stick a banana down your undies too?'

Jake gave him the finger. Xen grabbed Paddy's wrist, presumably worried that he might take the same approach he'd taken to checking Jake's abs.

'No,' Xen told Paddy.

Paddy batted his eyelashes. 'No what?'

'Just no.'

They had, in fact, given Jake a sort of foam cup to shove into his briefs. That had been nice. He was used to being naked in the locker room, but there was being naked in the locker room and then there was people in several major Australian cities knowing what your dick looked like. Turned out he did have some boundaries.

'Good break, though?' Paddy asked, with a suggestive lift of an eyebrow.

Jake hadn't really meant to come out to Xen and Paddy at the end of their first year on the Falcons together. He'd had a firm belief that the appropriate number of teammates to know he wasn't straight was a big fat zero. But then they'd been in Spain in September (no finals run for the Falcons), and one night in Barcelona Paddy had pointed out that a very hot man was leaning against the bar and checking Jake out in a way that was clearly meant to catch his attention.

'Um,' Jake had said.

'Hey, if you're not interested, let me know. I'll have a shot.'

Jake had been silent for longer than he meant to. 'You're . . .'

Paddy had shrugged. 'I don't really do labels.'

'Just sometimes dudes?' Xen had asked.

'I appreciate all the stars in the gender constellation,' Paddy had explained.

Jake had blurted out 'I'm gay' before he'd had time to second-guess himself. Which, let's be real, Xen and Paddy had already guessed. Saying it out loud had felt itchy and vulnerable, but then Xen had pulled him into a one-armed hug and Paddy had held out a fist for him to bump.

'Thanks for telling us,' Xen had said. 'We've got your back.'

'Yeah, this is cute and all,' Paddy had agreed, 'but are you gonna go talk to that guy?'

Jake did. Although after exchanging names, there hadn't actually been a lot of talking.

He should tell Xen and Paddy about breaking up with Kyle. Except he didn't want to tell them on the bus. Later. He'd tell them later. 'You know any of the new people?' he asked instead.

There had been five new names on the camp list. Their new draft picks, whom Jake had met a couple of times through the Falcons development academy. Jason Stevens had come from Perth, Nathan Rigger had done a couple of VFL seasons with the Harriers, and Theo Bestavros came from the Sydney Sharks as part of the trade for Jamie Collins.

Theo Bestavros.

Jake wished he'd never done that stupid fucking interview. *Full Forward* had always been a bit borderline, but he hadn't realised they were going to stick his interview next to a skit that had definitely crossed the boundary into actually racist. He hadn't needed Xen to explain just how problematic it was, but Xen had done so. A number of times, and in detail.

He'd thought about messaging Bestavros about it, but it wasn't as though they were friends – or likely to see each other again. Everyone had known Bestavros was done. Messaging him in order to be told to fuck off had seemed a bit pointless. Except apparently not, because now Bestavros was here, on the team bus, and presumably not ready to plait Jake's hair and make friendship bracelets.

Once they were well underway, and the bus driver had given up telling them all to sit down, Jake made his way down the bus to check in with everyone. It was good to be back.

Bestavros was sitting with Morgan Reyes. Not surprising; Raze was, at heart, a heavily tattooed mother hen. He already had Bestavros smiling.

The smile vanished when Bestavros saw Jake.

Raze returned Jake's fist bump. 'Hey, Jaze.' He turned to Bestavros. 'He's Jaze because we already had a Cunno.'

'And because it's cute that we rhyme,' Jake added.

'Hi,' Bestavros said. He didn't smile.

Bestavros was hot. Jake had known that, theoretically. He'd seen Bestavros on the field, but he didn't register other players as anything more than physics and geometry while he was playing. Angles and momentum. He broke them down into their component parts; pure form and function.

Bestavros was wearing tailored shorts and a cream linen shirt with short sleeves. It was a good look on him. His curly hair was shaved close on the sides, but he'd left it long on top and it was falling forward into his hazel eyes. He wasn't as built as Paddy, but he'd clearly been putting in the work over the off-season. He didn't look particularly touchable, but he did look good.

There was a beat of silence. Was Raze also thinking about the skit? He hadn't said anything about it, but that was probably because everyone knew that Yelks had already pulled Jake aside for one of his chats. Jake would have taken one of his mum's lectures any day over one of Yelks' not-angry-just-disappointed chats.

Jake hesitated. Should he apologise? He should probably apologise. Bestavros was right there, looking at him. Looking at him kind of expectantly. But this didn't seem like the time for an apology. On a bus, in front of Raze. There would be other moments when he could apologise. Or maybe apologising would make it worse.

He shouldn't apologise.

Cunningham hadn't apologised. Theo had been willing to give Cunningham a chance – only one chance, because the arrogant shit didn't deserve more than one – and Cunningham had blown it. He'd said 'hey' to Theo as though he hadn't sat his smug ass down in front of a camera six months ago and laughingly critiqued Theo's probably career-ending performance for the benefit of thirty thousand *Full Forward* subscribers.

The great mystery was why everyone acted as though the sun shone out of Cunningham's ass. He wasn't even *that* good-looking. He had the generic surfer charm that Aussie boys who grew up near the beach all seemed to have in spades; it soaked in with the sunscreen. Theo would have bet every cent in his bank account that Cunningham had spent most of the summer paddling around in the surf with a couple of other identical guys (maybe one brunette for variety). He probably had an equally boring, generically pretty girlfriend. He wasn't special.

What he was, though, was fucking irritating.

Cunningham had been the last to arrive for the bus, rumpled in a way that had to be deliberate. Nobody who wasn't trying could have picked board shorts and a singlet that clashed like that. He'd been late, but that obviously hadn't deterred him from stopping for coffee. And he'd brought a surfboard. To development camp.

Instead of shamefacedly retiring to the back of the bus and shutting the fuck up like a normal person, he seemed determined to remain the absolute centre of attention. He was in perpetual motion up and down the aisle, exchanging jokes and ridiculous handshakes with his teammates, constantly intruding into Theo's peripheral vision. Impossible to ignore. The sunlight sparked off the gold of a fidget ring on his left index finger as he gesticulated.

He hung on to the luggage rack as he chatted to various players, his singlet riding up to expose part of a tattoo on his hip. It hadn't been visible in the Naked sneaker ads – it must have been under a layer of mud. Theo couldn't quite work out what it was, which was even more irritating because then he was just staring at Cunningham's exposed hip.

He texted Priya to let her know they'd clearly touched up Cunningham's abs in the advertisements.

Priya

How have you seen his abs already?

Theo

His shirt rode up

Priya

> Were you making out in the bathroom
> of the bus at the time?

Theo

> This fantasy of yours is not the
> hill you should die on

Cunningham subsided into a seat every time the bus driver growled at him, but never for long. It was like being locked in a room with a very energetic puppy, except that Theo liked puppies.

The only saving grace of the bus ride was Morgan Reyes, who'd glanced around the bus and then dropped into the seat next to Theo. He was almost comically different to how he was on the field. Theo had only played against him once, but his abiding memory of that game was of Reyes, with his sharp undercut and sleeve tattoos, flattening Sharks midfielders like they were made of papier-mâché. Off the field he turned out to be softly spoken, with a ready smile and a laugh that crinkled the corners of his eyes. It was his third year with the Falcons, and he'd given Theo a quick rundown on what to expect.

Johnny Xenos had also given Theo a fist bump on the way past. Theo remembered Xenos – vividly – because it had been Xenos's broad chest that he'd hammered the ball into at the end of that last, awful game for the Sharks. He'd wondered if he'd be ribbed about it, wondered how he was going to pretend those barbs weren't hitting raw skin, but Xenos just gave him a friendly smile and said, 'Good to have you on board,' as though he really meant it. Maybe he did.

Cunningham was obviously tight with Xenos and Riley. The three of them were tactile in a so-homo-there's-no-homo way.

At one point Riley had literally shoved his hand up Cunningham's singlet.

By the time the players had unloaded their luggage in front of the Torquay Athletics Centre, Theo had decided that this was basically school camp. Weird bus trip where no one knew who to sit with: check. At least two or three people who were way too excited: check. At least one person arriving with triple the amount of luggage reasonably required: check. At least one person arriving with significantly less than the amount of luggage reasonably required: check.

He'd never been quite this anxious about school camp, though. The medication helped, but it didn't tamp down the thrumming current of *don't fuck this up, don't fuck this up*, punctuated by the occasional vicious *you're going to fuck this up*.

Kat clambered onto a bench to direct operations. She had a clipboard in one hand and a whistle around her neck. Apparently, players were going to be sharing rooms. Theo assumed the rationale was that it would help them all bond, because the club could definitely afford to give them their own rooms.

Kat's voice cut through the babble of conversation. 'Bestavros and Cunningham, room seven. Bestavros, Cunningham knows where to go.'

Oh *hell* no.

Theo looked across at Cunningham. The smile slipped off Cunningham's face for a moment, replaced by an almost cartoonish look of dismay.

Nice. *Feeling's mutual, dickhead.*

'Riley and Xenos, room eight.' The two exchanged a fist bump.

Theo grabbed his bag and approached Cunningham. He caught the tail end of the conversation between Cunningham, Riley and Xenos.

'Cold, bro,' Cunningham was saying.

'I live with you,' Xenos said. 'You can't blame me.'

'Besides,' Riley added, nudging Jake with his shoulder, 'he likes me best.'

Xenos snorted. 'I wouldn't go that far, but you're definitely more house-trained.'

Great. I bet Cunningham snores. Or smells. Or takes annoyingly long showers.

Cunningham's aviators had slid down to the bridge of his nose. He took them off and hooked them on the neck of his singlet. 'Hey, roomie,' he said as Theo stopped in front of him. Which still definitely wasn't 'sorry'.

'Hi. Kat said you knew the way?'

'I do.' Cunningham swung a duffel bag over each shoulder. He gave Theo's free arm a speculative look. 'Give me a hand with the board?'

Theo couldn't find words for a moment. Then he found 'sure', which wasn't the word he wanted, but was the only sensible option. He hoped Cunningham couldn't hear in his voice that he was gritting his teeth.

'Oval in thirty,' Kat yelled after them.

Theo unzipped his suitcase and extracted the packing cube with his training gear in it. Cunningham had tossed both his duffel bags onto one of the beds (the only one with a bedside lamp, Theo noticed) and vanished into the hallway. The muffled sounds of combat from the room next door suggested he'd gone to visit Riley and Xenos.

The room was pleasant, if a little faded. It was wide enough that there was a decent amount of space between the twin beds, and there was a desk under the window. The navy curtains billowed gently in the sea breeze. Theo changed quickly, pulling on shorts and one of his new training singlets. That done, he flopped back onto the bed and texted Priya to let her know he'd made it. A couple of other friends had messaged. His parents hadn't.

Priya responded within seconds.

Priya

How's it going? Any ab updates?

He sent her a thumbs up. She hated that.

Priya

Sharing a room?

Theo

Yeah. The theory is it helps with team bonding

Priya

Who's your roommate?

Theo

Guess

Priya

😂 not your nemesis?

Theo

Nemesis is a strong word

Priya

Idk seems fitting.

They texted back and forth until the door bounced open and Cunningham re-entered. Was he constitutionally incapable of moving through the world without making it a performance?

'We've got another ten minutes, right?' Cunningham said, unzipping one of the duffel bags.

'Yeah.' *Ten minutes you could use to apologise.*

'Sweet.'

Cunningham pulled off his singlet and shoved his shorts down. He was wearing yellow boxer briefs covered in pink flamingos. He opened the other bag and began excavating the contents, item by item. A couple of lip balms rolled across the floor and Theo stopped one with his foot. Watermelon flavoured.

Cunningham unearthed some shorts and a training singlet. He made a sound of satisfaction, then started tossing individual football boots out of the second bag.

He didn't seem to be in a hurry to put clothes on. Theo got a good look at a tattoo on back of his left thigh: a pelican with a footy in its mouth. It looked like the sort of tattoo you got in the golden haze of a grand-final victory.

Theo decided to take the opportunity to assert entitlement to the desk. Cunningham didn't seem likely to use it for its intended purpose, but it did seem likely that he would spread his shit all over it.

Theo unpacked a couple of Law textbooks, his laptop and a box of stationery. Studying during development camp hadn't been the plan, but the inconvenient thing about a mental-health crisis was that it tended to derail your plans. He'd gotten academic accommodations so he could finish his subjects, but that was going to involve grinding out some assignments over the course of pre-season.

'You studying?' Cunningham asked from behind him, and Theo turned. Cunningham still hadn't put his shorts on. The tattoo on his hip was of a 1950s pin-up-style mermaid.

That tracked.

'Yeah.' He couldn't be rude to Cunningham. The last thing he needed was to get a reputation for being a problem with the other players. But that didn't mean he had to be chatty.

'Cool, what're you doing?'

'Law.'

'Nice.' Cunningham prodded *Introduction to Torts*. 'I thought a tort was a cake.'

He was close enough that Theo could smell his cologne. Or, more likely, his body spray.

Someone banged on the door. 'Come on,' Xenos called, saving Theo from having to reply.

'On our way!' Jake yelled back.

'Bestavros, with me.'

Theo peeled off from the other players – running warm-up drills in groups – and jogged over to Kat. She'd changed into compression tights and a Falcons t-shirt. The muscles in her thighs could have crushed a person's head like a melon.

'Let's jog and talk,' she said, gesturing to the track around the edge of the oval. They fell into an easy pace, skirting the boundary line.

'Don't worry,' she told him. 'I'm going to pull each of the players out for a chat. You're just first in the alphabet.'

'Good to know I'm not in trouble.'

'Have you done anything that you should be in trouble for?'

'Not yet.'

'Just don't fall under Cunningham's malign influence. He loves a prank.'

No danger of that. 'Noted.'

Kat waited until they were out of earshot and passing the

expanse of purple wisteria that coated the side of the gym before she continued. 'I know when we last talked you had good reason to be a bit guarded about your time with the Sharks,' she said. 'But I'd like to hear more about it.'

'Sure.' Theo tried to sound relaxed. Professional.

'How did you find Gary Hunt as a coach?'

'I have a lot of respect for him. He's a very experienced and capable coach.' Theo didn't look across at Kat, although he could see from the corner of his eye that she was looking at him.

'True,' she said. 'But not the answer to my question.'

'Sorry, I might have misunderstood.'

She looked across at him, eyebrows sceptical, but didn't call bullshit. 'Do you feel like his coaching made you a better player?'

Theo watched the aerial acrobatics of a seagull as it circled the goal posts. He and Priya had toasted to new beginnings, but what did that mean? He was here to do a job. Kat didn't know him and he didn't know her; he didn't have any way to gauge the potential cost of honesty. The trade had been her idea (she'd copped it enough in the media for him to be sure of that), so she clearly saw something in him. Was that enough? Except, her first loyalty had to be to the team. She wasn't his friend, or his mentor. She had no reason to cut him any slack.

They jogged on in silence and Theo knew he should answer. Kat spoke again before he'd made up his mind. 'You know, a coach like Gary Hunt nearly made me give up footy.'

'I can't imagine you giving up anything.'

She laughed and nodded towards the cluster of players in the goal square. 'Players like Cunningham and Ryan, if you give them a real tune-up and tell them "this isn't good enough", they'll go out with a fire under their arse to prove you wrong. Because they think they're the best.'

As they watched, Tommy flicked a ball up from the ground with his foot, then spun in a circle, executing some sort of roundhouse kick. The ball thumped into the netting behind the goals and Cunningham hooted with glee.

'I wasn't like that, though,' Kat continued. They veered around a smattering of balls and cones spilling out of a bag on the boundary line. 'When my coach said "this isn't good enough", what I heard was, "you're not good enough". And I guess that's what I believed, deep down. So every time he said it, I believed it a bit more, until it was true. I wasn't playing well. I dropped marks, made mistakes – and the more he tried to make me stand tall, the smaller I got.'

'What happened?' It was hard for Theo to force the words out past the lump in his throat and the tightness in his chest.

'I quit. Threw in the towel after the first AFLW season. Went back to full-time teaching – taught Cunningham, actually.'

That startled a laugh out of Theo. 'Model student?'

She snorted. 'What do you think?'

They came around behind the other goals and Theo ducked a ball as it sailed between the posts.

Once they were out of the danger zone, Theo asked, 'And then?'

'I went away with some mates and some mates of mates. I hadn't touched a footy for nine months. But we were just stuffing around on this country oval – taking pot shots at goal, playing nines – and I forgot about everything that had happened. I started having fun again. Took the best hanger of my life.' She grinned. 'One of the mates of mates was Cindy Johnson, the new Geelong coach that year. One night we all had a few beers, and I found myself talking to her about it. Spilled my guts, really. She convinced me to give it another shot at Geelong.'

'Bet you're glad you met her.'

'For lots of reasons.' She glanced across at Theo and grinned even brighter. 'We're married now.'

Theo winced. 'Sorry. I should know these things, but I've never really followed all the footy news. Poor form, I know.'

'Nah, to be honest I think it's better. Easier to ignore the garbage if you're not tuned in all the time.'

They ran another half lap in silence. Theo had always found running meditative: the thud of his footsteps, the rhythm of his own breathing. It had always helped him think. But this time it didn't bring him any closer to making a decision. His instincts told him he could trust Kat. He *wanted* to trust her. But he hadn't talked to anyone about this, not really. Not someone who would understand the messy guts of it.

'Let's stretch,' she said, slowing to a walk and then resting a hand on the boundary fence. Theo dropped into a deep lunge. 'You don't have to tell me anything you don't want to. But I'll be able to coach you better if I know what's on your mind. It doesn't take a genius to work out that you were having a shit time. I don't want you carrying that.'

Priya would have told him to 'talk, goddammit', but she'd be biased because Kat was her type.

'I think I had a panic attack.' He hurried the words out and almost stumbled over them. 'When I lined up to take that shot. I don't think I was . . . in a good place.' Saying it felt good, for a second, and then the worry ate in at the edges. He looked across at Kat, trying to read her face.

She nodded, looking thoughtful. 'Have you had panic attacks before?'

'I don't think so. I've gotten nervous but . . . it was different.'

'That must have been horrible.' The empathy in her voice was so palpable and unexpected it almost knocked the breath out of him.

'Yeah.' He managed to keep his voice steady. 'I guess . . . I guess I knew it was my shot. Do or die.'

'That's a lot of pressure.'

'That's just the game, right?'

'Well, yes and no. Most players don't line up for a goal after the siren thinking their career is on the line.'

'Plenty of other players would have slotted it.' He tried not to glance towards Cunningham.

She looked at him levelly. He had the uncomfortable sense that he'd given away more than he'd meant to. 'Maybe. But maybe not.'

Theo switched legs, reaching one arm up and feeling the pull up his side. 'Bet you'll think twice about giving me a game now.' He tried for a joking tone.

Kat's eyebrows formed an unimpressed V (they were expressive eyebrows). 'I'm not going to send you out there if you're not in the right headspace, that's right. But you wouldn't have made that joke if we were talking a niggly hamstring or a sprain that hadn't come good. As far as I'm concerned, there's no difference here. What happened to you in the past means that there's something getting between you and your best footy. I'll do everything I can to give you the tools to manage it. All I expect from you is for you to work with them.'

He nodded, half convinced.

'You boys are all the same,' she told him, shaking her head. 'You think you're the first person in the world to need some help. You're not, trust me. Not the first, won't be the last.'

Theo rose to his feet and moved into a quad stretch, holding the fence so he had a reason to turn away. He wasn't quite ready to meet her eyes. 'So what do I do?'

'Well, all our players see one of our club psychs. I'd like to send you to Jenny, if that's alright with you. She's worked with lots of players around anxiety. She has a background with performers of all kinds – I think after opera singers, footballers are easy. But if you'd rather talk to a bloke, Mick is also great.'

'Jenny sounds good.' Priya would be delighted. She could stop sending him links to psychologists based in Melbourne.

Kat dropped into a pigeon pose and Theo followed suit.

'I'm not going to grill you about how you ended up in a bad place. Jenny's the one who's qualified to help you unpack that. But remember that you can always talk to me. If something's going on, if you're having trouble, come and say something.' She reached out a hand. 'Deal?'

He took it. 'Deal.'

He wasn't sure if he felt better, but something had changed. Had unravelled, or at least loosened. The anxiety was still there, waiting behind his ribs, but it had receded.

Kat got to her feet. 'Have you ever played on the wing?'

Back to business, then. 'A bit, not for a while.'

'I want to try you out there.' She gave him the type of look he usually saw on the faces of women in Birkenstocks sizing up produce at the farmers' market. 'Not necessarily forever, but I think it might suit you.'

On the one hand, playing on the wing put him a comfortable distance from the big sticks. On the other, it tasted a bit too much like failure. He'd always played forward, always kicked goals.

'Sounds good,' he said.

Kat clambered to her feet. 'It will mean playing a more defensive role, but you'll adjust. If you manage to shut down Jaze or Tommy, you'll be ready for anyone. Just don't hit them too hard. We need them.'

'I'll do my best.'

Chapter Three

'He officially hates me.' Jake tipped his head back against Xen's bed and closed his eyes. Xen was sprawled on top of the covers and had banished Jake to the floor. It was too hot to share, apparently.

They'd been given an hour to themselves before dinner. Jake was too wrecked to do anything except flop onto a comfortable surface. Or a flat surface, at least. He hadn't *slacked* in the off-season, but maybe he hadn't done as much as he could have.

Bestavros clearly hadn't slacked. He'd smashed the running drills, and he hadn't needed to throw up into a bin afterwards. It had been impressive. Notes had been taken on clipboards. Kat had nodded more than once. For the first time, Paddy had been beaten in the two-kilometre time trial.

So, Bestavros: hot, good at running, not a fan of Jake. That last part wasn't a surprise, but Jake wasn't used to his teammates not liking him. Sure, he was a pest. It was pretty much his whole deal. Opposition players didn't like him. Opposition fans *hated* him. But his own team: they liked him. He might be a pest, but he was *their* pest.

'Yeah? What did he say?' Xen was bouncing a tennis ball off the wall. It was probably very irritating for Bestavros next door.

'It's vibes.' Jake twisted the fidget ring around his finger. It had been an ironic gift from Keeley, his best friend since they'd been in kindergarten, but the joke was on her, because he liked it.

'Have you apologised?' Xen asked.

'No. Why would I bring it up?'

Xen bounced the ball off Jake's forehead.

'Ow, that fucking hurt.'

'It was meant to.'

Jake retaliated by throwing a sock at Xen's head. Xen was obviously wiped out too, because he caught the sock but didn't return fire.

Jake flicked the fidget ring again. Maybe he should have apologised. But suddenly they were two days into the camp and he hadn't brought it up, and he wasn't quite sure *how* to bring it up. It seemed safer to just leave it. Bestavros hadn't brought it up either. Then again, he hadn't said a word to Jake except in response to direct questions.

Paddy emerged from the bathroom wearing only a low-slung towel. 'What's up?'

'Bestavros hates me,' Jake told him.

Paddy grabbed a second towel from the foot of his bed and flicked it over his head to dry his hair. 'Maybe he hates everyone. That guy is *intense*,' he said, slightly muffled. He surfaced from the towel a moment later.

Paddy wasn't wrong. Bestavros wasn't unfriendly, exactly, but he kept to himself. Jake's mum would have called him 'reserved'. Bestavros' game was like that, too. He worked hard, hitting drills with a focused intensity, but he wasn't playing *well*. Not like he used to. Jake had spent some time looking at old footage of Bestavros playing in NSW, from back before he got drafted. He'd wanted to see what Kat had seen – and it was there in spades. Bestavros had the type of raw athleticism that Jake had always envied.

He only had a couple of inches on Jake, but he played much taller, and he'd mastered a fearless, aerial game that complemented his accuracy in front of goal.

Or it had.

'I like him,' Xen said. 'He works hard, seems nice. We've chatted a bit.'

Of course they had. Xen could talk to anyone. He wasn't *chatty*, but he put people at ease.

'I don't *dislike* him,' Paddy said, turning away from them both and pulling underwear out of his suitcase. He dropped the towel and Jake choked.

'What the fuck is that?'

Paddy looked over his shoulder. 'My ass?'

'On your ass, dickhead.' Paddy definitely didn't have a tattoo on his ass last time Jake had seen it. But there was one there now: a large blackwork piece spreading from Paddy's lower back over his ass and down to the backs of his thighs. It looked almost like an explosion of abstract flowers, the lines bold enough to show clearly on Paddy's dark skin.

Paddy pulled on his briefs. 'Keep looking and I'll start charging.' Jake flipped him off and threw a sock at him. It bounced off the ass in question. Paddy grabbed it and tossed it back towards Jake, who lobbed it at Xen. Xen threw the ball at Paddy and the sock at Jake.

'No,' Xen said, as Jake reached for one of Xen's discarded footy boots. 'Don't even think about it.'

Jake raised his hands in surrender. 'Think about what?'

Xen turned back to Paddy. 'Do people get tattoos on their asses if they *don't* want people to look?'

Paddy wiggled his ass and pulled on some shorts.

'Back to Stavs,' Xen said. 'Being on a new team is tough. Takes time to adjust.'

'We're great, though,' Paddy said, dropping back onto his own bed, still shirtless. 'Shouldn't he be happy to be here? Bet he didn't think he'd play another game after that shitshow last year.'

'I wasn't talking about whether or not he's happy to be here,' Jake said. 'I was talking about the fact that he hates *me*.'

'Of course, sorry to make it not about you.' Paddy folded his arms behind his head.

'Just apologise,' Xen told Jake.

'For what?' Paddy asked. 'You weren't in that stupid skit.'

Which, to be honest, was how Jake felt about it. Xen made a noise that meant he disagreed but wasn't going to say anything about it.

'Question,' Paddy continued, rolling over and propping himself up on one elbow to look down at Jake on the floor. 'Why do you *care*? Got a crush?'

Jake rolled his eyes. 'Yeah, sure.'

'It's okay, we won't tell Kyle.'

And there it was. The conversation he didn't want to have. The one he'd been avoiding since the start of camp. He wasn't sure what his face did, but Paddy's look changed from teasing to questioning.

'What happened?'

Jake ripped the band-aid off and took a layer of emotional skin with it. 'We broke up.'

'Jesus, Jaze!' He heard the rustle of the bedspread as Xen sat up. 'When?'

'Three weeks ago.'

Xen thumped down onto the floor next to him, nudging his arm up against Jake's.

'Why?'

Jake sighed and leaned into him. 'He said if I wasn't going to come out publicly, we were done. I said I wasn't coming out. He said we were done.'

'That's fucked,' Xen said.

Jake hated the part of him that still wanted to defend Kyle, that wanted to say *It was hard* and *I get it* and *He's not a bad guy.*

'Bro,' Paddy said. He'd also slid down to the floor, leaning back against his bed. He extended one leg and nudged Jake's calf with his foot. 'You should have said something.'

Jake closed his eyes for a moment. 'Not much to say.'

'Yeah, but we could have cheered you up.'

'You were on the other side of the world and had family shit to focus on.'

And telling the boys would have made the break-up seem permanent. Would have let it slip out of the sandy haze of the off-season and into reality – like it was now. Telling them meant that he was never going to get another flirty text from Kyle, or call Kyle while he was curled up in bed, or feel Kyle's lips pressed against the side of his neck.

'Did you at least talk to Keeley?' Xen asked.

'Yeah – I talked her out of killing him.' Jake hadn't asked her about Kyle's mysteriously slashed tyres.

'What do you need?' Xen asked. 'You wanna talk about it?'

Abso-fucking-lutely not. 'Just wanna play some good footy.'

'Can do,' Paddy said. 'Gonna be a good year.'

'Don't jinx it.'

Xen nudged Jake with his shoulder. 'We're here if you want to talk.'

Jake knew he probably *should* talk about it. He'd talked a bit with Keeley, but she knew him so well that she could fill in the gaps. He hadn't had to say much at all. She'd just put on *H2O* and ordered fish and chips.

He kept waiting to get angry. He knew he should be angry. Angry that he didn't know whether Kyle had been lying from the beginning when he'd said he understood. Angry that Kyle had said,

'We'll still be friends if it doesn't work out,' which had turned out to be bullshit. Angry that Kyle had spent two weeks sticking his dick into Jake's mouth and ass at every opportunity while counting down the days to dumping him – because Kyle had known, *must* have known, that Jake would say no to coming out.

Though maybe he should be grateful for the pre-break-up sex. He wasn't going to get laid again anytime soon.

Jake looked down at his phone. 'Gotta call Mum,' he said, levering himself to his feet. 'She was having scans today.' He had another ten minutes before she was expecting his call, but he'd also had enough of sharing.

'Say hi from me,' Xen said. 'Hope it's good news.' He squeezed Jake's shoulder. He was *definitely* going to make Jake talk about his feelings at some point.

But not today.

Jake ducked out through the fire escape and up the stairs. There weren't many places at the training centre where you could get both privacy and phone reception. The second-floor balcony was the best: shaded enough that it was usually a few degrees shy of roasting, but out-of-the-way enough to be a good place for a chat. It was only November, but this week felt more like January.

Jake was slipping through the door when he heard laughter. It took him a second to realise it was Bestavros. Bestavros hadn't seen Jake – the curve of the balcony hid the door from view.

'You know I wouldn't miss catching up with all of you,' Bestavros was saying.

A group call, Jake assumed. Personally, he tended to stick with group chats. He didn't even call Keeley more than once a month.

He hesitated for a second. Maybe Bestavros was wrapping things up. Jake didn't really fancy trying to find a better spot, and he still had a few minutes. He sat down on one of the deckchairs and pulled out his phone.

'. . . yeah, I thought that would be a good way to bond.' Bestavros' voice was dry. 'Nothing like a blowjob between bros.'

Okay, what? And yes, listening was wrong, but also, maybe if Jake listened to a couple more sentences he'd get a better idea of whether Bestavros was about to end the call.

There was a silence, then Bestavros spoke again. 'Yeah, and bad blowjobs wouldn't be good for team morale.' He snorted. 'Sorry, Rach, but there have been no blowjobs. As far as I know, anyway. My bisexuality remains valid but theoretical.'

Jake's brain shorted out. *My bisexuality remains valid but theoretical.*

'Oh, sharing a room with Cunningham,' Bestavros said. 'Yeah, except he's also a showboating hack.'

Wow, okay.

'He can't put anything away, he's allergic to wearing a shirt, and he fucking ducks *constantly* . . . no, Rach, it's a footy thing.' There was another pause. 'The abs aren't real, Priy. Trust me, I've seen them.'

Ouch. So now Jake was definitely eavesdropping, but come on. How could he not?

'He doesn't take it seriously,' Bestavros said. 'He fucks around constantly, and he gets away with it because he's got natural talent. He skips reps in the gym, he's always stuffing around in drills, he just cruises on his talent. He's a flog *and* he leaves wet towels on the floor.'

Okay, so Jake occasionally skipped a set. *Fucking sue me.* It wasn't like he was ever going to dominate one-on-ones. He knew his strengths and played to them.

The towel criticism was fair – he'd heard it before – but he'd never heard a teammate call him a flog before, and he didn't fucking like it. He'd worked *hard* to get here. Logged hundreds of kilometres on the road, driving to and from games. Even fallen asleep at the wheel once, only waking when his tyres hit gravel.

Left shit early – parties, birthdays, family lunches. Got to stuff late. Stayed sober when his mates weren't. Kept his stupid grades up, as much as he could, because his mum believed in him, but she also knew what footy could be like. Watched from the sidelines during what should have been his debut season, rehabbing an ACL day by agonising fucking day.

Oh, yeah, and he'd gotten his ass dumped because he wouldn't risk his career.

Where did Bestavros get off, acting like he knew *shit* about Jake?

'No, it's not that,' Bestavros said, and Jake desperately wanted to know what *that* was. 'He's just a typical surfer-boy douchebag. I don't have to like him just because we're on a team together. People like him are why . . . okay, yes, subject change. Ah shit, I've got to go anyway, I need to shower before dinner.'

Jake exhaled slowly. Bestavros didn't like him. Who gave a fuck? Bestavros was going to be lucky to edge his way into the best 22. Why would Jake give a shit what he thought?

Theo closed his laptop and tipped his head back against the stone wall. The sky was starting to colour and there was a soft evening breeze, lifting the heat of the day. He lingered for a couple more minutes, enjoying the smell of the sea. It was a nice spot, but if he didn't head back soon he wouldn't be able to shower before dinner, and that was definitely a necessity.

He'd almost bailed on the group video call. Priya, Rachel and Lee were his oldest friends, but he hadn't really wanted to answer the questions he knew they'd have for him. *How's it going? How are you feeling?*

He'd managed to divert them, initially, at the expense of Nathan Rigger, who'd seen that Theo was taking the vegetarian meal at lunch and had kindly volunteered that there were halal options. It actually *had* been quite nice of Rigger. Theo had cleared up the confusion – 'I'm vegetarian, not Muslim' – and Raze had choked on a mouthful of mashed potato. Rigger had looked like he was longing for the sweet embrace of death.

From there, Theo managed to steer the catch-up to Rachel's most recent dating sagas, then Lee's career crisis, and then Priya's current trial. In the flurry of their news, he'd gotten away with the sort of vague 'yeah, good so far' answers that would not have flown if the other three had been paying more attention. When the conversation eventually turned to Jake Cunningham, Priya had narrowed her eyes a couple of times, so he was probably going to hear from her later.

He walked around the corner and stopped dead. Cunningham was lounging on one of the deckchairs, apparently engrossed in whatever he was doing on his phone. He tipped his head back to look at Theo. The omnipresent aviators were hooked into the neck of his t-shirt.

'Hey,' Cunningham said.

'Hi.' *Fuck*. Theo's brain ran the conversation in reverse. *Fuck*. Was there a subtle way to ask *Did I just out myself to you?* 'What are you doing here?'

'Same as you, I guess. Reception's shit inside and I gotta make a call in a couple of minutes.'

'Yeah,' Theo agreed, only half listening. The follow-up question to *Did I just out myself?* had to be *Did you just overhear me bagging you out to my friends?* There was no way to know how long Cunningham had been there. And Theo, well . . . he hadn't held back.

'Did you —' He stopped.

'Did I what?' Cunningham asked. There was something in his voice Theo hadn't heard before. Then Cunningham closed his eyes for a second and sighed. 'I won't tell anyone.'

Theo's hands were a little clammy. He thought about saying *About what?*

'Why?' he asked instead.

For a moment, something like annoyance contracted the corners of Cunningham's eyes. Something sharper than annoyance, maybe.

'Because whatever you might think, Bestavros, I'm not that much of an asshole.'

'I didn't —' Theo started. Except he had said several things that pretty much meant 'asshole', and Cunningham must have heard some of them. 'Thanks,' he finished.

Cunningham shrugged. 'Sure.' He stood. 'Listen, I gotta make that call.' He looked pointedly towards the door.

'Uh, yeah, of course. Sure.' Theo was going to leave as soon as his brain unfroze and gave him back control of his feet.

Cunningham turned away and walked around the corner of the balcony, out of sight. Theo retreated, and heard Jake say, 'Hey, Mum, how'd it go?' before he closed the door.

Theo wasn't surprised when his phone started buzzing as he headed back towards his room. He thought about ignoring it, but then Priya would *know* something was wrong.

'Hey, Priy.'

'Are you good?' she asked, cutting to the chase. 'You were cagey.'

'Yeah,' he said, stopping to lean against the trunk of one of the jacarandas. 'No. I just accidentally outed myself to Cunningham.'

'What?'

Theo explained.

Priya made a thoughtful noise. 'That sucks, but it sounds like he won't tell anyone. I know you don't like him, with good reason. But outing you – that would be extreme.'

Theo had sent Priya the *Full Forward* episode after she'd made some gentle noises about the possibility of moving on and mending fences. It had put an end to those suggestions, and also to the jokes about Jake.

'If he overheard that then he overheard what I said about him.' Theo cringed internally. Calling him a flog had been pretty harsh. He'd been exaggerating a bit, maybe, for the benefit of the group, but Cunningham didn't know that.

'Yeesh.' There were a few moments of silence. But Priya had never been one to beat around the bush. 'Are you worried he'll out you out of spite?'

'Yes.' Theo hesitated. 'No. I don't know. Like you said, it'd be pretty extreme. And Kat, the one I was telling you about – she's queer. I think she'd come down pretty hard on anyone who did something like that. He is a star, though, so who knows. Nothing I can do about it now.'

'Should you apologise?'

'That might just make it worse. I mean, he hasn't apologised for the skit. So maybe we can just pretend it never happened. An eye for an eye.'

'How's everything else?' Priya asked. He appreciated the question, because he knew she wanted to tell him that he should take the initiative and apologise, and it was probably physically paining her not to give him that good advice.

'It's —' He stopped.

'Theo.' Her voice was a little wry and very warm, and Theo suddenly missed her so much it actually hurt.

'It's just . . . hard. I want —' He stopped again. Priya stayed quiet.

'I want to make this work,' he admitted. 'To fit in here. But it's like I've forgotten how to do that. It seems like a good group, and there's a lot of social stuff, but I just . . .' He shook his head, as though she could see. 'I can't seem to do it. And I'm not playing well. Better, I guess, but not well enough.'

'You were really excited when you got drafted to the Sharks,' she said. It was a mark of how seriously she was taking this that she didn't even pretend she'd forgotten the name of his first team.

'Yeah,' he said. 'I was.'

Shame pulsed up from his stomach, tightening his throat. He'd been naive. Hopeful. *Stupid.*

'You know,' Priya said, choosing her words carefully, 'the fact you were excited about that and it didn't work out doesn't mean you can't be excited about this.'

Theo closed his eyes. 'I don't know if I've got excitement in me,' he said. 'I just . . . I don't know. It's better, though. Kat is great. You'd like her.' Massive understatement. 'And the medication is still helping. It's better.'

'Good.' She didn't sound convinced.

'Really, Priy, I'd tell you if it wasn't.'

'Okay,' she said with a sigh. 'I just wish I could give you a hug.'

'Right back at you.'

Priya made the sort of noise she usually made before bringing up something serious. That was alarming, because they'd already covered *I accidentally outed myself to my least favourite teammate* and *my generalised anxiety disorder and accompanying depression might ruin my career.*

'And . . . you're okay not being out to the team?'

'What?'

Priya had never *said* she didn't approve of Theo staying closeted, but she'd been quick to raise it as a silver lining when his AFL career had looked like it was over.

'What you said about your bisexuality being valid but theoretical. The *way* you said it. I suppose I just wonder if you'd feel better if you could . . . be yourself. Be out.' She made a noise, and he could almost see her regretting her words. 'Not that anyone has to be out. You know what I mean.'

Would being out make him feel more like himself? He knew, intellectually, that the fact he'd only ever been with women didn't make him any less bisexual. He was out to his close friends, but that had happened organically, in the mess of teenage feelings and exploration. There were at least a dozen really good reasons he didn't want to come out to anyone else. But even if there hadn't been, he couldn't imagine telling his parents – let alone the team – without a partner to introduce. *Abi, Ommi, just a quick PSA to let you know that the Rafael Nadal poster I had above my bed wasn't there because I liked tennis.*

He knew what Priya would say if he told her he thought about it like that.

'It doesn't feel like a big deal right now. Honestly.'

She sighed. 'I hate that you have to hide it.'

'It's not like I've got a boyfriend stashed somewhere.'

'In a closet, for example?'

'I didn't say that.'

'It was building to a very obvious punchline.'

'You're mean.'

'What if you want to date men? Or hook up with them?'

Theo wasn't sure why Priya had a bee in her bonnet about this topic *now*.

'I'll cross that bridge if I come to it.'

Which I won't. Sure, in an alternate universe he might have taken the opportunity to broaden his horizons if it presented itself. But he liked women, and it wasn't as though dating was currently a priority in his life.

'It just feels like the opportune moment for . . . experimentation. Before you re-engage with serial monogamy,' Priya said.

'I don't think getting some dick will fix my depression.'

'Not the object of that exercise. Also, you don't have to get a dude to get some dick.'

'Point taken. You know what I mean, though. And seriously, I'm good. Go back to your trial prep. I know you need to highlight.'

'I do need to highlight,' she conceded. 'I'm going to call you on Tuesday after court. Talk then? Take care. Love you.'

'Love you too, Priy.'

Chapter Four

Jake scrambled for the ball and grabbed it, spinning to the right. He felt a hand on his shoulder and leaned in, bending his knees just enough that the hand slipped up, catching the side of his neck.

Kat's whistle shrilled. 'High!'

Jake turned, grinning.

Bestavros did not grin back. 'He ducked.'

Kat gave Bestavros a look over her sunglasses. 'Then tackle him lower.'

Jake winked at Bestavros, paced back and took the kick. They both jogged after the play, and Bestavros gave him a nudge with his shoulder as they ran. From Xen or Paddy it would have felt friendly. It did not feel friendly.

It wasn't yet a *hot* day, but it was warm enough that everyone had worked up a sweat early in the session. There was a damp sheen on Bestavros' neck, and he reached up to shove his hair out of his eyes.

'You need a headband,' Jake said.

Bestavros glanced across at him. 'I think I'm good.'

Things with Bestavros had been weird in the few days since Jake had overheard the phone call. Jake had tried to make it clear, without actually saying anything, that Bestavros' secret was safe with him. That he was chill about bisexuality.

He was also trying to be chill about Bestavros thinking he was a showboating hack. Getting into it with him about wearing a headband wouldn't help with that.

His dick, however, was not being chill. Mainly, Jake blamed the yoga. Bestavros was good at yoga. *Really* good at yoga. He practised every morning, before breakfast, in a corner of the courtyard clearly visible from where Jake liked to eat. Xen had nearly had to call an ambulance when Bestavros moved into some sort of pretzel position just as Jake took a sip of coffee.

Knowing Bestavros was queer made it trickier, somehow. Jake had learned a long time ago that other athletes were treats you didn't look at, because you weren't going to get to eat them. But then there was Bestavros. A treat who, in different circumstances, might have been interested in being eaten by Jake. Or whatever. They didn't pay Jake because he was good with words.

Bestavros didn't practise shirtless – it was worse than that. He practised in trackies and a t-shirt that slipped to show his flat stomach every time he was in a position that put his head below his hips. Whenever he moved into something like a lunge, his track pants pulled tight across his thighs and glutes, and – well, Jake had to avert his eyes for his own good.

It wasn't as though he'd never had queer teammates before. He had queer teammates *right now*. But the general *you're hot* sensation he'd experienced when he'd seen Bestavros on the bus had changed into a specific and inconvenient *I wonder*, which was definitely not going to become an *I know*, because: (a) Bestavros didn't like him; (b) Bestavros didn't seem as though he'd be into hate sex; and (c) Jake wasn't that much of a fucking idiot.

Jake refused to think of it as a crush. He wasn't twelve. But he was keeping out of their room as much as possible. Being in close quarters with Bestavros had tipped from awkward into *get me out of here* at the point when Bestavros glaring and nudging

Jake's things back onto Jake's side of the room had started to be a turn on.

It wasn't Jake's best training session. He just couldn't quite get his head into it. Bestavros took him high again – Jake was pretty sure it was an accident – and then they got tangled up in a tackle and the studs on Jake's boot left indents on Bestavros' calf. Bestavros scowled at Jake as though he'd done it deliberately, which was fucking rich coming from someone who'd nearly ripped his head off in *training*. Then they had a little tussle for the ball during a marking drill and Bestavros' elbow got Jake in the ribs in a way that definitely *wasn't* accidental, and which was definitely going to bruise.

The animosity only made the situation worse.

His dick had issues.

Theo knew he shouldn't have jammed his elbow into Cunningham's ribs. It was not the sort of thing you did in training. But Cunningham had spent the whole session getting in his face and Theo was *done*.

The chat with Kat had made Theo feel better – right up until he'd seen the pile of balls at the end of the first day and known it was goal-kicking time. By the time he'd picked up a ball, he felt a bit clammy.

He'd missed three of the four shots he took that day and the pattern had continued. He was *trying*, and he was still fucking it up. He was being supported, and given time, and it *wasn't working*. The Falcons weren't running a charity for washed-up second-round draft picks; if he didn't get his shit together, he wasn't going to get within cooee of a game.

Cunningham had slotted all four that first day, and the second day, and the third, and so on, and here was Cunningham again:

always talking, always grinning, always acting as if everything was one big joke. So, yeah, Theo shouldn't have rammed his elbow into Cunningham's ribs, but nobody could prove it hadn't been accidental.

And it had wiped the grin off Cunningham's face.

'You good, bro?' Xen asked, as Cunningham poked an exploratory finger into his side.

'Just a flesh wound.'

'Try not to fuck anyone up in training, Stavs,' Xen told Theo. Theo had wanted to be wary with Xen – he was too close to Cunningham – but it was very hard not to be friendly with someone who was just so *nice*. He'd noticed Theo liked to have a banana before their gym sessions, and had actively prevented Cunningham from getting the last one earlier that day so Theo could grab it.

Theo nodded. 'My bad.'

Cunningham's eyes flicked up at that. He'd noticed the lack of an actual apology. Shoe was on the other foot, then.

They finished the session with a friendly shots-on-goal competition. Again. Theo shanked a kick so badly that Cunningham wolf-whistled. He would have done it to anyone, but the jibe dropped like a stone down Theo's throat and settled in his churning stomach.

Ryan won, at least, after Cunningham smacked a kick from the pocket into the post.

Theo tried to keep the satisfaction off his face as he grabbed a Gatorade and listened to the post-session feedback. He knew there'd be more coming for him. Kat didn't seem to want to play him as a forward, but he still needed to be able to *kick a fucking goal*.

He was fucking this up.

Sometimes it felt as though there was a schism between his body and his brain. His brain told him, *You can do this, you've been doing this for years, Kat gets it*, but all his body had now was muscle memory and anxiety. They were eight days into camp and maybe it was a bit better – *maybe* – but nobody was going to sit around and give Theo unlimited time to sort his shit out. He was supposed to be a professional.

He threw his empty bottle at the bin and missed.

Jake didn't mean to walk back with Bestavros, but they ended up leaving the oval at the same time. Bestavros stalked next to him, silent, jaw set. If it had been anyone else, Jake would have said something reassuring. Sometimes you just had a shit day with the posts. But he didn't think Bestavros would want to hear it, and he wasn't in the mood to be told to get fucked. Or to be reminded that he ducked.

They got back to their room and Jake decided to make a strategic retreat. He grabbed a towel and a change of clothes – he was soaked with sweat – and headed for the door. He had to swerve around Bestavros to get there.

Bestavros rounded on him. 'Don't worry, I'm not going to make a pass at you.'

The fuck? 'What?'

Bestavros gestured to the room. 'You think I haven't noticed you've been avoiding the room ever since you overheard my phone conversation?'

Jake was rarely speechless. This did the job.

'Being bi doesn't mean I don't have standards,' Bestavros continued. He was scowling at Jake.

Jake wasn't finding the animosity hot anymore. He felt weird. Like he was having the conversation and also watching it from somewhere overhead. He tried to keep his voice even. 'I was trying to give you some space because you seem pretty pissed.'

Bestavros snorted. 'Sure.'

Jake knew he should just leave. Bestavros was picking a fight. It wasn't about Jake, it was just that Jake was here. Kyle had done that, sometimes. Bestavros had the yips in front of goal, in a major way, and he wanted to be pissed at someone other than himself.

Jake had always been a good target for that sort of anger.

He didn't leave. Instead he leaned back against the wall, crossing his arms. 'You think I have a problem with you being bi?'

'You've been pretty absent for the last few days.'

'Usually I don't hang out with people who hate my guts.'

'Sharing a room isn't hanging out.'

It was almost funny how wrong Bestavros was. But what was Jake supposed to say? *Ever since I found out you're queer I've been thinking about what it would be like if we fucked?* Bestavros would probably punch him in the face. Bestavros had 'standards', after all.

'I don't have a problem with you being bi.'

'Why would I believe that?'

The anger hit Jake in a sudden rush of heat. He was *done*. He was sick of every shitty journalist and random fan, and now apparently his *queer teammate*, making assumptions about him. The words were out before he could stop them. 'Because I'm gay, you asshole.'

Theo's stomach clenched. 'That's not funny.' It was low, even for Cunningham. Although Cunningham didn't look as though he was joking. There was no sign of his usual lazy smile. No mischief in the curve of his mouth. He was looking at Theo like he wanted to throw down.

'I'm not joking.' He held Theo's gaze.

Shit. 'That's . . . don't do that.' Theo felt like his heart was in the back of his throat. Some part of him was screaming at him to shut his mouth. That he'd radically, irreparably misjudged the situation. 'Stop fucking around.'

'What, need me to suck your dick to prove it?' Cunningham's voice was different, too. Clipped and a little mean.

Cunningham was *furious*, Theo realised. He felt a bit nauseated. Was Cunningham actually —

'Um, no?' he said. *Why the fuck had that come out like a question.* 'I mean . . .'

He had no idea what he meant.

Cunningham turned and opened the door enough to stick his head out. 'Paddy!'

Theo heard a door open and then Paddy's voice in the corridor. 'Yeah?'

'Come in and shut the door,' Cunningham said, stepping back to let Paddy in.

Paddy put his back against the closed door. His eyes flicked between them, then narrowed. 'What's up?'

'Tell Bestavros I've sucked a dick.'

Paddy blinked. To his credit, his voice stayed neutral as he answered. 'He's definitely sucked a dick.' Paddy paused. 'Not mine, if that's relevant.' He looked at Theo, then back at Cunningham. 'Everything okay?'

'Yeah,' Cunningham said. 'I just needed some help convincing Bestavros that I'm gay.'

'Sucking a dick doesn't necessarily make you gay,' Paddy pointed out. 'For example, I —'

Cunningham cut him off. 'Yeah, I know. And thanks.'

Paddy nodded once. 'Cool. I'm going to leave you to . . . whatever this is.' He waved a hand between them.

Then he looked at Cunningham, and his face softened. He reached for Cunningham's forearm, wrapping his fingers around Cunningham's wrist.

'You good?' he asked. The concern in his tone made guilt blossom under Theo's breastbone, unexpected and unwelcome. He'd really fucked this up.

'I'm good,' Cunningham said.

Paddy looked at Theo once more before he left, his gaze measuring. 'I hope so.' He closed the door behind him.

Cunningham was still looking at Theo, his chin slightly raised. He didn't look angry, now. He looked like he was waiting for Theo's next move.

'You're gay.' Theo said.

'Yeah.'

And now would be the time to apologise. 'I didn't realise,' he said instead.

'No shit.' Cunningham pushed himself off the wall. 'This has been a great chat, but I'm gonna go.' His voice hardened again. 'Don't run your mouth about it. I'm not out to everyone.'

Theo bristled, the guilt receding. 'Is that a threat?' Was Cunningham really going to go *mutually assured destruction* on this?

'It was a fucking request,' Cunningham said. 'I wouldn't out someone.'

'Okay.'

Theo needed to explain. He needed to fix this. He might not like Cunningham, but Cunningham was an integral part of the team, and pissing him off had been a terrible idea. And also he'd just *come out* to Theo, and Theo had . . . well.

'I didn't know —'

'Yeah, it's cool,' Cunningham snapped. 'You just assumed I was a complete cunt for no reason.'

Theo snorted. 'Sure, no reason.'

Cunningham rolled his eyes. 'I'm sorry I went on that fucking show, okay? I didn't know about the skit. It's not like they asked my opinion first.'

'I don't give a fuck about the skit,' Theo bit out. 'I give a fuck about you sitting there telling everyone I didn't have what it takes.'

Cunningham blinked at him. 'What?'

'The interview.'

'What about it?'

'You sat there and said I didn't have what it takes.'

Cunningham looked like he had to think about it before he remembered what he'd said, which was in itself infuriating. Theo had thought about it every day since, and Cunningham had *forgotten*.

'I think I said *some people* don't have what it takes.'

'Oh, sure, you definitely didn't mean me.'

Cunningham looked almost confused. 'What did you want me to say? Was I supposed to pretend you didn't choke?' There was an edge back in his voice that Theo couldn't place. Laughter, maybe.

Theo couldn't catch his breath. He didn't want to be here, having this conversation.

'I —' *I wanted someone to tell me it was okay. I wanted someone to say it happens to everyone. I wanted someone like* you *to understand.*

'Sorry I hurt your feelings,' Cunningham said. He didn't sound sorry at all.

'Fuck off.'

'I was trying to do that.'

'For the record, if someone accidentally outs themselves, it's probably best not to act like you're going to catch cooties from them.'

'*For the record*,' Cunningham said, 'when you bag someone out and they overhear it, they might try and keep out of your way.'

'Like you give a shit what I think of you.'

'I give a shit about this team.' Cunningham's blue eyes were locked with Theo's. 'I get you were pissed at me for going on that show. And maybe I should have talked to you and cleared the air or whatever when you got here. But I'm not the reason you choke every time you see a goal post, and my problem with you isn't that you're bi.'

'Look,' Theo started. He might have been about to apologise. 'I —'

'Fucking save it,' Cunningham said. He slammed the door behind him.

Jake was out on the oval when Paddy found him. There was always a bucket or two of balls for anyone who wanted to practise. Jake was channelling his anger into taking shots at goal from increasingly tricky positions, jogging in to collect the balls whenever the buckets were empty. He wasn't kicking particularly *well*, but the thud of his boot against the ball was making him feel a lot better, and it beat punching a wall. Or slamming Bestavros into one.

'So,' Paddy said, coming to stand beside him while he lined up a kick. 'Did you suck Stavsy's dick?'

Jake ignored the question and took the kick. The ball ricocheted off the point post and Paddy caught it. Jake grabbed another ball. He got it through this time, but now he felt a bit pathetic. Like a kid having a tantrum.

Paddy flopped down on the grass beside him, unperturbed. 'Yeah, I guess not. You'd be happier if you had.'

'Fuck off,' Jake griped half-heartedly, lowering himself to the ground too. He didn't like being alone with his feelings. And, unlike Xen, Paddy probably wouldn't try to make him talk about them.

'You gonna tell me what's going on?'

I've fucked up my life badly enough that my boyfriend dumped me for being closeted and the new queer player on the team assumed I was a massive bigot.

'Nothing's going on.'

'Are you sure? The two of you are going to have to play nice this season, and you're not looking super friendly.'

'Like he's going to make it out of the twos.'

Paddy gave him a look. He tucked one foot up against his thigh and leaned down towards the other one. He wasn't as bendy as Bestavros. 'Come on, bro. What the fuck was that? You're the one who called me in and just sprang dick sucking on me.'

'Thought you liked that.'

'Not with Stavs standing there looking like he was going to boke.'

Jake sighed. He *had* gotten Paddy involved. And Paddy would accept it if Jake told him to fuck off, but that would be a bit of a dick move.

'You know how I overheard him talking shit about me? Well, he mentioned some other stuff on the call. Personal stuff. He thought I was avoiding him because of that.'

Paddy would probably put the pieces together. He might have already clocked Bestavros as queer – he had an eerie sense for when people might be interested in fucking him.

'Bit of a leap from that to dick sucking,' Paddy said.

'Can't help you.'

'Mm.' Paddy stared in the direction of the goal posts. 'But you came out to him?'

'Yeah.' Jake leaned his chin against his knees. 'I guess I did.'

'Is he going to be a dick about it? Because if he —'

'I . . . no. I don't think he will.'

'Are *you* going to be a dick about whatever went down?'

Jake looked at the balls scattered behind the goal posts. There was the right answer to that question, and then there was the accurate one. He settled for honesty. Paddy wouldn't have believed him if he'd lied.

'Maybe.'

Chapter Five

The four weeks of pre-season that followed development camp made Theo miss the period when he and Cunningham had mainly ignored each other. It turned out Cunningham held a grudge. Maybe Theo should have apologised, but that went both ways.

The only thing they'd seen eye-to-eye on was profound relief that camp had come to an end. Theo really regretted accusing Cunningham of avoiding their room, because of course Cunningham spent the last four days of camp doing the opposite, making it impossible for Theo to study unless he found a quiet spot somewhere else. The couple of free mornings where Cunningham had gone off to surf had been *bliss*, even if he had an uncanny ability to spread sand onto everything once he got back.

But Theo had gotten through it, and even in his lower moments he couldn't think of the camp as a failure. He'd played well on the wing (he wasn't going to think about his accuracy in front of goal). He'd made, if not friends, then friendly acquaintances. The numbers said he was the best runner on the team, and it was hard to argue with numbers. He was never going to be stronger than someone like Raze, but he was putting in good work in the gym. Better work than some other people. Things were going . . . well, they were certainly going.

If he woke up every day with a thrumming pulse of anxiety in his chest, at least it wasn't stopping him from getting out of bed. He was deliberately not thinking about the first game of the season, though some malicious part of his brain was running a countdown and whispering, *You have to be better, you have to be better*. He'd since met the rest of the coaching staff, including the head coach, Davo. He wasn't sure what to make of him yet, but so far he hadn't said anything either homophobic or racist, so Theo was going to take the win.

The guys seemed like a good bunch. Although there were a few pretty old-school players. Barry Loin – known as Tenders – had cracked a couple of off-colour jokes during training, and Theo remembered that Bruce Archer – nicknamed Sheds for inexplicable reasons – had posted a couple of unfortunate things on social media in the past. The CEO, Randy Jones, wasn't known for being a bastion of progressive views either, but Theo doubted they'd ever actually meet.

Jenny, the psychologist Kat had sent him to, was not what he'd expected. She was a petite woman – maybe 5'2" to Theo's 6'4" – with a razor-sharp black bob, tattoos on the backs of her hands that stretched up her forearms, and an eyebrow piercing. Her handshake was firm and she smiled with her eyes first. She could have been anywhere between thirty and fifty. He'd been surprised to find that she sat on the bench at games to keep an eye on things.

He liked her better than the psychologist Priya had dragged him to. He couldn't quite put his finger on why. Maybe it was her directness, the pragmatic way she'd draw her eyebrows together and say, *Well, I think we can do something about that*. She didn't talk to him like she was his mum or a primary-school teacher. He'd spent every spare moment in their first session staring at her lanyard, which was in the colours of the pansexual flag, and wondering if he should tell her he was queer.

He hadn't.

It was a stinking hot Tuesday morning – just on the borderline of weather that would have had them doing something inside – and he could feel the sweat trickling down the back of his neck. They were running game-simulation exercises and Cunningham was taking every opportunity to get up in Theo's space. As per usual. It had taken Theo a few days after camp to realise that Cunningham had made it his personal mission to piss Theo off as much as possible during training. The coaches liked to pit the two of them against one another in drills, which just gave Cunningham plenty of opportunities to be a pest. His primary skill.

It was petty, and pathetic, and Theo was not going to let it get to him.

The next time they tussled for the ball, it spilled free. Theo went to scoop it off the ground, but Cunningham was there, blocking Theo with his body. Cunningham was smaller, and not as strong, but his positioning was ridiculously good. Cunningham emerged victorious and got the handball off to Raze, who was running past.

They reset to start the drill again, and Theo jostled Cunningham for position. A little harder than he would have if it had been someone else. Cunningham just turned and winked at him.

Theo exhaled, ignoring it, and reminded himself that he just needed to get through the next hour and then he would be inside in the air conditioning.

Except then he gave away two frees for high contact against Cunningham in quick succession – both tackles perfectly legal until Cunningham bent his knees. The second time, after he got the kick off, Cunningham turned to Theo and grinned. He was making Theo look like an idiot. He was *enjoying* making Theo look like an idiot.

'Your mum get on her knees that easy?' Theo snapped. He never sledged much, but it wasn't like he didn't know how to.

He expected Cunningham to bark right back, but instead he grabbed two handfuls of Theo's jumper and shoved him. Theo grabbed Cunningham's jumper right back. It felt *good* to get a rise out of him. To see that fucking smile drop off his face.

'The fuck is your problem?' Cunningham's voice was loud, and in his peripheral vision Theo saw Xen's head snap around.

'You know what my problem is.' This close, Theo had to look down to glare at Cunningham. Cunningham was looking right back up at him, blue eyes narrowed.

Cunningham shoved him again. 'Fuck you.'

'You wish.'

Theo's better judgement tried to regain control. He didn't *do* this. He'd never picked a fight with an opposition player in a game, let alone *a teammate during training*. He wasn't that sort of person. The problem was, he did have a temper, it just had a high ignition point.

Cunningham's gaze flicked to both sides. 'Don't,' he said, his voice softer.

'Like I would,' Theo said, matching his tone and tugging him in closer. Cunningham resisted, but Theo was too strong for him. Theo was breathing hard enough to stir Cunningham's ridiculous floppy hair where it was falling into his face. 'Worried you wouldn't be everyone's favourite if they knew?'

He needed to stop talking. He needed to stop talking before he said something he couldn't take back. But he was sick of Jake Cunningham, and his smug smile, and the way he made everything look so *easy*.

'Like you can fucking talk.' Cunningham tried to break Theo's grip again, but Theo wouldn't let him.

'Everyone who likes you doesn't even really know you. Reckon you'd still be a star if they did?'

Something shifted in Cunningham's face, and Theo realised he was about to get punched.

He probably deserved it.

Jake hadn't meant to do it. He'd been getting shit on the field about all sorts of things for years: his parents, his performances, his hair. Getting called names that were accurate, even if guys didn't know it. It usually slid right off. When you heard it day in, day out, it lost the sting. He should have laughed it off. Some dumb shit about his mum, nothing to see here. He might have shaken that one off, after a couple of seconds – even knowing the phone in his locker probably had unread messages about her oncology appointments. But of course Bestavros knew right where to land one, because of the one thing they had in common.

Jake didn't realise he'd pulled one hand back, fist clenched, until someone grabbed it.

'Jaze, stop it,' Xen panted into his ear. He raised his voice. 'Stavs, let go. Step back.'

'Cut it the fuck out.' Raze shouldered his way between them, forcing them apart. Xen wrapped an arm around Jake and pulled him backwards.

'Both of you, enough,' Yelks said in his captain voice, cool and authoritative. He had Bestavros by the arm. He hadn't been anywhere near them when the scuffle broke out, but he had a captain's nose for trouble and impressive closing speed for someone his age. He looked between them. 'What's this about?'

Fuck. Jake had nearly *punched his teammate.* 'Difference of opinion,' Jake ground out.

'Difference of opinion,' Bestavros agreed.

Davo was stalking towards them from the goal square. He was going to blow a fucking gasket.

'You can let go of me,' Jake told Xen. Xen did.

Bestavros met Jake's eyes for a second, then looked away. He looked like he might be sick.

'What is going on here?' Davo asked. He'd been red in the face all session from the heat, but he'd gotten much, much redder. Kat was standing back, her face unreadable, with the two assistant coaches. 'Well?' Davo insisted.

Jake had been with the Falcons long enough to know that the gentle tone indicated an imminent explosion.

'Difference of opinion,' Yelks said. 'I'll deal with it.'

Yelks took interpersonal stuff very seriously. Jake and Bestavros were probably going to get sat down in a room together and made to talk it out.

Hell fucking no to that.

'Right,' Davo said. He looked around at the group that had assembled around them. 'You being paid to stand around?'

The players began to disperse and Davo turned back to Jake and Bestavros. Jake braced for impact.

'As for the two of you,' Davo continued, looking at them like dog shit on a sneaker, 'you can both *get the fuck off this oval*. I don't give a flying fuck what the problem is, but you can come back out here once you're ready to behave like adults.' He took a deep breath. 'You've got extras for the next four days. I want you here at six every morning, and I will personally make sure you're too fucking tired to get into it again.'

Fuck. They each had individual programs, but tomorrow was supposed to be the last training session of the year. Jake had planned to leave for home directly afterward. To spend some proper time with his mum. His anger had trickled away, and now all he could think about was having to call his mum to explain why he couldn't come home until Christmas Day, why he wouldn't be there to do everything they'd planned.

'But,' Jake started. 'It's —'

Davo went even redder. 'Yes, Cunningham, it's Christmas. Do I look like I give a fuck? If you wanted a Christmas break, you shouldn't have fought one of your teammates.'

'Right,' Jake managed. He realised, on an awful inhale, that he was on the verge of tears. He bit the inside of his mouth, trying to keep it together.

'And as for you,' Davo said, turning to Bestavros, 'I suggest you spend more time earning a place on this team and less time getting into it with someone who's proved he deserves his.'

'I understand,' Bestavros said, stony-faced.

Davo waved a dismissal and Jake headed towards the rooms without looking back.

Fuck.

A combination of panic and trembling rage got Theo off the oval and into the gym before his brain really had time to process what had happened. They may have been kicked out of the rest of training, but Theo still had a conditioning workout he was supposed to do. He wanted to be done and out of the gym before the others got off the field.

Lifting weights turned out to be a good outlet for the sick energy crackling under his skin. His brain fell into a spiral of every shitty thing that might flow from that one stupid snipe. Lodged, every now and again, on the way Cunningham had looked at him when he'd said *don't*. He could almost taste the horrible blend of guilt and satisfaction every time he thought about the fact he'd finally *gotten* to Cunningham.

Except maybe he'd done that better than he'd meant to. And since when had he sledged using misogynist bullshit? It had been the kind of sledge packed in layers of everything he loathed about footy culture. Let alone taunting Jake for doing *exactly the same thing Theo was doing.*

Just as he realised he was benching slightly more than he should have been without a spotter – though if he crushed all his ribs at least he wouldn't need to deal with the consequences of his actions – hands appeared and grabbed the bar. Yelks looked down at him, frowning, and helped Theo rack it.

'Thanks,' Theo wheezed.

He hadn't had much to do with Yelks yet. The Falcons captain was a big guy – 6'5" according to the stats sheet – with long, dark-blond hair and striking green eyes. He was softly spoken off the field, almost gentle, as though he was acutely aware of how much space he took up. On the field he was a towering presence at fullback: the last line of defence, known for his physicality and his uncanny sense for the game. Theo didn't know what to make of him.

Theo sat up, swinging his legs around so he was sitting sideways on the bench. Yelks sat down beside him and handed him a protein shake.

'Thanks.'

'No worries. You want to tell me what happened out there?'

Theo popped the lid off the shaker and took a sip to avoid answering. Once he'd swallowed, he said, 'Did you ask Cunningham?'

'I would have if I'd been able to find him. I still will. But I'd like to hear it from you.'

Theo took another sip.

Yelks folded his hands in his lap. 'Davo is happy for me to handle this. I can tell you that no matter what it was, you're not looking at any serious disciplinary consequences, because it's the first time there's been an issue. But.' He pinned Theo with those eerie green eyes. 'This is a close-knit group. You and Cunningham have been needling each other for weeks – I'm not that oblivious. We need to fix it before it becomes a real problem.'

Theo put the shake aside and stared at the floor between his feet. The jittery energy he'd carried into the gym had drained away and now he just felt hollowed out. There was no good answer to that question. *He pisses me off.* God, he was an *adult*. A professional.

Yelks seemed content to sit in silence for as long as it took.

'I guess we got off on the wrong foot,' Theo said, finally. 'And things . . . escalated.'

'Okay. Why the wrong foot?'

'I . . . that episode of *Full Forward*. I wanted Cunningham to apologise.'

Yelks nodded. 'That's fair enough. And he didn't?'

'No.'

'Did you raise it with him?'

'No.'

'And things escalated?'

Theo managed to get out a version of the truth – one that omitted several of the important points – painfully aware that half the story sounded even worse than the full story. Yelks looked like he suspected Theo was holding something back, but he didn't say anything about it.

'And what did you say to him today?' Yelks asked, gentle but implacable.

Theo would have given most of his salary to sink into the ground. He managed to explain what he'd said about Cunningham's mum, though he made it sound as though that had been all – like he'd doubled down on that.

'Right,' Yelks said, brow furrowed.

'I know it wasn't okay,' Theo said, forcing himself to meet Yelks' eyes. 'I wouldn't . . . it's not the sort of thing I'd usually say. He . . .' *He rattles me. He gets under my skin.*

Yelks nodded. 'I'm glad to hear it.' He spent a few moments studying one of the elliptical machines and then seemed to come to a decision. 'Look, Theo, I'm not telling you anything that isn't already pretty well known, but I am going to tell you this because it might help mend fences.'

Theo froze. He couldn't mean —

'Jake didn't have the easiest time with his parents. His biological father was . . .' Yelks' mouth twisted. 'Not a good guy. He left when Jake was very young. Jake's mum raised him, and when he was in prep, she, uh, came out as a lesbian, and started a relationship with a woman. I don't think he had an easy time. To be clear, I'm not telling you anything confidential, he's talked about this openly.'

'Shit,' Theo said. If he'd wanted to sink into the floor before, now he wanted to sink into the middle of the earth. Did Cunningham think he'd known all that?

Yelks sighed. 'He's very close to his mum. I know he hears plenty about her on the field, and it doesn't usually bother him. But for whatever reason, it got to him today.'

'He probably didn't . . . expect that from a teammate.' Theo felt shame crawling all over his body. When had he forgotten how to be a team player? He'd played with guys like Cunningham before. Guys who were *worse* than Cunningham. But he'd never goaded one of them into taking a swing.

'Probably not.' Yelks paused again. He spoke certain words with a very faint accent; Eastern European, Theo thought. Something like that. 'Listen, Theo, I know settling in here can't be easy. I understand that you had reason to dislike Cunningham, and I'm going to speak to him about his behaviour. But he's not a bad guy. He loves this team, and he loves his teammates. I don't need you to be best friends, but you need to be able to work together. I should have intervened earlier, and that's on me, but I thought you boys might sort it out, especially with Xen and Paddy in the mix.'

Theo nodded. Yelks put a hand on his shoulder. It was the sort of paternal gesture Theo's own father never went in for. He wondered if Yelks ever got tired of being the dad to fifteen men in their twenties with large salaries and underdeveloped frontal lobes. Probably.

'I'll apologise,' Theo said, and meant it. 'I . . .' This felt like a vulnerable admission to make, but it wasn't as if anything he said was going to make Yelks think worse of him after what had happened that morning. 'I've been struggling a bit with my game, and the way Cunningham plays . . . it makes it harder, sometimes.'

Yelks smiled. 'He is that type of player. Nobody is comparing you to Cunningham, though. There's a real place for you in this team. You've got something we need, and you've got time to develop it. You just focus on running your own race, and I'll tell Cunningham to cool it in training. There've been days where I thought you might be the one to punch him, and I think he might have deserved it.' He gave Theo a conspiratorial smile. 'Don't tell anyone I said that.'

Theo smiled back. 'Deal.' This was a weird team. He liked it. 'I'm still going to have to do the extras, aren't I?'

Yelks slapped him on the back. 'They'll give you a good appetite for Christmas lunch.'

The problem with your captain living close by was that if, say, you were ignoring his calls, he could rock up on your doorstep with two boxes of takeaway pierogi and a sixpack of craft beer. Jake opened the door and let Yelks in. He'd never shut the door on Yelks' pierogi. Nobody knew where he got them, but they were *good*. So good that Xen and Paddy had once spent several weeks visiting every Polish restaurant they could find, trying to track down the source. They hadn't, though Paddy had discovered he really liked borscht.

Jake shouldn't have been ignoring Yelks' calls, but he'd just . . . needed a minute. Several minutes. Aiming a punch at Bestavros had been a stupid overreaction, but his mum was waiting on results from the follow-up scans and he'd just . . . cracked.

When he got home from training, he'd started sorting out the stuff in his room that belonged to Kyle. He'd already been having a terrible day, so why not double down? He didn't know what he was going to do with it. Post it back to him? Throw it away? Set it on fire? Except somehow he'd found himself sitting on the bed, his face buried in a cashmere sweater Kyle had left, trying not to lose his shit.

Jake, Paddy and Xen had worked out a system when they'd moved into their house. Anyone could go anywhere, unless a door was locked or (because Jake's bedroom didn't lock) he put out the *Do Not Disturb* sign that Paddy had filched from a fancy hotel. Ideally, he would mainly have used it when he was having great sex. Life was full of disappointments.

Xen had knocked twice (their signal for 'I'm leaving something here and fucking off') and left Jake a pot of some sort of herbal tea that would probably balance his aura (Xen's girlfriend was into alternative medicine) and a mini Picnic bar. Xen must have been really worried; he never tempted anyone off the diet plan.

Paddy had texted him a sequence of memes.

They both knew what was really the matter – he'd told them that the first scans had needed follow-up – but neither of them would push it. He didn't know if he wanted them to push it. He hadn't wanted to talk about Kyle, but he *couldn't* talk about his mum maybe being sick again. If he talked about it, that would make it real.

Yelks looked at him in the entryway. 'Deck?' he asked. They'd had a few team parties here, so Yelks knew the layout.

The back deck was Jake's favourite thing about the house. You could sit there and watch birds fight it out in the couple of fruit trees that Xen hadn't netted. On summer evenings you could see the sunset and hear laughter and music from the other backyards. The neighbours over the fence had kids who liked to play footy and occasionally Jake kicked a stray ball back to them.

Xen was the only one of them who was really interested in the fruit trees – every now and then he bullied Jake and Paddy into helping pick the fruit, and then Jake into driving buckets of blood oranges, lemons and mandarins to his yiayia's place. After a week or so, Jake would go and pick up the same boxes, now filled with jam and relish and other things they were only allowed in small quantities. There was now an allocated spot at the club for Xen to put the jars and bottles they were giving away. If football didn't work out, Xen and his yiayia could probably start some sort of preserves business.

Jake swiped some cutlery for him and Yelks on the way through the kitchen and they settled into the two best chairs on the deck. Xen and Paddy were nowhere to be found. Jake suspected Yelks had texted them and asked them to stay clear.

Traitors. At least he wouldn't have to share the food.

'I talked to Bestavros,' Yelks said, once they'd made a good start on the pierogi. Fuck, they were tasty.

'Yeah?'

'He didn't know about your family situation.'

'Okay.' *Good for him.*

'What's going on, Jaze? You get along with everyone, and Bestavros isn't a bad guy. To be honest, I thought he'd slot in with the three of you.'

'Did you ask him?'

Yelks smiled. When he first joined the Falcons, Jake had a crush on Yelks for about three weeks purely on the strength of his smile. Maybe also his thighs. 'Yes, but I want to hear it from you as well.'

Jake thought about it. He was going to have to come clean – but in a way that didn't out either of them. He managed to stumble his way through a version of the truth while Yelks gave him an *I know you're leaving shit out* look.

Yelks tended to let people sort out their own stuff rather than pushing. People did talk to him, though. Not really Jake, because Jake didn't usually have shit to talk about, or at least not shit he was going to talk to Yelks about. But he knew at least four people who'd cried onto one of Yelks' broad shoulders. Yelks had also been great with Xen from the word go; hadn't blinked when Xen had admitted he was having panic attacks, had just pulled him into a hug and then set up a sequence of appointments for him.

Sometimes Jake wondered if he should tell Yelks he was gay. Like, maybe it would be a relief. Some stupid part of him thought that if he could tell Yelks, and if Yelks said it was okay, then it really would be okay.

Feelings were fucked up.

Yelks waited once Jake finished. Expectantly.

'I'll apologise,' Jake said, finally. 'And I'll . . . um . . . stop provoking him?'

'Yes.'

It had gone a bit far. But Bestavros just *got to him*. All those fucking disapproving looks under those ridiculous lashes. The way he smashed everyone's times in the running drills. The way the training shorts looked on his thighs when he propelled himself into the air off the marking bag.

'This can't have been an easy transition for him,' Yelks said. 'I was hoping you boys would look out for him. He's got a lot of talent, but the Sharks obviously weren't a good fit. To really deliver on his ability, he needs to loosen up. Have some fun. Feel like part of this team.'

That was absolutely true. And Jake definitely hadn't done anything to help with that.

'Yeah,' Jake said, prodding the last pierogi. 'I'll do better. I don't know if he's gonna want to be friends, but I'll try.'

'That's all I can ask.' Yelks stretched. God, his arms were *ridiculous*. He was in his mid-thirties and he probably had the best body on the team. There was an Insta (which Jake definitely didn't follow on his burner account) devoted purely to pictures of Yelks in trackies. 'You've still got to do your extras though.'

Jake knew that if he explained what was going on with his mum, Yelks would go in to bat for him, and he'd be allowed to go home as planned. But he didn't want to explain. He already felt raw and scraped out. He didn't want to deal with Yelks being gentle and kind, the way he'd say something like, 'Whatever you need.' He didn't want Bestavros to think he'd gotten out of the extras because he was a brat, but he also didn't want him to know *why* he'd gotten out of extras.

So he said goodbye to Yelks, locked the door, and yelled, 'It's safe to come out,' down the hallway.

He'd cope.

Chapter Six

The first day of extras passed uneventfully. Theo apologised. Cunningham apologised. They both focused on not throwing up during the sprint session. And sure, the convivial back slaps felt a bit forced, but at least nobody tried to punch on. Also, Theo had observed at camp that Cunningham was not a morning person.

Davo took the session himself, unsmiling, but Theo detected a slight thawing by the end. Apparently the back slaps had done their work.

On the second day, Theo woke up half an hour before his alarm and decided he might as well head to the club. He could make a coffee there without waking up Eva, and the pre-workout options in the communal kitchen were good. He would say this for the Falcons: they had money, and with money came awesome facilities. There was a gorgeous player lounge with a view of the oval, extremely comfortable couches and booths, and an endless supply of snacks and smoothie ingredients.

He made a coffee and a protein shake, then realised he hadn't brought a headband with him (Cunningham had been right, damn him) and went to retrieve one from his locker. The club was a little eerie at this time of day, lights clicking on one by one as Theo walked through the silent corridors.

He walked into the locker room and froze. Cunningham was

slumped in front of his locker, elbows on his knees and face in his hands. He was definitely crying. Before Theo could decide whether to back the hell up and pretend he hadn't seen anything, Cunningham looked up. His eyes were red-rimmed and swollen, his cheeks wet with tears.

'Great,' Cunningham said, dragging the back of his forearm across his face.

Theo took a step into the room and hesitated. 'Are . . . are you okay?' Stupid question.

'Yup.' Cunningham popped the 'p'. 'I'm fine,' he said, looking about as far from fine as it was possible for a person to be. 'I'll meet you out there.'

It was the out Theo needed. He could leave, head to the oval, and they would never have to acknowledge this had happened. But also, something was wrong. *Really* wrong, maybe.

Theo didn't move any closer, but he didn't leave either. 'Did you need . . .' he started.

Cunningham let out a slow breath. It shook. His eyes looked even bluer than usual. 'You don't have to pretend to give a fuck,' he said, without rancour. He sounded exhausted. There were purple marks like bruises under his eyes. Had he slept? 'I just need a sec. Like I said, I'll meet you out there.'

It was definitely none of Theo's business. He should leave.

'Fuck,' Cunningham said, curling in on himself a little more, his shoulders shaking.

Theo almost turned away – he was intruding. Then Cunningham sobbed, just once. A harsh, animal sound of real grief that hooked under Theo's ribs.

He crossed the room and dropped to his knees in front of Cunningham. Cunningham looked up, startled.

'Okay,' Theo said. 'I know you'd probably rather this was anyone but me, but I'm not just going to leave you here.'

Cunningham looked at him. 'I don't want to talk to you about this,' he said, quietly, as though he was talking to himself.

'You don't have to. I know you think I'm an asshole, but I'm not leaving you alone when you're this upset. Do you need me to tell Davo that you're sick? Do you need me to call Xenos or Riley?' Although presumably Cunningham could have talked to one of them before he left the house. 'Yelks?'

'No,' Cunningham said, with conviction. 'I'll get it together.'

'Okay,' Theo said again. God, this was awkward. 'Um,' he started.

Cunningham's eyes met his, and then Cunningham started to laugh. There was an edge of hysteria to it, but it made Theo laugh as well, and then he couldn't stop. He grabbed the bench to keep himself upright (and so he didn't grab Cunningham's thigh). Cunningham got himself under control and scrubbed at his face. Theo leaned across to pull a towel out of his own locker and handed it to him.

'Thanks,' Cunningham said. 'Sorry, I didn't think you'd be in here. Xen and Paddy were up stupid early to get ready to go hiking and they would have noticed if I'd . . . lost my shit,' he finished.

'I'm sorry I walked in.'

'Yeah, I'll bet.'

'I mean, if you wanted privacy.'

Cunningham bit his lip. 'I don't know what I want. But thanks.'

'For what?'

'Giving a shit? Or giving me a towel, at least.'

'No problem.' Theo levered himself up and sat down on the bench next to Cunningham. Not close enough that their thighs were touching, but closer than he would have a couple of days ago. 'You sure I can't get you anything?'

'Yeah.'

They sat in silence for a few moments, Cunningham's breathing getting steadier, even though there were fresh tears sliding down his cheeks. Theo put a hand on his shoulder before he could second-guess himself.

Cunningham sighed, leaning into the touch a little.

'My mum has cancer,' he said, staring at the wall across from them. 'She had it, it went away, it came back. It probably won't go away again.'

Jesus. Theo didn't know what to say.

Cunningham was still staring at a spot on the wall. 'I was supposed to be home yesterday for the telehealth appointment she had with her oncologist.'

'I'm sorry.' That seemed very inadequate.

Cunningham rested his head against the side of his locker. 'The news . . . anyway, you don't need to hear about it. But I didn't sleep much.'

'Can I go and say something to Davo? I don't think you should be training this morning.'

Weirdly, that made Cunningham smile. It was a very damp, trembly smile, but it was a smile. 'Mum'd give me a spray if she knew I'd used her to get out of extras. So no, but thanks.'

'All good.' Being nice to someone whose mother was potentially dying seemed like a pretty low fucking bar. 'You want a coffee or anything?' At least that would be something he could *do*.

'You volunteering to make me one?'

'Sure.'

'That would be good, actually. Thanks.'

'How do you take it?'

'Reckon you can manage a cappuccino?'

'Uh.' Theo drank black coffee at the club partly because he didn't want to have to learn how to make the machine do anything more complicated.

'I like a lot of choccy sprinkles.' Jake's face broke into a smile. 'I'm joking,' he said, after a moment. 'There's a button for a latte, but I'm not picky. If it's coffee, I'll drink it.'

By the time Theo returned, Cunningham – Jake, maybe, at this point – had obviously washed his face and made a significant effort to get his shit together. Theo handed him the coffee. He was fairly sure it was a latte. He'd also brought them each a banana. Nature's energy snack.

Jake polished off his coffee and his snack while Theo finished his own coffee. The silence didn't feel awkward, even if the whole situation was objectively incredibly awkward.

They made it out onto the oval with plenty of time to spare. Davo grunted a good morning and then they were off. By the time they were done, Theo was dripping with sweat. Davo was taking the punishment dimension of these extras very seriously.

'Stretch,' Davo said, then stomped off towards the club and his office. Jake looked like he was a couple of breaths away from vomiting.

'I'm going to grab us both a Gatorade,' Theo told him, and jogged off. He'd stayed with Jake when he was distraught, but it was only decent to give someone the chance to spew privately into a bin.

By the time he got back, Jake was looking less green but more clammy. Theo handed him a water first and he rinsed his mouth out before he accepted the Gatorade.

'I think he's trying to kill us,' Jake said, flopping down onto the grass. 'Which I guess is one way of solving the problem.'

Theo followed him onto the grass, though less dramatically, and folded forward into a hamstring stretch.

'I'm sorry about the skit, and the interview,' Jake said. He was lying on his back, staring up at the soft morning sky. Maybe stretching was beyond him. 'And sorry I didn't apologise before.

It felt awkward as fuck to bring it up when you joined the team out of nowhere.'

'Thanks,' Theo said, because it still wasn't really okay, but he did get it. 'I'm sorry . . . about what I said. And for being a dick.'

Jake rolled over to look at Theo. 'Thanks.' He sat up and propped himself against the boundary fence, still not looking like he had any intention of stretching. He watched Theo get into a pigeon pose and then said, 'Does that mean I'm not a showboating hack?' His grin was all mischief again.

'I'll take back the hack part.'

'Fuck off,' Jake said, but not like he meant it.

'Like you can deny it.'

Jake shrugged. 'If you've got it . . .'

Theo rolled his eyes.

'Wanna grab breakfast?' Jake asked. 'The place around the corner will be open.'

Theo was sure he meant to say *No thanks*, but instead his mouth said, 'Yeah.' Then he clarified. 'I want a word with Davo, can you wait?'

'Sure, I wanna shower. Meet you in the foyer in twenty?'

'Sounds good.'

Once they parted ways, Theo took a steadying breath. He could do this. He wasn't going to be the reason Jake didn't get to spend the two days before Christmas with his sick mum.

Jake wasn't sure what Bestavros had said to Davo to get them out of the remaining extras – he obviously hadn't said anything about Jake's mum, because Davo would have bailed him up about that – but whatever he'd said had worked. Yelks had called him to deliver the good news around lunchtime, and Jake had been in his car and headed for Phillip Island an hour later.

Breakfast at Jane Orangutan had been nice. A bit weird, but nice. Stavs reminded Jake a bit of Xen back when they'd first become friends: kind of reserved with new people, funny as hell when he opened up. He had a great smile when he smiled properly, and an even better laugh. Jake had spent quite a lot of breakfast trying to get a smile.

He pulled in at his mum's place a bit past 3 pm. The house had looked the same for as long as he could remember: the eucalyptus in the front yard that he'd fallen out of when he was six (broken collarbone), his mum's beat-up Subaru in the driveway because she never put it in the garage, the pots on the verandah that Lydia filled with herbs and flowers, the deckchairs you couldn't sit in until you'd turned them upside down to check for spiders.

The front door opened as he got out of the car and Keeley hurtled down the front steps, Plugger hot on her heels and barking ecstatically. Keeley's parents liked to take a cruise at Christmas, so she'd gotten into the habit of spending Christmas with Jake. She flung herself at Jake and he caught her, spinning her around. She wrapped her legs around his waist and hugged him, burying her face in his shoulder while Plugger leaped all over them both. Jake's thighs were going to be scratched to hell.

'I missed you, dickhead,' Keeley said into his t-shirt.

'Missed you too, shortass,' he said, trying not to get a mouthful of her hair.

She kicked one foot into his back, and he pretended he was going to drop her. They were both gasping with laughter by the time he got up the steps. She hopped down once they made it to the door so he could wrap Lydia in a tight hug.

She always smelled of paint and jasmine. She'd never tried to be a parent – had installed herself gradually into cool aunt territory – but she gave the best hugs and made the best cocktails.

'I'm so glad you're here,' she said.

'Where's Mum?'

'Out on a walk. She thought she'd beat you back.' They exchanged looks. An apocalypse could be heading for Rhyll and his mum would still get her afternoon walk in.

Jake grabbed his stuff from the car and lugged it through the house and out to his den – also unchanged from when he'd left home at eighteen. Keeley followed him in and handed him a beer.

'Thanks, love,' he said, and dodged her elbow. She flopped onto his bed and he gave her a short version of the last couple of days. They texted almost constantly, so she'd been across the Bestavros situation. In that she'd mainly sent him the eyeroll and/ or eggplant emojis.

They were drawn back into the kitchen by the smell of melted cheese. Lydia plonked two trays of nachos onto the kitchen counter (one of them vegan, for her and Keeley). 'Save some for Debbie,' she ordered.

'You snooze, you lose,' Jake said, trying to avoid burning his fingers on the melted cheese. He'd just put a salsa-laden chip into his mouth when the front door opened and there were footsteps in the hall.

'Look what the cat dragged in,' Lydia called as Jake's mum walked into the kitchen. She was in a Falcons t-shirt, her favourite footy shorts and some sneakers Lydia had been trying to throw out for years.

'Welcome home,' she said, and if Jake couldn't talk past the lump in his throat while he hugged her, nobody was judging.

Chapter Seven

Did you text *Happy Christmas* to someone who was spending it with a parent who might be dying? Theo typed it out, deleted it, typed it out again, and deleted it again.

He was probably overthinking it.

It was 25 December and he'd retreated to his bedroom because their parents were arriving to spend ten days in Melbourne and Eva was treating it like a royal visit. As though Eva had anything to worry about. Eva was a model child. Basically, all three of his siblings were model children. But every time he went near her, she either snapped at him to get out of the way or made him clean something. Retreat had seemed sensible.

His family would never spend actual Christmas in Melbourne – Coptic Christmas was in January, and they'd have to be in Sydney for the festivities – but Eva and Theo had both said they couldn't make it back this year, so their parents had decided to make a trip to see them. Or to see Eva and to quietly disapprove of all of Theo's choices. At least if he'd gone back to Sydney there would have been enough chaos to diffuse some of the disapproval. Maybe one of his cousins would have committed a worse sin than becoming a professional footballer.

His phone buzzed in his hand. Jake had texted him *happy xmas* and a selfie: a golden retriever wearing a lot of tinsel was in the process of trying to lick his face. Jake looked so happy that something in Theo's stomach flipped over, and he found himself smiling back at the phone.

He'd known going to Davo had been the right thing to do, but that hadn't made it *easy*. The coach had studied him intently as Theo had asked for Jake to be excused from the additional days of extras – Theo said he'd do them, do double, that the altercation had been his fault. He'd thought his heart was going to beat out of his chest; his sweaty hands shoved into his pockets.

'Alright,' Davo had said, after what had felt like an eternity, though must have only been a few seconds.

'Thanks.' Theo had wondered if he should say anything more, if he should try to explain further. But any explanation would just sound like an excuse.

He'd been about to walk away when Davo had said, 'You're doing well, Bestavros. Keep it up. We'll treat this one as an outlier.' Then, more sternly, 'It had better be an outlier.'

Theo had nodded and fled.

Happy Christmas, Theo sent back, along with a picture of their tree. Theo's contribution had been to put up the lights under strict supervision. It had taken three attempts before Eva was satisfied. It was the sort of tree that looked like something out of a David Jones catalogue: all matching ivory ornaments, except for a couple of tastefully placed antique ones.

Jake

Theo

Not my work

Jake

yeh I figured

Theo

Rude.

Jake sent him a picture of a much less coordinated Christmas tree. A lot of the ornaments had obviously been made by Jake in school. Many of them were football themed. Junior-primary Jake had a vision for his future.

Theo hesitated, then wrote *I hope your Mum is doing ok.*

Jake sent him a picture of a woman with buzzed grey hair and Jake's eyes, sitting on the beach, holding up a stubby in a cheers gesture. She was in a grey Falcons singlet and there was a familiar mermaid tattoo on her left bicep, faded but still clearly distinguishable.

Theo

You have the same tattoo as your mum?

Jake

my mum is cool

Jake sent him another picture. He'd angled the phone so his mum's tattoo and his own were in the frame together. He'd hooked a thumb in the waistband of his rainbow-lorikeet board shorts and pulled them down to expose the whole tattoo, as though Theo hadn't seen it before.

Theo flicked the fan on. It really was a warm day.

Theo

Nice boardies

Jake

> present from lydia

> (mum's gf)

Jake sent him a sequence of pictures – one of a woman who must have been Lydia wearing a kaftan in the same print as Jake's boardies, an impressive beach tent, the golden retriever splashing gleefully in the waves with a girl in a yellow bikini (Jake's sister? Jake's friend?). Jake's Christmas Day seemed very focused on the beach and not very focused on anything to do with Christmas. Theo sent him a picture of the unhinged Nativity icon that had been in the family for a good few decades. It had lost a bit of its gilt over the years, but none of its character. The colour combinations on the robes of the Magi weren't dissimilar to some of Jake's outfit selections.

Jake sent a sequence of emojis that Theo interpreted as amusement.

Jake

> do ur family do church shit
> on xmas?

> not that its shit if ur into that

Theo

> My parents + extended family do,
> I don't usually go

> Christmas for us isn't until Jan 7

Jake

cool

like xen

Xen's family were Greek Orthodox, but Jake probably didn't want to hear about Monophysitism versus Miaphysitism. Theo shifted to arrange himself more comfortably on the bed. He wasn't sure why Jake was texting him instead of swimming, or surfing, or messaging one of his million mates, but at least it was a distraction from the imminent arrival of Theo's parents.

Jake

wat kind of church do they go 2?

can i ask that?

im not being a dick im just curious

paddy says i can ask qs about race and stuff if they come from a 'place of genuine curiosity' and if i cant google the answer

paddy talks a lot of shit tho

Theo snorted. He wouldn't have picked Jake as an over-texter. Or maybe he would have, given that Jake always seemed to say the first thing that came into his brain.

Theo

Haha it's fine. We're Coptic

My parents had to get out of Egypt in the eighties

Jake

cool

well not cool

u kno wat i mean

Theo did. For once.

Jake

wat r u doing 2day then

?

Theo

Hiding from my sister. Our parents are arriving today and she's lost it

Jake

?????

Theo

She wants everything to be perfect

Jake

Theo

She shouts at me whenever I try

Theo was about five chapters into *Death on the Nile* when Jake messaged him again, post-surf. By the time Theo felt it was safe to venture out of his room, he knew that the dog was called Plugger, that Jake's friend Keeley (of the yellow bikini) was a better surfer than Jake was, and that Lydia refused to cook turkey on Christmas because, 'Nobody likes it and it's too hot.' He didn't realise how long they'd been texting until he got downstairs and discovered his parents were ten minutes away and Eva wanted him to put on a nicer shirt. He thought about arguing – there was nothing wrong with his Falcons polo – but arguing with Eva was usually fruitless, so he went to change.

Jake was sprawled on the back steps, full of prawns and smoked salmon, scrolling while he got some afternoon sun. His mum, Lydia and Keeley had all flopped onto the couch to watch a detective Christmas special, and Jake had opted for some quality time with Plugger.

The message banner popped up as he was looking at some vintage sneakers.

Theo

I wish I could pull a fire alarm rn

Jake blinked at the text. Plugger took advantage and wrenched the rope toy out of his hand. He ran a triumphant lap of the backyard, trying to bark around the mouthful of hemp, then hurled himself at Jake's feet, tail thudding. Jake gave him a belly scratch with one bare foot as he considered the message.

He could text back, or he could just . . . call Stavs. Which he'd never done before, but the text did seem like a cry for help. Or at least for rescue. Jake wasn't going to leave a teammate high and dry.

Also, he wanted Stavs to be his friend. Stavs clearly needed some friends, and Jake liked him. They were going to be friends, whether Stavs thought he wanted to be friends or not.

Jake called him.

Theo's phone buzzed against the table, interrupting his father's question about his Law degree. It was always good to see his parents, except for the way it made something in him ache a little, like a broken bone that had never healed quite right. It didn't help that, apart from a little silver in their hair, they looked the same as when he was a kid.

Jenny the psychologist had gently introduced the concept of 'mind-reading' to their last session, talking him through all the problems of making assumptions about what other people were thinking – but knowing that's what he was doing didn't really help when his parents exchanged a look he knew meant *He'll get his head on straight eventually*. Maybe he was mind-reading, but he was reading their minds right.

His parents were the sort of people who managed to get off flights looking completely unrumpled. Maybe it was just practise. They were also the sort of people who could come on a ten-day trip with only carry-on baggage. Priya was convinced they'd exchanged their souls for magically capacious carry-on cases.

They were having drinks in the living room and 'catching up', which meant that his parents were asking Eva about work, updating both of them about their siblings, and pretending that Theo didn't have a job. Normally that meant Theo just avoided a loving but intense interrogation, which is what Eva got, but this year his parents *did* have Theo's studies to ask about. The degree was going fine, but the questions and suggestions were starting to feel like pinpricks: bearable individually, but painful in accumulation. No, he didn't have time to pick up a couple of additional subjects. No, he didn't think he'd be able to get involved in extra-curriculars. No, he wasn't going pick up some work experience. *Work experience*. As though he were a fifteen-year-old and not a professional fucking athlete.

He picked up the phone as it continued to vibrate, expecting to see Priya's face on the screen. She was good at responding promptly to an SOS; it wouldn't have been the first time she'd strategically called him on a holiday. His parents loved Priya, of course. They'd definitely spent a period of time hoping they'd get her as a daughter-in-law. They could conceivably *still* get her as a daughter-in-law, but only if Eva had a change of heart about heterosexuality.

It wasn't Priya. Theo stared at the screen for a few seconds. Why was Jake calling him? A butt dial?

'Everything okay?' Eva asked.

A life raft was a life raft. 'I should take this . . . it's someone from the team. Excuse me.'

He ducked out the back door into the garden before anyone could tell him off for checking his phone. It was a blisteringly hot day, but there was a nice nook of shade under the majestic gum tree that shaded the back courtyard.

He answered the call. 'Hi.'

'Hey.'

Theo waited for Jake to explain why he'd called.

'You said you wanted to pull a fire alarm,' Jake said, just as Theo was about to ask if he was still on the line.

Well, that explained it. 'Oh shit, sorry. I meant to send that message to someone else.'

'I kinda figured. But I didn't want to leave you, like, stranded or whatever.'

'You called me on Christmas so you could be a figurative fire alarm?'

Theo could almost hear Jake's shrug. 'Well, yeah, I'm not gonna ignore a cry for help.'

'Thanks.'

'You gonna tell me why you wanted to pull the alarm?'

'No,' Theo said, the horror of explaining his family to Jake overcoming his manners.

Jake just laughed. 'Fine,' he said. 'I'll make something up.'

'What?'

'I'm just gonna assume it was something really dramatic.'

'Like what?'

'I'm not gonna tell you.' There was a muted woof through the phone and Jake said, 'Alright, alright . . . Sorry, Plugger was pissed I stopped patting him.'

Needing to be the centre of attention was clearly a Cunningham family trait.

————

'So, it worked?' Jake asked, shifting to scratch Plugger's belly with his other foot. The dog wriggled happily, and Jake was definitely going to have to de-grass-seed him before they went inside.

'It did. I told everyone that it was probably something important about the team.'

'Yeah, super-important team business.' Jake considered his options. 'Like, maybe if I don't call all my teammates on Christmas then our whole season is cursed.'

Stavs snorted.

'Or . . . hmm . . . I needed to discuss the theme of our New Year's party with you. Because if we don't get the theme right —'

'The whole season is cursed?'

'Got it.'

'Or you could be discussing tactics with me?'

'Nah.' Jake said. 'I'm not the strategy guy. We need Xen on the phone for that.'

'I mean, my family don't know that.'

'Yeah, but I don't wanna have to pretend to be talking game strategy to you. You'll judge.'

'Who says I'm not judging already?'

Plugger barked, because he liked to get involved in conversations.

'Is that Plugger?' Stavs asked.

'Yeah, wanna see?'

Stavs did want to see, so Jake switched to a video call and got Plugger into the frame. That was never difficult – it was usually more difficult to keep Plugger's nose more than two centimetres away from the camera.

'He's just like you,' Stavs said.

'Excuse me?'

'No sense of personal space.'

Jake dodged a barrage of licks directed at his mouth. He loved

Plugger, but there was a lot of drool, and Plugger *really* needed one of his doggie toothbrush chews.

'Hey, I don't slobber on my teammates.'

'Not much.'

Jake didn't trust himself to respond to that – he wasn't really sure where he and Stavs were sitting on the *Oh shit we both like dudes* spectrum. In Jake's experience, the spectrum went from *Let's never speak about this, or to each other, again* (1) to *Let's fuck immediately* (10). They definitely weren't at either extreme, but they could have been basically anywhere else. Jake was at about (8) if he was honest, but Stavs was a mystery.

'Also, I brush my teeth,' Jake said, before he could say something stupid. Stavs had turned his camera on as well, so Jake could see his face and a bit of a cute-looking courtyard. Stavs was wearing a shirt with a collar. Madness.

'I know, you never rinse the basin after.'

'Wow, you *really* hold a grudge. You could have just told me at the time.'

'Then I would have had to stop being annoyed.'

That was . . . surprisingly honest. 'Maybe I was seeing how long it would take you to crack,' Jake admitted.

'You're —'

'A dick? I know.'

'It's not as charming as you think it is.'

'Hey, you're still talking to me.'

'I can hang up.'

'So do it.'

Stavs didn't do it.

'Are you doing anything for New Year's?' Jake asked. Plugger was now on the step next to him, panting his doggie breath into Jake's face.

'Probably not.'

'You are now. Paddy, Xen and I always have a party. Just bring yourself and some beer or something.'

Stavs' eyes narrowed. 'Is there a theme?'

'No theme,' Jake promised. 'We save that for Mad Monday, and birthdays.'

'Thanks for the warning. I don't know —'

Keeley called Jake's name from inside, and Jake cut Stavs off before he could come up with a bullshit excuse. 'Sorry, Stavs. I gotta go. You good?'

'I'm good,' Stavs said. 'Thanks, by the way.'

'No problem. See you at New Year's.' Jake ended the call before Stavs could argue.

Chapter Eight

If someone had asked Theo a year ago where he thought he'd be the following New Year's Eve, the answer would not have been *a house party at Jake Cunningham's place*. But here he was, knocking on the door of a dilapidated bungalow in Coburg. Maybe Jake wasn't as unbearable as Theo had first thought. Or maybe Theo was building up a tolerance. Like microdosing arsenic.

At least the New Year's Eve party had given him an excuse to escape his family. It hadn't been *bad*, exactly. It just always felt as though there was something they were all pointedly *not* talking about (his choices, his ex-girlfriend, him moving back to Sydney). A fretful, unfair part of him was worried that Eva might spill the beans about the *incident* that had landed him in hospital. She'd promised she wouldn't, but he wasn't certain. He hadn't spent proper time with Eva in years, and some days she felt like a stranger.

On top of the usual prickle of parental disapproval, he kept thinking about coming out. Maybe it had been the conversation with Priya, but he turned it over in his mind, again and again. He didn't think his parents would react poorly. But it would be one more item on the list of things about Theo to be *accepted*, or *indulged*.

It would be worse if he were really estranged from his parents, he *knew* that, but that didn't stop the way things were from feeling fraught. He knew they loved him, but they still looked at him like they didn't understand him at all. He'd stopped talking about the things that mattered to him until they didn't really have anything to say to one another. They didn't really know him anymore.

The night of the incident, even if they'd been in town, he still would have called Priya for help. Probably even if they'd been in the house with him.

He shook his head. These were not New Year's party thoughts.

There was a doorbell, but someone had pasted a sticky note above it that read *fucked*, so Theo knocked.

'It's open,' someone yelled from inside. 'Come in, turn left.'

Theo stepped into a tiled hallway with a worn runner that had definitely come from Ikea and stopped. Blinked.

There was a shrine to the Virgin Mary in a nook next to the door, complete with one of those waxy statues wearing a baby-blue robe and an expression of blank benevolence. It stood on a lace doily alongside a set of rosary beads and a couple of candles in pink plastic holders. All standard (though unexpected in this house). What was less standard was the array of other objects: Falcons footy cards, several seashells, a battered green rosette and a scattering of middling origami.

Theo wondered if he was dreaming. Maybe his mind had merged the homes of various elderly relatives with what he'd imagined Jake's house to be like. Maybe his parents had asked one question too many and he'd had some sort of stress blackout.

'Don't worry,' Jake said, materialising next to him. He was wearing fireworks-pattern board shorts and nothing else. 'You brought beer, so she approves.'

'I . . . Do I want to know?'

'It was here when we moved in, so we just left it.'

'Hey, bro,' Paddy said, joining them in front of the little oratory. Theo handed him the beers; he wasn't going to drink any of them, but it would have felt rude to show up empty-handed. 'Thanks. Nice of you to say hi.' Paddy gestured at the statue.

'That's a lot.'

'Felt weird to chuck it out.'

'That . . . I get it.' Good to know the tenets of a Christian childhood crossed cultural barriers.

'Mainly it's to stop Paddy fucking anyone in the hall,' Xen said, coming up to join them. 'Hey, Stavs.' He pulled Theo into a friendly hug.

Paddy snorted. 'Maybe she'd be into it.' He ducked past them to greet a couple of newcomers before Theo could reply.

Theo followed Xen and Jake deeper into the house. It was exactly what he would have expected from Jake, Xen and Paddy: huge TV, giant sectional couch, wall-to-wall Ikea. There were a handful of Falcons players in the living room – mainly the younger guys and several of the AFLW players. He could have amused himself guessing whose friends were whose; there were definitely some people who were too cool to be there for anyone other than Paddy.

Jake and Xen got pulled aside by some people Theo didn't know, so Theo joined a group that included Tommy and Raze. He didn't know any of the AFLW players well. He'd spotted for the captain, Gabriella D'Ambrosio, a few times during early morning gym sessions. He knew a few of the others from the sort of casual chats you had in between sets or when you were both making a cup of tea at the same time. They were all friendly, but he had the sense that they were a little wary about the men's team. Probably with good reason.

He came into the conversation in time to join a spirited argument about indie pop. He found an unexpected ally in one of the AFLW players, who was rocking a lot of facial glitter and the most impressive mullet Theo had ever seen.

'I'm Dex,' the player said in a lull in the conversation. 'They/them.'

Theo took the hand they offered. Dex held on just long enough to let Theo know that they weren't *not* interested.

He didn't find it hard to smile back. 'Theo. He/him.'

'Ooooh, *you're* Theo. Interesting.' Dex gave him a once-over.

'What?'

Dex shrugged. 'Nothing, just heard about you.'

'That's alarming.'

'Dex is usually pretty alarming,' one of the other players chimed in. Yağmur Kaya, Theo remembered. She was wearing denim shorts and a crop top that read *Fuck NYE*.

'Theo, this is Drips, she's my least favourite teammate,' Dex said.

Drips – Theo had questions about that nickname – rested her chin on Dex's shoulder. 'Mean. Why are you alarming this nice boy, Dexy?'

'I just said I'd heard of him,' Dex protested. 'Good things only.' They tipped their head towards Gabby. 'Gabs likes you, and Paddy hasn't said anything that bad about you.'

'Wow, good to know.'

It actually *was* good to know. Theo knew he'd gotten a couple of black marks against his name with Paddy.

They slipped into easy conversation about the AFLW season. The party, overall, was more chill than Theo had expected it to be. There was a very aggressive *Mario Kart* tournament happening in the living room, but nobody was going too hard on the substance front (at least, not obviously). The sliding doors at the back had been thrown open to connect the open-plan living room to a covered deck and the backyard. The playlist had clearly been put together by people with diverse and divergent musical tastes, but it was kind of working.

Theo stuck with the group of players, drinking kombucha while everyone else drank beer and got louder and looser in increments. He got pulled into the *Mario Kart* tournament eventually.

'Should have known you'd be fucking good at this,' Paddy griped as Theo emerged victorious from the first race. Theo lost the cup to Jake, who was the sort of player who moved his whole body as he played, his shoulder pressing into Theo's every time he leaned to one side. Theo maintained that Jake had deliberately jostled his elbow at a crucial juncture, but he had to take the L.

He surrendered his controller and went to grab another kombucha, lingering for a moment in the empty hallway, taking a deep breath. He was hit by a sudden feeling of dislocation. Everything had changed so much in a year. When he blinked, he could almost catch snatches of last New Year's. Sarah's hand in his, pulling him out onto the balcony to watch the fireworks. The pulse of the bass. The flickering of the coloured lights in her friend's Kirribilli penthouse. Increasingly incoherent voice messages from Priya and Rachel, demanding that he go out with them after. Thinking, *This will be my year, this year will be better*, as golden starbursts blossomed and fell into the dark water, light pouring in an endless waterfall off the Harbour Bridge.

His chest tightened. He headed for the backyard rather than the group he'd been talking to.

There were a few people smoking outside and a couple sitting on the grass, wrapped up in each other. Theo ducked around the corner of the house and found it quiet, away from the glow of the outdoor lights. The only seating option was one of those ridiculous swinging love seats, so he lowered himself onto that and focused on his breathing, counting in and out, then on the feeling of the cold bottle against his fingers, then the points where his thighs touched the seat. There were coloured fairy lights wrapped around the frame of the seat. He counted those, too.

He wasn't sure how long he'd been out there when he heard footsteps – a few minutes, maybe. He straightened as Jake rounded the corner and stopped.

'Hey, this is my hiding spot,' Jake said.

'Sorry.' Theo made to get up, but Jake waved him back down.

'It's all good, but you gotta share.' Jake dropped down onto the seat beside Theo, sending it rocking, then stretched his legs out. 'And you gotta tell me why *you're* hiding.'

'I'm not hiding.'

'Yeah, sure.' Jake rocked the seat again.

'Why are *you* hiding?'

Jake crossed one ankle over the other and took a sip of his beer. 'My ex and I got together on New Year's the year before last,' he said eventually, picking at the edge of the label on the bottle with his thumbnail.

'Oh.' Theo felt like he was intruding, again, but Jake had told him to stay. He suddenly wanted to know what the deal had been with Jake's ex: his name, what he'd been like, why they'd broken up. Not that he was going to ask any of that.

Jake continued pulling at the label. 'His parents have this place on the Peninsula. So then the year before last he invited me down and got this fancy dinner delivered and set up the table with candles and shit. It was . . . it was nice.' Jake took a long pull of his beer. 'I was trying not to think about it, but I also don't want to get too fucked up, so now I'm thinking about it.'

'I feel that.'

'Yeah?'

Theo sighed. 'I was thinking about my ex today too. She really liked New Year's.'

Theo hadn't – not before Sarah – but she'd loved the excuse to plan and set goals. Sometimes he'd wondered if Sarah had created a relationship spreadsheet the same way she'd had spreadsheets for her professional goals and her running. He'd always been a planner, too, so they'd planned together, and every time they'd done it Theo had felt the settled kind of comfort that came with being on a good team.

Harvard had always been in her plan, but he'd thought when the time came they'd work something out. Hadn't thought it would come down to a yes or no.

Last New Year's had been a good night. He'd been doing well at the Sharks' pre-season camp and Sarah had just published a paper in a prestigious journal. They'd gotten drunk on champagne and when he'd looked at her, smiling up at him under the fireworks, he'd thought *I'm going to ask her to marry me*. Had thought about asking right then and there, except she would have thought a public proposal was tacky.

He wasn't still in love with her. He didn't even really miss *her*, anymore, but sometimes he missed having a partner. Someone to come home to, and wake up with. Someone to talk to, to share with. Someone who knew all the little things about him, the things you only learned through time and proximity.

'So, you've only ever dated girls?' Jake asked. It was the first time since their scuffle at training that he'd alluded to the fact Theo was queer.

Theo hesitated. But Jake didn't sound judgemental, just curious.

'Yeah. I dated a bit in high school, then my ex and I got together our first year of uni and we were together for five years.'

'Wow, sounds serious.'

'It was.'

'What happened?' Jake rocked the seat again. He glanced across at Theo. 'You don't have to talk about it.'

Theo shrugged. 'It's fine. She got into Harvard to do her PhD. She wanted me to move to the US with her.'

'Right.'

It sounded very simple, when he put it like that. And maybe it had been, in the end. They hadn't even fought about it. She'd been incredulous, initially, that he wasn't willing to leave, and then they'd both been resigned to breaking up. It had been amicable, and maybe that hurt as well, in its own way.

'Is it . . . It must be hard, dating guys,' Theo said, because he didn't really want to talk about Sarah. 'While you're not out,' he clarified.

'I mean . . .' Jake shrugged. 'Nobody I was fucking around with in school or whatever wanted to be out either, so it was fine. And then I was with Kyle – my ex – and that was fine until it wasn't. We broke up a couple of months ago.'

'What happened?' Jake had asked first, so turnabout was fair play. 'You also don't have to talk about it.'

Jake lifted his bottle to his lips and took another sip of beer, then set it aside. 'He told me we were done if I didn't come out. I said I wasn't coming out.'

'Jesus. I'm sorry.'

'I mean, thanks, but don't be sorry. I'm pretty pissed with him.' Jake sighed. 'I kinda miss his dick, though.'

Theo choked on air. It was a good thing he hadn't been drinking. 'Right.'

'Or maybe just dick in general,' Jake said, as though the statement had needed clarification.

'Fair.' Theo was conscious that he didn't sound totally normal.

'What?' Jake asked, laughter creeping back into his voice. 'You saying you don't . . . actually, probably not. I guess it's easier if you also like girls.'

Theo hadn't been with anyone since Sarah, but sex didn't feel like a priority. Or at least it *hadn't*, except now he was very aware of the warmth of Jake's thigh next to his. He hadn't known you could get board shorts with a five-inch inseam, but here they were, the fireworks fabric stretched over Jake's thighs, the hem barely brushing the top of the pelican tattoo.

'I'm sure you could find dick elsewhere?' *What the actual fuck.*

Jake rocked them on the seat again. 'It's kinda hard . . . I'm not on Grindr or whatever because I don't trust randoms, and it's not like I really meet people who aren't on the team. And I don't shit where I eat, you know.' He paused. 'Anymore.'

Theo was not going to think about what *that* meant. 'Right.'

Talking about this with Jake was not a good idea. Not when Jake was bare-chested and slouched beside him, loose and relaxed. Jake had a good body – everyone on the team had a good body – but Theo thought he probably would have been just as attractive if he didn't spend half his life exercising. He was so comfortable in his own skin, so quick to smile and laugh.

Jake took another drink of his beer. 'I thought we'd get a dog, maybe,' he said, staring at the ground. 'Like, it's dumb, because we weren't even living in the same city, and we hadn't been together that long, but sometimes I thought about us getting a dog and walking it or whatever.' He paused. 'Just, I don't know. Having a dog. Together.'

'It's not dumb.'

'It was my fault we didn't get a dog, though.'

The last thing Jake should be talking about was Kyle. He wasn't even supposed to be *thinking* about Kyle. He especially shouldn't be talking about whatever stupid thoughts he'd had about getting a dog.

It would have been a golden retriever. A girl. They would have called her Daisy.

'I . . . I don't know your ex,' Stavs said, after a long pause. 'But giving someone an ultimatum like that is . . . that's not okay.'

Jake shrugged. 'He thought I was gutless for not coming out.'

Stavs winced. 'I'm sorry I . . . said what I said. About that.'

'It's all good. Well, I mean, it wasn't, but you just wanted to piss me off.'

'Yeah.' Stavs laughed softly, then shifted restlessly. 'And I guess sometimes I feel that way about myself. So I said it to you, because I knew —'

'I get it,' Jake said. It wasn't like he had a big chunk of moral high ground here. But also, he didn't want to talk about it. 'So, what's your New Year's resolution?' he asked, setting his empty beer down off to the side so he wouldn't kick it over. He dug in his heels, sending the swing into a gentle rock.

'Who says I have one?'

'Yeah right.' Jake did not believe that for a second. Stavs definitely had a colour-coded planner. 'I bet you have a set of SMART goals written in your journal somewhere.'

Stavs flipped Jake off instead of answering, which was as good as a confession.

'What's yours?' Stavs countered.

'Do I seem like a resolutions person?'

Stavs rubbed an imaginary beard. Jake bet he could actually grow a proper beard if he wanted. It would be hot. 'Hmm. I bet you do have one. I bet it's "win the Brownlow" or "kick a hundred goals" or something like that.'

'Those are specific, measurable . . .' Jake tried to remember what the other letters stood for.

'There's an "achievable" in there for a reason.'

'Fuck you.'

Jake did have one resolution – it was *befriend Stavs* – but he wasn't going to tell Stavs about that. That would take all the fun out of it.

———

Sitting with Jake was comfortable. Theo wouldn't have expected that. They could have joined everyone inside for the countdown, but Theo didn't really want to move. The night was just warm enough to be pleasant, and there was something lovely about being on the outside of all the activity: hearing the murmur of voices and the thrum of the music without being caught up in it, smelling citrus and night jasmine alongside the barbecue happening next door.

Jake didn't seem to want to move either. He was looking into the middle distance, his expression pensive. The fairy lights gilded his fair hair. Someone had switched across to a radio station before the countdown, and Theo could hear the thud of shoes on the deck as people danced to the last song before midnight.

The radio announced one minute to midnight, and they still didn't move. Theo gave the seat a nudge this time, swinging it back. It made an alarming creaking noise.

'Ten,' Jake said, when the radio countdown started, and Theo joined him on 'three'. There was an explosion of noise as everyone cheered in the new year, and then a sequence of cracks and bursts of colour as someone nearby set off some backyard fireworks.

'Happy New Year,' Jake said, shifting on the seat to face Theo. 'Wanna make out?' He was grinning, almost laughing, but a little bit of the earlier sadness lingered on his face.

Yes, unfortunately. For a moment, as their eyes met, Theo wondered whether Jake was at least half serious. If Theo leaned across, would Jake close the distance between them? He thought about Jake's lips, soft and warm and tasting of the watermelon lip balm he was always using. Wondered how Jake liked to be kissed, whether he'd want it slow and sweet, or if he'd wrap a hand in Theo's hair and bite at Theo's lip, eager and demanding. Wondered whether Jake had kissed many people at midnight, and if a kiss would chase away that bit of sadness.

The moment stretched, and Theo almost did it – almost thought that Jake started to sway towards him. But then there was the thud of footsteps, heading towards them, and Paddy appeared around the corner.

'There you are,' he said, and dumped himself onto the seat between them, practically onto Jake's lap, and handed Jake another beer.

'Happy New Year,' Jake said as Paddy pressed a drunken kiss to his cheek. Theo got one as well, and it was probably an accident that Paddy nearly got him on the mouth. Probably.

Theo held up his bottle.

Jake clinked his beer against it.

ROUNDS 1–3

Chapter Nine

Jake liked doing social-media shit. Usually. It was funny. Or at least, the process was funny. The quality of the actual content varied. Jake had no idea why the Falcons didn't find someone under the age of forty to do team media, but maybe Greg had worked in marketing for so long that the Falcons couldn't fire him. Jake had to explain TikTok to him at least once a fortnight.

Jake didn't have a good feeling about Valentine's Day–themed social media, though. At least not Valentine's Day social media curated by Greg. He also probably shouldn't have engineered for Stavs to get dragged in as well, but . . . he wanted to at least have some fun with it, and Stavs was definitely going to hate it more than he did.

Jake had followed through with his New Year's resolution: he and Stavs were definitely friends now. Stavs looked happier in training these days, although he did go a bit quiet whenever anyone mentioned the pre-season games coming up at the end of February. Putting him on the wing had been an inspired move: his closing speed was insane and he didn't get beaten one-on-one very often. He was looking good. Looking like he had in those old videos.

Now he just had to do it in a game.

Jake had been collecting details about Stavs. He hadn't meant to, but they stuck. His coffee order (soy flat white). His preferred snack (banana, sometimes with peanut butter). The fact he always had a battered old book in his gym bag. His real smile, which started out as a quirk on one side of his mouth and then spread over the rest of his face from there. The way he laughed in training when he forgot he was worried and got caught up in fooling around. The way his hands had felt on Jake's back when Jake had jumped into his arms after a goal in a match sim. The way he'd been able to take Jake's weight with no effort at all.

Jake knew that Stavs hadn't *wanted* to like him, which just made every smile Jake got out of him – and every laugh, every time he said yes when Jake suggested coffee or a drink – that much more satisfying.

Stavs being hot, though, was becoming a problem. Or more of a problem. Jake had, historically, mixed results when fucking around with teammates. On the one hand, it was very convenient, and normally both participants were committed to secrecy. There was little risk of a relationship-ending fight about, say, coming out. On the other hand, the probability of things getting weird was high. He'd had a bit of a thing with one of his Falcons teammates in his first year, but Taylor had been traded to Brisbane and that had been that. And, like he'd told Stavs, he didn't shit where he ate anymore.

But try telling that to his dick.

Fucking around with Stavs would be a bad idea. Even if it was a possibility, which it probably wasn't. Stavs did not seem like a bros-with-blowies kind of guy. He'd overheard Stavs say that his bisexuality was only theoretical, so if Jake sometimes spent time in the shower thinking about giving him some *practical* experience, well . . . he was only human. Stavs had really good biceps, and those *eyelashes*. And he was wound tight in a way that made Jake want to mess him up. Or to rile him up enough that he decided to mess Jake up. That would probably be even better. Jake wanted . . . well, he wanted things he wasn't going to get.

And shouldn't be thinking about. Stavs had obviously had a bad time, was trying to shake off whatever had happened last year, and he needed to feel comfortable in the team. Fucking one of his team-mates was not the way to accomplish that.

Jake locked his car and jogged across the car park. Stavs was waiting for him in the foyer of the training centre, looking like he was going before the AFL Tribunal, not filming social-media content. Because he was a good boy, he'd put on a pink polo for the occasion (Greg had told them to 'dress in theme'). Pink was a good colour on him. A really good colour. He'd had his hair cut as well, and the newly crisp fade did things to his cheekbones.

Jake was wearing a Taylor Swift *Eras* singlet. Stavs gave it a judgemental look, because his taste in music was shit.

'Ready?' Jake asked.

'I don't know why they wanted *me* to do this.'

Jake knew, but he wasn't going to confess. 'Come on, Greg'll bitch if we're late.'

Greg had put a high round table and two bar stools in front of a whiteboard that he'd draped in a pink picnic blanket. Jake wondered if he'd meant to make it look like they were on a date. Probably not. It had probably never crossed Greg's mind that two men who played football could date each other.

Greg looked very pleased with himself. A bad sign. As was the stack of love-heart-shaped cards in the centre of the table.

Stavs arranged himself on the stool, looking more and more like he was at his own wake. Jake hopped up and looked at Greg for instructions. Nothing to do but get it over with.

'You're going to ask one another questions,' Greg explained. 'They're Valentine's Day themed.'

'Great,' Jake said.

'Okay.' Theo looked like he was considering faking illness. Or 'accidentally' falling back off the stool.

Greg gave Theo a concerned look. 'Are you alright? Jake said you were very keen, but if you're not —'

Whoops.

Stavs no longer looked ill. He looked murderous.

'I'm fine,' Stavs ground out, giving Jake a *we'll talk about this later* look that definitely wasn't *intended* to be sexy.

Jake needed to get laid. He needed to find some hot, anonymous man and get this attraction to Stavs railed right out of him.

'Right,' Greg said, straightening the cards. 'Let's get started.'

He pulled one out of the pack and handed it to Jake.

Jake took a second to read it, then looked at Stavs, who was still looking murderous. 'What's your favourite type of first date?' *Boring.*

Stavs visibly forced the scowl off his face. He'd obviously decided to make an effort, probably because he didn't want Greg to tell anyone that he wasn't a team player. He even smiled a little while he pretended to think before he answered. 'Something low-key, I guess. If I don't know the person that well, going for a coffee or brunch and then a walk somewhere nice. If I do know them, maybe dinner – nothing wrong with a classic.'

'Yeah, you're so chill, bro,' Jake teased.

Stavs kicked him under the table and then had to reach out to grab him so he didn't topple off the stool.

'What's *your* favourite type of first date?' Stavs asked, even though he was supposed to get a new question from the next card. Greg wouldn't like that.

'Walk on the beach,' Jake said, instead of the truth, which was *I've never been on one.* 'A swim if the weather's good.' Maybe the New Year's thing with Kyle counted as a date. But it didn't feel like it. *Dating* seemed like something you did where people could see you. It didn't count if you couldn't even hold hands in public.

Stavs rolled his eyes. 'Of course.'

'What's wrong with the beach on a first date?' *Was* there something wrong with the beach on a first date? It seemed like a fine first date to him.

Theo gave the camera a *seriously* type of look. Maybe you weren't supposed to take girls to the beach on the first date? Was that the sort of first date that felt a bit murdery if you were a girl? He'd ask Keeley.

Greg handed Stavs a card. A little pointedly.

'Flowers or chocolates?' Stavs asked.

'Both, duh.'

'For you or for your date?' Stavs had cheered up a bit now he'd gotten a dig in and nearly knocked Jake off the stool. The smile was starting to look real.

Greg – bloody Greg – snorted. 'For his date, obviously.'

Obviously.

The smile froze on Stavs' face and his brows drew together. 'What, can't Jaze have flowers?'

It was the first time he'd called him *Jaze*. Not that Jake had been paying attention.

Jake pouted a little at the camera. 'Yeah, what if I want flowers?'

Greg looked baffled. And all of a sudden Jake was tired in a way that felt like a kettlebell on his chest. Most of the time it wasn't hard to pretend, because he'd been pretending his whole life, and he didn't have to with the people he really cared about. The people who really cared about him. But for some reason, sitting in front of a stupid whiteboard for a stupid jokey video, he was exhausted.

His smile didn't slip, because it was a reflex at this point.

'You gotta bring flowers for Jaze on a first date, he's worth it,' Stavs told the camera, pulling Greg's attention away from Jake.

Stavs nudged the cards across the table and Jake took one. This was probably what he deserved, karmically, for roping Stavs into this.

'Stavs,' Jake said, reading from a new card. 'How many languages can you ask someone out in?' It was lucky Stavs had gotten this one, because Jake's answer was *One, kinda.*

'Oh.' Stavs sounded surprised. It was actually a pretty interesting question. Maybe Greg had googled for suggestions. 'Um, I think four.'

'Really?' Greg looked like he was about to call bullshit. Jake might have thought the same thing a few weeks ago, but he didn't now.

'English, obviously. Then I speak some French and Spanish, and . . .' Jake wondered if he was imagining the slight hesitation in Stavs' voice. 'I speak Arabic with my family.'

'Give us a demo?' Greg said.

Stavs shifted, as though he was uncomfortable that everyone was finding out he was a fucking genius who could take a wicked contested mark *and* knew about law shit *and* casually spoke more than one language.

'Yeah, you can pretend to ask me out,' Jake said, because he was a fucking moron. 'Come on.'

Stavs looked as though he was torn between laughing along and running away. 'Sure, okay,' he said, which took Jake by surprise. Then he leaned across the table and *took Jake's hand.* Jake regretted all of the choices in his life that had led to this moment.

Theo said something in, like, proper French. As far as Jake could tell. Which he probably couldn't. But it was a couple of sentences, not just *bonjour* or whatever.

Jake had always had a bit of a thing for hot guys speaking different languages. Maybe it was just that, apart from his relationship with Kyle, most of his sexual experience had been with guys in Europe, so it was Pavlovian at this point.

'Uh, oui?' Jake said, trying not to sound turned on.

Theo grinned at him. 'Great. And, uh . . .' He paused for a second and switched to Spanish. Again, multiple sentences.

'Claro, guapo,' Jake said, because he had learned some Spanish. Mainly variations of *Yes, like that* and *Can I?*

He couldn't believe this was happening while he was being filmed by Greg. Or maybe it was a good thing it was Greg. If Jake popped a boner, Greg would assume he was thinking about his best goals or something. But that was not going to happen, because Jake was a grown-ass adult and *in control of his dick.*

The Arabic was definitely the worst. Or the best. Maybe it was just that Stavs said more in Arabic. But he still had Jake's hand in his, and he looked into Jake's eyes as he said it, and Jake tried to look like he was on the verge of laughter rather than on the verge of grabbing Stavs by the collar and sticking his tongue down his throat.

'What did you say?' Greg asked.

Theo's eyes widened for a second. 'Oh,' he said. 'Um, I said *You're the most beautiful person I've ever seen, Rumi would have written poetry about you, your eyes are like the ocean, please let me take you to dinner.*'

'Smooth,' Jake said, and they both dissolved into laughter. *Thank God.*

Jake grabbed another card before the situation could get even more out of hand – under Greg's oblivious fucking nose.

'What's the most romantic place in the world?'

'I think any place in the world can be romantic if you're with the right person,' Stavs said.

'Gross.' Except it wasn't. It really was romantic.

Stavs picked the next card. 'Best date you've ever been on.'

That put out Jake's good mood like a wet blanket over a campfire. 'Nah, too hard to pick,' he said. 'Don't want to hurt anyone's feelings.' He winked at the camera and didn't look at Stavs, because Stavs would know he was a fucking liar.

The questions continued. Jake was pretty sure the published video would be just what Greg wanted: a bit of banter between teammates, some low-key thirst content, nothing that the main body of the supporter base would dislike. Very safe.

Jake fucking hated it.

Jake was silent as they walked back towards the foyer. That was ominous. Jake was *never* silent. Theo didn't think anyone watching the video would notice Jake's face had shuttered when Theo had asked about the best date he'd ever been on. Theo might not have noticed a month ago, but at some point he'd just started noticing things about Jake.

It had occurred to Theo, as Jake's smile had shifted from real to fake, that Jake might not have gone on dates with anyone except his ex. Hell, maybe he hadn't even gone on dates with his ex – Jake might not have wanted to risk being seen on a date.

Was it possible that Jake Cunningham had *never been on a date*? The possibility was enough to distract Theo from having told him 'Your eyes are like the ocean'. (What the fuck.) There was something fundamentally wrong with a world where Jake Cunningham couldn't go on a date. He was the sort of person who'd *like* dating.

'Want to grab a coffee?' Theo asked, as they approached the main doors.

'Sure,' Jake said.

The silence continued while they walked. It was unsettling.

They ended up at Jane Orangutan. The staff knew all the Falcons players, but they maintained their allegiance to the Collingwood Currawongs. Theo ordered for them both while Jake grabbed his favourite booth. After a moment of deliberation, Theo got Jake one of the weird peanut-butter protein balls he liked.

When he reached the table, Jake was staring at his water glass rather than scrolling. Even more ominous.

The silence continued through the arrival of the coffee. Theo decided to drink his coffee and not ask any questions. It was a strategy Priya sometimes used on him when she wanted him to spit something out.

'Kyle and I didn't really get to go on dates,' Jake said to his latte, after a few minutes. He hadn't drunk any of it. 'We went out and stuff, but we weren't coupley, you know.'

'You don't have to talk about it. But you can.'

Jake took a sip of the coffee, then pushed it away. 'It . . . I don't know. It was . . . I just . . .' He trailed off again, looking out the window.

Theo let the silence unfold between them again, trying to make it clear that he was listening but not pushing. That Jake could change the subject if he wanted to. Except somehow it was important that Jake *didn't* change the subject. Theo wanted Jake to trust him with whatever it was that was bothering him. Wanted to make it better, if he could.

'I thought he meant it,' Jake told the protein ball. 'When we first got together he said he got that I wouldn't come out, and he didn't mind. He said he could wait, that he wouldn't push. I believed him, you know?'

Theo had realised, after six or so weeks of getting to know Jake properly, that Jake didn't say things he didn't mean. He could be careless, and a bit of a dickhead, and he was definitely used to getting what he wanted, but he was honest. It was like he didn't know any other way to be, like he'd never learned to lie, except for the one big lie of omission they had in common. Jake took other people at face value, and Theo felt indignation tighten his chest when he thought about someone knowing that and lying to Jake to get what *they* wanted.

'I don't get why he said it if he didn't mean it,' Jake said quietly, this time to the cactus in a jar on the table. 'Like, I get it, it sucks having to hide it or whatever. I *know* that.' His voice cracked. 'But he . . . he said I was worth it. And then he changed his mind.' His blue eyes were very bright. 'And I still don't know . . . was it something I did, did it take him a while to realise I wasn't worth it, or did he never mean it at all?'

Theo didn't think Jake had intended to say all that. He knew the feeling; the words like something you'd ripped out from somewhere under your ribcage and plopped down bloody on the table.

'I'm sorry he did that,' Theo said. He wanted to reach across and touch Jake's arm, to pull him into a hug. Paddy or Xen would have done it, but Theo hadn't quite worked out the effortless intimacy they had with one another.

'I need a fucking hug,' Jake said.

'From me?'

'Do you see anyone else volunteering?' Jake was still looking at the protein ball.

Theo shuffled around to Jake's side of the booth, wrapped an arm around Jake's shoulder and pulled him in. It was the sort of awkward side-hug that shouldn't have worked, except Jake relaxed into Theo's embrace and it just *did*. Theo felt Jake exhale, felt some of the tension in his back and shoulders release. He'd turned his head so his cheek was nestled against Theo's chest.

'You're a good hugger,' Jake said against Theo's hoodie. Theo was very consciously not noticing the smell of citrus shampoo and skin-warmed body spray, something light and spicy.

'Don't tell anyone,' Theo said. Not quite into Jake's hair.

Jake snorted. It verged on a snuffle. Theo realised that he wanted to kiss the top of Jake's head, which was . . . it was absolutely not a thing he should want, or be thinking about. Even if

Jake had settled into his arms as though he was meant to be there, even if Theo could feel every breath he took.

'This is cute,' a familiar voice said. Theo looked up. Xen and Paddy were looking down at them. 'Can't believe the two of you snuck off to snuggle without inviting us,' Paddy continued, sliding into the booth next to Jake. Xen took the other side of the booth.

'I wanted a hug,' Jake said. Xen and Paddy didn't seem to think that was out of the ordinary, so presumably Theo wasn't the first person to be asked for a hug in a time of need. He wasn't going to have any feelings about that.

'You okay?' Xen asked. Theo wasn't sure if it was directed to him or to Jake, so he answered for both of them.

'We just did some Valentine's Day social media. With Greg.'

'Yikes,' Xen said.

Paddy wrapped an arm around Jake from the other side and Jake transferred the snuggle to him. Which was for the best, even if Theo felt oddly bereft without Jake pressed against his chest. He still had one arm around Jake's shoulders, so he left it there while Jake nestled into Paddy's side.

'It was a kind of quiz,' Theo explained. 'Questions about our best-ever dates and stuff.'

'Ah,' Xen said, clearly getting it. 'I don't think they should make us talk about our personal lives like that on the socials. It's shitty.'

'I think it was just supposed to be cute and funny,' Theo said, trying to be fair. 'It wasn't Greg's fault he picked two players in the closet.'

There was a beat of silence and *whoops* – well, that was one way for him to come out, Theo supposed.

'I'm bi,' he said.

'Cool.' Paddy reached around Jake for a fist bump.

'Thanks for telling us.' Xen smiled. 'Sorry you didn't really mean to.'

'I meant to,' Theo said, and realised he had. 'Maybe not right then, but – I was going to say something, at some point.'

'Three out of four.' Paddy turned to Xen. 'You sure you don't want to join the club?'

'I think it's the sort of club you get appointed to at birth,' Xen said.

Paddy looked at Theo. 'I don't like labels, but I'm not straight.'

'Cool, thanks for telling me.'

It wasn't exactly a *surprise*. Paddy had the air of someone who'd transcended earthly concerns like sexuality.

'Did you guess?' Jake asked, perking up a bit.

'I mean . . .'

'Was it when he tried to plant one on you at New Year's?' Jake asked, in the tone of someone taking a bit of revenge.

'I kissed his cheek,' Paddy protested. 'I kissed *your* cheek,' he said to Jake.

Jake snorted and turned his attention to the latte – probably cold by now – which Theo took as a sign of convalescence. They didn't talk about anything serious while they finished their coffees, just gossiped about the club and the league and inconsequential things, then headed back to the club together.

Paddy slung a friendly arm over Theo's shoulder as they walked and Theo leaned into him. Paddy was very attractive, objectively, but having Paddy's arm around him didn't make Theo's stomach flip the way it had when Jake's head had been on his chest.

Jake looked back over his shoulder. 'Stop flirting,' he called.

Paddy rolled his eyes and let Theo go, nudging him towards Jake. 'I was just borrowing him.'

'Give him back,' Jake said.

Theo decided not to think about why a tension he hadn't even been aware of eased when Jake wrapped an arm around his waist.

Chapter Ten

Theo's phone buzzed insistently on his bedside table. He ignored it.

He knew he should get up and face the day, but he didn't want to. He didn't want to look at this phone. He didn't want to see the posts he'd been mentioned in, the messages everyone was sending. It had been a bad game. There wasn't any more to be said. One bad game.

Another fucking bad game.

The first pre-season game, too, so people had been paying attention to his debut performance as a Falcon. He'd been so determined not to fuck it up. He'd thrown up beforehand and run out still tasting vomit and choking down the nausea of anxiety, focused on *do better, be better.*

It just hadn't clicked. Part of his brain – the rational, analytical part – knew it hadn't all been his fault. They'd been playing the reigning premiers, they'd been trying out some new things, the structures hadn't come together. But that didn't make it *feel* any better.

He rolled over and stared up at the ceiling. There was light spilling in from the gap in the curtains, painting golden strips across the cream walls. Maybe he'd go back to sleep if he lay still and did some deep breathing. Maybe he'd forget that he'd managed to be in the wrong place over and over again. Maybe he could excise from his mind the one-on-one contest he'd lost that had led directly to a goal.

The phone started buzzing again. Theo picked it up to check whether it was someone he couldn't ignore.

It was Jake. Jake must have filched his phone at some point, because he came up as 'Jake 🔥🦋🍂🧦 Cunningham.'

Another buzz, this time a text.

Jake

pick up

r u alive?

Theo winced. That hit a bit different, these days.

Jake

??

i'll ring the bell

ur sis is eva right???

That made Theo roll over and peer out the window. Sure enough, Jake's ute was parked outside the house. It was pretty distinctive. Theo picked up the phone when it buzzed again.

'Jake,' he started.

He couldn't think of anyone he wanted to see less, but he also couldn't think of anyone he wanted to see more. He wanted to see Jake's smile and hear Jake's laugh. He wanted to watch the way Jake bit his lip and tipped his head when he was thinking. Maybe he wanted Jake to hold him until he felt better, which was not a thing he was going to get, even if he went along with whatever Jake was about to suggest.

Jake cut him off. 'You've got ten minutes. Wear bathers and shoes you can walk in.'

'What?'

'We're going to the beach.'

'I don't like the beach.' Theo did like the beach, but this seemed like an easy objection. 'Also, the beaches here suck.'

'Now you have to come so I can prove you wrong.'

'I said I don't like the beach.'

Jake sighed, long-suffering. 'I don't care.'

'It's not beach weather.' Melbourne was doing that thing where it decided to put some weather from one season into the middle of another one. It had been unseasonably chilly for several days, which meant it would probably be baking hot tomorrow.

'Bro, it's February.'

'Jaze, I —'

Jake cut him off. 'Out in ten or I'll come in and get you. I'll talk to *Eva*.'

Theo stared at his phone. He did not want to go to the beach, but he also didn't want to stay here. And he definitely didn't want Jake knocking on his door. He didn't doubt that Jake *would* march up to the door, flirt politely with Eva, and then bully or cajole Theo out of the house. The lower-energy option was to bow to the inevitable and stave off Eva finding out that anything was wrong. That he was fucking up *again*.

'Tick-tock,' Jake said, and hung up.

Theo threw the phone down on the bed, but he also got up. He fossicked in a drawer to find some board shorts and pulled on a ratty t-shirt.

He managed to get out of the house without running into Eva, so he texted to let her know where he was going.

One of the windows of Jake's ute rolled down as Theo approached. 'Get in, loser,' he said, looking at Theo over his aviators. 'There's coffee. And snacks.'

There was. Theo sipped his coffee and pretended not to be delighted by the bag of warm cinnamon doughnuts. It was . . . quite thoughtful, really.

They were both quiet on the drive. At one point Theo made the error of reaching for Jake's phone to change the music and was shouted down – apparently the K-pop wasn't some sort of algorithm misfire.

'I don't know how you listen to this,' Theo said.

'Better than the sad-boy indie shit you're into.'

Jake drowned out Theo's reply by joining in with a rap break. There were accompanying dance moves, which Jake performed with one hand. Theo found himself smiling, even if he did wish Jake would drive with two hands on the wheel.

'Where are we going?'

'You'll see.'

They turned off the highway forty-five minutes later and proceeded down a network of country roads, then finally onto a dirt track. It was probably a good thing that Jake drove a stupid ute – Eva's hatchback couldn't have handled the potholes. They pulled up, finally, in the sort of car park that had evolved organically rather than through planning permits. A hand-painted sign read 'Take your litter away with you, you dirty cunts'.

Jake parked and unclipped his seatbelt. 'Phone,' he said, holding out his hand.

'What?'

'Phone.'

Theo handed it over, confused, and Jake shut it in the glove box. 'You won't need it.'

'I'm not twelve.'

'So you weren't on socials this morning like a muppet?'

Theo *had* been on socials that morning. Like a muppet. A sad, pathetic muppet. 'Fine.'

Jake retrieved a backpack from the back seat and led Theo across the car park to the beginning of a track. Theo trailed after him, feeling a little bit like a reluctant puppy being taken on a walk.

'I used to come here all the time during school holidays,' Jake said, sure-footed on the rough path. Theo was really hoping neither of them was going to break an ankle. Davo would be pissed as hell. 'Most people don't know about this track, so it was a good place to go and . . . hang out.'

'Hang out, huh?'

Jake gave Theo a wry look over his shoulder. 'Yeah.'

It wasn't a hard climb, but Theo could appreciate why you wouldn't make it if you had a gaggle of children or a whole lot of gear. Just as Theo was about to ask how much further they had to go they came up over a rise and there was the beach, the restless ocean stretching out to the edge of the pale-blue sky.

He'd been wrong. It *was* beach weather, even if it was a little cool.

They both kicked off their sneakers and walked down the sand. Theo inhaled. He'd missed being close to the beach. Sometimes you just needed to submerge yourself in salt water. Not that he was going to admit that to Jake.

Jake unfolded his towel and tossed his stuff on top of it. Theo followed suit and sat down.

'I'm getting in,' Jake said, pulling off his t-shirt.

Theo actively dragged his eyes away from the mermaid tattoo. He'd seen tattoos before. There was no reason this one should exert a magnetic pull on his eyeballs.

'It's not warm enough to swim.'

'Yeah, it is,' Jake said, unbuttoning his shorts. He was wearing budgie smugglers underneath. They were neon pink with an eggplant-emoji pattern.

'I am not getting in.'

'Yeah, you are.' Jake nudged his toe under the hem of Theo's t-shirt and Theo wriggled away.

'Get your gross feet away from me.'

'Hey, my feet are fine. Xen and I get fucking pedicures all the time, okay?'

The foot intruded under Theo's t-shirt again and he grabbed Jake by the ankle. Jake hopped free, laughing. 'Come on.'

'This is not swimming weather.'

'Don't make me make you.'

'Like you could.'

Jake's eyes narrowed.

'That was not a challenge,' Theo said, rolling to his feet, because he was absolutely not going to get into a situation where he and Jake were grappling and Jake was trying to *remove Theo's clothes.*

'Sounded like one.'

'I'm bigger than you.'

'I'm meaner.'

'I'm faster.'

'I bought you doughnuts.'

'I'm sad.' It came out almost like a joke.

'But *I'll* be sad if you don't come in.'

'I'll be sadder if I do.'

'Fine.' Jake pouted. Actually pouted. 'I'll go for a swim and you can just sit here on the sand like a loser.'

'A loser who isn't going to freeze his balls off.'

'Thanks for the concern about my balls.'

Theo resettled on the towel as Jake waded into the water. He spun back around, stretching his arms wide. 'It's nice!'

'I don't believe you!'

Jake gave him the finger then turned, took a few running steps and plunged into the surf. He surfaced a few seconds later, shaking out his hair. 'Refreshing!'

Theo realised he was smiling. 'Fine!' he yelled back. He did want to get in. He could never be on the sand without wanting to get into the water.

He took his usual approach to getting into an ocean that might be cold, which was to run in and submerge himself before his body could register the actual temperature. Which might have been an error, in this case, because it was *freezing*.

'You're a fucking liar,' Theo shouted as he surfaced. This water must have come straight from the Antarctic. He wasn't sure he'd ever been in colder water.

Jake was laughing, his hair turned darkly golden. He threw his arms out, tipping his head back. 'It's the fucking best.'

'I might die.'

'Nah, I'd rescue you.'

'Not if I drown you first for being a lying shit.'

Jake grinned at him. Sometimes looking at Jake when he smiled was a bit like getting winded. It wasn't just that he was good-looking, it was that he didn't hold anything back when he was happy. His smile made Theo think of summer sunshine, and freshly squeezed orange juice, and also the time he'd run flat out into a goal post trying to take a mark in under-16s.

Then Jake splashed him, and he stopped thinking about Jake's smile. They spent a few minutes making spirited attempts to drown each other, then, a truce reached, swam along the shoreline for a while. Jake looked absolutely at home in the water, occasionally flipping onto his back to do backstroke or diving to cut through the water like a seal.

They got out when Theo realised he'd lost feeling in his toes, then jogged back to their towels. Jake had packed extra towels, two Falcons hoodies, beer and two thermoses of coffee. Theo suspected Xen's intervention.

They lay in silence for a while, Jake sprawled on his back and Theo on his stomach with his head resting on one elbow.

'Why the beach?' Theo asked eventually. He'd dried enough to sit up and pull on a hoodie. The breeze was nippy.

Jake was still looking at the ocean. 'The beach always makes me feel better.'

'I . . . thanks.' Theo hoped Jake wasn't going to look at him. He was sure his face was doing something stupid.

'You wanna talk about it?' Jake asked. He'd pushed his hair back off his face and it was drying in tangles. His eyes were the same colour as the sky.

Theo thought about the last time he'd been at the beach, barefoot in the shallows with Priya walking beside him.

'Not really.' He realised it wasn't true as he said it. 'Maybe.'

Xen would probably have been the better pick for this conversation. He was a good listener, and he always knew the right questions to ask. Jake was not always a good listener, and he had no idea what questions he might have to ask. But Stavs looked like he needed to talk, and maybe he'd do it here with his hair drying in windblown curls and sand clinging to his bare calves. Jake had always found it easier to talk when he could smell the salt. When he could look at the ocean instead of whoever he was talking to. When he was thirteen he'd come out to Keeley on the beach, drinking stolen strawberry Cruisers, staring at the seagulls.

He'd thought about bringing Xen and Paddy as well. But he was more likely to get Stavs to the beach if he rocked up alone and made it harder for him to just say no. The three of them had had a post-game conference in Jake's car about how to cheer up Stavs. Raze had called him as well, because apparently Jake was suddenly the resident Stavs expert. He'd told them all he'd talk to him.

Stavs didn't look at Jake. He'd rolled onto his back as well and was staring up at the sky, one hand resting on his stomach and the other above his heart, like he was in yoga or something. Jake gave him a moment, digging a bottle of beer out of the backpack and putting a kombucha next to Stavs' towel. Jake looked out at the waves, waiting, nursing his beer.

'Things weren't good,' Stavs said, after a few minutes. 'Last year, I mean. After that game. Or before it as well, I guess.'

'Yeah?'

'I'd moved back in with my parents after Sarah and I broke up, because I didn't know what I was going to do. The apartment we'd been living in was hers. My parents were away, and I was . . . I was pretty low. After all of that.'

Jake realised where the story was going with the skidding sensation of losing control of a car on a dirt road: you knew what was happening, but there was no way to stop it. And you couldn't slam the brakes, no matter how much you wanted to.

Stavs couldn't seem to look at Jake. He'd turned his head, but his eyes skirted over Jake's face and away.

'I—' He stopped. 'It doesn't—' He stopped again, and Jake stayed quiet. 'Well,' Stavs said, his voice soft, 'things were . . . things got a bit messed up.' He swallowed. 'I took a lot of paracetamol and chased it with a lot of vodka. I still don't know . . . I didn't really want to *die*. I just needed to . . . I don't know. I needed to do *something*. To turn the way I was feeling into something other people could see. But I called my friend Priya, and she came and got me to the ER.'

Jake wanted to reach for him. He didn't, but he shifted so their wrists were touching. 'I'm sorry you were feeling that way.'

'Thanks . . . I just . . . I want this to work out. It *has* to work out.'

'Why?' Jake asked.

Theo met his eyes, then. 'What do you mean?'

Jake tried to find the right words. 'I get why you want to play footy, obviously. But, like, you're smart. You do Law and you speak different languages and shit. You could do lots of things that aren't footy. If I didn't play footy, I'd probably be stacking shelves at Woolies. You'd be a big-shot lawyer or a diplomat or something. If footy doesn't work out you've got options.'

'That's . . . so do you.'

Jake snorted. 'I mean, not really. I'm not bitching about it. This is what I've always wanted to do. But you could do heaps of things. Why does it *have* to work out?'

'It's hard to explain.'

'I've got nowhere better to be,' Jake told him, taking another sip of beer and gesturing at the beach around them.

'I didn't pick up a footy until I was fifteen,' Stavs said, staring up at the sky. There were a few patchy clouds racing across the sun above them. 'I did athletics, and one day the footy coach came up to me after training and asked if I'd ever thought about playing footy. I was a bit bored, so I said I'd try it.'

Jake could imagine a footy coach spotting a teenaged Stavs doing the high jump or whatever and being unable to believe his luck.

'My parents liked us – my siblings and me – doing sport as an extracurricular, but they didn't think about it as a serious thing. They're both academics in medical fields, and they wanted us all to work towards getting good jobs, being financially stable, all that. So sport was only part of being well-rounded, something for job interviews.' Stavs sounded almost defensive. 'They're good parents. But they can be set in their ways.'

Stavs shifted and sat up, crossing his legs. He cast a longing look at Jake's beer and Jake offered it to him. To his surprise, Stavs took it, and Jake tried not to notice the way his lips wrapped around the mouth of the bottle, the line of his throat as he swallowed. He handed the beer back and Jake took a sip as well.

'I loved footy from my very first training session,' Stavs said, his smile a little sad. 'It was . . . it's such a weird game when you haven't grown up watching it, but it was *fun*. It didn't make any sense, but I loved it. And I was good at it, too. I didn't really think about the AFL until I was in the under-18s and suddenly people were asking me about nominating myself for the draft.' Theo swiped the beer from Jake and took another sip.

'You can have that one,' Jake told him, and got himself another.

Sharing was going to give him ideas.

'My parents talked me out of it. So I went to uni and did an Arts degree and played in the VFL. But I kept thinking about putting my name in for the rookie draft, seeing if I could make it work. So I did, finally, and then instead of starting my JD full time, I got drafted.' He laughed, but not as though anything was funny. 'My parents were . . . well, they didn't shout or anything, they're not like that, but they made it clear they thought I was making a big mistake. They just don't take footy seriously, you know.'

Jake didn't know, because his mum took footy more seriously than almost anything else, but he could get it on an abstract level.

'And then last year it was like they were proven right. That it was a stupid idea. I fought with them for so long to try to convince them that this was worthwhile, and Sarah and I broke up because I wouldn't leave Australia, and I just . . . I want to prove to them that I can *do this*. That I haven't *failed*.'

His voice wavered on the last word and Jake hesitated, then shifted so they were sitting closer together, their shoulders touching as well as their wrists. Stavs leaned back into him, just a little.

'Would . . . I mean, even if you were voted All-Australian or whatever, would that convince them?' Jake asked.

Stavs looked, briefly, absolutely miserable. Jake cursed himself for not sending Xen in his place.

'I'm not saying it wouldn't,' he said quickly. 'I just mean . . .' What the fuck did he mean? 'You thought footy was a worthwhile thing to do, and I think you're right, and heaps of other people think you're right. So maybe they're just wrong, and you can't really do anything to stop them being wrong, so you've gotta do this for yourself and fuck what anyone else thinks.'

Stavs gave him a look. 'You say that like it's easy.'

'I know it's not, but . . .' He wished he was better with words. He wished he could say something to fix this, to get Stavs untangled from all this bullshit. Wished Stavs could read his mind, for a few moments, so he'd just get what Jake wanted to say.

Although he didn't want Stavs reading *too* much of his mind.

'Look,' he said finally, conscious that he sounded like his mum. 'You had the balls to give this a shot, even when people told you not to. You got drafted, and you've played at the highest level – that's not *failing*. You've kinda already made it. And if you decide you don't like it after all, or if it doesn't work out, you can go off and make bank doing something else. But you're here now, and you tried real fucking hard to get here, so maybe you've just gotta let yourself have some fun. Because not many people get to do this, and it doesn't matter what your parents think, or what I think, it matters what *you* think. And I think you want to play this game because you love it, and you're fucking *good* at it, and you've just got to get out of your own fucking way.'

Stavs blinked at him, and Jake's cheeks felt a bit hot. Was he *blushing*? He'd never blushed in his life, but he also wasn't sure he'd said that many words in a row before. Stavs was looking at him intensely, like he'd never really seen Jake properly before. Which wasn't helping the whole blushing situation.

'Sorry,' Jake said, fiddling with his fidget ring. 'Pep talks aren't really my thing.'

'It was actually pretty good.' Stavs was smiling properly now.

'Really?'

'Really,' Stavs said, putting his beer aside. 'Sorry, that was a lot to unload on you.'

'All good,' Jake said. 'Thanks for talking.' That didn't feel like enough. 'I get that it was hard to talk about. I'm glad you . . . trusted me.'

Stavs blew out a breath. 'You want to share a deeply personal secret to make me feel better?'

'Kinda did that already.'

They both laughed, and Jake unearthed a tube of Pringles from the backpack. They deserved a snack. They'd worked hard.

They didn't say much else, just lay on the beach until it was time to get in the water again, chased one another through the waves like they were kids, piled back into Jake's ute, sandy and exhausted, and drove home. And if Jake thought a bit about Stavs' lips wrapped around the mouth of a beer bottle, about his wet board shorts clinging to his strong thighs . . .

Well. Nobody had to know.

Chapter Eleven

Theo was spotting for Drips when Dex came into the gym. Drips was on her last rep, straining to re-rack the bar, and Theo was focused on staying ready to grab it if he had to (but not grabbing it too soon, which would be almost as grievous an offence as leaving it too late). They'd started chatting between sets a few days earlier. He'd asked about the tattoos stamped down her arms, and she'd started asking him to spot if none of the AFLW players were around. She didn't like encouragement, just a pair of hands and someone paying attention. He'd asked about her nickname, and she'd explained that that Yağmur meant 'rain' in Turkish. 'It's better than "YaYa",' she'd said.

He'd worked out, from their conversations – mainly conducted in intervals of one to three minutes – that her conservative Turkish father hadn't been impressed by the tattoos, or footy, or the fact she had a girlfriend. It made Theo feel an odd blend of kinship and guilt. He understood chafing against parental expectations, but he had it much better than Drips. It felt petty to gripe about his parents when he'd never *really* had to worry. If anything, sometimes he wondered if he and his parents would be better off if they'd learned to shout at one another, let it all out, and then move on.

Dex walked purposefully towards them as the bar thudded into place and Drips sat up, breathing hard and grinning.

'Nice job,' Theo told her. Encouragement was prohibited, praise was not.

She blew out a breath and reached for her water. 'Thanks for the spot.'

'Any time.'

He hadn't been dropped for the second pre-season game, and even his anxious brain had to concede that he'd played well. The wing suited him, and he'd banged in a goal from the fifty-metre arc. He knew he wasn't going to be in the best 23 at the beginning of the season – he hadn't needed the *managing expectations* chat Kat had given him – but she'd also made it clear that if he maintained his form in the VFL, he'd get a run sooner or later.

Dex stopped beside them, hands on hips. 'Good, two of you. Jaze is teaching me some of his tricky shit and we need more bodies. You done? Jaze said he specifically needs you, Stavs.'

'Does he?' The prospect was disconcerting.

'We're done,' Drips said. It was clear that resistance would be futile.

He followed Drips and Dex down to the oval, and he felt his heart rate kick a little as they headed towards the group gathered in front of the goals. He still wasn't enjoying anything involving goal-kicking. He could hit a target on the run, but as soon as he was kicking for goal he felt like a baby giraffe on uncertain legs.

Jake, Paddy, Xen and Gabby were gathered by one of the point posts, handballing a footy around while they chatted.

'Good,' Jake said when they arrived. He tossed the ball to Xen. 'Xen's gonna kick it to the two of you in a contest' – he pointed at Gabby, then Theo – 'and you'll knock it down for us.'

'Be gentle,' Dex told Gabby. 'Don't break him.'

Gabby showed some teeth. 'No promises.'

Theo wasn't stupid enough to underestimate Gabby. She was only a couple of inches shorter than he was, and while he might have had a few kilos on her, he suspected she had about a tonne of raw determination on him. She'd also definitely deck him if he didn't go as hard as he would with a dude.

He crushed his chivalrous urges as the ball came off Xen's boot (*Chivalry is just polite patriarchy*, Priya said in his head) and went hard for the ball, the same way he would with any of the boys. He could tell Gabby was loving it, relishing the opportunity to use all her physicality. They knocked it down, again and again, as Jake showed Dex how he liked to run through defenders (Paddy and Drips) at stoppages, how he angled his body to the goal, how to knock the ball forward and run on to it. The kind of stuff he'd been practising since he was six years old.

Dex had played soccer before they'd switched to AFL, and Theo could see they were still trying to drill in the sort of skills you only learned through playing, hour after hour, until your body knew what to do before your brain caught up.

Theo enjoyed watching Jake when he wasn't the one in charge of stopping him. He read the ball so well; he thrived on the chaos of a ground ball. Knew when to pick it up and when to tap it on.

He was a surprisingly good teacher as well. Theo knew a lot of people who couldn't explain things they were good at. But Jake didn't try to explain what he *did* so much as what he *saw* – what to look for, what cued each movement. He'd call 'Stop!' every now and again, and Drips and Paddy would freeze in place so Jake could show Dex what they needed to look for.

The drill devolved into chaos in the end. Dex started it with a solid tackle on Jake that Xen called as holding the ball, and then they were all playing an ad hoc game that was mostly keepings-off, switching teams and positions as they played.

'Stavs!' Gabby yelled, and then the ball was in Theo's hands. He had his back to the goals, but he got it on his boot and snapped it over his head without thinking. He just *knew* where the goal posts were, in a way he hadn't for months. He didn't have to look to know it had gone through.

Jake wolf-whistled and Gabby ran over for a fist bump.

After that, he couldn't miss. It felt like for months he'd had to tell himself to take every breath, and now he was doing everything on autopilot again. Something inside him that had been knocked awry had clicked back into place. It was easy, the way it had been when he was seventeen, the coach working with him on his set-up, on his ball drop, on his follow-through, until one day it just *happened*.

They took shots from weird angles, and Theo argued with Jake for a solid five minutes about how far was too far to kick round the corner (Theo was declared the winner after Jake missed two in a row).

Gabby called time and they all flopped down to stretch. Or, in Jake's case, to roll on the grass.

'Hey, Jaze, I didn't know your mum was a fucking *legend*,' Dex said, sprawled on their back. 'There are a stack of pictures of her up in the exhibition about the women's game at the National Gallery.'

'What?' Drips asked.

'Jaze's mum is Debbie Cunningham,' Dex explained. 'She won *five* premierships with the Woolamai Tiger Sharks and then coached them to another three. She's, like, a pioneer of the game. She still runs clinics for girls who want to play.'

'She's pretty cool,' Jake agreed.

'What happened to you?' Gabby asked, nudging Jake with her shin. He stuck his tongue out.

'Here,' Dex said, and handed their phone around. Debbie must have been in her twenties in the picture, dressed in muddy game gear and holding a trophy. There was a striking resemblance between her and Jake: same wavy blonde hair, same strong jaw and stubborn chin, something similar in the way they stood. She had more tattoos than Jake: a big piece on each thigh and a full sleeve on one arm in addition to the pin-up on her other bicep.

'Wow,' Drips said. 'She's *hot*.'

'She should come in and talk to us,' Dex suggested. 'That'd be sick. She could do a pre-game address, if she'd be down for it.'

'Oh, she would be,' Jake said. Theo saw him hesitate. 'She has to come down to Melbourne every couple of weeks for chemo, so we could maybe work around that.'

There was a beat of silence.

'Shit, bro, I'm sorry,' Dex said. 'That's rough.'

'Thanks.'

'How's it going?' Gabby asked. 'Unless you don't want to talk about it, in which case, no stress.'

'No, it's fine,' Jake said, leaning his elbows on his knees and propping his chin in his hands. 'She had uterine cancer a few years ago. It was in remission, but . . . yeah. It's back. It's too early to know if the chemo is working.'

'I'm really sorry,' Gabby said. Drips and Dex murmured agreement. 'Let us know if there's anything we can do.'

'Thanks,' Jake said.

Jake hadn't said much about the chemo, at least not to Theo. Maybe he was talking to Paddy and Xen about it, but Theo doubted it. He stuck to the facts when he did talk about it: *Mum's feeling shitty today, Lydia says Mum's off her tucker, Mum's pissed she fell asleep and missed the last quarter.* He spoke about it with a matter-of-factness that might have been convincing if Theo hadn't seen him so distraught in the locker room that morning before their second extra.

'If she did want to come and chat to us, we'd love that,' Gabby added. 'It doesn't have to be a formal thing. She could just come and hang out. I want to make sure we don't forget our history, you know?'

'She'll be keen.' Jake grinned. 'Good luck getting her to stop talking.'

'It's hereditary, then,' Theo said.

He wasn't sure whether Jake tackled him due to the provocation or to end the conversation.

'Stavs will be playing his first real game as a Falcon.'

Stavs froze for a second before he started to stand. Jake stuck his fingers in his mouth and whistled as loud as he could. Stavs looked surprised – he must have been the only one in the small auditorium who was. Jake had known it was a sure thing as soon as Rigger hobbled out of training early with hamstring awareness.

Stavs had been playing well in the VFL. *Really* well. He'd relaxed, too, now that he'd remembered where the goals were. Jake had seen him *smile* during a goal-kicking drill. He'd *laughed* in a game when he went for a hanger, missed it, and did a full somersault on the way down. Jake was going to take at least some of the credit. If it hadn't been the beach, it had been the fucking around with the footy until Stavs had forgotten to be stressed about it.

Jake, Xen and Paddy had all agreed it had to be Stavs coming into the team – there was nobody else pushing as hard for selection, and it was a like-for-like swap. Stavs was smiling as he clambered over Jake and Tommy and jogged down the few steps to the front of the room, but he looked a bit green around the gills. He took the jumper, shook hands with Davo, and managed to grin for the camera that Greg shoved in his face. But as soon as he sat back down, he flipped up his hood and crossed his arms across his chest.

Jake kept an eye on him throughout the rest of the session.

He sat very still, folded in on himself. He was up and out the door as soon it was over, turning his face into the side of his hood.

'Should I?' Xen asked, jerking his head in the direction of the door.

'I've got it,' Jake said, deciding that he couldn't see the meaningful look Paddy and Xen exchanged. As he headed for the door, he saw Paddy catch Raze's arm. Probably telling Raze that he didn't need to chase Stavs himself.

Jake left the meeting room and turned right down the corridor. There was an equipment room a couple of doors down that was always unlocked and didn't have anything in it anyone was likely to need. It was, unofficially, the *I'm having a meltdown* or *I need to have a manly cry* or *I need to hit a marking bag repeatedly so I don't punch someone in the face* room.

Stavs looked up when the door opened. He was sitting on one of the benches, his head near his knees. Jake slipped in and shut the door behind him. The only sound in the room was Stavs' breathing, harsh and ragged. Too fast, with an edge of a whine on every inhale. The jumper was balled up in his clenched fists.

'I'm good,' Stavs wheezed before Jake could open his mouth. 'Just need a sec.'

He did not sound good.

Jake crossed the room and sat down next to him, not too close. Stavs might think he didn't need anyone here with him, but Stavs hadn't left Jake alone when they'd barely been on speaking terms, so he could fuck right off if he thought Jake was going to leave him now that they were friends. If he didn't want Jake, Jake would get Xen, or Kat, or call one of his friends, or *something*.

'You're having a panic attack,' Jake said.

'No fucking kidding,' Stavs said.

So, not his first rodeo. That was probably good, as much as it also sucked.

'Let me help?'

'No,' Stavs said. Then, 'Okay. Yes.'

Jake slid down to kneel between Stavs' thighs. He thought about the last time they'd been in this position, the way Stavs had tentatively reached out to put a hand on Jake's shoulder as though Jake might push him away. Stavs looked down at him, his breathing shallow. In slightly different circumstances Jake would have made a joke.

'Can I touch you?' he asked instead.

'Okay,' Stavs said again. He was staring at the jumper in his hands.

Jake put his hand on Stavs' shoulder, curling his fingers around the spot where it met his neck, his other hand resting just above Stavs' knee. The position brought their faces close together – so close that Jake could see every one of Stavs' stupid lovely eyelashes.

'Breathe with me?'

'Okay.'

Jake started to count through each inhale and exhale, rubbing light circles over Stavs' hoodie with his thumb. Touch had always helped Xen calm down, but Jake wasn't sure if it might be too much, too intimate. Stavs shut his eyes for a second and exhaled, long and slow, then inhaled again.

Jake felt it under his palm when Stavs started thinking about it all again; he felt the hitch in Stavs' breath at the same time he heard it.

'It's okay,' he said. 'You're okay.'

Stavs gasped, his eyes losing focus.

'Stavs. Look at me, I got you.'

For a second, he thought Stavs wouldn't do it. Then his eyes locked with Jake's. They'd never been this close before. He could see that Stavs' dark eyes were hazel with flecks of gold.

'I've got you,' Jake said again.

Stavs followed his lead when Jake started to count again, his thumb still tracing circles on Stavs' shoulder.

'You're good at this,' Stavs said, once his breathing started to even out.

'Xen used to have panic attacks before every game.'

Stavs blinked. 'He . . . he's so calm though?'

Jake could see why he thought that. Xen had a careful pre-game routine, and he was good at looking like he was focused rather than shitting bricks.

'Yeah, well, he wasn't. Still isn't, probably. Not that you could tell.'

Jake hadn't been sure what to think about the club psychologists until he'd seen what Jenny had been like with Xen. He knew Stavs was seeing Jenny as well; he hoped he'd told her about the panic attacks. Wondered if he'd told Jenny he was queer.

Jake saw Mick every now and again, but they didn't usually have much to talk about. He hadn't told Mick he was queer. He probably *should* tell Mick about his mum, but he wasn't going to.

They breathed together while Jake kept counting. Jake wasn't sure for how long. The position he was in meant he had to look at Stavs' face: the sweep of his eyelashes every time he blinked, the slight bump where his nose must have been broken in the past. He smelled good, like the posh candles Lydia brought home from local markets. Jake wanted to touch his face, wanted to feel the rasp of his stubble, to kiss the delicate skin of his eyelids.

Then Stavs exhaled, long and steady, and Jake watched him deliberately unclench his fingers from around the jumper.

'I'm good,' he said, and Jake realised that he was still rubbing circles on Stavs' back, their faces only a handspan apart.

Jake shuffled back and levered himself up onto the bench again. He resisted the urge to wrap an arm around Stavs, but he let their shoulders press together.

'I can get Xen in here if you need a pep talk.'

Stavs smiled. It wasn't a very convincing smile, but it was something. 'The one you gave me at the beach was pretty good.'

'First and last.' Jake was never going to be a pep-talker. It was why he'd never be leadership material. Not that he minded. He'd have to be less of a pest if he was supposed to inspire people and shit.

'Come on.' Stavs picked up the jumper and folded it neatly. His hands were still shaking, but he was starting to smile for real. 'I have faith in you.'

'Okay, here goes.' Jake pretended to pick up some grass and throw it into the air like he was preparing to take a shot at goal. 'You've killed it in the last couple of games.'

'In the VFL.'

'Yeah, well, it's all footy.'

'Hmm.' Stavs smoothed his fingers over the part of the number on the jumper still visible. 'Maybe.'

Jake watched him trace the outline of the '2' and the '7'. 'Did you pick 27?' he asked, deciding a distraction might work. 'Or are you one of those weirdos who doesn't care what number you wear?'

Stavs glanced up. 'It's my friend Priya's favourite number. I've been wearing it since high school.'

'Cute.'

'Why do you wear 9?'

'It was my mum's number. When I was a kid, I wanted to be just like her. Wasn't tall enough to ruck though.' He sighed. 'Crushed my dreams.'

'You seem to be doing alright.' Stavs' smile faded. 'Must be nice.'

More pep talk was going to be required. 'Are you gonna go out there and do your best?'

Stavs gave him a look. 'Yeah.'

'Well, that's all anyone wants from you.'

'It's professional footy. You don't get participation trophies.'

That was true, and it was something Jake had been reminded of by a succession of shitty school coaches. Maybe Jake had even said it a couple of times himself.

He knocked his shoulder against Stavs'. 'You're not supposed to fight me on this. It's a pep talk, you gotta let yourself be pepped.'

Stavs sighed. 'The media stuff last year messed with me,' he said. 'I just . . . I don't want to go through that again.'

'Seriously, fuck them,' Jake said. 'They just want a story. They say fucked-up shit about *everyone*. Last week they ran a story about how Yelks is past it because he dropped a mark. *One* mark. Every third week some hack says Xen's too short to play footy or that Raze is overweight. They don't know shit.'

'It's just . . . it's never *just* about me.' Stavs was twisting his fingers through the drawstring of his hoodie. 'They say you have to *see it to be it*, right? I get that. Maybe I would have gotten into footy as a kid if there had been more players who looked like me. And now here I am, and they're just watching me fail, and seeing racist shit people put on social media.'

Jake was absolutely not the person who Stavs should talk to about this. It wasn't that he didn't kind of get it, because he felt the same way about coming out – what if he couldn't take it, what if it just proved to a whole lot of queer kids that they *couldn't* be queer and play AFL? But he did not feel like he was the person to have *this* conversation with.

'You could talk to Raze or Paddy, you know,' he offered, hoping it didn't sound like *please talk to Raze or Paddy about this*.

Stavs looked amused, so Jake was going to take that as a win. 'I shouldn't talk to you about it?'

'Well, you can, but I'm real fucking white.'

Stavs actually laughed then. 'You're not wrong.'

Jake shrugged. 'Not usually. Paddy says I'm the whitest person imaginable.'

'Not gonna argue,' Stavs said, reaching out to hook the corner of the seashell necklace Jake was wearing. His finger brushed Jake's throat as he did it and Jake felt like the temperature in the room had shot up several degrees. He looked across and found Stavs looking back, still holding the necklace, his knuckles resting on Jake's bare skin. Stavs' eyes flicked down to Jake's mouth for a second.

For a single, glorious moment Jake thought Stavs might reach for him. Then Stavs swallowed and let go of the necklace, pulling back.

'Is the pep talk over already?' His voice was a little rougher than usual.

Jake stretched his legs out. 'I reckon whatever I say, you're gonna find a reason to disagree. So I'm not going to waste my breath.'

'That's a novel approach to a pep talk.'

'I know what I know, though,' Jake told him. 'You're not gonna talk me out of it: you're fucking good at this. You've got what it takes. And you're going to show them.'

Stavs met his eyes. He was smiling. *Don't look at his mouth.*

'Jake,' he started.

There was a knock on the door and Stavs jumped. Jake couldn't decide if he was pissed off or relieved that the moment had been interrupted.

'Yeah?' he called.

The door opened, and Jake wasn't surprised to see Xen and Paddy.

'Ah,' Paddy said to Stavs. 'You found Xen's quiet spot.'

'What?'

'Xen comes here when he needs a break from Jaze,' Paddy told him.

'So, every day?' Stavs asked, standing and stretching. His t-shirt rode up to expose a strip of stomach and Jake was absolutely not looking.

Based on the look Paddy shot him, he'd been caught not looking.

Jake made a wounded sound. 'You know, because this is such a special day for you, I'm going to let that comment go.'

'Come on, Stavs,' Paddy said. 'Celebratory lunch, and Tommy says he's buying. Hustle.'

Chapter Twelve

They won the game. In the rooms, Theo got shoved into the centre of the circle of players and showered in Gatorade. He shouted along to the team song with a savage satisfaction that didn't make any sense: it was one game, it was so early in the season, there were still a million ways it could go wrong. He'd put in a respectable performance: twenty disposals, eleven kicks, 350 metres gained. It wasn't anything special.

It felt like *everything*. He was sticky, and he was pretty sure there was Gatorade in his eyes, but Jake had an arm wrapped around him and for the first time in forever he felt wiped clean of the clinging grit of dread.

'Drinks at ours,' Paddy yelled. It was early enough in the season that they weren't on a drinking ban, and it was only recovery tomorrow. Theo half expected Yelks to intervene, but he just shook his head and gave Paddy a tolerant smile.

Jake drove them back to Coburg with the windows down, cranking a playlist he'd named *All we do is win, win, win*. Xen spat out Eminem's verse on 'Drop the World' with an unexpected proficiency while Paddy laughed at the look on Theo's face. A good few of their teammates followed in a loose convoy.

Theo felt a little drunk when he got out of the car, high on adrenaline and the joy of relief. Then he felt actually drunk, because Xen unearthed a bottle of something that tasted like rocket fuel and they did shots from appalling novelty shot glasses Paddy produced from a kitchen drawer. Theo turned down the third – he hadn't been drinking at all, and two already had him loose and buzzed, sprawled on the couch, eating pizza and shouting encouragement as Paddy and Tommy duked it out on the Nintendo.

There were enough people that the living room felt pleasantly full – all the younger guys who didn't have families to get back to after the game. Dex, Drips and Gabby rocked up with a couple of tubs of ice-cream, and *Mario Kart* took a turn for the vicious. Theo took another shot when Xen poured him one. The alcohol was warm in his veins and just for tonight he was going to let himself feel good.

Also, Jake was flirting with him.

Not obviously. Not in a way that stepped outside the realm of plausible deniability. But he was definitely flirting: leaning into Theo when they ended up next to each other on the couch, nudging their thighs together, finding excuses to touch him.

After that third shot, Theo let himself flirt back: putting a hand on Jake's thigh when he leaned across the couch to snag a slice of pizza, letting his eyes drift to Jake's mouth while Jake trash-talked him in between races, twisting his fingers to brush Jake's when Jake handed him a fourth shot. He was looking, and Jake was looking back, and there was no way this was anything other than a bad idea, but Theo couldn't find a single fuck to give.

He wanted to know what it would be like to kiss Jake. Wanted to know how Jake kissed, what he liked. Wanted to know whether he'd moan if Theo kissed up his throat to his jaw, if Theo traced the edges of that mermaid tattoo with his tongue.

Everyone started to crash around 10 pm, worn out from the game and the drinking. Nobody had been going *too* hard, and

Theo ended up on the end of the couch between Jake and Paddy, still battling for *Mario Kart* supremacy.

'Gonna crash,' Paddy said, after a resounding loss. He levered himself to his feet and retreated, leaving Theo and Jake on the couch.

'We gotta finish this round,' Jake said.

'I should go.' Theo wasn't sure whether he'd be relieved or disappointed if Jake agreed.

Jake just looked at him, tipping his head back against the back of the couch. 'Come on. We're even. We need a decider.'

'It's pretty late.'

'You can crash here if you like.'

Theo felt like he was teetering on the edge of a precipice, looking down. Jake's singlet had ridden up to show a strip of tanned skin and the waistband of his underwear. The sensible part of Theo's mind was screaming at him to say goodnight and go home, but every other part of him was humming with the need to stay where he was, to see what would happen. Because *something* would happen if he stayed. He knew it, and Jake knew it, and Jake was looking at him with a challenge in his eyes.

'Alright, let's go,' he said, and Jake's smile made his stomach turn over.

They were one-all and Theo was winning the last race when Jake – the *asshole* – grabbed Theo's controller right out of his hands and held it out of his reach. Theo lunged to reclaim it and Jake kept him off with one hand and a knee, gasping with laughter as Mario spun out and crashed on the screen. Jake lost his own controller in the scuffle, Princess Peach going the same way as Mario. Then Theo was sprawled on top of Jake, struggling to keep both of Jake's wrists pinned to the couch, their legs tangled together, both of them shaking with laughter.

'You're such a shit,' Theo said, trying to catch his breath.

Jake grinned up at him. 'You like it.'

Theo needed to stop looking at Jake. Needed to stop looking at his mouth, specifically. He let go of Jake's wrists and Jake shifted, his hands going to Theo's waist as though to push him off. Theo's shirt had slid up in the struggle and he couldn't stop his breath from catching as Jake's fingers brushed his bare sides.

Theo wasn't sure who kissed who. One moment he was trying (failing) to tear his eyes away from Jake's lips, to pull away from the heat of Jake's body, and the next he'd kissed Jake or Jake had kissed him – someone had kissed someone, and someone was kissing back.

Jake kissed the same way he did everything: confident, a little messy, sweeter than Theo had expected. Theo cradled the back of his head, getting his hands into Jake's hair. He tugged, gently, and Jake pressed closer, one hand on Theo's jaw and the other on Theo's hip. There was nothing sweet about the way he moaned into Theo's mouth, the way he nipped at Theo's bottom lip like he wanted Theo to bite back.

Theo was so familiar with Jake's body on the field, taut and resisting, and Jake's easy tactility with his friends, but this was something else entirely: Jake yielding underneath him, Jake's fingers tightening like he needed to hold on to something, Jake's mouth against his, hot and open and demanding.

Jake was a good kisser, because of course he was. Or maybe it was just that he kissed exactly how Theo liked, not caring if Theo knew how much he wanted this, how much he wanted *Theo*. Theo had always loved kissing, and kissing Jake Cunningham was turning out to be a revelation. It had been so long since he'd kissed someone for the first time – kissed someone and worked out what they liked from the way they kissed back, the way their body responded, the way they shivered.

It was different to kissing a woman, but not in any way that felt significant. Jake's stubble against his mouth when he moved his lips to Jake's jaw, then his neck. The hard planes of Jake's chest when Theo trailed a hand up his torso. (Why the fuck did Jake have a shirt on – for *once* – when Theo needed it to be gone?)

Theo made do, because he was good like that: got the tips of his fingers under the hem of Jake's singlet and waited until Jake breathed, 'Yeah, come on,' against Theo's mouth. Then there was warm skin under his fingers and he could feel the tense and tremble of Jake's abs beneath his palms, the way Jake shuddered when Theo slid his hands over Jake's ribs.

Theo shifted on the couch, one of his thighs pressing between Jake's legs, and Jake hooked a leg around the back of his thigh to urge him closer, to bring their hips together. Theo tried to bite back a noise he was sure was going to be embarrassing – failed, because he felt Jake's lips curve into a smile. They were both wearing trackies and Theo could feel the hard line of Jake's dick against his thigh. That was new, too, but all Theo could think was *Thank God*, because he was painfully turned on and all they'd done was roll around on the couch and make out.

'Is this . . . are you . . .' he said against Jake's mouth. Jake seemed very into it, but he'd also been unusually quiet.

Admittedly, his mouth had been pretty occupied.

'Yeah, yeah, *yes*, I'm good,' Jake said, tangling his fingers into Theo's hair to pull him into another kiss. 'C'mere.'

So apparently the key to shutting up Jake Cunningham had been to just kiss him.

Theo thought maybe he could kiss Jake for hours. Days. Maybe it had been hours, or days, and he'd just lost track. Every little thing that had annoyed him about Jake – every infinitesimal way he'd gotten under Theo's skin – and then every little thing that he'd come to like about Jake – had crashed together and caught alight. He wanted to hold Jake down and touch him until he begged for it.

They broke apart and Theo took a moment to just look, Jake sprawled underneath him, his hair dishevelled by Theo's fingers and his lips swollen. Jake quirked an eyebrow at him, smirking, so Theo had to press a kiss to the edge of Jake's jaw, under his ear, and then set his teeth to the same spot, just to remind Jake that he wasn't in charge. Jake's eyes slipped shut and he sighed something that might have been Theo's name.

Theo shoved at the hem of Jake's singlet and Jake took the hint, wriggling back to sit up a little so he could pull it off.

'You too,' he said.

Theo unbuttoned his own shirt with shaky fingers and then they were chest to chest, Jake's thighs bracketing Theo's hips, Jake sliding his hands over Theo's arms and chest and back like he couldn't decide what he wanted to touch more.

The kiss felt different when their mouths met again, more like they were building towards something else. Jake had lost a little finesse, but all it did was make it hotter, make it even better when Theo ground his hips down and Jake's fingers tightened on his biceps, hard enough to bruise.

Theo broke the kiss again so he could do what he'd maybe wanted to do since the day they'd met. He kissed his way down Jake's torso and put his mouth against that tattoo, revelling in the way Jake gasped, in the way Jake's body arched towards him. Jake sighed when Theo traced his hipbone first with his thumb and then again with his mouth.

It felt natural, from there, to kiss along the edge of the waistband of Jake's trackies, to slide a hand up Jake's thigh and pause, just for a second, to let Jake say, 'Shit,' and, 'You're fucking killing me.' Theo hesitated. He'd known he was bisexual for a long time, but part of him had always wondered if he might get weird about it if he got up close with someone else's dick. If he'd get to that point and just think *Nope*.

He didn't.

He palmed Jake's dick through his trackies and Jake groaned, tipping his head back against the arm of the couch. When Theo curled his fingers and felt the shape of him through the fabric, Jake made a noise that Theo was going to remember forever.

'We should . . . bed,' Jake said, his hips chasing Theo's hand even as he pushed Theo back.

'Yes,' Theo agreed. He'd forgotten that Xen or Paddy might walk in at any moment. They might've walked in and out again without him noticing, he'd been so caught up in Jake.

He sat back on the couch, not missing the way Jake's eyes slid down his body, and let Jake roll to his feet. Jake held out a hand and Theo took it and rose, stumbling a little as he came to his feet. The room spun for a second and Jake grabbed him by the arm to steady him.

'How drunk are you?' Jake asked, frowning.

Theo didn't like it. Jake should never frown. He should always be smiling that annoying, smug smile, just so Theo had an excuse to kiss it off his face.

Theo took stock. He was . . . definitely drunk. Though not *that* drunk.

'Drunk enough to think this is a good idea.'

He'd meant it as a tease, but Jake took a step back to put some space between them. His hand slid down to Theo's wrist but he didn't let go.

'We're . . . I didn't . . . we should stop,' Jake said.

'What?' That was definitely not what they should do. They should do the opposite of that.

'We're not going to fuck while you're drunk,' he said. 'Or *because* you're drunk.'

That little twist of sadness was back at the corner of his mouth. Theo hated it.

'I didn't . . . that's not what I meant.' He stepped in, and Jake didn't pull away when he reached up to cradle Jake's cheek with one hand, didn't turn his head when Theo pressed a soft kiss to his mouth. An apology.

'We're still gonna stop,' Jake told him.

Theo wasn't drunk enough to pretend Jake wasn't right about this, and he wasn't the sort of person to try to tempt Jake into *yes*, even if keeping distance between them felt like it physically hurt. There was a hickey darkening the side of Jake's neck and Theo wanted, desperately and viscerally, to push Jake down onto a horizontal surface and see what he looked like when he came.

'Does that mean no more kissing?' Theo asked. Trying not to sound like he was sulking.

Jake shook his head, but not in a way that said *no*, more in a way that said *you're silly*. His eyes fluttered shut as Theo leaned in, and the kiss this time was slower and sweeter. Or it started out that way. By the time they stopped kissing, Jake was pressed back against the wall with his legs around Theo's waist and both of Theo's hands on his ass.

The kissing got better every time they tried it. They should keep trying it, to see if that kept happening. For science.

'We're still not gonna fuck,' Jake said against Theo's mouth, breathless. He dropped his head down onto Theo's shoulder.

'I know.' Theo stepped back to let Jake slip his feet back down to the floor. 'I can go,' he said, even though every part of his body wanted to stay as close to Jake as possible. Even though he didn't want to go, because as soon as he stepped out of the house he knew the reality of what they were doing would crash over him like a bucket of ice-water.

Jake leaned back against the wall and Theo tried not to look at the way his dick was tenting the front of his trackies. 'You can still stay,' he said. 'It's late.'

'I can take the couch.' He wasn't actually sure he could. Wasn't sure he could be ten metres away from Jake's bed without begging to be let into it.

Jake rolled his eyes. 'Do you *want* to take the couch?'

'No, but I . . . if we're not going to . . . I didn't know . . .'

Jake pushed off the wall. 'You're an idiot. Come to bed. If you behave, I'll blow you in the morning.'

That went straight to Theo's dick. He must have made some sort of noise, because Jake looked smug about it.

'Such a romantic,' Theo told him, reaching out to hook a thumb in the waist of Jake's trackies to pull him closer.

'You won't be complaining tomorrow,' Jake said. He tilted his head up for a kiss, but broke it before it could get heated again. 'Come on,' he said, grabbing Theo by the hand and tugging him down the hall. 'I'll get you a Gatorade.'

He did get Theo a Gatorade, and he also retrieved Theo's abandoned shirt from the living room, gave Theo a spare t-shirt to sleep in and put some water on the bedside table, then pulled him down onto the bed and into another kiss, lazy this time, like they had all the time in the world, like there wasn't every chance that they'd wake up tomorrow and pretend this had never happened. But Theo wasn't going to think about that now, not when Jake was here, his hands gentle in Theo's hair, his mouth tasting of toothpaste.

It was Jake who stopped the kissing, in the end, lingering for a moment with his forehead resting against Theo's. Then he shifted to the side and tucked his head against Theo's shoulder, one arm draped loosely over Theo's torso.

'G'night,' he murmured.

'Night.'

Theo wondered if he'd struggle to sleep – he didn't always do well in strange beds – but Jake's mattress was comfortable, and he felt himself slipping towards sleep, lulled by the rhythm of Jake's steady breathing and the smell of his shampoo.

Chapter Thirteen

Jake woke up with his cheek pressed against the warm fabric of Stavs' t-shirt. He always wrapped himself around anyone sleeping beside him. Paddy said he was like a fucking koala and made him sleep next to Xen if they ever had to share. Kyle had found it irritating.

In this case he'd managed to curl up with one leg over Stavs' calf, his face pillowed against Stavs' pec. He couldn't believe Stavs hadn't shoved him away. But here he was, next to Jake, his breathing even, his face softer than Jake had ever seen it.

Jake resisted the urge to nestle even closer and instead reached out to tap his phone. It was half past seven, and they had nowhere to be until midday. He was . . . not nervous. It would be stupid to be nervous. And he was very comfortable. It was nice to wake up next to someone again. At some point in the night they'd thrown off the doona and shoved the sheet down so it was tangled around their thighs.

Stavs was sleeping with one arm flung out above his head, and Jake let himself just admire his chest and his shoulders and his *arms*.

It wasn't like he didn't see Stavs naked or half-naked all the time, but it was different like this. Different to have Stavs here, in his bed, and to be able to *look*. To be able to look, after touching.

The t-shirt Jake had loaned him was a bit small on him and it was a whole situation.

It was probably a good thing they hadn't fucked. If it all went sideways, Jake could walk it off. He didn't think Stavs was going to be a dick; he might be awkward about it, maybe, but not a dick. Still, however Stavs reacted, Jake could probably manage to get them back into 'friends' territory. They'd been drunk, they were fired up after the game, shit happens. It didn't mean anything.

Lying propped up on one elbow to watch Stavs' sleeping face didn't mean anything either. Anyone would look at that face. At those ridiculous eyelashes. People paid good money for eyelashes like that. And Stavs had a nice mouth. Jake had been *not* looking at it for weeks, but he could look at it now, look at the strong line of Stavs' jaw, the dip of his throat, the fading bruise above one collarbone. He had a scar just under his left eye, a tiny pink line against his dark skin. Jake wanted to know how it had happened. He wanted to know lots of things about Stavs. It was a problem.

Jake felt the moment that Stavs woke, felt the sudden tension in his body. He wanted to press a kiss to Stavs' chest, in case it was the last one.

He didn't.

'Hi,' he said.

Stavs blinked a couple of times, as though he was trying to work out where he was and why. 'Hey.'

Stavs' voice was rough with sleep and Jake felt it somewhere in the vicinity of his stomach. There was a dark shadow on Stavs' jaw and cheeks. Jake wanted to feel that stubble against his skin.

He shuffled back to give Stavs some space. He probably didn't want to process the situation with Jake's morning wood pressed against his thigh, even if the sheet had been pushed down far enough to show that Jake wasn't the only one with that problem. He didn't *think* Stavs was going to be pissed about this. True, Jake wouldn't have kissed him if he'd been a little less buzzed himself and had stopped to think about the fact that Stavs didn't usually drink. But Stavs hadn't been obviously fucked up, and Jake hadn't realised until they'd stood up that he was drunk.

Maybe at that point he should have taken a harder line against more kissing, but he was weak.

Stavs blinked a couple of times and ran a hand through his hair. He was, unfortunately, extremely hot when he was sleep-rumpled and a bit bleary.

'I figure you've got some options,' Jake said, before Stavs could say anything. 'You can bail, or we could get breakfast, or we could get off. Or a combo of those things. And we can pretend this never happened, if you need to. Whatever option you pick.'

The part of Jake that listened to Xen knew that fucking and then having Stavs bail and pretend it had never happened was not a good idea. It would have made a worried little line appear between Xen's eyes. But Jake was only human. Stavs was *hot*, and he smelled great, and he was here in Jake's bed, and maybe if Jake knew going into it that Stavs was going to fuck and duck, it would all be fine. It wasn't like Jake hadn't fucked people before on the understanding that they'd never speak of it again. It wasn't his favourite way to do things, but he was the one in the closet, so. Yeah.

'What do you want to do?' Stavs asked, his voice still husky. He shifted slightly, propping himself up on one elbow.

Jake continued not to look. Much. 'I asked first.'

Stavs rolled his eyes.

Jake sighed. But it wasn't as though he hadn't put his cards on the table already. 'I'd like to get off, get breakfast, and then not pretend this didn't happen.'

Stavs was looking at his mouth. That seemed like a good sign. Jake sat up a little, stretching. Maybe flexing a bit. Just because he was being responsible didn't mean he wasn't going to put his best foot forward.

Stavs was definitely not looking at his face anymore, so mission accomplished.

Stavs licked his lips. 'Hooking up . . . is a bad idea.'

There was a hint of a question. Just a hint, but Jake could roll with it. He wasn't going to try to talk Stavs *into* anything, but he wasn't going to try to talk him *out* of anything either.

'Why?'

'We're . . . teammates. We don't want it to get weird.'

'Then we don't make it weird.'

'If we . . . it shouldn't happen more than once,' Stavs said, his gaze sliding down Jake's torso.

Yeah, they were going to have sex. Stavs just needed to work out that he'd already decided, maybe that he'd decided last night on the couch, when they'd wrestled for that controller.

Jake realised he hadn't said anything in response to Stavs' comment, so he shrugged.

'It shouldn't,' Stavs said, sitting up a little more. As though that was going to help Jake concentrate on Stavs' words and not his dick. Or his shoulders. Or the trail of hair vanishing into the top of his briefs.

'I wasn't arguing,' Jake said.

'You didn't agree.'

'If you don't want it to happen again, it won't happen again.' Jake shifted, and if it had the effect of pulling his boxers tighter over his crotch then, well, these things happen.

Stavs narrowed his eyes, like he thought Jake was tricking him. 'You want it to happen again?'

'Dunno, it hasn't happened the first time yet.'

That made Stavs stop thinking about a hypothetical next time. His eyes narrowed. Competitive motherfucker.

'I didn't hear any complaints last night,' Stavs said.

'I'm gonna start complaining now if you don't make up your mind.'

'Yeah?' Stavs shifted towards him, but they still weren't quite touching. The look in his eyes made Jake's stomach flip. 'What have you got to complain about?'

'Well,' Jake said, and finally, *finally* let himself reach out to put a hand on Stavs' hip. 'There's this hot guy in bed with me and all he's doing is *talking*.'

'Wow, that must be really hard for you.'

'That's not what's hard.' With someone else, Jake might have grabbed their hand and pressed it against his dick, let them feel how fucking hard he was from just sleeping next to them, but he wasn't quite sure where Stavs was at with . . . well, with dicks. He'd seemed pretty keen on Jake's dick last night, but there was last night and then there was this morning.

Stavs' eyes tracked down Jake's body, slowly. Jake had never minded being looked at, had always *liked* being looked at in bed, but something about Stavs' focused attention made him feel hot and shivery at the same time. He remembered the way Stavs had pinned his wrists to the couch, the way he'd pressed his teeth just under Jake's ear. The effort of not kissing Stavs, not touching him, not doing *something*, was going to kill Jake. But this wasn't his call to make. He'd made it pretty clear what he wanted, and if Stavs was going to bail, better now than in ten minutes.

Stavs didn't bail. Instead, he reached up to set one hand against Jake's cheek. It was sweet in a way Jake hadn't expected, and he turned his head to kiss Stavs' palm, then his wrist.

'I think I'm done talking,' Stavs said.

'Fucking *finally*,' Jake said, and kissed him.

———

Theo was sure there were very good reasons he shouldn't have sex with Jake Cunningham. He'd had a good grasp of them a few minutes ago. He'd really almost taken the *bail and pretend this never happened* option.

But now Jake was straddling him – his bare thighs on either side of Theo's hips – and the grin that had annoyed Theo so much the first few times he'd seen it was having a very different effect. Or maybe the same effect, but he wasn't lying to himself about it anymore. He wondered, for a second before their lips met, whether kissing Jake would be as good as he remembered from the night before. Whether some of it had just been the buzz from the game and the alcohol. But if anything it was even better this time, both of them sleep-warm and still a little lazy, Jake's mouth opening under his, hot and eager. The way Jake had been laughing, just a little, the second before they'd kissed.

They kissed for . . . Theo wasn't sure how long, time buckling around them as he explored Jake's body, the breadth of his shoulders, the way the muscles in his back flexed under Theo's palms, the way his abs tensed under the pads of Theo's fingers when Theo got a hand under his t-shirt, the way Theo could tell what he liked from the way he kissed back. They kissed until it wasn't lazy at all, until Theo couldn't remember a single reason they shouldn't do this.

Theo rolled them over, pinning Jake underneath him, and Jake made a noise somewhere between startled and pleased. He had both his hands in Theo's hair, and Theo made a stupid, needy sound when Jake's dick pressed hard against his own. Jake broke the kiss and then his mouth was on Theo's neck and he was shoving at Theo's t-shirt.

They had to break apart for Theo to get the t-shirt off and Jake followed suit, tossing his in the direction of the laundry hamper. Jake pulled him in for another kiss and they were chest to chest,

Jake's body hot against his, Jake's tongue in his mouth. Theo could feel Jake's dick hard against his stomach. He managed to get a hand in between them to wrap his fingers loosely around Jake's dick through his boxers and Jake groaned, his hips jerking upwards. Theo liked the way Jake felt in his hand, the way his kisses got sloppier when Theo touched him like this.

'How's practical bisexuality?' Jake asked when they broke apart, sounding as ragged and strung-out as Theo felt. Theo was still stroking him lightly through the fabric, Jake squirming and rocking up into his grip.

It took Theo a moment to remember that Jake had heard him describe his bisexuality as theoretical. 'It's good,' he managed. 'But I think I need more data.'

Jake took that as an invitation to roll them over again. Theo went with it, letting Jake straddle him. Jake pushed himself up with one hand on Theo's chest and grinned down at him, his lips swollen and his hair tousled. Theo couldn't look away.

Jake leaned down to kiss Theo's jaw, then his neck, and Theo gave in to the urge to grab Jake's ass. Jake moaned, gently biting under Theo's ear, his hands in Theo's hair again. Theo was suddenly conscious of how close he was to the edge, how desperately he needed Jake to touch him. There was a very significant risk that he was going to come just from grinding up against Jake.

'Wanna blow you,' Jake said, his mouth against Theo's neck. 'Yeah?'

Theo's brain went offline, file not found, and it wasn't until Jake said, 'Stavs?' that he realised he hadn't said anything.

'Yeah,' he said. 'Yeah, yes.'

Jake was smirking again, so Theo ran two fingers over his lips. Jake opened his mouth for them, eager, and Theo was going to die. How had he been foolish enough to think that sex with Jake Cunningham wouldn't be a completely overwhelming experience?

What a way to go, though.

Jake took mercy on him; he nipped at Theo's fingers and then pulled back to look at him. Theo felt . . . not self-conscious, exactly, because it wasn't like Jake hadn't seen him naked before, but definitely *conscious*. Conscious of Jake's gaze, hungry and appreciative, that look racing through him and lighting up every nerve.

'So fucking hot,' Jake said, grazing his thumb over one of Theo's nipples. Theo closed his eyes for a moment. It was almost too much. Jake's eyes, Jake's hands, having someone look at him like *that*.

Then Jake's mouth was back at his throat, his collarbone, his ribs. Jake took his time, as though he was daring Theo to hurry him up. By the time he got to the waistband of Theo's briefs, Theo's hands were fisted in the sheets and there was a wet patch where his dick was straining against the fabric. He might have been embarrassed about it, but Jake just made a soft, pleased sound as he hooked a thumb under the waistband.

'We good?' he asked, and Theo felt the warmth of his breath like a touch.

'Yeah,' he said, because he was incapable of any other words.

'Can't fucking wait to get you in my mouth,' Jake said, which was . . . a lot. It was also a lie, because it turned out Jake *could* wait. He pressed his mouth to the wet spot on Theo's briefs and dragged his tongue over the fabric, exploring the shape of Theo's dick while Theo tried not to shove his hips up or moan or just beg him to *hurry the fuck up*. Of course Jake was a fucking tease.

By the time Jake eased off Theo's briefs, tugging them down his thighs, Theo was as turned on as he'd ever been in his life. But if he'd thought that Jake might be about to *get the fuck on with it* he'd been wrong, because it seemed like Jake had forgotten all about Theo's dick in favour of exploring the soft skin of Theo's inner thighs with his lips and his tongue and his teeth.

'Fuck, Jake. You . . .' he said finally, and Jake stopped what he was doing to look up at Theo.

'Who's complaining now?'

'It wasn't a complaint,' Theo said, resisting the urge to push Jake's head down. 'It was . . . it was a request.'

Jake grinned up at him, sweaty and dishevelled, and it was going to be a miracle if Theo lasted more than thirty seconds once Jake actually started to blow him. *If* Jake ever started to blow him.

'Haven't heard you ask yet. You gonna say please?' Jake pressed his mouth to Theo's inner thigh, tantalisingly close to his balls.

Theo tried not to writhe. 'Please,' he managed, because maintaining some semblance of dignity was only a distant priority compared to getting Jake's mouth on his dick.

Jake grinned. 'Since you asked nicely,' he said.

It had been . . . well, it had been *a while*. And it had been even longer since someone had gone down on him like *this*, like there was nothing else they'd rather be doing, getting off on getting him off. (If he was being honest with himself, he wasn't sure anyone had *ever* gone down on him like this.) Jake was *good* at giving head, but it was more than that; it was the way his fingers tightened on Theo's thighs, the way he pulled off to say, 'You're allowed to move,' and then made an appreciative noise when Theo rolled his hips up. Theo realised that Jake was stroking himself through his boxers, slow and teasing, while his mouth was driving Theo insane. His fingers were in Jake's hair and he couldn't remember moving his hands there, but he managed to find the presence of mind to say, 'That okay?'

Jake pulled back and grinned. 'Yeah,' he said.

Theo shouldn't have distracted him, because instead of going back to what he'd been doing he set out to drive Theo out of his mind again with teasing kisses and licks that were nowhere near enough, pressing Theo's hips down whenever Theo tried to chase some proper friction. Theo definitely said *please* again, *please, Jake*, and God knew what else. He was a fucking mess, and he was probably going to be embarrassed about it afterwards, but he couldn't bring himself to care, not when it felt this good and when he was so fucking close.

'Jake, I'm gonna —' he managed to get out, and Jake just took him deeper and sucked harder, his fingers digging into Theo's thighs. Theo came harder than he could remember coming in years, his body bowing off the bed. He managed not to shove Jake's head down, managed to keep his hands gentle in Jake's hair while Jake sucked him through it.

'Stop,' he had to gasp, finally, and Jake pulled away, wiping his mouth on the back of his hand. He rolled to the side and propped himself up on one elbow while Theo tried to get his brain to reboot.

'Fuck,' Theo said, once he was capable of speech. 'That was . . .' He realised that Jake had a hand down his boxers and that made him lose track of what he was going to say. He watched Jake's hand move, watched the way Jake's eyes dropped shut as he twisted his wrist. He needed see Jake looking just as wrecked as he felt.

'Take those off,' Theo said.

'Bossy.' Jake didn't sound like he thought that was a bad thing.

He wriggled out of his boxers and tossed them off the bed.

Theo didn't know if there was such a thing as looking too much. But he wanted to look, because he might not get to see Jake like this again, flushed and sex-rumpled, his dick hard and leaking against his stomach. He wanted to make sure he remembered it, even if it would probably be safer to forget.

'Like what you see?' Jake said, knowing the answer, and Theo had to kiss him to shut him up, then kiss him some more for the hell of it. Jake might have had the upper hand before, but he wanted it just as much as Theo had; he hitched one leg over Theo's hip so he could press closer, grinding against Theo's thigh.

Theo rolled them again, pressing Jake down on the bed by his shoulders, and then shifted so he was on all fours above Jake, looking his fill.

'That's mean,' Jake panted. He reached for his dick and Theo knocked his hand away.

'Be patient.'

'Don't wanna.'

Theo had to kiss him again, then, hard and sloppy. Had to kiss his mouth, then his neck, then down to the tattoo on his hip. Had to trace that with his tongue. Had to put his mouth on Jake's abs, the inside of his thigh, and . . .

Theo didn't freak out. He *didn't*. It was just . . . his brain still felt like it had melted and dripped out of his ears, and now he was abruptly certain that he was going to be terrible at blowjobs. He was going to give Jake a terrible blowjob, and Jake would have to be nice about it because he would know that Theo had never given anyone a blowjob before, and —

'Stavs?' Jake asked.

Theo realised that he'd sort of frozen in place. Staring at Jake's dick.

'I'm good,' Theo said.

'You're staring at my dick like it's gonna bite you.'

It would be poor form not to reciprocate; Jake had pretty much obliterated Theo's central nervous system. Theo *wanted* to reciprocate. Except he also didn't, and he was stuck, tangled up in all of it. The wanting and the not-wanting, all at once. The feeling that he *should* do it washing away the fact that he wanted to.

'Stavs?' Jake carded his fingers through Theo's hair and Theo looked up at him.

'I'm sorry,' he said, 'I'm not . . . I . . .'

'Come back up here,' Jake told him, giving his hair a gentle tug. Theo went, and Jake shuffled back to prop himself up against the headboard. He nudged Theo back so they were sitting almost side by side, facing one another.

'You're freaking out,' Jake said. There was something in his voice that hit an answering chord in Theo's brain. Not quite fear, but something a little like it.

'Not because of . . .' Theo gestured at the two of them.

'Okay,' Jake said.

Theo was suddenly aware that they weren't touching anymore. He reached for Jake's hand and intertwined their fingers. It was too intimate, maybe, too *much* for whatever they were doing, but some of the tension drained out of Jake's shoulders.

'I'm . . . stressed about not being good at it,' Theo admitted. Jake burst out laughing.

Theo tried to pull his hand away and Jake wouldn't let him. Theo pulled harder, which only meant that he yanked Jake into his lap.

'You're . . . I . . .' Jake started, grinning at him. In this position they were eye to eye.

Theo glared, because he was being *vulnerable* and Jake was *laughing,* but then Jake's hands were on his shoulder and he was leaning in for a quick kiss, just a chaste press of his lips.

'Stavs,' Jake said, very seriously. 'You're an idiot.'

'I just . . .' He didn't have the right words.

'I get it,' Jake said. 'The first time I . . .' He paused. 'You wanna stop, or you wanna do something else? Because I'm not gonna tell that story if we're still going.'

'I'm not just going to leave you like that.' Theo gestured at Jake's dick. He was slightly indignant that Jake thought he would jump ship after Jake had made him come so hard he'd seen the universe on the back of his eyelids.

'It's cool,' Jake said, though it sounded a bit strained. 'It's all good, if you want to stop.'

'I don't want to stop.' Theo let go of Jake's hand to trace his fingers over Jake's ribs. 'I'm sorry, I just . . . had a moment.'

Jake shifted restlessly under Theo's hands. 'Nothing to apologise for.' He trailed his fingers down Theo's chest as Theo's slid his hand down Jake's back. 'What do you wanna do?'

'I . . .' Theo had never been tongue-tied in bed before. He was twenty-four years old, and he'd had plenty of sex. There was no reason he should be embarrassed just because Jake was a man, and just because they weren't *dating*. And sure, he'd never been really into *talking* in bed, but he could at least articulate what he wanted. 'I want you to come,' he said.

Jake sighed, dramatic, but there was only laughter in his eyes. 'Me too.'

Theo rolled his eyes.

'You wanna watch me get myself off?' Jake suggested.

Yes. Theo did want that. Even if it felt like having his training wheels put back on. But he'd never watched someone like that before. He'd thought about it, sometimes, but it had always felt like asking his partner to do all the work.

Jake fumbled in the bedside drawer for a bottle of lube and flicked the cap open. Theo's anxious brain wondered, for a second, whether this was going to be awkward as fuck, but then Jake was squeezing lube into his palm and looking across at Theo with that wicked grin, and Theo's anxious brain fucked right off.

Jake wrapped his hand around his dick and Theo made a sound like Jake was touching him. Jake had softened a little as they talked, and Theo watched as he stroked himself back to hardness, watched how Jake liked it. The only sounds in the room were the wet slide of Jake's hand and his breathing, turned quick again. Then Jake planted one foot on the bed, raising his knee and shifting so Theo could see him reach down to play with his balls.

'Fuck,' Theo said, without meaning to.

Jake looked at him, his thumb circling the head of his dick. 'Yeah?'

'Yeah.'

Theo wasn't sure if Jake liked to tease himself or if he just liked to put on a show. He didn't keep his eyes on Theo the whole time; he let his head fall back on the pillow, let his eyes flutter shut, but then he'd look across, his teeth catching his bottom lip, and Theo's dick was definitely getting back in the game.

Jake's breathing was getting more and more ragged, his hand speeding up. He looked at Theo watching him. 'Fuck, Stavs,' he said, eyes blown dark.

Theo wanted to touch him, wanted it to be his hands making Jake feel like this. Wondered if Jake sometimes got a finger inside himself when he did this, what it would be like to watch that. He almost asked, but he didn't want to interrupt, not when Jake's hips were arching off the bed, his eyes closed almost as if in pain, his dick leaking in his fist.

He looked so good, and Theo needed to touch him so badly.

'Can I kiss you?' he asked, not sure of the rules.

'Yes, fuck, *yes*,' Jake said, and they were kissing again, Theo's hands in Jake's hair. He could feel Jake getting closer to the edge from the way he kissed, messier by the moment, his tongue pushing into Theo's mouth. Theo couldn't stop touching him, stroking his hair, cradling his face, trying to kiss him and touch him and watch him all at the same time.

'Next time,' Theo said, against his mouth. 'Next time I'll —'

Jake shuddered as he came and Theo wanted to see it, but he couldn't stop kissing him, and maybe it was better like that, better to feel the frantic press of Jake's mouth and the way he trembled.

Jake broke the kiss, chest heaving. He flopped an arm over his head and exhaled. Theo dragged his fingers through the mess on Jake's stomach without thinking, and Jake murmured happily, his eyes still closed, mouth a little slack.

'Sorry you had to do all the work,' Theo said.

'Yeah, I'm real mad about it,' Jake murmured, his eyes closed. Theo ran his thumb over the mermaid tattoo and Jake opened one eye. 'What is it with you and that tattoo?'

It was . . . it was something he'd misunderstood, something that had only made sense once he'd gotten to know Jake a little better. Something that was very *Jake*. He couldn't say that, though.

'Just can't believe you've got the same tattoo as your mum,' Theo told him.

'I can't believe you're getting off on me having the same tattoo as my mum.'

'Gross,' Theo told him, and kissed him before he could reply.

Kissing Jake really was a very satisfactory way to shut him up.

Chapter Fourteen

Jake needed to get his shit together. He needed a shower and a coffee, and he definitely needed to stop kissing Stavs like they'd snuck away to make out after the school formal. There had been way too much kissing for *we can't do this again* or for *bros just fucking around.*

Why had there been so much kissing? Maybe casual hook-ups with girls were different. Maybe there was, as a rule, more kissing. But by Jake's standards, there had been an unexpected amount of kissing.

Still, Stavs was a very good kisser, and if they kept kissing for much longer they were definitely heading for a second round. Jake felt good about that. He felt good about almost everything with Stavs' mouth against his, though he probably should have mopped up a bit before they'd gotten pressed up together again. Stavs didn't wax his chest, and Jake was a bit obsessed with the dark spread of hair across his pecs.

'Hey, Jaze,' Paddy said from the hall. Jake opened his mouth to say something, but the door bounced off the doorstop before he could get a word out.

It was Jake's fault, really. He'd been too caught up in Stavs to flip the do-not-disturb sign on the door.

Stavs almost yeeted himself out of the bed in surprise, narrowly avoiding kneeing Jake in the balls. He managed to burrito himself in the sheet, which of course meant that Jake was very much not covered by the sheet.

There was no possible explanation for what was going on other than *We just fucked*. They were both naked, there was come drying tacky on Jake's stomach, and Jake was pretty sure there was a growing bruise on the side of his neck where Stavs had really gotten his teeth in at one point.

Oh, and his dick was still at half-mast. That too. Paddy's entrance had had a chilling effect, but not chilling enough.

'Shit, sorry,' Paddy said and retreated, pulling the door shut behind him. Jake heard him dissolve into laughter in the hall. 'You want breakfast, Jaze? Stavs?' he asked from the other side of the door. 'Or did you already eat?'

'Go fuck yourself,' Jake called. 'But yeah, give us twenty. Gotta shower.'

'Keep it down in there, I don't want to hear it.'

'Like you wouldn't love it.'

Paddy's footsteps receded down the hall. He was still laughing. Jake grabbed the nearest item of clothing – hopefully it belonged to him – and took stock while he did a quick clean-up. Stavs looked like he'd taken a hard knock to the head, so round two was probably off the table. He was still wrapped in the sheet. He looked a bit like one of those confused rescue animals swaddled in a towel, eyes wide.

'It's fine,' Jake said. 'Paddy won't say anything.'

Stavs blinked. 'Okay.'

'Are you good?'

'I'm . . . yeah.' Stavs didn't sound very convincing. Jake hoped it was because Paddy walking in on them had been a surprise, not because he was freaking out about boning a dude. Jake usually tried to be gone prior to any post-sex identity crises.

'Seriously, Paddy won't say anything. Well, probably to Xen, but not to anyone else. We might cop it a bit from those two.'

Paddy rarely passed over an opportunity to give people shit. He wouldn't gossip, but Jake was confident they were both going to be roasted over breakfast like a couple of vine-ripe tomatoes. Assuming breakfast was still on the table.

'I know.' Stavs closed his eyes for a moment, then opened them and shook his head. 'We . . . should we talk? About . . .' He made an expansive hand gesture.

They should probably talk. 'Or we could get breakfast?' Jake suggested.

'Sure.' Jake wasn't sure whether Stavs looked relieved or not. *Jake* was relieved. He needed to recover from it before they talked about it, or alternatively not talk about it ever.

He could be chill. He *was* chill. He'd hooked up with a teammate before. Until Taylor got traded, the two of them had a good thing going. Although, thinking about it, Jake wasn't sure they'd ever *kissed*. It hadn't been a kissing kind of thing.

He and Stavs showered – one at a time, unfortunately – and Stavs got distracted from whatever was going on in his head when he realised that it was *his* shirt that Jake had mopped up with. Jake gave him a spare Falcons t-shirt and resisted the urge to kiss the irritation off his face.

There was not going to be any more kissing.

Xen arrived back from a run as they got into the kitchen. Paddy was sitting on one of the kitchen stools, grinning like the Cheshire Cat. Xen gave him a puzzled look, but Paddy kept his mouth shut. The four of them managed to get out of the house, snag a premium spot in the cafe courtyard and order food without disaster. Jake was almost relaxed by the time the food arrived. Stavs seemed relatively chill – as chill as Stavs ever seemed. It was a beautiful morning, and he'd gotten off. No complaints from Jake, except that he'd been denied the chance to get off again.

He hadn't expected Xen to be the one to bring it all unstuck.

'So who ended up on top?' Xen asked, slicing a neat corner off his toast.

Paddy snorted orange juice all over his scrambled eggs and started to cough.

'Sorry?' Stavs was choking on a mouthful of bagel.

Xen handed Paddy a serviette. 'In *Mario Kart*?'

'Yeah,' Paddy said, emerging from behind his serviette. 'You guys were heading for Rainbow Road when I went to bed, right? Or was it Peach Beach?'

'Funny,' Jake said, attempting to project *Shut the fuck up* at Paddy.

'It was a tie,' Stavs said. He was studying the remains of his latte with grim intensity.

If Paddy was the reason Stavs decided they shouldn't fuck again, Jake was going to *murder* him.

Paddy took a sip of his coffee. 'No tie-breaker? Did you get all tangled up in Sweet Sweet Canyon or something?'

'We got tired,' Stavs explained.

Paddy grinned at him. 'Giant Goomba too much for you?'

Stavs got to his feet so quickly the table shook. 'Bathroom,' he said, and escaped . . . not in the direction of the bathroom. He was going to have to circle back.

'You're a dick,' Jake told Paddy, and swiped the last mushroom off his plate. 'Save it for me. Don't be mean to him.'

Paddy put his hands up. 'Fine, fine.'

Xen looked between Jake and Paddy, then glanced at Stavs taking the long way around to the bathrooms to avoid walking past their table. He looked back at Jake. 'You didn't.'

'I didn't what?'

'He did,' Paddy said. 'He definitely did.'

Xen sighed, rubbing the bridge of his nose. 'Well, I guess it was inevitable.'

'What?'

'You've been batting your lashes at him like an anime heroine for weeks,' Paddy said, and demonstrated.

'I have not!' Jake speared a piece of haloumi off Paddy's plate. The best piece.

When Stavs returned, he was holding his phone in front of him like a shield. 'I forgot I had a, um, brunch this morning. I'm going to jump in an Uber. See you tomorrow.'

He was gone before Jake could manage a *bye*.

Fuck.

Paddy started to laugh again.

'Bro.' Jake glared at him. 'That was *your fault*.'

'How was it my fault?'

'Did you have to keep fucking bringing it up?'

Paddy blinked at him. 'The situation is objectively very funny.' He turned to Xen. 'Jaze didn't flip the sign.' He quirked an eyebrow at Jake. 'Sorry for interrupting. Though it looked like —'

'You don't get it.' Jake realised he'd raised his voice, so he lowered it. Xen was frowning now. 'It was . . .' He stopped. It was Stavs' business. Jake wasn't going to tell anyone that it had been Stavs' first time with a guy. 'Forget it,' Jake said.

Xen was still frowning. He was too fucking perceptive for his own good. For Jake's good. 'Is Stavs okay?'

'I'm sure fucking Jake isn't *that* —' Paddy started.

'Seriously, would you *can it*?' Jake hadn't meant to sound that angry. Hadn't realised he *was* that angry.

Paddy raised his hands again. 'Sorry,' he said, and Jake knew he was. Paddy wouldn't be a dick about something like this on purpose.

'It's fine.'

Xen put a hand on his arm. 'Jaze, it's okay,' he said. 'It will be okay.'

'Sure,' Jake told him, and started on his eggs. 'Stavs said he didn't want it to be weird, so I'm sure it will be chill.'

He wasn't even convincing himself.

———

Theo

Hi

Sorry I had to bail on breakfast, I forgot I was meeting friends

I know we didn't talk about it this morning, but I don't think we should hook up again. We don't have to pretend it didn't happen but I just want to stay focused on the team and my game, and I don't want to mess up our friendship

To be clear, I'm not assuming you would want to hook up again, I was just thinking about it because we didn't really clarify this morning

I had a good time

I hope you also had a good time

Well, shit.

Jake didn't throw his phone down onto the bed, because he was an adult. He threw himself down onto the bed instead.

He was sore from a particularly brutal physio session, and he just wanted to curl up and nap. It was stupid to be in his feelings about this. Stavs had said it shouldn't happen again. He was even right. But he'd also panted, 'Next time,' against Jake's mouth, and some stupid part of Jake had gotten its hopes up.

'I don't want it to get weird,' he mimicked, rolling onto his back and glaring at his phone. It had been really fucking weird. From the second Jake had arrived at the club for post-game recovery until the moment Stavs had bolted out of there. When Jake had brought Stavs a coffee, he'd looked at it like the froth might be hiding an unsolicited dick pic.

The little typing dots appeared, disappeared, then appeared again.

Disappeared.

Appeared again.

Disappeared.

Appeared.

Jake

its fine bro no sweat, i get it

Jake closed his phone and shoved it out of reach. He did get it. People said things after they'd just come down his throat, and then they thought better of them later.

'Bro, what did you *do*?' Paddy asked, five days later.

For a person who hadn't wanted to fuck up a friendship, Stavs was doing a pretty good job of fucking up a friendship. It was hard to be friends with someone who avoided being within talking distance.

Paddy was sitting with his back against one of the goal posts, drinking a smoothie. They could have gone home after the morning's training, but it was a stunning day and the oval was empty, so they'd made snacks and headed for the goal square. Sitting near the goals always made Jake feel like he was back in school.

'I didn't *do* anything!'

'Are you sure? Did you bite him on the dick or something?'

'Fuck off.'

In truth, Jake was starting to wonder if he *had* done something. Had he been pushy? Had Stavs wanted to bail all along?

Xen knocked his shoulder gently against Jake's. 'You okay?'

Jake blew out a breath. 'I'm fine.'

'Sure,' Paddy said.

'Well, Stavs is being weird as fuck, but other than that it's all good.'

'Yeah,' Paddy agreed. 'He's playing okay, though.'

That was, luckily, true. Stavs had taken all those victory vibes and channelled them into some truly stellar form in the last few training sessions. Or maybe he'd just needed to get laid. Maybe Jake should take the credit.

'Did the sex suck?' Paddy asked.

'The sex was good.'

The sex *had* been good, but so had the kissing, and the waking up together, and the period of time when Jake had thought maybe they were going to be chill about it and that maybe it would happen again. He didn't want a boyfriend, obviously, but it could have been good.

'Then what's his problem?' Paddy asked.

'How would I fucking know?' Jake knew he hadn't managed to keep the hurt out of his voice.

Xen was making the face he made when he thought Jake and Paddy were both being oblivious. 'Maybe he hasn't hooked up casually with a lot of people,' Xen suggested. 'So he's freaked out. Especially because you're his friend, Jaze.'

Paddy looked a bit incredulous. 'Have you seen him?'

'Being attractive doesn't mean you have a lot of casual sex,' Xen said.

'Yeah, but he hooked up with Jaze, so obviously he *is* down for some casual sex,' Paddy pointed out.

Xen shrugged. 'He's talked about one long-term girlfriend, and then maybe another girlfriend during high school. I'm just speculating. But maybe he's freaking out because you're friends, and he doesn't know how to act around a friend he's had sex with.'

It seemed . . . possible. Jake preferred it to most of the explanations he was coming up with. It was much less bad than *he regrets having sex with you*.

'Okay, Yoda, so what do I do about it?'

'Talk to him,' Paddy said, at the same time as Xen said, 'Give him some space.'

Paddy gave Xen a hurt look. 'You *always* say to talk to people.'

Xen put his smoothie aside and lay back on the grass. 'I don't know, I'm just guessing. But I'd say trying to *make* him talk will probably freak him out more, so give him a couple more days, keep being chill about it, and if he doesn't come to you, *then* try to talk to him.'

'So wise,' Paddy told him. Xen rolled his eyes, but he looked pleased with himself.

'Incoming,' Paddy said, and Jake glanced back towards the club. Raze was walking purposefully towards them. 'Bet he's coming to ask why your boy is being a freakshow.'

'He's not my boy,' Jake said. And he wasn't going to be. Clearly.

Chapter Fifteen

Theo was aware that he was making it weird. He couldn't seem to *stop* making it weird. It should have been easy to be normal, because Jake was acting like nothing had happened. That was making it worse. Jake totally unfazed, when all Theo could think about was the fact they'd had sex. He laid eyes on Jake and sex klaxons went off in his brain.

At least he was playing okay. It had taken him a couple of games to get used to being on the wing, but he felt settled there now. Being able to accelerate away from an opponent down the boundary line was a particular kind of satisfying. For the first time in his career, there had been positive articles about his performance. He'd even gotten an email from a Falcons fan podcast asking if he'd come on and have a chat. (He'd filed that one in the 'maybe' basket.) He'd also dropped back to one Law subject for the trimester, which was keeping the study side of things manageable.

He couldn't decide if it was a blessing or a curse that Priya was in Melbourne for a trial. On the one hand, she was his best friend and he wanted to talk to her very badly. On the other hand, she was very thorough in her cross-examination.

He didn't think he was going to hold up in the witness box.

Priya had requested they go somewhere 'as Melbourne as possible', so he'd gotten some advice from Paddy and now they were in a second-floor bar just off Sydney Road that didn't have a name, just a give-way sticker on a purple door. The furniture was mismatched, the lighting was soft and there was a neon sign over the bar that said *fuck transphobes*.

Priya was delighted. She made the bar look like it had been decorated specifically to provide contrast to her patent-leather loafers and pussybow blouse. They ordered strawberry daiquiris, to the visible distress of the ambiguously gendered and extremely attractive bartender. The bartender looked even more upset when Theo asked for his to be virgin.

'Debrief daiquiris,' Priya explained, leaning on the bar and smiling at the bartender. 'They're traditional.'

The bartender smiled back. 'Can't mess with tradition.'

'Shameless flirt,' Theo told her as they made their way from the bar to find a table.

'Always,' she said.

It was the sort of place where you were basically sitting with the people on either side of you unless you managed to snag one of the two booths, both of which had reserved signs on them. Priya doubled back to chat to the bartender and returned to shepherd Theo towards one of the booths.

'Do I want to know?' he asked.

She grinned. 'I'm just charming. Besides, we have things to talk about, and we can't talk about them if Karen and Jan over there are sitting on your lap.' She inclined her head towards two middle-aged women who looked like they weren't sure how they'd ended up in a bar like this.

They sat down and she pushed the complimentary bowl of wasabi peas across the table towards him. At least, he assumed they were wasabi peas. They were the right colour, but something was off about the shape.

'So, what's up?' Priya asked.

'Who says something's up?'

She arched an eyebrow. 'That's what you're going with?'

No. He wasn't. He waited until the straw was in her mouth, then said, 'I had sex with Jake.'

Priya froze, her lips still wrapped around the straw. Theo watched the level of the daiquiri drop. Then drop more. Then more.

It took her less than ten seconds to finish the whole thing. She raised her head once she was done and pushed the glass away. Theo recognised her expression, because he'd seen it many times before. Not usually directed at him. With a couple of notable exceptions, he wasn't the one in their group of friends who made terrible choices.

Priya retrieved the bowl of alleged wasabi peas. 'Right, first thing's first, are you okay?'

'Why wouldn't I be okay?'

'I don't know, because you slept with someone you couldn't stand a few weeks ago?' She popped a pea into her mouth, crunched it, then winced. 'What is this?'

Theo tried one. It definitely wasn't a wasabi pea, but it wasn't unpleasant. 'I have no idea.' He took a handful. He needed to fuel. 'And I don't hate him. We've been hanging out. You know that.'

'You definitely hated him three months ago.' She leaned forward across the table. 'I say this with love, but have you lost your entire mind?'

'Probably.' Theo prodded at one of the maraschino cherries in his daiquiri, trying to skewer it. Maraschino cherries did not belong in a strawberry daiquiri, but they were tasty.

'At least you're self-aware. So, what happened?'

Theo gave her a precis – the game, the win, the party, the couch. He got to the kissing part before she interrupted.

'Were you drunk?' Theo could hear in her voice that she was about to declare war on Jake Cunningham and all his demesnes.

'No! Well, we both were, a bit, and when we kissed, yes, but he . . . he realised and then he, uh . . .' Theo was assaulted by a vivid image of Jake, his lips kiss-swollen and his hair rumpled from Theo's fingers, saying, 'If you behave I'll blow you in the morning.' And then a sort of highlight reel of Jake doing just that.

'I don't want to know what you're thinking about,' Priya said.

'Noted. I stayed the night, and then in the morning we, you know.' He raised his hands to gesture and realised there was no appropriate gesture.

'Morning sex without night-before sex. Your dream.'

'Get stuffed.'

Not that she was wrong. He did like morning sex, because the fact you were already in bed, and frequently already naked, smoothed out some of the awkward steps between *not having sex* and *having sex*. He liked waking up next to someone, warm and close, and the type of sex you had when that leisurely closeness turned hot.

Sarah, who had been a dedicated morning runner, had not felt the same way about morning sex.

'So, how was?'

'Was good.' He wasn't sure why he was being cagey. He and Priya had always been open about the details of this sort of thing, often to the peril of people sitting nearby in cafes and restaurants. This felt different, though. Maybe because men were not a shared interest.

'Here's to bisexuality,' she said, raising an imaginary glass.

'I don't know if I'm very good at it,' Theo admitted.

Priya blinked at him. 'What do you mean?' She held up a hand. 'Actually, give me a sec, I need another daiquiri first. Minimum of two daiquiris before I hear about dicks attached to men.'

She secured another drink, pausing to flirt with the bartender some more, and when she sat down immediately put her mouth on the straw. Presumably ready to start chugging. 'Hit me,' she said, a bit muffled.

'I kinda freaked out. About, uh, you know.'

'I absolutely don't know.'

'About blowing him.'

She let the straw fall out of her mouth. 'Was it . . . weird-looking or something? Does he not manscape?'

'No! I mean, it wasn't weird-looking. Also, *manscape*?'

Priya shrugged, unapologetic. 'It's a good word.'

'If you're *Cosmopolitan* circa 2012, yes.'

'You're deflecting.'

He sighed and got it out there. 'I freaked out about not being good at it,' he said into his glass.

Priya snorted. 'Theo.'

'Don't laugh at me.' It felt unfair, her laughing at him after Jake had laughed at him. Even though he knew neither of them was really laughing *at* him. Jake had sucked his dick, and teased him, and been hot and understanding, and the only thing Theo had done was be weird about it after the fact.

Priya was studying him. 'You like going down on girls. What's the difference?'

'It's not that I don't like the idea, it's just —'

'— you don't want to be bad at it?' She shook her head. 'You are the worst perfectionist I know.'

Those were fighting words, coming from her.

She took a sip of her daiquiri. 'I mean, the first couple of times you went down on girls weren't smooth sailing, and you persisted. Why is this different?'

Priya knew about that because the internet had not been a useful resource for troubleshooting. Priya had been a useful resource. There had been diagrams.

'I guess . . . it just feels different now. I'm in my mid-twenties, I should know what I'm doing.'

Priya gave him a deeply unimpressed look. 'Now who's imbibed a whole lot of shit from *Cosmo*?'

'I know, I know.'

'I think it's a pretty common experience for queer people to feel like this,' Priya said, not teasing anymore. 'Jake wasn't a dick about it, was he?'

'No.'

That was part of the problem. If Jake had been even just a little annoyed, Theo might have been able to stop thinking about the whole situation. But, instead, he'd been sexily sympathetic. Now, rather than putting the whole experience in a box labelled *embarrassing, do not open*, the memories were just roaming unchecked around Theo's brain. 'He was chill about it. We . . . managed.'

'I'll bet. So what's the problem? It sounds like it was fine.'

'I'm being weird about it. Weird around him.'

'You? Never.'

'I don't like you.'

'How are you being weird about it?'

'I think about it every time I see him!' he blurted. He lowered his voice. 'It's so fucking distracting.'

'Mm,' she said. 'And?'

God, her eyebrows were cruel. 'When I texted him to say we shouldn't do it again, I said I had a good time, and that I hoped he had a good time. When he replied, he didn't say he had a good time.'

'When you . . . *texted* him to say you shouldn't do it again,' Priya repeated, slowly. 'Can I see the messages?'

Theo handed over his phone. Priya perused the messages while Theo finished his daiquiri and wished for death.

'Well,' she said finally, 'I think I like him after all.'

'Why?'

'I mean' – she tapped the phone – 'he gave you what you wanted, right? You said you wanted to forget about it, and he didn't bring it up after that. It would have been a bit much if you'd been like, *I think we should forget about it*, and then he'd followed up with, *I had a really good time sucking your dick, I'm sorry you don't want to do it again.*'

'I guess.'

Priya narrowed her eyes at him. 'You're so salty about this. Why?'

'I'm not.'

'Yeah, you are. Are you all sad because he wasn't like, *Oh em gee, that was the best sex of my life, I'm so pleased we fucked and then you told me we shouldn't do it again over text, I just want you to rip all my clothes off and put your mouth all over my —*'

Theo threw half a maraschino cherry at her. He missed, which was for the best, because her blouse was definitely silk.

'I didn't want him to say *that*,' he protested. 'It just would have been nice if he'd said he also had a good time.'

'But you *know*.'

'I guess.' Theo nudged disconsolately at the remaining cherry. The paper straw had lost the structural integrity required to act as a skewer.

Priya was watching him. Her eyes narrowed, and then she grinned. 'You *like* him,' she sing-songed, as though they were back in the mall after school, drinking iced coffee and gossiping.

'Of course I like him, we're friends.'

Priya's eyebrows had become a fully-fledged participant in the conversation. 'Uh huh.'

'I *can't* be into him, Priy. He's my teammate.'

'Yes, nobody has ever been into someone they *can't be into*.' She did a very uncharitable impression of his voice.

'Sometimes people have casual sex with their friends,' he tried. 'And then go back to being friends who don't have sex. That is a thing that people can do.'

'*People* can do that, but in this case there is no evidence that you are people.'

The problem with Priya was that she'd known him for too long. She knew about every person he'd ever had sex with (three people, before Jake). And she also knew that each time he had been in a relationship with those people. Sex always made the most sense to him in that context.

Or at least it *had*, until he'd been playing *Mario Kart* with Jake Cunningham.

'What are you going to do?' Priya asked. She was using the tone he sometimes heard her adopt with agitated solicitors who called her out of hours.

'Not do it again,' Theo said firmly. Very firmly. With implacable firmness.

'Are you going to be able to survive without showing him you're good at giving head?'

'Yes.'

'Sure,' she said. 'Now, I'm getting us another round, and we're going to talk about how you can be less weird tomorrow.'

APRIL / MAY

ROUNDS 4–12

Chapter 16

Was Jake hallucinating? He *thought* he saw Stavs beckoning him over to a booth in the player lounge. But he also hadn't started on his coffee, so it was possible that he was having a caffeine-deficiency delusion. He'd brought a flat white for Stavs as well, because he'd planned to find him, corner him, and then bully him into being normal again.

He hadn't run this plan past anyone else. But something had to be done, before he gave Stavs a fright and copped the blame for him dropping a barbell on his chest or falling down some stairs. Thank God his on-field performance hadn't suffered.

Jake had thought a lot about what Xen had said. Sex had never really been a big deal to Jake, except during the couple of years when he'd been pretty focused on finding people to have it with. As a kid, his mum had given him a very comprehensive sex education at the kitchen table. It had been more useful than the sex education he'd gotten at school. Sex education from school did mean that he could label the fallopian tubes on a diagram, though. If that ever became relevant.

Sure, he'd had a couple of sexual experiences that he didn't *dwell* on, but they were kind of funny. In retrospect. Sex was fun. Having it with people you genuinely liked was more fun. He'd never found hooking up with friends difficult to navigate, and the good thing about sex with people you weren't dating was that they didn't expect you to do things like announce your sexuality to the whole world.

He wasn't naive enough to think that everyone thought that way about sex. Xen obviously didn't – though they'd never really talked about that. And it did seem like Stavs' family were kind of religious. Maybe Jake should have talked to Stavs about it before he'd had a chance to get in his head about it. Jake hadn't done that, though, so they were going to talk about it now, even if Jake had to lock them in the equipment room and tie Stavs up with a skipping rope.

'Hey,' Jake said, handing over the coffee. 'One soy flat white. There was a love heart in the foam but the lid has probably fucked it. That was a message from the barista, to be clear. I think she likes you. She remembers your name.' He stopped himself from talking.

'Thanks.' Stavs took a sip and seemed to brace himself, staring at the fried mushrooms on his plate. 'Can we talk?'

'Good idea.' Jake slid into the booth. 'You wanna start, or should I?'

'I'll start,' Stavs said. Jake waited. 'Sorry I've been so awkward.' Stavs didn't quite manage to meet Jake's eyes. 'I guess I just freaked out a bit.'

'Yeah, I got that. Because I'm a dude?'

'What? No!' Stavs did meet his eyes then.

He looked so shocked that Jake felt like someone had grabbed a weight he'd been struggling to get back onto the rack and lifted it for him.

Stavs managed to keep looking at Jake's face. 'I guess I've been . . . I haven't really . . . hooked up with a friend before.' He swallowed and glanced away again. 'And I've been finding it hard to, uh, not think about it. When I see you.'

'Think about it?' That sounded worrying.

'In, uh, in a good way.' Stavs was back to carefully looking everywhere except Jake's face.

Smirking would be inappropriate. Jake knew that.

'Are you . . . are you *smiling?*' Stavs was obviously trying to sound annoyed, but one corner of his mouth twitched.

'No,' Jake lied.

'You're the fucking worst.' Stavs was laughing a bit, though, and Jake wanted him to keep laughing, wanted it to turn into a proper laugh.

'It's just nice to know I left an impression.'

Stavs swallowed, the smile fading. 'I guess I was kinda embarrassed, too.'

Well, they were really whole-assing the talking. 'Why?'

'Because I didn't . . . you know.'

Jake blinked. 'Bro, it's all good, I told you.' It had, in fact, been *great.*

'I kinda bailed halfway.'

Jake was starting to feel like he'd screwed up the *location* of this talk. They probably shouldn't be discussing the quality of the sex they'd had in the player lounge.

'You really didn't, though.' Jake said. Stavs looked down, and Jake really needed him to stop looking *sad.* 'Look, I get that it can be . . . kinda complicated, or whatever,' he continued. 'But I had a great time, and if you had a good time too, then it's all good. There's not, like . . . if it feels good, it's good, right? And hey . . .' He reached across to touch Stavs' hand with his own. 'It felt good.'

Stavs looked at Jake's fingers resting on the back of his hand. 'Yeah.' He took a slow breath. 'Yeah, it did.'

His eyes met Jake's, then dropped to Jake's lips. That was a problem, because now Jake knew they were *both* thinking about it.

He was remembering the way Stavs had felt under his hands, the way he'd kissed, how good it had been when he'd lost it a little, his hands on Jake's ass, on Jake's thighs, a little clumsy.

Stavs coughed. 'We, uh . . . that doesn't mean I think we should . . .'

Jake moved his hand. 'I get it. Really.' And he did. He didn't *agree*, but he did get it. Stavs was pushing the last few mushrooms around his plate. They looked good. 'You gonna eat those?'

Stavs blinked at him. 'Um, no?'

He sounded unsure. 'You snooze, you lose,' Jake told him and speared a mushroom.

'Hey, Jaze. Oh, hey, Stavs.'

Jake looked up. He'd missed Paddy and Xen coming through the door. Jake expected a comment about the fact he and Stavs were sitting together, but instead Paddy just held out his phone. 'Have you two seen this?' He didn't sound like his usual self.

Stavs leaned across the table and Jake tried not to be conscious of the spot where their arms were touching. Why did Stavs have to smell so good? It wasn't fair.

But it only took about five seconds of the video for Jake to forget all about how good Stavs smelled.

It was a *Full Forward* clip. Jake felt Stavs go tense next to him. One of the hosts eyeballed the camera, smiling unpleasantly. 'And we all know the most exciting thing that's happening this week,' he said. 'Let's give you a reminder.' He gestured and a video spun up onto the screen and started playing.

Someone had obviously gone to a lot of effort to put together thirty seconds of the worst AFLW bloopers; most of them were from at least a couple of seasons ago. It was mean, and unnecessary, and a shitty way to ring in the first week of AFLW pre-season games (the Falcons were playing tomorrow), but he wasn't sure why Paddy was looking like he wanted to kill someone.

Then the video vanished, and he got it. The hosts of *Full Forward* were on the screen again, dressed up in what Jake wasn't going to call 'drag', because drag was awesome. One of the hosts was obviously meant to be Gabby, and another was wearing Dex's number.

For a second Jake thought – hoped, maybe – that the skit was going to be a spoof of all the horrible takes on the AFLW on social media.

Yeah, nah.

He wanted to reach down and turn it off. He didn't. He was going to watch it, and then he was going to do something about it. Paddy looked like he was going to storm the *Full Forward* studio with an axe.

'What the *fuck*,' Stavs said when the video ended.

Jake should say something. He wanted to say something. But all he could think about was his mum, and Keeley, and all the AFLW players who worked their asses off only to get laughed at by losers.

'We have to do something,' Paddy said. 'We've got to get around them.'

'Yeah,' Jake agreed. He looked around. Yelks was making himself breakfast in the kitchen, his headphones on and his hair up in a messy bun. It was unusual to see him in the club so early; he usually had breakfast at home with his wife. Jake pushed to his feet and Stavs followed suit. 'Let's go.'

Yelks wasn't a guy who got angry very often. He also didn't get loud when he got angry. But as he watched the video, Jake recognised the way his jaw tightened and his eyes narrowed.

Yelks handed the phone back to Paddy. 'Right,' he said. 'We've got work to do. And not long to do it. Let's get moving.'

———

Theo leaned forward on the fence and watched as the AFLW team warmed up. Jake was next to him, wearing a rainbow headband, sunglasses with pink, heart-shaped frames, a Falcons training hoodie and tiny gym shorts. Somehow, it was a good look on him. Theo could admit he might have lost objectivity.

'Hey, boys.' Kat joined them at the fence, Paddy moving over to give her some space. She was holding hands with a tall woman who had a toddler in a Falcons onesie balanced on one hip.

'Hey Kat, hey Cindy,' Jake said. He extended his arms. 'Hey, kiddo.'

Cindy handed Jake the toddler. The toddler immediately made a grab for the necklace of shells he was wearing.

It wouldn't be a great loss if the kid destroyed it.

'Riley, this is Stavs,' Jake said, gently nudging Riley's hands away from the shells. 'You gonna shake hands?'

Theo wasn't sure whether that was directed at Riley or him, so he extended a hand. Riley grabbed one of his fingers, beaming up at him with Kat's blue eyes.

'Hi, Riley.'

Theo never knew what to do with children. He was the youngest in his immediate family, and while he'd grown up with plenty of cousins, they were all older as well. Babies and toddlers were a mystery. His niblings were very cute, but he saw them infrequently and in short bursts. He'd always figured one day he'd probably become a parent, but how to interact with children was a problem for future Theo – and future Theo's prospective co-parent, who'd hopefully know what the fuck they were doing.

'He likes you,' Cindy said. 'I'm Cindy, by the way. I'd shake your hand, but —'

'It's Riley's now,' Theo confirmed. Riley had some strength in those chubby little fingers. 'Theo. Good to meet you.'

Yelks came to join them at the rail and Riley's attention turned to his hair. It was up in a half-bun, but there were strands falling loose around his face. Theo got his hand back as Riley reached out to make a grab for it.

'Captain's prerogative,' Yelks said, holding out his arms. Jake handed Riley over, and Riley made delighted noises. Theo couldn't remember if Yelks had kids or not, but he seemed relaxed about babies. Jake snapped a couple of pictures as Yelks hoisted Riley into the air. Yelks was so *big*, and Riley was so small.

Jake was running a very aggressive AFLW support campaign on his socials, ably assisted by Paddy and Raze. They were doing a better job than the club, truth be told. Greg wasn't actively being shit, but he didn't really seem to understand that a show of force was required, or what that might look like.

Theo waved to Gabby as the players finished their warm-up and headed down to the rooms, and she jogged over to the fence. She'd braided her hair and coiled it up around her head. She looked even more like an ancient Greek goddess than usual: Athena, if Athena had worn footy shorts and had tattoos on her muscular thighs. She was the sort of woman who Theo had always found both terrifying and catastrophically attractive. She could probably break Theo over her knee and he'd thank her for it.

'Thanks for coming out,' she said. She was grinning, but there were dark circles under her eyes.

'Least we could do.'

She shrugged. 'Still, we appreciate it.'

Jake pulled her into a selfie. She gave Riley a quick kiss on the cheek, then jogged off to rejoin the team. She'd been doing the brunt of the heavy lifting in the media. Greg had interviewed her for the Falcons' socials, and Theo knew she'd done a lot of work on the statement the club had put out. She'd made time for journos and radio appearances.

He'd seen her and Dex briefly the day before; he'd given them both a hug and told them how fucked up it was. He'd wanted to say other things as well, tell them how much he admired them for keeping their heads up, how courageous they were, but he wasn't sure how to say that without the risk of sounding patronising.

Theo joined the honour guard that assembled for when the team ran out. Most of the men's team was there, plus a lot of the coaching staff, trainers, spouses and kids. They cheered the team out, then retreated to a spot close enough to the bench that they'd be visible on the livestream any time it cut to the bench. A few people came over to chat and get autographs, but in general the crowd seemed to sense that the men's players were there to watch the game, that it wasn't about them.

Theo had always assumed Yelks was a bit old school, no matter that he was a good captain and seemed like a good guy. But Yelks had taken control of the *Full Forward* situation with the same quiet competence he displayed on the field. He'd even managed to get Tenders and Sheds to show up.

It was a great game. The Falcons AFLW team had been solid the previous season, but it was like all the shit over the last couple of days had kicked things up a notch. It was only a pre-season game, but it looked like a final; the Currawongs were a good team, and just as determined to show what they could do.

The AFLW Falcons played a different kind of game to the AFL team, and Theo enjoyed seeing the game plan unfold: watching how good Gabby was on the rebound from halfback, watching their new full-forward compete hard against the Currawongs' All-Australian fullback. Jake kept up a steady stream of encouragement, sometimes under his breath, sometimes at full volume.

It had been a long time since Theo had been to watch a football game. He'd forgotten how much fun it was. It was a close game, too, the lead flipping back and forth, and he found himself leaning out over the fence, yelling just as loud as Jake.

Jake grabbed him by the arm as Gabby put a high kick towards the goal square, then wrapped an arm around his shoulders when Dex came down with it. His sunglasses had gone a bit askew, and when he turned to say, 'Fucking beauty of a mark,' Theo wanted to kiss him so badly he was pretty sure it was written all over his face.

'Yeah,' he said instead.

The Falcons managed to get two goals up in the fourth quarter and held on for the win from there. The handshake line was convivial, players from both teams laughing and joking. There was a palpable sense of satisfaction from the players and the supporters. Both teams dispersed along the boundary to chat to the fans, players signing things and posing for selfies. It was a nice vibe. One of the Falcons players took possession of Riley, galloping off as Riley cackled.

There were a few journos roaming around, searching for sound bites. They interviewed Gabby close enough that Theo could hear every word. He didn't know how she did it. She was a consummate professional, smiling at the camera as the journo tried to bait her into saying something controversial. Theo could see Jake watching as well, his eyes narrowed a little (one of the ALFW players had nicked his sunnies).

The journo eventually gave up on Gabby and came over to the fence. Theo recognised him as one of the innumerable footy journos who cooked up provocative pieces. He'd written a few pieces about the AFLW, Theo remembered. Mainly *we're all thinking it, I'm just saying it* bullshit.

'Cunningham!' He sounded delighted. Yelks flinched next to Theo. Jake smiled, but there were a lot of teeth in it. He clearly fucking *hated* this journalist.

'Surprised to see you here, Hunter,' Jake said. 'Didn't think you followed the AFLW.'

Brayden Hunter, Theo remembered. He'd played a few games for the Sharks, then slid into footy media. His dad was the CEO of one of the Perth clubs, he couldn't remember which one.

'I do when there's a story,' Hunter said. He held the mic to Jake's face and the camera person stepped in closer. 'You've been pretty active on social media over the last couple of days,' he said. 'Anything you want to say to a wider audience?'

'Yeah, actually,' Jake said. 'Though I'm not sure you've got a bigger audience than I do, mate.'

There was a note in Jake's voice Theo remembered from months ago, in their room before Jake had come out to him. Yelks looked like he wanted to yank Jake bodily away from the camera.

'Go ahead.' Hunter looked thrilled.

Jake looked straight at the camera. 'Women and non-binary folks have been playing footy for decades, even though everyone tried to stop them. They've played on shit grounds with shit facilities at shit times. They've been called names and laughed at and they've kept playing because they love the game – love it enough to put up with all of that so they can put their boots on and get out there.'

He took a breath. Theo could feel Yelks basically vibrating with tension beside him.

'I saw that piss-weak skit,' Jake continued, 'and I reckon if you're a Falcons fan – or a footy fan – and you're laughing at that shit, or dragging the AFLW while your ass is stuck to the couch, then you can fuck right off.'

Hunter looked like Christmas had come early. Yelks looked like he couldn't decide whether he wanted to wring Jake's neck or high-five him. Theo knew exactly what he wanted to do to Jake, but he definitely couldn't do it in front of a camera.

'Cheers,' Jake said, grinning at Hunter. 'Go Falcons.'

Chapter Seventeen

Theo had known Jake was a controversial player. It was impossible to play football and not know that, even if you avoided the footy media. There had been a protracted period a couple of seasons ago when you hadn't been able to turn on a game without running into a wall of commentary about the way Jake Cunningham played for frees. There had been an actual rule change as a result of Jake's game.

Knowing it was one thing. Seeing it up close was another. Theo had never witnessed a camera operator chase someone across a car park before. Every pundit had a view. Every fan on social media had a view. Greg had a view. Randy Jones and Davo had a view. The AFLW players had views.

Yelks had stepped in to manage Jones and, as much as he could, the media. Theo had liked Yelks, but he'd developed a new respect for him after seeing the way he handled drama. He soothed ruffled feathers, fixed his earnest green gaze on journos as they asked leading questions, and somehow managed to back Jake up without putting a toe outside the hastily circulated media strategy.

Jake had been sent to Greg to 'discuss his media presence'. As far as Theo could tell, the meeting seemed to entail Greg using terms like *traditional fanbase* and *moderation* while Jake drank a bubble tea. Jake was shrugging it all off – or, to be more accurate, shrugging off journalists and continuing his enthusiasm for the AFLW team on social media – but Theo could tell something was bothering him. He was brazening it out, because that was what Jake did, but there were moments when Theo saw his energy flicker.

'I did the right thing,' he'd said to Theo in the silent locker room one evening. They'd each stayed back late for appointments with Jenny and Mick.

'Yeah,' Theo had agreed.

Jake tossed his phone into his bag. 'Imagine if all these people calling me a fag knew the truth.'

Theo winced. 'Jake —'

Jake shook his head. 'Let's not.'

Theo had nodded and left it. He'd followed Jake home and had dinner there, watching Paddy make Jake laugh while Xen cooked them pasta.

Jake had done the right thing in the interview with Hunter, no question. The problem was that Theo had watched that interview more times than he would ever admit. If he'd thought it was hard to be around Jake without being distracted *before*, it was nothing compared to *now*. There was the interview, and then there was Jake swaggering across the car park with an AFLW cap on backwards, smirking at importunate journalists. There was the way his face had settled into serious lines for a moment when Tenders had called him a shit-stirrer, and then he'd said *just sticking up for my mates*. It all made Theo want to . . . he didn't even know. Kiss Jake breathless. Beat the shit out of every homophobic asshole on the internet.

A game against the Ogres wasn't usually rowdy; they were an interstate team without a massive fan base. But today a group of Ogres fans had come to the game holding giant cardboard snowflakes with Jake's face pasted into the middle of them. Jake waved to them as the Falcons warmed up.

Jake had spent the whole week leading up to the game crackling with an intensity that had made the hair on the back of Theo's neck prickle. On top of Jake's normal pre-game energy, it made the situation feel explosive.

There were other fan-made signs, too, though nothing quite bad enough to get anyone ejected. Jake just pointed them out, laughing, and practised his shots.

Theo tried not to watch him, tried not to think about how Jake's eyes looked up close, the freckles across the bridge of his nose, the way he'd pushed his sweaty hair out of his face when they'd been in bed.

That became untenable after Jake kicked his third goal of the first half.

Even Theo had to accept that his own kick to set it up had been a beauty – low and perfectly weighted so it thudded straight into Jake's chest as he ran hard on the lead. The whistle shrilled and the beaten defender said something that made Jake grin.

Jake's goal-kicking routine was surprisingly low-key, all things considered. No grass throwing, no weird sequence of steps, no colossal run-up. It was understated and economical.

Jake nailed the goal. It was a beautiful kick from forty-five metres out, straight through the middle. A stunning reminder that, for all his filthy snaps and trick shots, he could flush a set shot with the best of them. Theo wished it wasn't a turn-on. It was going to be very inconvenient if Jake kicking goals became a turn-on.

Theo only had a moment to contemplate that chilling possibility because Jake was running towards him, arms in the air. Jake's post-goal celebrations were *not* understated or economical. The crowd roared and Jake leaped into Theo's arms in celebration, his legs wrapped around Theo's waist. Theo grabbed him to hold him up, looking up into his jubilant face, and he knew he was smiling back.

'Let's do it again,' Jake said.

It took Theo a moment to realise he was talking about the goal.

They did do it again. Ten minutes into the fourth quarter, Jake had five. The Ogres were looking murderous. The fans with snow-flake signs were getting very loud.

The ball got punched out of the stoppage and Theo, with a couple of metres on the Ogres player who'd been drawn into the contest, scooped it up. The wing was open in front of him and he took off. Felt the heart-pounding satisfaction of knowing his opponent couldn't catch him. Felt the burn in his legs as he pushed harder. He took a bounce, then another one.

Jake hadn't managed to lose his defender, but he pointed up and to the forward pocket. Theo didn't think, just steadied himself and put the ball up high.

Jake didn't usually take speccies. He wasn't a particularly aerial player. In this case, he got his boot into the hip of the tallest Ogre's defender as he went up. He juggled the ball in the air for a second, suspended, and then managed to yank it to his chest.

He kept hold of the ball but didn't stick the landing, and for a second Theo worried that he'd hurt himself. But then he was laughing, levering himself up onto hands and knees. Paddy was there to pull him to his feet, and Theo was trying to catch his own breath. From the running. Obviously.

Jake took his time, then snapped the kick around his body with signature accuracy. Even if it was too far out for anything other than a drop punt, really.

The crowd went berserk and Jake ran forward to get right into the faces of the Ogres cheer squad behind the goal. They screamed back at him, furious, as he pointed at the fans with the snowflakes and blew them a kiss.

It was exactly the sort of performance that, six months ago, would have pissed Theo off. Yet here he was, grateful that his compression shorts were . . . compressing.

They won the game decisively. In the rooms afterwards, Theo knew he was looking at Jake too much, but he couldn't *stop*. Jake stretching, laughing with Yelks. Jake stripped down to his shorts, chatting to one of the trainers. Jake with a microphone in his face, grinning at a reporter. Theo needed to stop, because he wasn't being subtle about it, but he couldn't *not* look.

He went through the motions of showering and getting dressed without registering any of it. He got a thump on the back from Yelks and a nod of approval from Davo, both of which should have made him feel good about the game. But all he could feel was a restless ache in his stomach.

It was a bad idea. It had been a bad idea the first time, and it was a bad idea now. In fact, it was an even worse idea now, because at least that first time he'd been drunk when they'd started it. This time he was stone-cold sober and perfectly able to see all the ways it could go wrong.

He managed to intercept Jake on the way out to his car, jogging a little to catch up with him, hauling his half-zipped gym bag.

'Hey,' Theo said, a little breathless.

Jake was still grinning. 'What's up?'

Theo took a deep breath. 'My sister is away for a conference this weekend. You wanna come over tonight and, uh, play some *Mario Kart*?'

Jake's slow smile made Theo feel a bit drunk. 'Sure,' he said. 'I've just gotta drop Xen and Paddy home first.'

'Cool.'

Jake's fingers brushed Theo's wrist. The gesture would have looked entirely innocuous to an onlooker, but it made Theo feel like he might burst into flames.

'See you later,' Jake said.

'Yeah,' Theo said, knowing that it was a terrible idea and not giving a damn.

Jake jogged up the steps to Stavs' place and rung the bell. He'd thought Stavs might get cold feet and send him an 'actually . . .' message. But he hadn't, and even some serious side eye from Xen hadn't stopped Jake from dumping his bag at home, changing, and then heading straight back out the door.

Jake heard footsteps, then the door opened. Stavs was wearing a threadbare navy skivvy and grey trackies. His hair was a little damp, messy like he'd been running his hands through it.

'I want the yellow controller,' Jake told him, stepping inside and kicking off his sneakers. 'And I'm sitting on the right.'

Stavs looked, for a second, like he genuinely believed that Jake had driven over at 11 pm on a Saturday night after a game to play *Mario Kart*. It was great. Everything was great. It had been a great day, and now Jake was going to have some great sex.

'Um,' Stavs said, and Jake took a couple of steps into his space, nudging him until his back was against the door. His eyes dropped to Jake's mouth. 'What if there's no yellow controller?'

'Guess we'll have to find something else to do.'

'Oh yeah?' Stavs' hands moved like he'd thought about reaching for Jake's hips and then changed his mind.

'Any ideas?'

'A couple.' Stavs leaned in and Jake gave in to temptation and tipped his face up for a kiss. Stavs' hands went to Jake's waist right away, tugging him in.

The way Stavs kissed wasn't fair. His lips were warm and gentle, almost teasing, until he reached a hand to Jake's face to tilt it just how he wanted it. Then the kiss turned hard and hungry,

Stavs' hands under Jake's jacket, sliding around to snug in the small of his back and pull him even closer.

It was almost enough to make Jake forget what he'd decided in the car. Things had gotten a bit intense last time and Stavs had freaked out. The solution was obviously drawing a bright line between the zones of *we're friends* and *DTF*. Less kissing, less staring tenderly into one another's eyes.

Jake broke the kiss, feeling a little unsteady. Lucky his hands were on Stavs' shoulders already. He wasn't getting weak at the fucking knees after a bit of kissing up against a door, he was just tired from the game.

He slid his hands under the hem of Stavs' skivvy, Stavs' skin warm under his fingers. 'Do you even have a Nintendo?'

Stavs huffed out a laugh. 'No.'

Jake sighed. 'Guess I'm leaving then.'

Stavs' hands skimmed down Jake's back to his ass. 'You sure?'

Jake slid one of his hands down and over the front of Stavs' trackies. 'I mean, if you let me play —'

Stavs pressed a hand over Jake's mouth. 'If you make a joystick joke, I'll throw you out.'

Jake widened his eyes, then licked Stavs' palm. Stavs pulled it away, but only so he could replace it with his mouth. And there he went again, sabotaging Jake's plans. But two could play that game, so Jake got one hand down the front of Stavs' trackies and his mouth on Stavs' neck. Stavs moaned and then the only sound in the hall was their breathing, fast and rough.

'Jake, fuck,' Stavs said. He had one hand in Jake's hair and the other on his ass. 'Bedroom?'

'That's one idea,' Jake said, glancing down. There was a nice, thick runner in the hallway. Perfect. Stavs' eyes widened a little as Jake dropped to his knees. Jake looked up at him. 'I've got a better one.'

'God,' Stavs breathed, one of his hands settling back in Jake's hair. He didn't grab at it, just stroked his fingers through it. Jake didn't quite know what to do with that, so he turned his attention to something he *did* know what to do with. He pressed his cheek against the bulge in Stavs' trackies and Stavs exhaled, a little shakily.

'Been thinking about you,' Jake told him, because it was true, and also because Stavs clearly liked it when he ran his mouth a bit. 'Thinking about doing this.' He got Stavs' trackies and briefs down just far enough to get his mouth on Stavs' dick. Stavs groaned.

Jake didn't try anything fancy. He got his hands on Stavs' hips, shoved him back against the door and then took him as deep as he could. He'd noticed, last time, that Stavs had liked that Jake had gotten off on blowing him, the way his eyes had gone dark when he'd looked down and seen that Jake was touching himself. So he let himself moan, made it hot and wet and a little messy because that made Stavs' hips stutter against Jake's hands, made him pant and say Jake's name.

Jake had always liked giving head, but he especially liked giving head like this, feeling Stavs coming apart under his mouth, the muscles trembling in his thighs, the way his fingers felt in Jake's hair as he tried not to pull.

'Jake, I'm going . . .'

Jake could tell. He pulled off for a moment to say, 'Yeah, give it to me,' and then got straight back to it.

'Jesus *Christ*,' Stavs said, and came. Jake stayed where he was until Stavs' legs had stopped shaking, then pulled off, pressing an open-mouthed kiss to the inside of Stavs' thigh. Stavs was panting, eyes a bit glassy, and he didn't seem to realise that he was still carding his fingers through Jake's hair.

———

Theo managed not to slide down the door onto his ass. It was more effort than it should have been. His legs felt like he'd just maxed out on the squat rack, and he was breathing hard. He hadn't had a clear idea of how the night was going to go, but he would have predicted making it past the hallway before coming his brains out.

Jake wiped his mouth on the back of his hand and grinned. He looked a little wrecked, his mouth swollen and his chin wet, his hair a mess from Theo's fingers, his hoodie askew where Theo had been pulling on it.

He also looked extremely pleased with himself.

Theo offered him a hand and helped him up, tugging him into a kiss. Jake kissed him back, then turned his head to kiss up Theo's jaw.

'Gonna give me a tour?' Jake asked. 'Let's start with the bedroom.'

Theo led him in the direction of his bedroom, relieved his legs still seemed to be working. He probably didn't need to keep hold of Jake's hand, but Jake didn't say anything, just followed him down the hall.

Jake looked around when they got into the bedroom, his eyes drifting over the photos on the desk, the colourful throw on the end of the bed, the stack of books and notes next to the bedside table. Theo had left a lamp on in the best approximation of mood lighting he could manage.

'No sexy playlist?' Jake asked, walking over and sitting down on the edge of the bed. He shrugged off his jacket. 'I'm kinda disappointed.'

'I've got speakers if that's what you need.' Theo let himself just enjoy, for a second, how good Jake looked on his bed.

'Nah, I just wanted to know what tunes get you in the mood.' Jake leaned back, propping himself up on his elbows. 'You gonna come here or you just wanna watch?'

He slid one hand down the front of his shorts, his eyes fluttering closed for a second, then shuffled back a little and rested on his elbows, head tilted. Theo didn't answer. He crossed the room and stepped between Jake's thighs, nudging them wider. Jake looked up at him, smiling, and Theo lowered himself so he was kneeling between Jake's spread legs. He pushed the hem of Jake's hoodie and t-shirt up so he could kiss the warm skin of Jake's stomach.

'Yeah,' Jake sighed. 'So good.'

'You're wearing too many clothes,' Theo murmured against Jake's hipbone. He felt Jake's laugh under his lips, and then Jake tugged off his hoodie and t-shirt in one go.

'You too,' Jake said.

Theo pulled off his skivvy and went back to kissing Jake's stomach, working up his ribs, brushing a thumb over one of his nipples, then the other.

Jake was still propped on his elbows, unable to touch, and Theo let himself enjoy the rare sensation of having Jake quiet and pliant, letting him explore. He tasted the sweat in the hollow of Jake's collarbone, then pressed a kiss to the spot where his shoulder met this throat, grazing it with his teeth. Jake shuddered.

'Can I blow you?' Theo asked, letting his hands travel up Jake's thighs.

'You don't have to,' Jake said, voice rough.

'I want to.'

He must have sounded convincing, because Jake said, 'Yeah,' and lifted his hips so Theo could pull off his shorts. He wasn't wearing underwear. Theo bent his head to lick a stripe over Jake's stomach and Jake made a soft, needy sound, his hips rocking up. Theo took pity on him, wrapped his fingers around Jake's dick and stroked him, watching the way it made his eyes flicker shut.

'One sec,' Jake said, and Theo stopped, looking up. Jake wriggled himself into a sitting position, his hands settling on Theo's shoulders. 'Wanna touch you,' he explained. 'As you were.'

He was grinning, and Theo wondered if he'd ever get used to the way Jake was just as playful in bed as he was everywhere else. How easily he laughed.

Theo leaned in and pressed his mouth to the side of Jake's dick. He liked the way it felt against his lips, under his tongue. Liked the way it tasted. Jake said, 'Fuck,' under his breath and Theo felt the abortive twitch of his hips as he held himself still.

He hesitated. He didn't want to be *bad* at this. Not when Jake was definitely *good* at it.

'You're overthinking it,' Jake said.

'Am not,' Theo said, aware that he sounded petulant. He got his hand around Jake's dick again, because Jake talked less that way. He was going to do it. He *wanted* to do it.

'Can you . . . tell me what you like?' He glanced up at Jake, who was looking down at him, amusement crinkling the corners of his eyes.

'Having my dick sucked goes alright.'

'Fuck you.'

'Sure, if you wanna.' *That* briefly distracted Theo from stroking Jake's dick, and Jake made a dissatisfied noise. But then Jake had one finger under Theo's chin, tipping it up. 'Like I said, it's all good if you don't want to,' Jake said. 'There's plenty of other shit we could do.'

'I'm just . . . I told you, I don't want to be bad at it.'

Jake gave him a look that was fond in a way that made something in Theo's stomach flip. 'Stavs, you go to *law school*. This has gotta be easier than that cake-law stuff.'

Theo forgot he was worried, because *what the fuck*. 'Cake law?'

'That book you had at camp.'

Theo was speechless.

'Tortoise law?'

Theo put his mouth on Jake's dick just to get him to stop talking.

It was effective.

About twenty seconds later, Theo decided that sucking dick wasn't that hard. Or, at least, it wasn't complex. Sure, there was a bit to coordinate with his hand and his mouth and his breathing, but it was equipment that Theo was used to, and Jake was communicative about what he liked. Not necessarily *eloquent*, but communicative.

Theo could feel the effort it was taking for Jake to keep himself still; Jake's thighs trembled under Theo's hands while he kept up a soft stream of encouragement that was mainly variations of *fuck yes*, *yeah* and *like that*. Theo liked the feel of Jake in his mouth, the taste of his skin, the way it felt when it was on the brink of too much. He gagged once and had to pull back, feeling the spit dripping down his chin, and he liked the messiness of that, too. He liked the way Jake's hands felt in his hair, the way Jake made a sort of wounded, desperate noise when Theo remembered he had two hands and cupped Jake's balls gently while he tried to get him a little deeper. He wasn't sure how long it was before Jake got incoherent, his fingers clenching on the sheets like he didn't trust himself not to push Theo down or pull his hair. Theo looked up, and their eyes met for a second.

'So fucking close,' Jake gasped. 'Fuck, Stavs, I'm gonna come.' Theo decided a moment too late that he was going to pull off, and instead of coming into his mouth, or into his hand, Jake got the lower half of his face and his neck. It was startling . . . and sort of hot. Theo managed to keep his shit together enough to stroke Jake, shuddering, through the orgasm. Then he started to laugh, because he really hadn't thought they'd get to *facials*.

'What?' Jake said, opening his eyes. They widened. 'Fuck,' he said, his voice hoarse. 'Shit, sorry.'

'I think this one was on me.'

'I mean, it wasn't meant to be.'

'You did warn me.' Theo licked his lips without thinking and Jake's softening dick twitched.

'Jesus,' Jake said, almost as if to himself. He grabbed a handful of tissues from the bedside table. 'Here,' he said. 'I got you.'

He cleaned up the mess, gently, and Theo levered himself up onto the bed. He was *exhausted*. The game, the adrenaline, the orgasm – all he wanted to do was sleep.

Jake binned the tissues and joined him. 'Sorry,' he repeated, tracing a finger down Theo's cheek. 'I would've asked before I did *that*.'

'I know,' Theo said. 'I . . . didn't mind.'

Jake raised an eyebrow. 'Oh yeah?'

Theo's reply was swallowed by a huge yawn.

Jake stretched out next to him, one arm tucked behind his head, apparently completely unbothered by the fact he was still naked. 'So, I gotta kick six and you'll blow me?'

'Imagine what I'll do if you get seven.'

Theo was pretty sure he hadn't meant to let Jake stay the night. That felt like a *dating* thing, or a *couple* thing, and they weren't doing either of those things. But it was very, very easy to reach down and pull a sheet up over them both. 'You going to stay?' he asked.

Jake nuzzled in closer to him, tucking his head against Theo's chest. 'Mmm. That okay? I'm wrecked.'

'Yeah,' Theo said, into his hair. 'Yeah, it is.' They were silent for a few moments.

'Hey Jake, was —' Theo started.

Jake pressed his lips against Theo's collarbone. 'Ten out of ten, no notes,' he murmured. 'Go to sleep.'

JUNE / JULY / AUGUST

ROUNDS 13—23

Chapter Eighteen

It was bucketing with rain and Jake was busy taking screenshots of the really messed-up shit in his direct messages. The storm had started after lunch – the type of apocalyptic downpour Melbourne saved up for afternoons when the morning had been sunny. Jake didn't like the winter, but he did like being warm and cosy with the rain hammering down on the roof. It helped that Stavs was sprawled on the bed beside him, still naked, a blanket pulled up over his legs. They didn't usually get lazy afternoons, but the Falcons had played a Thursday-night game and Davo had given them Sunday afternoon off. Jake had managed to lure Stavs into bed after lunch and Stavs had passed out about thirty seconds after coming.

The Falcons were playing well. Even better, *Stavs* was playing well, and he'd also managed to bounce back from a quiet game without getting sad. Rigger was back from his hamstring injury, but Davo had left Stavs on the wing and put Rigger into the middle.

Jake brushed his fingers over Stavs' shoulder and Stavs murmured sleepily as he rolled over, nestling closer. He was much cuddlier than he pretended to be. That was the type of small Stavs detail Jake had been storing up. He had three weeks' worth of them now.

The sex was . . . *really* good. And only seemed to be getting *better*. At some point, Jake was going to raise the fact that there were options other than hands and mouths on dicks, but hands and mouths on dicks were pretty great, and he didn't want Stavs to feel like Jake was pushing.

Jake leaned down to kiss the nape of Stavs' neck and Stavs opened his eyes, blinking once or twice like he wasn't sure where he was. It was extremely cute. Jake resisted the urge to kiss him on the head.

'What're you doing?' Stavs' voice was a little husky with sleep.

Jake told him.

'What?' Stavs no longer sounded sleepy.

'The club told me to send them any threats and shit on social media. So they can keep track, I guess.'

Stavs wriggled to prop himself up on the pillow, pulling the blanket up with him. Disappointing, but it was chilly. Jake could probably persuade him to give up the blanket later.

'Should you be doing that? Can't someone else scan through them?'

'I'm not giving Greg access to my DMs.'

'Who's DMing you?'

'Why, you jealous?'

Stavs gave him a look that said *I know what you're doing and I'm not rising to the bait*. 'It seems wrong that you have to look at it all.'

Jake shrugged. 'I don't really care.' Most of it was just bullshit. Some of it was a bit fucked up.

His phone buzzed on the bed and he checked it, then grinned.

Stavs quirked an eyebrow.

'Some of the AFLW players have a group where they share the shit they get on social media,' he explained. 'Gabby added me after we chatted about it in the gym.'

In fact, Gabby had been sending him commentary on the screenshots he'd sent to the group, sometimes complete with annotations. The group was very funny, as long as he didn't think too hard about it.

'They get fucked-up shit,' Jake said, sliding down the bed so he could rest his head on Stavs' thigh. He had to take advantage of this sleepy, agreeable Stavs. 'Dex doesn't even use social media anymore because it got so bad after they came out as non-binary and had their top surgery and stuff.'

'That's terrible.'

'Yeah.'

'Are you okay?' Stavs asked, his fingers settling in Jake's hair. Jake pressed his head into the touch and thought about it. 'Yeah, I'm kinda used to it. It's worse now, but it's fine. People have been saying gross shit to me since the first season I played. Before then, even.'

'People suck.'

'There are nice messages, too. I have an album. And Greg's been sending me supportive stuff people send to the club. Plus some players from other AFLW teams have messaged me.'

'Can I see?'

'The good ones or the bad ones?'

'I'll take the good ones, thanks.'

Jake opened the album and handed him the phone. Stavs took it, but kept one hand in Jake's hair.

'I feel kinda bad,' Jake admitted. 'I didn't do shit, and people are acting like I was really brave or something.'

Stavs' fingers stilled in his hair. 'It was brave. Nobody's said anything like that before. You could have been disciplined by the club.'

'What were they going to do? Be like, *Oh yeah, actually, we don't support the AFLW team?*'

Stavs was quiet for a little while, flicking through the album. Some of the messages were really kind. Jake wasn't sure what to do with the way they made him feel; whether he wanted to lean into the feeling or flinch away from it.

'Can I see the bad ones?' Stavs asked, finally.

'If you wanna.'

Stavs handed back the phone back and Jake opened the album. He hesitated. 'They're . . . are you sure you wanna?'

Something in Stavs' face got determined. 'Yes.'

Jake put his head back on Stavs' thigh because it was very comfortable.

Stavs made little noises of outrage every now and again. 'This is fucked,' he said, finally. 'You shouldn't have to deal with this.'

Jake sighed. 'It's chill, seriously. I just screenshot it and block people.'

Stavs made another unhappy noise.

'I've been thinking about what it would be like to come out,' Jake said. He didn't want to look at Stavs' face. He didn't want to see what Stavs was thinking.

'Yeah?'

'Like, not now, obviously.' He wasn't sure what he wanted Stavs to say. To agree with him? To tell him that he *should* come out?

'The team would have your back,' Stavs said.

'Yeah, but I'm not the right person to be first, you know? I'm not, like, a model gay. But maybe if nothing happens in the next couple of years, it's better than nothing.'

'A model gay?'

'Yeah, like . . . people are gonna say shit about it, right? Because it's me.'

'I think they'd say shit about it no matter who it is. The mainstream media won't be too bad. There's a code of conduct.'

'*Full Forward* will do a skit about me taking it up the ass though. And . . .' He hesitated. 'I don't know. I wanna think that guys wouldn't say shit on the field. But they're gonna say shit on the field, and it's gonna suck.'

Stavs winced. 'Probably.'

It was kind of comforting, the way Stavs didn't try to tell him he was wrong. It wasn't like it had been a decade ago; probably most guys wouldn't care. Some would, though. The media probably wouldn't ask *How do you feel about sharing a locker room with a gay guy?* But there were lots of questions that were more subtly homophobic. *Is it a distraction? Why do you have to make a big deal out of this?* All that sort of shit. Like people came out because they wanted a fucking gift basket.

'It shits me, you know,' Jake said. 'I never told anyone I was straight. But if I do anything gay, it's gonna be a shitshow. People will say I want the attention.'

Stavs ducked his head and pressed a kiss to Jake's hair. 'You do like attention,' he said, gently teasing.

'Mm,' Jake agreed. 'You gonna give me some?'

He still wasn't sure what he'd wanted Stavs to say about coming out. Stavs hadn't said it, whatever it was. But it was a rainy afternoon, and they were in bed together, and Jake had a lot of practice not thinking about coming out.

Stavs handed the phone back. 'Reading those didn't really put me in the mood.'

Jake pouted. 'Fine. You can help me sort them. Sometimes it's kinda hard to tell who's being threatening and who's hitting on me. Is "suck my dick pretty boy" abuse or an invitation?'

'Is there a question mark?'

'Does that matter?'

'I think it's the difference between . . .' Stavs assumed what was supposed to be a threatening look. '"Suck my dick, pretty boy."'

Then he adopted an expression that really made the most of his eyelashes. 'And "Suck my dick, pretty boy?"'

'Yeah, but those were both kinda hot,' Jake said, putting his phone aside. 'Maybe you should order me around more.'

Theo snorted. 'You hate doing what you're told.'

'Only when I don't wanna do it.' Jake sat up, but only so he could throw a leg over Stavs' thighs and straddle him. It made him a bit taller and Stavs looked up at him, smiling. It was a strange smile. Soft.

Jake ran his palms down Stavs' bare chest. Stavs sighed, his hands settling on Jake's thighs.

'Well?' Jake asked. 'How's your mood now?'

'Might have changed a bit.'

It turned out Stavs wasn't very good at giving orders in bed. He couldn't get through, 'Suck my dick, pretty boy,' without starting to laugh. It was nice to see him laughing, though, so Jake sucked his dick anyway. Lazily this time, because they'd done it hard and fast earlier, and he liked the way Stavs gasped when he slowed it down. Liked the way he tried to keep quiet and couldn't.

At some point, Jake was going to raise the subject of fingering, and then he was going to have a good time making Stavs get louder.

Once he'd taken a moment, Stavs rolled them over and kissed his way purposefully down Jake's body. Stavs was a quick learner. Good attention to detail. He liked it when Jake got two hands in his hair, not pushing him down or pulling it, just gentle pressure against his scalp. He liked it when Jake talked to him, too, even though Jake had never been any good at talking dirty. He didn't even try these days, just said *yes* and *fuck* and variations on *so good*.

This time Stavs didn't pass out immediately after; he flopped back against the pillows and let Jake tuck his head against his chest.

'Hey,' Jake said, tracing a finger over one of Stavs' pecs. 'I'm going home for the bye weekend. Wanna come? Paddy and Xen are in.'

Stavs blinked at him. 'What, to meet your mum?'

Jake pushed himself up onto his elbow. Stavs was looking up at him. 'Well, yeah, my mum will be there, but that's not the point. The point is the beach. We'll teach you to surf.'

'It's *June.*'

'Wetsuits, bro,' Jake said. 'No stress if you've got shit on here. It'll be fun, though.' It occurred to him, too late, that Stavs might read too much into the invitation. 'Paddy, Xen and I usually go down for a few days when we can.'

Jake was pretty sure Stavs was going to refuse. He didn't know why the thought made something in the vicinity of his stomach sink.

'Sure,' Stavs said instead. 'Sounds great.'

Theo walked across the foyer feeling sick with dread. Was it too late to bail? Probably. The tug towards saying *sorry, family stuff* had been growing stronger every minute since he'd started packing an overnight bag.

They'd been hooking up for four weeks, and despite Priya's scepticism, he thought he was doing pretty well at the casual-sex thing. He mainly just followed Jake's lead. Jake had an uncanny ability to switch from *we're bros watching this game* to *I'm going to make you come so hard you see God.* Theo had decided he just needed to roll with it.

There was a corner of his brain that insisted that whatever version of *casual* they were doing looked a lot like *couple,* but it wasn't like that. Having a toothbrush at Jake's place was just practical, and he hadn't *asked* Xen to add him to the house group chat used for messages like *coffee?*, *where the fuck is the remote?* and *some of us are trying to sleep.*

(He *tried* to be quiet, he really did, but sometimes Jake didn't. Or sometimes Jake tried *really* hard, and that was the problem.)

Eva had asked a couple of times whether he was seeing someone. She hadn't looked very convinced by his 'Sometimes it's easier to crash with the boys.'

His thoughts snagged, every now and again, on the conversation they'd had the afternoon Jake had shown him the messages he'd been getting. Jake would come out. Theo wasn't sure how he knew it, but he did. Something in the way Jake had looked when he'd talked about it. Jake would come out, and then he could date whoever he wanted. And it wasn't as though he was going to have any trouble finding people to date. He'd be fending them off.

Theo knew Jake liked him – he didn't doubt they were really friends – and there was no doubt Jake was attracted to him. But the fact of the matter was that, at the moment, Jake didn't have many options. What they were doing made sense. It was ridiculous for Theo to experience pangs of jealousy about the idea of Jake coming out, because it wasn't as though Theo had suggested they make things official.

It had been very easy to say yes to Jake's suggestion they spend the bye weekend together on Phillip Island, because it was easy to say yes to everything Jake suggested, especially in bed. He regretted it now. It felt . . . it felt like too much. That was probably stupid. Paddy and Xen would be there, and apparently Jake's friend Keeley would be around, but it was still a *meeting of the parents*. Theo was typically good with parents, but he'd never met the parents of his friend-with-benefits before. If that was the right term.

All the small logistical things had combined into a rolling snowball of anxiety: where he'd be sleeping, how to behave with

Jake, how much privacy they'd have, whether Jake's mum and Lydia knew he was a vegetarian. And, yes, he should just ask Jake these questions, but he didn't want Jake to see how caught up he got on little things. Having a panic attack was one thing, but admitting that he couldn't stop thinking about the minute details of what was supposed to be a chilled-out weekend was different.

He wished he could flick an off switch on parts of his brain. Things were better, most days. The meds helped, Jenny helped, and a lot of the time the anxiety was a background hum rather than a roar.

Most days.

Some days just sucked, and no matter how many times he told himself *they're just thoughts*, he couldn't make his nervous system agree. There was no rhyme or reason to it. He could have a great game and then wake up the next day with a disjointed sense of unease.

He could still bail. It wasn't as if Jake would have to go alone; Paddy and Xen would be there. They were taking a separate car, because apparently two cars were necessary.

He pushed open the door to the gym and froze.

Jake had gotten into the habit of working out at the same time as Gabby, Dex and Drips once or twice a week. Theo didn't recognise the song that was playing, but Jake was dancing with Gabby next to the weight racks, both of them laughing, while Dex cackled and tried to hold their phone steady to capture it on camera. Drips was egging them both on. Gabby sat down on a weight bench and beckoned Jake closer. Jake stepped in between her thighs and stole her baseball cap, putting it on backwards.

If he'd been asked, Theo would have guessed that Jake *couldn't* slut drop. He would have been wrong.

Drips wolf-whistled, and Dex actually dropped their phone. Gabby was laughing so hard she almost fell off the bench and had to grab Jake for support. The song faded out and Theo recognised the first bars of Beyoncé's 'Partition' – that one he did know. Obviously Jake was in charge of the playlist.

Drips caught sight of Theo first and waved. 'Hey, Stavs, you're late for the show.'

Jake turned, smiling. 'Hey,' he said, and for a second Theo felt like he was choking on his own heart.

'I think I caught the best bit,' Theo said, walking over.

Jake grinned at him, skin sheened with sweat from his workout, his eyes dancing with laughter. 'Bet you haven't got moves like that.' He winked.

Instead of saying *I don't really dance*, Theo's mouth opened without him giving it permission and he said, 'I have moves you can't even imagine.'

Drips snorted. 'Shots fired.'

Jake rolled his eyes. 'All bark, no bite,' he declared.

'Yeah, come on, Stavs,' Dex said. 'Gotta back it up.'

'Jaze certainly did,' Gabby said.

'I'll dance with you,' Drips volunteered. 'I promise I won't try to cop a feel.'

Theo underwent his second out-of-body experience in half a minute and grabbed the hat from Jake. 'Sure.' He put the hat on – sideways, obviously – and Jake dropped back onto the weight bench next to Gabby, grinning.

The joke was on Jake, though, because Theo *could* dance. His sisters had had a long *Dance Dance Revolution* phase, and he'd spent a lot of time dancing with Priya at clubs and parties. Priya had a great sense of rhythm and did not tolerate half-measures.

He didn't want to get closer to Drips than she was comfortable with, but she made it clear almost immediately that she was game to get cosy in pursuit of the bit. He was trying to keep his face serious, which was just making it harder not to laugh. Then he glanced across at Jake, who was staring incredulously, and couldn't hold it back. He managed to keep dancing, though.

'Oh my God,' Dex said, nudging Drips out of the way. 'I want a turn.'

So, Theo danced with Dex, then with Gabby. Then Jake shouldered Gabby out of the way and they were dancing together, Theo trying not to just stare into Jake's eyes, trying not to run his hands down Jake's sweat-slick biceps. Jake was, of course, outrageous. Theo was going to murder him for the way he was jokingly grinding against Theo, as though that wasn't likely to cause Theo *problems*.

The door opened again and they turned to see Yelks and Tenders in the entrance, gaping. That did it. Theo lost it, grabbing onto Jake as he doubled over with laughter. Jake was no better, and Gabby was actually on the floor, curled into a ball.

'I'm not going to ask,' Yelks said, over the beginning of 'WAP'. Theo thought about turning the music off, but technically whoever got to the speakers first had dibs. He was sure Yelks had heard worse. He and Tenders retreated to the far corner of the gym, and they both had headphones on.

The workout was clearly over. Jake dropped down to the ground to stretch with the others and Theo joined them. There could never be too much stretching.

'This song is a public service,' Dex observed. 'Swiping your nose like a credit card.' They looked pointedly at Jake and Theo.

'Not really my area of expertise,' Jake said casually from his hamstring stretch. Dex's eyebrows drew together, and Theo knew *exactly* what they were thinking. Then Jake said, 'I don't mind when it hits the back of my throat, though.'

There was a brief moment of silence. Theo couldn't breathe. He felt a rush of something that might have been pride.

'Do you mean . . .' Gabby started, carefully.

'Yeah,' Jake said, like it was something he told people all the time. He shot a glance at Yelks and Tenders, but they were both on bikes and facing the other way. 'I'm, uh, gay.'

Drips rolled close and wrapped an arm around his shoulders. 'Awesome. Thanks for telling us.'

Then the other two piled on top so Jake was at the bottom of an enthusiastic and sweaty group hug. They disentangled themselves eventually. For all the grinning Jake did, Theo wasn't sure he'd ever seen that exact smile before.

Gabby glanced at Theo, something a little measuring in her eyes. He swallowed. He knew he didn't have to say it. But if he *did* say it, Gabby, at least, was going to work out what was going on between him and Jake.

'I guess, while we're talking about it . . . I'm also queer,' he said, before he could change his mind. 'I'm bi.'

'I fucking love this,' Drips said. 'This is great. I love you both.' She held out her fist for Theo to bump. 'Except I love you more, because bi rep.'

Jake glared at Theo. 'First the dancing, now you're one-upping me while I'm *coming out*.'

'Maybe if you're lucky he'll make it up to you later,' Gabby said, with a grin eerily reminiscent of Paddy's.

'I regret my choices,' Jake said, clambering to his feet. 'And we should get a move on.'

The two of them said their goodbyes – getting hugs from everyone – and headed towards the locker room so Jake could shower. Jake was walking very briskly.

'What's the hurry?' Theo asked. They had a while before they needed to be on the road.

Jake stopped in front of a door and tested the handle. It opened, and Theo saw a dingy room full of assorted equipment.

'Great,' Jake said, opening the door wider. 'Come here.'

'What are —' Theo didn't get the rest of the question out, because Jake had pulled him into the room and shoved him up against the door, and by then Theo knew *exactly* what he was doing.

He didn't have any complaints.

Jake felt like his heart was still going a bit too fast, bouncing up and down under his ribs as they set off on the drive. He wasn't sure why he'd done it. He hadn't really *meant* to do it, the words had just come out. And now he had the same jittery feeling he got after a good win – too much energy to contain.

Maybe it had been spending time with the AFLW players, seeing how open they could be, how they joked about queerness. Maybe it had been every stinging reference to him being a great *ally*. Maybe it had been that he didn't want to keep lying, not to them, even just one ongoing lie of omission. Maybe it had just felt safe.

He glanced across at Stavs in the passenger seat. He was still smiling in the dopey way that meant Jake had won at sex, his head tipped back against the headrest.

He'd actually thought Stavs was going to bail on coming with him to Phillip Island. He'd seemed stressed about the whole idea. But he hadn't bailed, and maybe a little bit of the excitement was the thought of having Stavs in the place that would always be home. A niggly part of Jake said that they should really *talk* about this, because whatever they were doing was not just fuck buddies, but Jake was ignoring that. Why risk messing up a good thing by talking about it?

They stopped at Jake's favourite bakery on the way, and Jake overcame Stavs' resistance to a vanilla slice.

'It's yellow,' Stavs said, giving it an experimental poke. The custard jiggled.

They'd taken their haul down to the inlet to eat. It was a spot where Jake had memories on top of memories: eating lamingtons here with his mum, eating doughnuts with Keeley, chilling out with his mates and pissing off anyone trying to have a nice, quiet time.

'They're supposed to be yellow.'

'This is not a colour found in nature, unless nature is very ill.'

'Just eat the slice.'

Stavs did eat the slice, though he also insisted he'd take Jake to some Egyptian bakery to learn about proper baking. Jake liked the idea so much that he almost forgot to defend Mrs O'Hara's Country Bakery. Liked the idea of going with Stavs to a place that was important to *him*. The way Stavs would look while he explained to Jake why his baked things were superior.

Occasionally, these sort of moments made Jake reflect that he might be a bit fucked.

Stavs was quiet in the car, but he seemed peaceful. He didn't even try to skip the K-pop on Jake's playlist.

'I wrecked my first car there,' Jake said as they came around a sweeping bend. 'Driving back after a game when I was sixteen. Fucked up some ribs.'

He shouldn't have been driving unsupervised at all – when his ride to the game fell through, he'd stuck P-plates on instead of his Ls and taken the chance that his mum wouldn't catch him.

Stavs glanced across, frowning. 'Yeah?'

Jake thought about it every time he drove down this part of the road. He didn't really remember the minutes before it, just how tired he'd been, driving with both windows down and Nickelback playing, telling himself to stay awake, too young and stupid to just pull over.

'I was playing for the Dandenong Dragons, so it was a couple of hours both ways. I usually got a lift, but there was this one night where the game got delayed and then I just couldn't keep my eyes open. I woke up when the tyres hit the gravel, just in time to feel my ribs crack.'

Stavs winced.

'After that I used to stay with mates, or someone would come and get me. Keeley used to, sometimes, and then sometimes . . . sometimes Kyle would drive me and Olly, his brother. He used to bitch about it, but I think he liked it.'

'Because he got to spend time with you?'

Jake snorted. 'No, because he liked to be a martyr.' That was probably unfair. It had been nice of him.

Stavs glanced across at him. Jake sometimes got the feeling that he had questions about Kyle. Jake would have answered them, if he'd asked, but as a rule Jake avoided discussing the last guy he'd fucked with the guy he was currently fucking.

'Did the crash interfere with you getting drafted?' Stavs asked, instead.

'Nah, it was early in the season and I was only in Year 10, so we were good. I did my ACL just *after* I got drafted, though.'

'Ouch.'

'Yeah. I thought I was going to go nuts, not being able to play.' He *would* have gone nuts without Keeley and Lydia keeping him entertained, even though Keeley had been flat out with uni. He'd started messaging Kyle, too. Sending him photos of the beach, Plugger, things he'd fucked up trying to cook. He could still remember the thrill of nerves every time his phone buzzed on the table. The way things had ended had spread back through all those good memories like poison. But it had been good, at the beginning.

He and Stavs chatted about nothing much for the rest of the ride: high school, Stavs' NSW team, what it was like to play in Sydney. Stavs never talked much about his family. Jake got why, after that chat on the beach, but he was curious.

Stavs went a bit quiet as they pulled into Jake's street.

Jake decided to stop pretending he didn't know Stavs was stressing. 'They'll like you,' he said. 'It'll be chill.'

'I know.'

Stavs had actually brought a proper gift for his mum and Lydia, like they were in *Bridgerton* or something. It was a little basket with tea and spices and things Jake couldn't identify. Lydia was going to flip.

Jake heard Plugger barking as soon as he got out of the car. Somebody opened the front door and Plugger exploded out, hurling himself at Jake, who just about managed to catch him. He put him down almost immediately, because Plugger was a big dog, and he wriggled when he was excited, but he knelt down to give him a proper cuddle. 'Hey, hey, say hello to Stavs.'

Plugger did say hello, and Stavs was pretty relaxed about being slobbered on. That was good, because it was hard to be in the house and not get slobbered on a lot.

Jake dropped his bag at the top of the stairs, trying not to trip over Plugger, and hugged his mum. He hadn't seen her in person since she'd lost her hair. She had a bandana wrapped around her head (she'd probably used it to flag, back in the day). He knew she hadn't gotten a wig – she said that if *she* didn't have a problem being bald, everyone else could fucking deal with it – but it was winter.

She hugged him just as hard as she always did.

'Fuck, it's good to see you,' he said, trying not to squeeze too hard.

'Good to see you, too.'

Stavs was shaking hands with Lydia. 'Thanks for having me,' he said, handing over the gift basket. It wasn't unprecedented for one of Jake's mates to bring gifts – Xen always brought jam or something – but this was definitely the poshest gift they'd ever received from a friend of Jake's. The tea was in *jars*.

Lydia beamed at him. 'You're welcome whenever you want,' she said, investigating the jars. '*Whenever* you want.' Jake sensed he was going to have to work to avoid drinking the type of tea that tasted like grass clippings soaked in hot water.

Stavs offered his hand to Jake's mum. 'Theo,' he said. 'It's lovely to meet you.'

Debbie shook his hand. 'Lovely to meet you, too. I've heard a lot about you.'

Stavs gave Jake an alarmed look. Debbie caught it and laughed. 'All good things,' she reassured him. 'At least recently,' she amended.

Stavs laughed, and Jake could tell he'd already started to chill out. It was pretty hard not to relax around his mum and Lydia.

Debbie ushered them both into the house, still laughing, and Jake felt, just for a second, the heat of tears behind his eyes.

Chapter Nineteen

Teaching people to surf was often a bit funny, but teaching Stavs to surf was hilarious. Jake had thought he'd pick it up quickly – he was athletic, and he had good balance and whatever from all of that pretzel yoga.

He did not pick it up quickly.

They'd headed to the beach after dumping their bags and sitting down for a cup of tea. Paddy and Xen had arrived a few minutes after Jake and Theo, and Keeley had come over for some lunch – and to eyeball Stavs. He hadn't told Keeley about what was going on with Stavs, but she was good at picking up clues, and he might have been mentioning Stavs more than was wise. He could tell her, of course, but then she'd probably give him some good advice, and he wasn't interested in getting any of that.

Stavs had been allowed to help Lydia assemble sandwiches in the kitchen – a rare privilege. Jake was not allowed to help with sandwiches because he 'mangled' the bread. Kyle had never been allowed to help with the sandwiches. Lydia hadn't liked Kyle, and while she'd never *said* that, she had her ways of showing it. Stavs sliced bread beautifully, of course, and actually seemed to enjoy the cup of grass-clippings tea. His mum had already given Jake a couple of looks that he knew meant *we're going to talk about him later.*

Jake had no idea what he was going to say.

He'd enlisted Keeley to help with the surfing lesson because she was a better teacher, and because it meant that Jake could watch while Stavs tried, and failed, to stand up on the board, his face twisted into an adorable expression of intense concentration. It also meant he could admire Stavs in the borrowed wetsuit.

Xen and Paddy had opted to go for a walk along the beach instead of getting in the water. The water *was* chilly. But Stavs couldn't show weakness, of course – not with Keeley striding in as though it were the middle of summer. Jake was going to go in as well, once he'd finished observing.

Stavs and Keeley had hit it off almost immediately. Jake knew – and maybe Stavs knew – that the surfing was a test. Some dudes weren't great about learning shit from women. But Stavs cheerfully deferred to her, and wasn't even getting that cranky about his consistent failure. Given what a perfectionist he was on the field, that was a miracle.

Jake went to join them, eventually, and the surfing lesson devolved when Jake pushed a triumphant and upright Stavs off his board. Keeley was drawn into the ensuing melee, and then Plugger plunged into the water to see what was going on.

Jake somehow ended up on Stavs' back, his legs wrapped around Stavs' waist while Keeley splashed them. Stavs was laughing so hard he was unsteady on his feet. He lost his balance and fell sideways, submerging them both. They surfaced, both laughing and gasping, and then Jake tackled him and they went under again while Plugger barked gleefully.

Jake didn't realise anyone was watching them until he heard Keeley say, 'Oh,' in the sort of tone you used when you realised the milk had gone off or you'd just tracked something gross into the house.

Jake turned to the shore. He already knew who'd be there.

Kyle was standing on the edge of the water, leaning on his surf-board. It wasn't a surprise; he spent plenty of weekends back with his family.

Jake hadn't seen him in person since they'd broken up. They'd started fighting in the car, taken the fight back to Jake's room, fucked against the wall, then ended things. His last memory of the two of them was Kyle turning back to look at him and saying, 'I'm not waiting around for you to realise you've fucked this up.' Jake had felt like someone had punched through his ribcage and grabbed his heart. And also like he wanted to crack Kyle's skull open and force the way he felt into Kyle's brain so he would under-stand and come back.

Now, he waited for a surge of feeling and got . . . almost nothing. Echoes of all the things he'd felt, for all those years. He'd never been one to try to hang on to things once he'd been forced to let go.

Plugger – the *traitor* – went splashing towards Kyle, who leaned down to scratch his ears.

'We can ignore him,' Keeley said.

Jake sighed. Kyle didn't like being ignored. If he wanted to say something, it was probably best to get it over with. And if he hadn't wanted to say something he would have fucked off into the surf.

'Is that —' Stavs started.

'The dickhead-in-chief?' Keeley said. 'Guess he likes having to replace his slashed tyres.'

Jake splashed her. 'Keeley.'

'Mmm.' Stavs' tone suggested he'd stand watch for her while she did it. It was kind of nice.

The three of them walked out of the surf together. Kyle was still hot. Unfortunately. Same wavy brown hair, same striking green eyes, same broad shoulders and good arms. He'd been the first guy Jake had ever *looked* at, even if Kyle hadn't looked back for years.

He wasn't as hot as Stavs, and Jake was petty enough to be pleased. Not that he and Stavs were *together*, but Kyle would definitely assume they were after all the wrestling in the water.

Stavs had grabbed his towel and was giving them some space. Keeley had joined him, steadfastly pretending Kyle didn't exist, even though they'd known each other for more than twenty years. She did not forgive.

'Hi, Jake,' Kyle said, but his eyes were on Stavs, who'd unzipped the wetsuit and pulled it down to his waist. It was a good look on him. His hair was getting a little unruly, tangled and drying in the breeze.

And now Jake was definitely staring at Stavs' bare chest. He returned his attention to Kyle. 'Did you want something?'

It wasn't like they'd agreed to stay friends.

Plugger looked at Jake balefully, but he trotted over to Keeley when she snapped her fingers. Plugger had always liked Kyle. Like Jake, he wasn't very smart around hot dudes who scratched behind his ears. So to speak.

Kyle was giving him the kind of look Jake had never learned to read. 'Just saying hi. I'm visiting Mum and Dad for the weekend.'

Jake nodded. 'Hi.'

Kyle tilted his head towards Stavs. 'Nice to see you moved on quickly.'

That was a lot, given that Kyle's Insta stories for the last eight months had been exclusively blurry club photos and low-key thirst traps.

Jake decided that, for once in his life, he was going to keep quiet. He didn't have anything to say to Kyle. He'd imagined, so many times, finding the words to shut Kyle up, to make Kyle realise he'd been *wrong*. But he'd never been able to match Kyle with words and he never would. It seemed less important now.

Stavs came over before Jake caved and broke the silence. 'Coffee time, Jaze?' he asked. He wrapped an arm around Jake's shoulders. It was the type of thing any of Jake's mates might have done. It still sent a little tendril of satisfaction uncurling in Jake's stomach.

'Hi,' Kyle said, turning all his charm on Stavs. 'Haven't seen you around before.' It wasn't flirtatious. Not quite.

'This is Stavs,' Jake said. 'One of my teammates.'

'Jake hasn't mentioned you,' Kyle said. 'New to the team? I'm Kyle.' He held out his hand.

'I know,' Stavs said. He looked at Kyle's hand like it was covered in dog shit. 'Jake *has* mentioned *you*.'

Keeley made a soft, choked-off noise that might have been the beginning of a laugh. Kyle looked genuinely taken aback. It was *great*.

Stavs kept his arm around Jake's shoulders, and Kyle was forced to let his hand drop.

'You done chatting?' Stavs asked. 'I can bring a coffee back for you if you want.'

'Nah, we're done here,' Jake said. 'Good to see you, mate,' he said to Kyle, and turned away. He didn't bother looking back. It was easy with Stavs' arm warm across his shoulders.

Keeley was almost skipping beside them as they walked up towards the kiosk. Jake knew that Stavs was a bit of a coffee snob, so the kiosk was going to be a problem for him.

'Wow, that was *rude*,' Keeley said to Stavs when they were out of earshot.

Stavs shrugged. 'He deserved it.'

'He *did*.'

Keeley bought them all coffee and handed Stavs his with a look of profound approval. Stavs did not look at the coffee with the same level of approval once he'd taken a sip, but he couldn't have expected much. The coffee machine had made him visibly upset.

They watched the ocean as they drank their coffees, sitting by the kiosk. There was a cluster of surfers out beyond the break. Stavs was looking thoughtfully in their direction.

'Are there ever sharks?' he asked.

Keeley started to laugh. 'Not usually.'

'Hmm.'

'I don't want Kyle to get eaten by a shark,' Jake felt moved to say. 'He's not . . . it wasn't all his fault, you know.'

'You're entitled to your opinion,' Stavs said.

They split a bag of hot chips and a couple of potato cakes between them. Keeley actually gave Stavs the last chip. *Gave* it to him. She would have put a plastic fork through Jake's hand if he'd tried to take it.

Jake let himself wonder what it would be like if Stavs was here as his boyfriend and not just the friend he'd been fucking daily. Then stopped, because he'd always been pretty good at just not thinking about things. He'd messed that up, at the end, with Kyle. He wasn't going to make that mistake again, no matter how good it felt to be sitting beside Stavs, their thighs pressed together, here in his favourite place in the world.

He wasn't smart, but he could learn.

By the time it got to dusk, Theo was tired in the satisfying way that came from being outside and active all day. As he'd suspected, he was definitely never going to be a surfer, but it had been fun. Surprisingly fun. He'd been so focused on trying to stand up on the bloody board that it had wiped his brain clean of everything else.

They'd collected Paddy and Xen, driven back to shower and then gone on a long walk along the headland. Jake had scorned sunscreen and gotten slightly sunburned on the walk. Sunburn should not have made him more attractive.

And yet.

They were barbecuing for dinner. The weather was cold but clear, and Debbie and Lydia had a couple of outdoor gas heaters that were keeping everyone toasty. A random assortment of people had arrived to join in. Theo had no hope of remembering who everyone was, except some of the children were Keeley's niblings, and everyone was very loud. Still, they were loud in the friendly way that made it easy to drift on the edge of the gathering without feeling left out.

Theo was perched on the steps, drinking a Sprite and watching a maelstrom of children swirl around Jake, who was clearly a favourite. Keeley came to join him and they sat in companionable silence as Jake, Paddy and Xen corralled the kids into a chaotic game of Marker's Up. Theo would have guessed that Jake would be great with kids after seeing him with Riley, but there was guessing it and there was seeing Jake hoisting one of his honorary niblings into the air so she could grab for the ball, screaming with glee. It made him realise that for all Jake's energy and confidence, in some ways he held himself back, just a little. You didn't notice it until he truly let go and *really* laughed.

He'd been laughing like that the night they'd first kissed.

Keeley held out her Corona and Theo touched the base of his Sprite to it.

'So, you and Jake,' she said.

Theo took a sip of his drink to avoid answering for a few seconds.

Keeley gave him a knowing look. 'Don't bother. I know him, and neither of you are *that* subtle. He's worse, though. A couple of times I thought I was going to have to spray him with the hose.'

Theo snorted. 'I guess he feels like he doesn't have to hide stuff here.'

'Yeah,' Keeley said, sounding a little sad.

He wondered if he was about to be threatened. Keeley was clearly a staunch defender of Jake.

'Are you going to threaten me?' he asked, because they might as well get it over with.

She burst out laughing, and Jake glanced across at them. She waved at him and he grinned and turned to fend off a spirited assault by one of the kids.

'No,' she said. 'I've assessed you as at equal risk of having your heart broken, so no threats.'

Theo felt like he should protest. They weren't supposed to be doing anything with the possibility of ending in broken hearts.

Before he could formulate a response, Keeley continued. 'Have you guys talked much about Kyle?' She was tracing shapes in the sand at the base of the steps with one of her big toes.

'Not heaps,' Theo said. On the one hand, he was burningly curious about Kyle, especially after the earlier encounter. On the other hand, trying to get information about him from Jake's best friend felt like a recipe for disaster.

Keeley studied him for a few moments, and Theo wanted to shift under the look. It was inquisitive. Measuring. Then she seemed to come to some sort of decision and looked away, her gaze tracking down the backyard again.

'I'm going to tell you some stuff about Kyle and Jake,' she said, voice quiet. 'Things I noticed, right? I'm not breaking his confidence but . . . I'm going to tell you because you seem like a

good guy, and whatever the two of you are doing, I think you care
about Jake. And because of what you said to Kyle today.'

'I do care about Jake.' It felt like a dangerous confession.
'We're friends.'

She wiped away the design in the sand with her foot and
started again. 'He told you about the break-up?'

'Yeah, a while ago. He said they broke up because Jake
wouldn't come out.'

Keeley sighed. 'I don't think Kyle ever thought Jake would say
no to him. I don't think he ever had before.' She caught Theo's
look and shrugged. 'I don't really mean like *that*. Though probably
that, too. I just mean – well, Kyle's four years older than we are.
Me and Jake, I mean. We were good mates with Kyle's younger
brother, Olly, so Kyle was around a fair bit, and you know what
it's like when you're a kid. Kyle seemed like he was so *cool*.
I used to give Jake so much shit because his crush was that obvious.'

Theo could imagine. He had developed a crippling and humil-
iating crush on his friend's older sister at the age of thirteen.
Recovery had been slow and painful.

'Kyle never looked twice at him – obviously, we were babies –
but then Jake turned eighteen and got drafted and came back
looking like . . . well, like *that*.'

She waved a hand at Jake, who was in the process of showing
the niblings how to take an overhead mark. He was, for once,
wearing a shirt, but it was an old footy singlet that didn't leave
much to the imagination.

'And nothing happened, not for ages, but there was just something different in the way he looked at Jake, you know? He was
suddenly keen to tell Jake all about his job and his glamorous
friends and whatever else. He was around a lot more, and then he
invited Jake down to the Peninsula for New Year's and, well, that
was that.' She scowled. 'Jake was so fucking *happy*. Whenever

I think about it, I want to go and punch Kyle in his stupid symmetrical face.'

That was an urge Theo shared.

'But it was like . . . like Jake felt he had to be *grateful* that Kyle wanted to be with him. And especially that Kyle was willing to be with him when he wasn't out. I don't know if things would have been different if he *had* been out, but there was just this . . . dynamic. Jake was always working to make up for the fact he was closeted. It was always Jake making the compromises, you know? Jake driving to Canberra, Jake dropping things to go and see Kyle, Jake making the time, Jake buying Kyle shit even though Kyle made plenty of money. Like Kyle never had to make any effort because he'd compromised on that one thing.' She grimaced. 'I *hated* it.'

'Kyle seems like a shithead.'

Keeley grinned. 'You won't hear any arguments from me. But I'm being unfair. He was . . . charming. Charismatic. Smart, and funny.'

'Hot,' Theo added.

'That too. He can be pretty irresistible when he wants to be.'

'I guess it would be tough being with someone closeted,' Theo observed. Cautiously.

Keeley glanced across at him. 'Of course. And to be honest, if Kyle had called it quits because of that, I would have understood. I still would've thought he was a dick, but I get it. It wasn't the fact he decided he couldn't do it – it was the ultimatum. You don't do that if you love someone.'

'I guess you don't.'

Theo thought about Sarah and the moment he'd known it was over between them. It felt like a lifetime ago.

'Jake, uh . . .' Theo paused, trying to frame the question in a way that didn't make it seem like he was fishing for information.

Even if he absolutely was. 'He hasn't mentioned any other boy-friends. As opposed to, uh . . .'

'Dudes he fucked?' she finished for him. 'Well, you should ask him. But yeah. Kyle was the only serious one.' She sighed. 'The prick.'

They lapsed into silence for a couple of minutes, watching Jake pretend to fight off a couple of the kids.

Keeley sighed. 'Sometimes I think he's convinced himself he doesn't deserve a real relationship because he hasn't come out.'

'Surely . . .' Theo started, and then stopped.

'Look,' Keeley said. 'It's all speculation on my part. I get that it's complicated, for both of you, and that it's not official or anything.' She gave him a wry look. 'I promise I won't slash *your* tyres. But just . . . be kind to him. Please. Sometimes people don't see that he needs that.'

Theo felt as though someone had wrapped their hands around his heart and squeezed. 'I will. I promise.'

She smiled. 'Thanks. He's lucky to have you.'

She was lucky Theo had good reflexes, because he just managed to punch the footy away as it barrelled directly for Keeley's face. The nibling responsible for the rogue kick was staring at them, frozen with horror.

'Thanks,' she said again. It was even more heartfelt this time.

'That's why they pay him the big bucks,' Paddy said, coming over to retrieve the ball. 'C'mon, Stavs, Keeley. We need you.'

Theo let himself be towed to his feet, and he only dropped a couple of marks because he was distracted watching Jake.

By the time they called it a night, Theo's stomach muscles hurt from laughing. Once the guests had all drifted away, they'd settled by the fire in the living room and Debbie had started to tell them stories about Jake as a child. She and Jake had spoken over each other and finished each other's sentences, arguing about the details of every anecdote with Keeley as moderator and instigator by turns. Jake didn't seem to have any shame about being the butt of the joke; he laughed at himself, sprawled on the worn carpet with one hand behind his head, gesturing with a mint slice in the other.

Paddy had joined in as well – he had enough siblings to have an endless supply of stories – and had made Lydia actually cry with laughter, clutching Xen's shoulder for support. Xen had turned out to be a surprisingly good mimic, and he'd chimed in with a couple of stories from his time in the VFL with Paddy and Jake. Theo had let it all eddy around him, warm from the fire and the shared laughter.

Theo helped with the dishes and then followed Jake out to what Lydia and Debbie called 'the den'. The den was a small granny flat that Lydia and Debbie had converted for Jake once he'd turned fourteen. To give him privacy, apparently. Theo wondered whether what they really meant was to give Debbie and Lydia privacy. Theo and Jake had dropped their bags in there earlier and the room was exactly what Theo would have expected. There was an artful array of surfboards, a guitar (possibly never played) in one corner, a spirited attempt at fuckboy LEDs, several football posters of varying levels of homoeroticism and a single rail for Jake's clothes but two cabinets stuffed full of footy memorabilia, all lovingly arranged.

Plugger watched them mournfully through the sliding door as they walked away from the main house. It had turned properly cold, the grass a little damp under Theo's bare feet. He broke into a jog to cover the last few steps.

They'd barely made it through the door when Jake's hands were on him, pulling him into a hungry kiss. Theo kissed him back and tugged him closer. Jake was still warm from the fire, his mouth tasting of chocolate and mint.

Jake broke the kiss, his hands in Theo's hair. He was smiling, the ridiculous lights threading red and orange through his hair. 'Thanks for coming,' he said.

Theo didn't know what to say, so he cradled Jake's face in his hands and kissed him again. Jake's mouth opened under his and they kissed until Jake was shoving at Theo's t-shirt and they broke apart so Theo could pull it off. Jake's hands were on his chest immediately, his thumb teasing one of Theo's nipples, his mouth on Theo's neck.

'Hey, so,' Jake said, breaking the kiss and tugging Theo towards the bed by his belt buckle, his smile mischievous. 'Wanna fuck me?'

'Uh.' Theo nearly fell over his own feet. He caught himself and let Jake pull him over to the bed. Jake sat down and Theo stepped between his legs, Jake's hands sliding up Theo's thighs.

Jake was still grinning, but it had gone sweet around the edges. 'You don't have to.'

It had occurred to Theo, obviously, that there were options beyond blowjobs and handjobs. He hadn't quite known how to bring that up, especially as he wasn't sure how he felt about anything going into his own ass. He knew, theoretically, that it was something many people did, and enjoyed, presumably without accident or humiliation. But still, the anxious part of his brain was apprehensive.

Reddit hadn't helped.

'I've never . . . done it like that. With anyone.'

Jake leaned forward and pressed a kiss just above Theo's waistband. His mouth lingered there, then he looked up at Theo. 'Do you wanna try? We can take it slow.'

Theo's answer to that was probably obvious, because Jake's face was level with his dick. 'Yeah,' he said. 'Yeah, I do.'

Jake's fingers were deft on Theo's belt buckle. He pulled the belt free with a hiss of leather and then flicked open the button on Theo's shorts. 'Get naked,' he said.

'You're the one with all your clothes still on,' Theo pointed out. He started to say, 'For once,' but Jake pressed his mouth against Theo's briefs and he lost the words.

Jake slid his hands around Stavs' ass to pull him in a little closer and Stavs sighed happily. He'd looked a little nervous, and Jake had figured that a bit of distraction couldn't hurt. One of Stavs' hands was in his hair now, the other on Jake's cheek, and Jake could feel him trying to hold himself back from pushing harder into Jake's mouth.

'Stop,' Stavs gasped, and Jake pulled back and licked his lips.

Stavs pushed him backwards onto the bed and followed him down. 'You're still not naked,' he said.

Jake kicked off his shorts and wriggled out of his singlet. Stavs leaned down to kiss him, slow and hot, and Jake got a foot behind his thigh to pull him closer. They both groaned when their dicks slid together, slick and perfect. Stavs knew, by now, exactly how Jake liked to be kissed, and he'd found all the places that made Jake shiver: the spot under his ear where his jaw met his neck, the hollow of his throat, the crease of his thigh. He kissed them, then kissed them again, because he was a cruel fucker who didn't care that Jake was so hard it was painful, his body humming with the promise of having Stavs inside him.

'This isn't fucking me,' Jake panted, squirming. Stavs had pinned his wrists against the bed.

'Not yet.'

'It won't be ever if I die of frustration,' Jake pointed out. 'Or come,' he added, when Stavs let go of Jake's wrists.

Stavs smiled in the way he only did when they were tangled up and naked together. 'I thought we were going slow?'

'I changed my mind.'

'I didn't.'

He hadn't. He kissed his way down Jake's body again, *so fucking slowly*, and, this time, took Jake's dick in his mouth. He didn't do anything that was likely to get Jake anywhere close to coming, just kept it languid and wet until Jake had one hand wrapped in the sheets and the other on Stavs' shoulder. It would serve Stavs right if his fingers left bruises.

'Fuck,' Jake said. He bent his knees, feet on the bed, and Stavs took the hint.

Jake made an inadvertent, wounded sound when Stavs took his mouth away, but then he was kissing the spot where Jake's thigh met his ass, dragging his tongue occasionally over Jake's balls, and Jake was undoubtedly saying a lot of dumb shit, trying not to actually beg.

'Lube?' Stavs asked, after a million years.

Jake fumbled the bedside drawer open. He'd lost a bit of manual dexterity somewhere along the way, but he managed to find the bottle and hand it over. At least Stavs was a bit shaky as well. Jake was going to have to get his shit together or he was going to come after approximately ten seconds of getting fucked. Which would be a fucking *tragedy*.

Stavs was generous with the lube in a way that was probably going to be fun for them and bad for the sheets. Jake rolled over, onto his knees and elbows, and Stavs ran the hand that wasn't covered in lube down his spine.

'Hey,' Stavs said, sounding a little hesitant.

Jake looked over his shoulder. 'Yeah?' He would be fine if Stavs had changed his mind. Totally fine.

'Can we . . . I'd like to be able to see your face.' Stavs was looking down at him in that way he did sometimes – the way that made something happen in Jake's stomach that definitely wasn't *butterflies*. Nothing about this whole situation was supposed to cause *butterflies*.

'Sure,' Jake said, shifting onto his back. He felt vulnerable in a way that he usually didn't during sex. He wasn't sure what Stavs might see on his face.

'What's . . . what's the best way like this?' Stavs asked.

'I don't know if this is something you can, like, optimise.'

Stavs narrowed his eyes and Jake really hoped that he was in trouble. He bent his knees up again. 'Have at it.'

Stavs choked on a laugh. 'You're absurd.'

'You l–like it.'

Stavs didn't reply, but he did run a slick finger down the crease of Jake's ass. Jake closed his eyes, let himself fall into the sensation. Stavs took his time, teasing, while Jake tried not to squirm, tried not to press against Stavs' fingers. Stavs dipped his head to kiss Jake's neck as his knuckle pressed just where Jake wanted it and Jake made an objectively embarrassing noise.

Stavs exhaled when he finally pressed a finger inside Jake's body, as though they were doing this the other way round.

It had been a while, and it felt so fucking *good*. 'Yeah,' Jake said. 'Like that.'

Stavs was so careful, so gentle, that it made Jake's chest go tight. He'd had people go slow before, to tease him or whatever, but he knew Stavs wasn't just teasing, he wanted to make sure it was good for Jake.

Stavs smiled when he found the angle that made Jake's body jerk, and Jake wanted to kiss him, wanted to feel that smile against his mouth. He realised he'd grabbed Stavs' free hand, twining their fingers together. Stavs was staring down at him like he couldn't quite believe Jake was real.

'We good?' Jake asked. *He* was certainly good.

'Yeah,' Stavs said, breathless. 'Yeah, you're so . . .' He slid another finger in beside the first.

'I'm so what?' Jake asked. They were still holding hands.

'You're so fucking hot, it drives me crazy.'

People had said way dirtier shit to Jake in bed, told him how hot he was, what they wanted to do to him, but he couldn't remember anyone ever saying something that had made him feel like this.

Stavs never really said much in bed, but now he was looking down at Jake, his eyes blown dark, his fingers inside Jake's body, and Jake regretted doing this face to face. It was too much, too intense. He knew his face was revealing things that neither of them should be thinking about.

'Stavs, *please*,' he said, because he had to say *something*, and then Stavs had another finger inside him and he wasn't going slow anymore, though he was still careful. He leaned down to catch Jake's mouth in a hard, messy kiss, and Jake was trying to touch all of him at once: his shoulders, his back, his biceps. He needed him closer, needed more of him.

'Condom?' Stavs asked, pulling his fingers free, and Jake gasped at the loss. It took him a second to register the question.

'In the drawer if you want. I'm on PrEP and I got tested after Kyle, so if you don't want to . . .'

Stavs hesitated. 'I'm good, too, but are you sure . . .'

'Yeah,' Jake said. 'Yeah, I want it like that, just *hurry up*.'

They'd managed to knock the lube onto the bed, so there was a brief scramble to retrieve it. Jake ended up finding it first and slicked up Stavs' dick while Stavs' breathing went ragged.

Jake almost got on his hands and knees, almost chickened out of doing this face to face, but Stavs had *asked*, and Stavs didn't ask for much. So he let Stavs cover him with his body and reached down to help guide him in.

Stavs went slow, and Jake exhaled, letting his body relax into it. It was quite a lot to take. Stavs was breathing hard, holding himself back.

'Are you okay?' Stavs asked when his hips were flush against Jake's body.

'So okay. You?'

'Nearly *too* okay,' Stavs said, in a voice that didn't sound like his own. That made Jake laugh a little. It was nice to know he wasn't the only one who was struggling to keep it together.

'Don't do that,' Stavs gasped, which made Jake laugh again. 'Fucking *menace*,' Stavs said, and gave his hips an experimental roll.

Jake stopped laughing, then, and groaned instead as Stavs thrust again, still careful. He ran his hands down Jake's ribs, gently, like Jake needed reassurance. Maybe he did, a little.

'More,' Jake said. Maybe a little sooner than he should have.

'I don't want to hurt you.'

'Every second you're not fucking me properly is hurting me.'

Stavs kissed him, and then he was moving, slowly at first, finding a rhythm. Jake let him work it out. It didn't take him long to get it right, to find the angle that made Jake shudder and clutch at Stavs' shoulders. Stavs had broken the kiss and was watching him. Jake closed his eyes because it was too much, but opened them again because *he* wanted to see what Stavs' face looked like while they did this.

'You can go harder,' he said, and hooked a foot in the small of Stavs' back. 'I want it, Stavs. Come *on*. Use those stupid muscles and *fuck me*.'

Stavs took him at his word this time. He snapped his hips forward just right, and then neither of them was keeping it together. They were kissing again, frantic, Jake's tongue in Stavs' mouth and Stavs' hands tangled Jake's hair, and Stavs was going to have scratches down his back from Jake's fingernails.

Jake reached for his own dick but Stavs knocked his hand away, instead pinning both Jake's wrists above his head with one hand. Jake choked on a gasp.

'That okay?' Stavs asked, letting his grip loosen for a second.

'So okay. So . . . yes, okay.'

Stavs brought their mouths together again, kissed Jake hard and got his lube-slicked hand around Jake's dick. Jake made a sound that came close to a whine, his legs tightening around Stavs' back. He didn't want to come, not yet, not before Stavs had, but it was too good, too much.

'So close,' Jake said against Stavs' mouth, and then they were kissing again, Jake's teeth on Stavs' bottom lip. 'Fuck, I'm gonna — *fuck*.'

He came hard, straining against Stavs' grip on his wrists. He felt Stavs hesitate and he managed to say, 'No, keep *going*, come on,' and then Stavs was coming too, burying his face in Jake's neck.

Stavs stayed where he was for a few seconds, panting, then lowered himself down so they were chest to chest. 'This okay?' he asked.

'Yeah,' Jake said. He liked staying close after sex. Liked feeling Stavs softening inside him. He let himself trace idle shapes on Stavs' back while their breathing evened out. Stavs pressed a gentle kiss to the side of his head, and Jake sighed happily.

'We should clean up.' Stavs exhaled, his breath warm against Jake's cheek.

Jake was already more than half asleep. He was going to get cold if he didn't get under the covers, but that seemed like a *lot* of effort.

'Mmm,' he agreed.

He winced a little when Stavs pulled out, and yeah, they were probably going to need to ditch the bedspread.

He heard Stavs cross into the bathroom, then the tap running. The bed shifted when he came back.

'I'm going to clean you up,' Stavs said softly. Jake murmured agreement, and then there was a warm flannel on his stomach. Stavs cleaned him up, gently, then bullied him under the covers.

'Sorry,' Jake managed. 'Dunno why I'm so wiped out.'

'I could hazard a guess,' Stavs said, getting under the covers as well. Jake nestled against him and Stavs wrapped an arm around him.

'Was that . . . It was good?' Stavs asked in the way he always did after he'd fucked Jake into semi-consciousness.

'Mm.'

'I guess it must have been if it's shut you up.' Stavs' fingers were gentle in Jake's hair.

The last thing Jake felt before he went to sleep were Stavs' lips brushing the nape of his neck.

Jake wasn't sure what woke him: maybe the winter sunlight streaming through the blinds he'd forgotten to close, maybe Stavs throwing an arm over Jake's stomach. He groped for his phone. Six thirty. Rolling over and going back to sleep was very tempting – his legs were tangled up with Stavs', and it would be easy to tuck his head onto Stavs' shoulder and go back to sleep.

He got up instead, careful not to wake Stavs. He was a little sore, but in a way that made him want to get back into bed and nuzzle his way down Stavs' chest. To keep him in bed all morning. To pin him down and ride him because it would hurt a bit and that would make it better.

His mum was sitting in the kitchen, lacing up her sneakers. She was wearing a ratty Tiger Sharks beanie, and the percolator was starting to bubble. Plugger was lying in front of her, his tail thumping on the linoleum. He scrambled up as Jake came in and whuffed quietly. Jake reached down to scratch his ears.

'You're up early,' Debbie said. 'Thought you boys would sleep in.'

'I woke up, fancied a walk.'

'Coffee?'

'Please.'

Debbie dug out another cup for the thermos while Jake found his sneakers and a puffer. Plugger scrambled down the hallway to sit by the front door.

'Sorry,' Jake told him. 'You're not allowed in the reserve.'

They managed to get out the door without Plugger, and walked in silence through the dewy grass towards the wildlife reserve. Debbie was walking slower than the last time they'd done this, and Jake tried to match her pace without making it obvious.

Stavs thought Jake should talk about his feelings about the cancer. But Jake didn't know how to talk about this. The thought of a world without his mum – without morning walks, the way she made coffee, her texts after his games – felt impossible.

Jake wasn't sure how many times he'd done this walk. Hundreds. Thousands, maybe. There were pictures of him at the entrance of the reserve on Debbie's back in a carrier, pointing at the wallabies. Then holding Debbie's hand as a toddler in a series of footy onesies. Riding his bike. Pictures with Keeley, and Olly. He'd walked it, run it, cycled it. Sometimes it felt like he'd made every important decision in his life somewhere along this track, stamping over the rough dirt, looking out for snakes.

They picked their way down to the lookout over the mangroves. The sun was only just up and there was barely any breeze. They could have been looking at a postcard.

Debbie unscrewed the lid of the thermos and poured them both a cup of coffee. Jake blew on his and watched the steam curl and evaporate.

'I'm thinking about coming out,' he said.

Debbie nodded slowly, like she wasn't surprised. 'Do you mean holding hands with someone while you get a coffee? Or a press release?'

Jake sighed and pulled his legs up, wrapping his arms around his knees. 'I think it kinda all ends up in a press release. But not all at once . . . like, maybe I tell the team first, and then even if I don't say anything publicly, I just stop being careful.'

Debbie made a *mm* noise. 'I see.'

'You don't think it's a good idea.'

She looked across at him, frowning. 'I didn't say that.'

'You didn't say I *should* do it, either.'

She sighed and took a sip of coffee. 'I'm not going to tell you what I think you should do,' she said. 'This one's only for you.'

He rested his chin on his knees. 'I know.'

'It's not that I don't think you should do it,' she said, as they watched a group of pelicans wing their way around the headland. 'It's just that sometimes I feel like these days it's all about *coming out*. Announcing it, labelling it. I don't want you to feel like you have to.'

'I just wanna be able to be open about it. Go on a date, whatever.'

'You didn't feel that way a few months ago.'

He'd told her about Kyle's ultimatum, of course. She'd given him a hug, gotten the ingredients for chicken soup (her remedy for all ills), and then taken him on an extra-long walk.

He shrugged. 'Yeah, I dunno. I guess I said that stuff about AFLW and I got shit for it. But I also got lots of nice messages. It meant something to people. I don't want to be some ambassador for queer AFL players, but I'm also sick of keeping it a secret. Maybe I tell the team, and then if people find out they find out.'

'And Theo?'

Jake tilted his head back. 'We haven't really talked about it. I don't know how he'd feel about it. I know he'd be supportive, but . . .' *But it might end things*. It was one thing for them to be hooking up in sort of secret, another to be doing that if Jake was out. Another thing altogether to *date*.

'You like him a lot.'

Jake blew out a breath. 'Yeah.'

'It's mutual.'

Jake shrugged. He thought so too, but. 'And complicated.'

'Why?'

Jake gave her a look. It was a question his mum only really asked when she already knew the answer but wanted Jake to talk something through. 'We're teammates. We're both closeted. His family don't know he's queer. Coming out to the team is one thing. Being in a . . . whatever with a teammate is another.'

'You've been around the women's game enough to know that teammates can date.' She grinned. 'I like the way he looks at you. Lydia says he's a good boy, but not *too* good.'

'Yeah.' Jake tried not to grin too broadly.

'I think whatever happens, you two would work it out. If it's romantic, or if he's a friend.'

'You've known him for twenty-four hours,' Jake pointed out. Not because she was wrong.

'I'm a good judge of character,' she said. 'I never liked Kyle.'

'That's because he called you Mrs Cunningham.'

'Maybe.'

They finished their coffee and watched the sun rise. Jake had always loved a winter sunrise. They picked their way back down the track in silence. Debbie even consented to lean on Jake's arm on one of the steeper parts.

'Look who's up,' Debbie said as they got back to the stretch of grass that led back towards the house.

Stavs was walking towards them, his hands shoved into the pockets of a puffer, following the trail of their footprints.

'Morning,' Debbie called, and Stavs looked up and smiled.

Wow, Jake was fucked.

Chapter Twenty

Jake was in a good mood. He'd had a couple of seriously good games, he'd been the subject of a whole week of bizarre controversy about his pre-game routines, and he was having more – and better – sex than he'd ever been able to have in his life. The rain was pouring, the birds were hiding, but Jake was having a good fucking day.

They'd done an indoor session because the coaching staff didn't want anyone to hurt themselves in the mud, and Jake had a few minutes to kill before he was due to see the physio. He'd gotten absolutely cleaned up in their last game, and his right shoulder was complaining a bit.

Kat poked her head out of her office as he walked past. 'Jake, time for a word?'

'Sure.'

Kat's office had probably once been a printer room. If Jake had to work in a space that small, it would have immediately descended into complete chaos. But Kat had imposed a rigid order over the books and papers. She had a standing desk and one of those little under-desk treadmills. She'd even managed to find space for a couple of plants, which were surviving despite the complete absence of sunlight.

Kat shut the door behind her and gestured to the chair

opposite her desk. She sat as well, steepling her fingers under her chin.

'You're not going to like this conversation,' she told him. 'But just hear me out.'

Ordinarily this sort of chat would be the precursor to being dropped for the next game. But there was no way Jake was being dropped. He was playing well. *Really* well. He was only three goals behind Sheds as the leading Falcons goalscorer, and *nobody* kicked more goals than Sheds.

'This is not a coach talk,' she continued. 'This is a talk from someone who's known you for a long time.'

'Yeah?'

She looked him in the eye. 'You need to think about what you're doing with Bestavros.'

Jake had never been very good at controlling his face. He did his best.

'What do you mean?'

Kat had known he was gay for years, but it wasn't something either of them really acknowledged. He knew she was supportive, but he'd always preferred to keep his sexuality away from his footy.

She fixed him with a look he remembered from primary school. 'I'm not asking you to tell me anything about what's going on, I'm just asking you to listen. And then to think.'

'Sure.' Jake could listen. He tipped the chair back, waiting. He knew that Kat hated it when people did that.

'So, let's just say there was something' – she hesitated – '*romantic* going on between you and Bestavros. All I'm saying is that you should think about the potential consequences. For him.'

That sounded bad. 'What do you mean?'

'He's a good player, and he's doing well. But if something happens, *he's* the one who's expendable. You're not going to get traded or delisted.'

Jake let the legs of his chair thump back to the ground. '"Something happens"?'

'If whatever is going on affects one or both of you on the field. If things end badly and you can't work together. If people find out and it affects the team dynamic. I'm not . . . you know I'd stick up for him. But it's not going to be my call. And putting the team first is going to mean putting you first.'

'Right,' Jake said, because she seemed to be waiting for him to say something. 'You're saying . . . if we were doing anything, we should stop.'

Kat sighed. 'No, Jake. I mean, I *married my coach*. I'm saying you should think about the risks and you should talk to Bestavros about them. Maybe you've done that already, in which case you can tell me to butt out.'

Jake shut his eyes for a second. He'd *known* he was going to have to think about this, but he'd been doing a pretty good job of pretending he didn't. Stavs had to know too. He was way smarter than Jake, and even Jake could see that whatever they were doing was no longer just friends fucking around. It could all go pretty pear-shaped.

Kat was talking again. 'I'm not saying you can't be together and play here, but I just . . . I like him, Jake. He's a good guy. I want him to succeed.'

So did Jake.

She continued. 'I've played with teammates who've been couples, and I've played with teammates who've broken up. It can work, but sometimes it doesn't, and there isn't always a better solution than one person leaving the club. You're both adults, and you can make your own choices. But just don't let it happen and then realise too late that you should have talked about it earlier.'

'Yeah.'

Stavs was going to want to stop. Jake knew how important this year was to Stavs – he wasn't going to want to risk it. Stavs was going to say *sorry*, and thinking about it gave Jake the same feeling he got when he saw a hit coming and couldn't stop it. When he knew it was going to *hurt* and there was nothing he could do but brace for impact.

'I'll think about it,' he promised.

'Jake,' she said, as he made to stand. 'I'm not saying you shouldn't . . .' She sighed. 'You two . . .' She seemed to change her mind about whatever she was going to say. Then she shook her head. 'I probably shouldn't say this, but you two seem good together. Maybe it's worth the risk. But you can't choose for him.'

'Yeah.' He hesitated. 'How did you . . . I mean, with Cindy. How did it happen?'

Kat's smile went a little dreamy. 'Well, we sort of . . . things happened in the off-season, and then we talked about how it would work. But it was a bit different. The AFLW was only just starting out, there wasn't much media, and it was already a very queer-friendly space. I was pretty much on the verge of retirement anyway, so I knew if something went really wrong, that was an option. We disclosed our relationship to management and the team and worked out some systems for any potential conflicts. It wasn't perfect, but we made it work, and then I retired at the end of the year and the issue went away.'

'Why did you decide it was worth the risk?'

Kat's eyes went to the photo on her desk. 'I don't really believe there's only one person for everyone,' she said. 'But I realised one day that I knew all the ways she pissed me off, and I still wanted to see her every day. Days when I didn't see her were always a little bit worse. Every time I thought about doing something – travelling, going to see my family, going to the snow, even just cooking a nice dinner at home – I imagined her there with me, without even meaning to. Having to compromise on my footy didn't feel like a big deal if it meant we could be together.'

Jake nodded. There was a lump in his throat, and he didn't think he could speak around it.

'You know,' Kat said, her voice uncharacteristically soft. 'If you two were together, I'd have your back. And if either of you, or both of you, wanted to come out, you'd have the support of the club. You'd have my support.'

'Yeah,' Jake said, and his voice didn't come out quite right. 'I don't think I'm cut out to be that kind of role model.'

Kat frowned. 'What do you mean?'

'Seriously? I can't even put on some headphones and chill before a game without someone writing about how I'm not taking things seriously. You reckon I'm gonna be a good poster boy for queer footballers?'

'Representation isn't about being perfect, it's about being there.'

'Sure,' Jake said. 'But . . .' He stopped. There was no point arguing about it. He wasn't going to come out any time soon, so it didn't matter what Kat thought.

Kat was still studying him. 'Look, whoever comes out first, it's not going to be easy. But *nobody* is going to be the perfect example.'

'There'd be some who weren't shit, though.'

'Jake. You're a star player, and you spoke out recently for the AFLW and for queer players. You coming out would be a big fucking deal for the queer community. In a good way. I'm not saying there wouldn't be a lot of chat about it, but you'd be a great role model. You *are* a great role model.'

Jake shrugged. 'Maybe. Kinda academic, though.' He glanced at the clock. 'Shit, I'm late.'

'Go,' Kat told him. 'And think about it.'

'I will.'

He was going to have to, now. No matter how much he didn't want to.

'Kat knows,' Jake blurted into Stavs' collarbone. He'd been trying to pick his moment. This was probably not it – both of them sweaty and tangled together on Jake's bed – but if he didn't spit it out he was going to go insane.

The conversation with Kat had been rattling around his head for the last few days. He'd kept meaning to bring it up. And, okay, maybe it was selfish and stupid, but he'd wanted a few more days of Stavs before they called it quits. He couldn't see any scenario where they *didn't* call it quits. They'd both been clear that it was casual, and it wasn't Stavs' problem that Jake had caught feelings. Even if Stavs had caught feelings as well. (Jake wasn't an idiot, he knew when someone was into him.)

Stavs went tense. 'What?'

Jake raised his head. He was half-sprawled over Stavs' chest. It was one of his favourite places to be, hearing Stavs' heartbeat under his cheek.

'Kat knows we're . . .' Jake gestured between them. *Fucking* felt like the wrong word.

'What? How?' There was a note of accusation in Stavs' voice that made Jake shift to roll off him and sit up.

'I didn't tell her,' Jake said. 'But she's like a sniffer dog for queer romance. She's always been like that. She pulled me aside to talk about it.'

'When?'

Oh, Stavs was not going to like this. 'Last Tuesday.'

There was a beat of silence.

'I think we should talk about this with our clothes on.' Stavs turned away from Jake and swung his legs off the bed.

Neither of them said anything as they found their clothes. Jake wasn't a stranger to awkward post-coital silence, but this one was particularly bad. He managed to find his shorts and singlet. He had no idea where his underwear was, and he wasn't going to crawl around bare-assed looking for it.

He got back onto the bed and leaned against the headboard. Stavs joined him. He'd buttoned his shirt wrong and his hair was still messy from Jake's fingers. Jake had no idea what he was going to do. What he was going to say.

'What did Kat say?' Stavs asked.

'She said . . .' Jake hesitated. He wasn't sure if there was a tactful way to summarise. 'She said that if there was something going on between us, we should make sure we were okay with the potential consequences.'

'Meaning?'

'Like, if we . . .' He couldn't say *break up*, because they weren't together. 'You know, if it affected our game. If something happened and we couldn't work together. Or if someone in list management found out and had concerns about it.'

Stavs had been smiling, earlier. Smiling against Jake's mouth. There was none of that smile left on his face. He looked a bit nauseous. 'What would happen to me, you mean. You're not going anywhere.'

What was Jake supposed to say to that? It was true and they both knew it.

'Kat said she'd have our back. But she's not in charge.'

Stavs was toying with the hem of his shirt, twisting the fabric between his fingers. 'You should have told me,' he said. 'It's been a *week*, Jake.'

Jake forced himself to look Stavs in the eye. 'I know, I'm really sorry. I was trying to find the right moment. I just didn't want . . .'

Had he just done to Stavs what Kyle had done to him? Fucked him on false pretences? Hung on to something, knowing it was over?

'This year is really important for my career,' Stavs said. Almost like he wanted Jake to disagree. 'I can't risk doing anything that might fuck it up.'

'Yeah, I know.' Jake waited for the blow to land.

'We need to stop,' Stavs said.

Jake had known it was coming, so why did it hurt as though it was a surprise? Stavs was doing well. He was having exactly the break-out season he needed to have. Even if Stavs did have feelings – and Jake was pretty sure he did – he had to put footy first.

Jake understood. It was the same decision he had made at the end of last year. Although if this was karma's way of making him understand how Kyle had felt, it fucking sucked.

Jake wished he could read Stavs more easily. He'd been getting better at it, but now he couldn't tell what Stavs was thinking.

'Okay,' Jake said, swallowing. 'Yeah.'

He was doing a piss-poor job of sounding okay about ending things.

'Jake . . .' Stavs reached out and took Jake's hand. He hesitated, closed his eyes. Opened them again. 'Would you want this to be more? If we weren't teammates?'

Jake should probably lie. Wouldn't it be easier for both of them if he lied? But he didn't *want* to lie. Not to Stavs, not now.

'Yeah,' he said. 'But we *are* teammates. I'm not gonna – there's no point thinking about it.'

'Yeah. You're right.' Stavs squeezed his hand, then let it go. 'But we're still friends, right?'

'Duh. Just don't be a fucking weirdo again,' Jake told him.

Stavs leaned over and kissed him. A gentle brush of his lips. He pressed his forehead against Jake's, lingering for a second. 'I promise.'

'Good.'

Jake had had his heart broken before. He'd let Kyle fuck him, knowing it was the last time, and then he'd watched Kyle walk away, trembling with rage and grief and the fucking *unfairness* of it all.

This was quiet, and gentle, and worse.

Stavs found his phone and his keys and left. Jake let himself slide off the bed and thump down onto the floor. It was for the best, he told himself. He'd get over it. He'd gotten over people before. Or, at least, one person.

It just *sucked*. He'd found someone he – well, what was the point in even thinking about what word he should use? He'd found someone he wanted for a boyfriend, he was seriously thinking about coming out, and it still wouldn't fucking work.

His mum always said, 'You don't do the right thing because it makes you feel good, you do it because it's the right thing to do.' Telling Stavs had been the right thing to do. Stopping what they were doing had been the right thing to do. He'd told Stavs the truth, and Stavs had walked away. Which was fine. Footy first.

Jake

u free? can we talk?

Debbie

of course, I'll call you.

'Hey sweetie,' Debbie said, as soon as he picked up. 'Everything okay?'

'Stavs and I broke up,' he told her, feeling like his throat was closing up. Because that was what had happened, even if they hadn't given it the right name. Stavs had been sleeping in his bed every second night. There was tahini in the fridge. A toothbrush for Stavs in his bathroom. He'd taken Stavs to the place he loved most in the world, to meet the people he loved most in the world.

'Oh, Jake,' she said. 'I'm so sorry.'

'Me too.'

He couldn't get any more words out. But he didn't need to. He just sat on the floor, on the phone, breathing and listening to his mum breathe. She didn't need to say anything either. She was there, and that had always been enough.

Except she might not be, soon. There wasn't any bad news, not yet, but there *could* be. He tried to choke back a sob and couldn't. There were tears on his cheeks, but he couldn't remember when he'd started crying.

'Jake?' she said. 'Are you alright?'

He couldn't speak. He knew he must be freaking her out – he must sound like he was dying – but he couldn't stop crying. It was like the safety glass that had kept him from thinking about his mum had shattered into a million pieces. Maybe next time he broke up with someone he wouldn't be able to call her. Wouldn't be able to hear her voice and feel safe. Loved. There wouldn't be a home to go to that was a place, and a feeling, but was mainly her – practical and indomitable, someone who took up so much space it was impossible to imagine a world without her.

'I'm texting Xen,' she said, and Jake couldn't get the words out to tell her not to.

The door opened and then Xen was there, kneeling down and pulling Jake into his arms. Jake buried his face in Xen's shoulder and let himself cry. Xen gently took the phone out of his hand.

'I've got him,' he said to Debbie. 'We'll look after him. I'll get him to call you later.'

'Sorry, Mum,' Jake managed.

Xen put the phone down and wrapped both his arms around Jake, holding him close. 'You're going to be okay,' he said. Not *it's going to be okay*. Because they both knew it might not be.

Jake gave up on getting his shit together and let himself cry, Xen rubbing soothing circles between his shoulder blades.

'What —' Paddy's voice, then footsteps. Another set of arms around him. It felt good to be held like this, close and warm. Even if they weren't the arms he really wanted.

'Hey,' Paddy said. He kissed Jake on the top of the head. 'We're here.'

'Thanks,' Jake managed, his cheek still pressed against Xen's t-shirt. Xen's damp t-shirt, now. 'Sorry.'

'Better out than in,' Paddy told him.

Jake managed to lift his head. 'You usually say that when someone's vomiting.'

'It's good advice in a range of situations.'

Jake felt like someone had grabbed him with both hands and wrung him out. They had a game tomorrow. He couldn't imagine managing to play a quarter, let alone a whole game.

'Can we watch a movie or something?' He didn't want to be alone, or to think.

'Of course,' Xen said. 'And I was making pot roast.'

'You're the best,' Jake said. He let Paddy pull him to his feet.

'Do I need to go and break Stavs' legs for breaking your heart?' Paddy asked.

'No!'

'Are you sure?'

'No, we . . . I mean, it was mutual.'

Paddy looked at him, incredulous. 'Are you serious?'

'It's . . . complicated. Can we not talk about this now?'

Paddy sighed. 'Fine. Come on, you need some carbs.'

Chapter Twenty-One

Theo arrived home to the smell of something delicious. Eva had texted to ask if he was free for dinner, but he'd assumed they'd order takeaway. He could hear her singing in the kitchen. She had a lovely voice, but in high school she'd given up her singing lessons for debating and mooting. She was singing an Egyptian pop song he hadn't heard in years. 'I'm home,' he called, toeing out of his shoes and heading for the kitchen.

Eva was in front of the stove wearing an apron he'd never seen before, her hair caught back in a colourful scarf. There was a bakery box on the table, tied up in familiar pink ribbon.

'I'm making koshari,' she told him. 'And there are snacks.'

She'd made fresh aish baladi and hummus.

He sat down on a kitchen stool and helped himself. 'This looks incredible. You didn't have to cook.' He couldn't believe she'd had *time* to cook. He'd barely seen her for at least a month; he mainly knew she was coming home in the evenings because there were rinsed dishes on the sink every morning.

'I wanted to,' she told him. 'Besides, you need koshari, and mine is better than anything we could order.'

'I need koshari?'

Eva turned to give him a look. 'You do. You've been sad. You need koshari *and* knafeh. Luckily I've got both.'

She wasn't wrong. He was sad, but he was also having to watch *Jake* be sad, which was much worse than dealing with his own feelings. It had been a deeply shitty ten days.

He'd been the one who made the choice. He knew it was the right one. But that didn't make him feel any better about it. Asking Jake what he would have wanted if they weren't teammates had been a terrible idea. Because Jake had told the truth – of course he had – and now Theo couldn't lie down to sleep without thinking about an alternate universe where he still got to see Jake's wicked smile and wake up with all of Jake's limbs wrapped around him.

They were still friends – Theo still got to hear Jake's laugh, roll his eyes at Jake's silliness, see Jake almost every day, and that was going to have to be enough. Except Jake hadn't laughed much since they'd called things off, and he was being meticulously careful not to touch Theo beyond a clap on the shoulder or a fist bump. Xen would occasionally look at Jake with a worried little crease between his eyebrows. Theo wanted to ask him if Jake was okay, but he already knew the answer.

They'd played a game the day after the . . . talk, Theo would call it. Jake had the kind of bad performance that happened to everyone once in a while: put a good opportunity straight into the post, fumbled a couple of pick-ups, argued with an umpire and gave away a fifty. Jake usually shrugged off bad luck, but he'd come off the field looking like he wanted to punch a wall and vanished as soon as he could.

Theo was sad, but . . . fine. He was playing well. This was what he had wanted. The ladder was tight, but the Falcons were on track to clinch a spot in the eight. He'd been able to reduce the dosage of his meds, although he didn't see himself coming off them entirely any time soon. This was what he'd wanted. It proved he'd made the right call.

'I thought we could watch some *Poirot*,' Eva suggested.

'It's not that bad,' Theo assured her. 'I promise.' Eva didn't find murder mysteries as relaxing as Theo did. She'd been forever scarred as a child by a particularly harrowing episode of *Miss Marple*.

'My mind is made up.'

She dished up for both of them, at the kitchen counter rather than the dining table. They'd never been allowed to eat at the counter as kids. She was the type of cook who cleaned as she went, and the kitchen was warm from the stove and smelled of spices.

Theo took a bite of the koshari. It was incredible. 'You're right, this is better than anything we could have bought.'

'Thank you.' She preened a little. 'Now, what's going on? I'm your older sister, I'm allowed to pry. And I know it's not work. You got seventeen disposals' – she paused, as though not sure she'd used the right word – 'in your last game.'

Theo dropped a spoonful of koshari back into his bowl in shock. 'You've been following my games?'

'I haven't watched them,' she said, as though he might be mad about it. 'I just can't understand them. But Rohan – one of the partners – is a big AFL fan, and he's been giving me summaries.' She sighed, nudging her koshari around the bowl. 'I'm sorry I haven't been around more. I knew you were having a rough time when you got here, but it seemed like it was getting better, and I've been a bit consumed by work. It's not an excuse, but there it is.'

'It's okay. I know I could have asked if I needed anything. Also, I'm living in your house for free.'

'I'm not sure you *have* been living here for the last few weeks.' She raised an eyebrow at him.

'I was seeing someone,' Theo admitted, fortified by the food. 'I really liked . . . them.'

'And they broke it off?'

'No, it was . . . mutual, I guess.'

Eva was studying him in a way that reminded him a lot of Priya. 'Do you want me to ignore the pronoun, or do you want me to ask about it? Just for the record, you know you're still going to be my favourite little brother, no matter who you're dating.'

He knew she wouldn't ask if he told her not to. And maybe that was why he suddenly wanted to tell her. He took a deep breath.

'*He* was an athlete as well, and he didn't want to come out. I don't know if I do, either. At least not publicly. We decided to call it quits before it got messier.'

'Oh,' she said, her eyes widening. 'I'm really sorry. I can see how that would make things complicated.'

'Yeah.'

'It seemed like he made you happy.'

'He did.' It *hurt*, knowing that she'd noticed. 'But I can't do anything to risk this year, you know? I'm not going to get another opportunity like this. I can't do anything to jeopardise it.'

She nodded. 'I get it.' He knew she'd been dumped before by men who hadn't liked the hours she worked. She'd been absolutely single-minded in pursuit of her career. He wanted to ask if she thought it was worth it.

'He got it, too.'

'Was he . . . Did you know you were interested in men? Before him?'

'I've known I was bi since I was about fifteen. But he was the first guy I've dated.'

She nodded. 'I'm sorry if you didn't feel like you could tell me you're bi. Priya knows, right? You could talk to her about it?'

'Yeah, she knows. And it wasn't that I didn't feel like I could tell you – I didn't want to tell Ommi and Abi, and I didn't want to ask you to keep it secret from them. Then I was with Rachel, then Sarah, and it didn't seem to matter. I always figured I'd say something if things got serious with a guy.'

'I really don't think you need to worry about them reacting badly.'

Deep down, he knew she was right. His extended family might not be accepting, but his parents had been in left-wing academic circles for years as they'd moved from practice into teaching. They went through the motions to stay connected to their culture, but they weren't socially conservative. At least, not about queerness. That wasn't really the problem.

'It'll be another reason I shouldn't be playing footy though, right? Not only is it not a real job, but I'd be one of the first out queer players – assuming I did come out.' He sighed. 'I'm just . . . I don't want to deal with it.'

'That's fair. You know I won't say anything to them.'

'I know.'

She tilted her head towards their food. 'Speaking of things our parents wouldn't approve of, we could eat the rest of dinner on the couch?'

He gave her a scandalised look. '*Eva*. The *idea*.'

She gathered up her bowl and the platter with the dips. 'Come on.'

'We really don't have to watch *Poirot*. How about . . .' Theo considered. 'We could properly go back to childhood and watch *The Road to El-Dorado*.'

'Done,' Eva said. She paused. 'Actually, I think I might be starting to understand why you watched that movie so many times. Also *Hercules*.'

'My interest in *Hercules* was completely innocent,' Theo protested.

She paused. 'And *Pirates of the Caribbean*? There was that time I walked in —'

'Oh my God, Eva, *stop*.' Theo had almost forgotten *that* incident, and wished he hadn't been reminded.

'Bring the knafeh,' she ordered.

'Yes, ma'am.'

Theo stared at the blinking cursor. He'd managed *Dear Abi and Ommi* and stopped. Maybe he should just ring them. But the thought of calling – of having to be on the line for whatever their initial response was – made his stomach churn. He didn't think they'd have a problem with him being bisexual, but he also didn't think it had ever occurred to them that he might be. He didn't want a box seat for their surprise, or incredulity, or whatever their first reaction might be.

Writing an email had been a suggestion from Jenny – not about his sexuality, he still hadn't told her anything about that, but she'd floated the idea of him raising some of his feelings about his family and his football in an email rather than in person. She said it would allow him to 'set clear boundaries' about their response. He'd been mulling that over.

He called Priya after a few more minutes of staring at the screen. She'd taken a two-week holiday in some lush mountain cabin and had been keeping him updated with observations about the scenery, the people in the other cabins, and her reading material. She liked to set a reading theme for holidays, and this time it was *tentacles*. It had led to a very varied selection of books.

'What's up?' she asked. Theo could hear jazz playing in the background.

'Nothing urgent, if you're busy.'

'I am so far from busy.' She sounded very pleased about it. 'I am lying in front of the fire with a whiskey and a book. I have never been less busy.'

'Sounds idyllic.'

'I needed it so badly. I have not checked my emails once. I am thriving.'

'Do you feel like thriving while helping me with something?'

'Of course.'

'I'm thinking about coming out to my parents.'

'Wow.' There was a moment of silence. 'Why now? Because it went well with Eva?'

Theo tapped his finger absently against the space bar. 'Maybe. I don't really know. I'm not going to do it today. I've just been thinking *how* I'd do it.'

'Or is this because of Jake?' That was Priya – right for the jugular.

He leaned back in his chair. 'I guess what happened with Jake made me think more about the fact I hadn't told them. And *why* I hadn't told them.'

'So what's the plan?

'I'm writing an email.'

'How's that going?'

'How do you think?'

Her laugh was sympathetic.

'It's *weird*. How do you tell people something like that? *Hi, how are you? I'm bisexual. Love, Theo.*'

'That would get the job done.'

'I feel like I need to tell them *why* I'm telling them now.'

Priya made a thoughtful noise. 'Do you? I mean, I don't think you owe them a big explanation or anything. You could just say it's important to you that they know and leave it at that.'

'They're going to ask how long I've known.'

'Maybe,' Priya acknowledged. 'But you could just say something simple, right? Like, *I've known for a long time, but haven't felt ready to share it.* And if they want to interrogate you, you can say you don't want to talk about it.'

'I think they'll be hurt I didn't tell them earlier.'

'I don't think that's a you problem.'

'It might *become* a me problem.'

'Why don't you enlist Eva? We work out what you want to say, then you talk to Eva about what you don't want *them* to say, and she talks to them and lays down some ground rules.'

It was a good idea. 'That might work.'

'Are you going to tell your whole family?'

'If I tell my parents, I'll also tell Simon and Alisa. And I think I'd tell them not to keep it a secret. It can just sort of – trickle out to the extended family. I'm not telling everyone individually, that would take years.'

There was a rustle of fabric. 'I'm getting another drink. Go make a cup of tea and get a snack. We've got some brainstorming to do.'

Theo got to his feet. 'Aye aye, Captain.' He left his phone on speaker on his desk and went down to the kitchen. He thought about Priya's question as the kettle boiled. *Why now?*

Talking to Eva about Jake (even without using Jake's name) had made him feel closer to her than he had in years. They hadn't talked about it again that night, they'd just watched movies until they were both yawning and stuffed full of knafeh, but afterwards there'd been an ease between them he couldn't remember feeling before. He'd let her in, and he was glad he had. Had taken the risk that she wouldn't react the way he wanted her to.

Maybe he needed to do the same with his parents. The conflict about his footy had resolved into a silent stalemate, and that silence had crept into everything else. He'd stopped talking to them about anything he cared about. There was nothing wrong with self-preservation, but it wasn't fair to behave as though they'd react the same way to everything. He didn't owe them the truth about his sexuality, but he *wanted* to tell them. He wanted them to know him, properly, even if they didn't always understand him.

By the time he'd made his tea and returned to his desk, he had a plan.

'I'm back,' he told Priya. 'But I think I've worked it out. Your services are not required.'

She sighed. 'I'm still taking the credit.'

'That's fair, you did suggest the tea. Enjoy your drink.'

'I will. Text me if you need anything.'

'Will do.'

Chapter Twenty-Two

Everyone had bad games. That was footy. It happened. You picked yourself up, you did whatever you needed to do to vent, and then you got the fuck over it. But Jake didn't like bad games, and two in a row felt like getting kicked when he was down. It was also a shitty time to be having bad games; the middle of the ladder was tight, and while the Falcons were on track to make the eight, it wasn't a sure thing.

They were playing the Sharks in the kind of weather that turned the ball into a heavy leather weight made to break fingers. It had stopped raining midway through the first quarter, but the ground was soaked and everyone was sliding and fumbling. The game had been scrappy and the score was tight. A few missed calls both ways – one that had left Yelks with a split eyebrow. Tempers were running high.

Jake didn't like the Sharks. He hadn't ever liked them, and he particularly didn't like them with Jamie Collins in their midfield. He hadn't been sad to see Collins traded from the Falcons, and he knew Collins was itching to mash him into the mud.

At least Stavs was playing well. It was like watching a totally different player. Maybe he wanted to stick it to his old team, or maybe he was just better than Jake at keeping shit compartmentalised.

Or maybe he didn't have much to compartmentalise. It had occurred to Jake – belatedly, as usual – that when he told Stavs he'd want more if they weren't teammates, Stavs hadn't said the same thing. And Stavs seemed fine. He was friendly, and it wasn't weird. It made Jake want to drown himself in the ice bath.

Not that he should be thinking about any of that during a game.

The ball had been stuck in the Falcons' D50 for what felt like eternity, stoppage after stoppage. Tenders finally managed to extract it – a thumping kick down the wing – and Jake started to move. The ball went over Stavs' head but he chased it down and took possession through sheer bloody-mindedness. A shepherd from Raze sent his direct opponent flying and then Stavs tried to get it in low, a spearing kick towards Tommy, but a Sharks defender punched it free and Tommy ended up at the bottom of a pile of players.

The umpire blew the whistle and Tommy was slow to get up. Jake moved closer, circling, his opponent hard on his heels.

There was a scuffle between a Sharks player and Paddy – Paddy had taken exception to Tommy being held down on the ground – but the umpire balled it up anyway.

When Sheds won the tap, Jake was already on the move. This was what he did. He reached for the ball, knowing exactly where he'd need to put the kick.

Everything went black.

Theo saw the hit as though it happened in slow motion. Jake had his head over the ball, bending to pick it up, when Jamie Collins came in hard from the side. Theo saw the moment when Collins stopped looking at the ball and looked at Jake instead.

Collins' shoulder caught the side of Jake's head and sent him flying. Theo knew Jake was unconscious even before he hit the ground like a ragdoll. The whistle shrilled. Jake didn't move.

The crowd roared its fury, and Theo could almost feel the rage of the Falcons supporters burning up his throat. He didn't even realise he'd moved until he had a hand wrapped in Collins' jumper. Collins was grinning. He had a couple of inches and about twenty kilos on Theo, and he grabbed Theo right back.

'What's wrong?' Collins was smirking. 'He your boyfriend?'

'Why, you jealous?'

Someone hit them hard from the side and Theo staggered, but he kept his hand in the front of Collins' jumper. Raze was shoving in between them, trying to push them apart, or maybe trying to shake Theo off so he could go at Collins himself, but all Theo could see was Jake's body hitting the ground and the smug little smirk on this fucker's face. Another Sharks player grabbed Raze's jumper and hauled him away, leaving Theo and Collins alone. Theo could see other players piling in around them.

'Fucking pussy,' Collins spat. 'You think everyone doesn't know that he's a fa—'

Theo tried to punch him in the face. Tried, because someone grabbed his arm before he could really take a swing. Paddy's voice was in his ear, but all he could see was Collins' red, furious face.

'Takes one to know one,' Theo snarled.

Collins slammed an elbow into his stomach and, *fuck*, that hurt. Theo struggled to break Paddy's grip, but there were more hands on him and on Collins. Theo wasn't sure how he ended up on the ground, or who was on top of him. Something bony got him hard in the nose and then there was blood in his mouth as well. He got a knee up, jammed it into something soft. There was a grunt of pain, so he did it again.

Then, suddenly, there was nothing on top of him. He rolled over onto his hands and knees, blinking tears out of his eyes and spitting out a mouthful of blood. There was blood dripping from his nose as well. He hoped it wasn't broken. It felt like it might be.

A hand appeared in his peripheral vision and he grabbed it. Tenders hauled him up and gave him a pat on the back. Raze was holding two Sharks players back with no apparent effort, and a couple of Sharks players were restraining Collins. One of them gave Theo a rueful shrug.

Xen had obviously pulled Paddy out of the scrum, Yelks was shoving players away from one another and Tenders looked like he'd deck the next person to make a wrong move.

But Jake was still on the ground, so the umpires hadn't been able to ball it up to distract everyone.

Theo took a step towards Collins without thinking.

'Stavsy.' Xen grabbed him by the shoulders and got in his face. He pressed their foreheads together. 'Stavsy, get your shit together.'

Theo opened his mouth and blood spilled out over his chin.

'Jesus,' Xen said. He pulled off his jumper and handed it to Theo. 'You're bleeding like a motherfucker.'

'My nose,' Theo explained, pressing the jumper against his face.

The Sharks captain had a hand on Collins' shoulder and was talking to him. He and Yelks exchanged a look that radiated comradely exasperation. Like two dads whose kids had been fighting in the playground.

There were trainers on either side of Jake, and Paddy had knelt down beside them. He was holding Jake's forearm, talking to him.

Theo removed the jumper from his face. 'Is he okay?'

Xen tugged Theo gently in the direction of the bench. 'They're checking him out. Come on, Stavs. We need to get you a towel and work out if *you're* alright.'

The trainer with Jake had signalled for the stretcher, and now two of the medical staff were jogging towards Jake with a spine board. Theo froze and stumbled against Xen.

'They always bring it out as a precaution if someone's knocked out,' Xen told him. 'He's probably fine. I saw the hit. It was nasty, but he'll be okay.'

A trainer ran out to meet Theo with a bag of ice and a towel. She tossed Xen's bloody jumper aside and forced Theo to sit down on the bench. He tried to see past her towards Jake.

'We'll get the doc onto you once he's done with Cunningham,' the trainer said, peering into his face. 'It doesn't look displaced. You might be lucky.'

The big screen showed a replay of the melee – of course – and Theo experienced the truly strange sensation of knowing it was him on the screen and yet not recognising himself at all. There was a low hum of anxiety in the back of his brain, buzzing behind the worried nausea. Jake had been so *still*.

The crowd murmured and Theo looked up at the screen again. Jake was conscious, and Theo felt the relief like somebody had cut his strings. Jake gave the crowd a thumbs up and there was a roar of approval. Xen sighed, long and shaky.

It took a while to get a neck brace onto Jake and then to get him onto the transport vehicle. Yelks and Paddy stayed close, and the Sharks captain lingered at a respectful distance. The rest of the players had retreated to their respective huddles.

The Falcons supporters were on their feet as soon as the transport started moving, and the huddle broke apart so that everyone could jog over to escort Jake off the field. Theo was cornered by the doctor before he could get across to see Jake, and he submitted reluctantly to having his nose poked at.

'Not broken,' the doctor told him, cheerfully, as Theo tried to hold still. 'So you're the second lucky one today.'

'Jake's okay?'

'He won't enjoy the concussion, but he'll mend. Now, I'm going to tape up your nose so you can go back on. Try not to get hit in the face again.'

'I'll do my best.'

With Jake out for the game, they couldn't sub Theo off, so he was just going to have to cope with the nose. Inevitably, every Sharks player would try to clobber him in the same spot again. He pulled off his bloody jumper and accepted a replacement. Fuck them.

After that, Theo played one of the best halves of football of his life. It was as though his rage and then his relief had seared everything else away. He managed a filthy goal from the pocket when two Sharks players collided, then slotted an absolute beauty from outside the arc. It came off his boot perfectly, sailed through the goal as the crowd screamed their approval.

He felt absolutely nothing.

It was after midnight by the time Theo parked Jake's car in the sharehouse driveway. They'd won the game, but it wasn't the kind of win anyone felt that good about. Jake was obviously feeling terrible. He hadn't even given Theo any shit about his driving. He sat slumped in the passenger seat, his eyes closed.

Jake had been sent to hospital as a precaution. He'd been discharged once Theo and Xen arrived and promised that they'd keep an eye on him, keep him fed and watered, and stop him from looking at screens. The Registrar had repeated the latter instruction several times.

Xen and Paddy hadn't asked why Theo had been the one to sit with Jake while they waited for an update, why he'd been the one to get Jake's keys, why he hadn't left Jake except to take the world's shortest shower.

Theo had expected to be the subject of a solid chewing-out from Davo, and then a quiet talk from Yelks. Instead, Davo had sat him down and asked, very seriously, whether he was alright. He'd managed to explain that yes, he was, and no, that wasn't how he'd normally react on the field, but it had been a very nasty hit. Luckily the hit had been so egregious that nobody seemed to think it was surprising that Theo had lost his shit.

That was good, but it didn't solve Theo's problem. He *hadn't* lost his shit because Jake was his friend. Yes, he would have gotten into anyone who'd hit Paddy like that, or Xen, or any of his teammates, but it wouldn't have felt the same. He wouldn't have tried to *punch someone in the face*. If Paddy hadn't stopped him, it would have been an eight-week suspension. It might have been the end of things with the Falcons.

He'd thought about that while sitting with Jake, holding a bucket for him while he threw up. He'd thought about it while Jake leaned on him on the way back to the car, unsteady on his feet and trusting Theo to support him. It was the closest they'd been in a fortnight.

There were sensible decisions and career planning, and then there was the warmth of Jake against his side, the way Jake had nestled closer, too tired to pretend he didn't want to. The way it had felt right to be the person waiting with Jake, the person who knew where he kept his keys, the person who took the doctor's written sheet of instructions and promised to take care of him.

Jake had been lucky, the doctor had said. He was going to be miserable, but it was his first bad concussion (somehow), and the doctor hadn't seemed too worried.

Theo knew, objectively, that AFL careers were short. That had been hammered into him. He'd be lucky to still be playing at thirty. A bad hit, some bad luck, and he'd be gone before then. He'd given up Jake as though that could somehow guarantee his professional longevity. As though being with Jake was inevitably the end of his career. As though it was as simple as *Jake or footy, pick one.*

Theo steered Jake towards his bedroom, then changed his mind and nudged him gently onto the couch. 'Stay here, I'm going to make your bed.'

Jake looked up at him, belligerent. 'Who says I didn't make it?'

'Data.'

Theo made the bed in record time and returned to the patient. Jake was lying back on the couch and looking miserably around the living room. Xen and Paddy had distracted him with a short rundown of the melee, but retreated to the kitchen when Theo reappeared.

'Xen won't show me the video of the fight,' Jake complained. Then added, 'I can't believe you tried to punch on.'

Theo decided to ignore the last part. 'Good. You're not supposed to be looking at screens. Stay there, I'm going to get you some water and something to eat.'

'I'm not hungry.'

'Tough.'

Jake pouted. It figured he'd be the world's worst patient.

Paddy was perched at the kitchen counter, eating the protein-powder-based horror he described as ice-cream. Xen was defrosting something in the microwave.

'Chicken soup,' he explained.

'Great.'

'How's the patient?' Paddy asked.

'Grumpy.'

'I can hear you,' Jake said from the living room. 'You'd be fucking grumpy, too.'

'You're the new favourite, Stavs,' Paddy said.

'What?' Theo put on some toast.

'The fans. You're their new favourite.' He cleared his throat. '"I take back every bad thing I ever said about Bestavros. He's my hero. About time somebody stood up for @jcjk9."'

'I tried to punch someone in the face. It was a bad thing to do.'

'Nah,' Paddy said. 'It was the right thing to do.'

'You stopped me,' Theo pointed out.

'You would've broken your hand *and* gotten suspended for ages.' He paused, still scrolling. 'They get better. "Bestavros can punch me in the face any time." "Bestavros could hit me with his car and I'd thank him." "My girlfriend and I have agreed that Bestavros is our hall pass." "Against all violence except the right-eous violence of Theo Bestavros."'

Theo managed a smile. Maybe he'd find them funnier in the morning.

'Are you okay, Stavs?' Xen asked, taking the soup out of the microwave. It smelled excellent, and Theo's stomach growled. 'You want some?'

'If there's some going. And yeah, I'm good.' It was a lie, and Xen probably knew it was a lie, but Theo wasn't going to talk to Xen and Paddy about it. He needed to talk to *Jake* about it.

Theo took two serves of soup and toast into Jake's bedroom on a tray – God knows why Xen owned a tray like they were in a period drama – and then helped Jake off the couch and onto his bed. It was like manhandling a helpless and very sulky kitten. If Jake had been able to go limp and dangle resentfully in Theo's grasp, Theo was sure he would have.

There wasn't anywhere to sit except the bed, so Theo dragged in a dining chair and used the nightstand as a table. He wanted, desperately, to get on the bed next to Jake. To wrap an arm around him and pull him close. He wanted to bury his face in Jake's hair and know he was safe and warm and alright. His skin would smell of the locker-room body wash Tenders had bought as a joke – mango and coconut.

He'd asked Jake what he'd want if they weren't teammates. But he hadn't asked Jake what he wanted outright. Maybe because he already knew, and he'd known he wouldn't be able to hear it and stick to his guns.

Jake took a spoonful of soup. Theo had never seen him look less enthusiastic about food.

'I'm sorry,' Theo said. Which was absolutely a cop-out.

Jake looked up. 'For what?'

'For losing my shit. We said we'd stop hooking up because we didn't want to risk something like this happening, and then I did it anyway.'

'I don't know why you're apologising to *me*. You're the one who could have been suspended.'

'You could have been seriously hurt!' Theo said. 'Punching Collins might have been worth it.'

He was, rationally, glad Paddy had stopped him. But not all of him was rational. Some part of him still wished he'd been able to punch Jamie Collins in the jaw, damn the suspension and the broken hand.

Priya liked to ask *what's the worst that could happen?* She really meant it, too. She wanted you to take the worst-case scenario and examine it from every angle. So he did. A worst-case scenario: they were together, then they broke up, and Theo got traded to somewhere awful. Or not at all and his career was done.

It was a risk.

Another risk: he could give up the chance of something with Jake, something *good*, and watch him fall in love with someone else. And maybe one day Theo would be at Jake Cunningham's buck's party, drinking a daiquiri through a penis-shaped straw, and watching Jake's whole face light up with the thought of someone other than Theo. Jake smiling at someone else the way Jake smiled at him.

He could give Jake up and, a year later, break his leg. He could lose footy any number of ways. And he was going to give Jake up without even *trying*? Give Jake up the way he'd never given up footy, because he loved footy, and he'd been willing to *fight* for it? Give Jake up because sometimes his anxious brain shouted loudly enough to make him believe his worries and insecurities were certainties?

Fuck that.

'I . . .' he started to say.

Jake had been staring into the soup. 'Yeah?' He took another disconsolate spoonful of broth.

'I didn't ask you what you wanted.'

Jake looked up, then. His eyes were very blue. 'What?'

'I asked you if you'd want more if we weren't teammates. But I didn't just ask what you wanted.'

Jake put the spoon down. 'What do you mean?' he said.

'What would you have said, if I'd just asked what you wanted?'

He looked away. 'I would've said I don't wanna be the person who ruins this for you.'

'You know that's not what I mean.'

'It's true.' Jake still wouldn't look at him. 'I know how important this year is to you.'

'Okay, answer this, then. Do you want to be with me?'

Jake closed his eyes. 'That's not fair. You already know the answer.'

Theo reached out to take Jake's hand. 'Tell me.'

Jake looked at him, and that made Theo's throat tighten. With hope, maybe. 'Yeah, I do. But I know —'

Theo tangled their fingers together. 'I want that too.'

'But we said —'

'I know what we said. We were wrong. Or I was, at least. I know it's a risk. It could go wrong. But it also might not, and I don't want to throw away something good because there's a risk of something bad happening in the future. I mean, if you don't want anything serious —' he stopped, because Jake was shaking his head.

'I do,' he said. 'Want something serious.' He was still looking at Theo intently, like he couldn't quite believe the words coming out of Theo's mouth. 'If you do.'

'I do.'

'Stavs, are you sure I'm . . . are you sure it's worth it?'

'You're worth it,' Theo told him.

Jake smiled, then, grey with exhaustion and sporting a blossoming black eye. That smile was the best thing Theo had ever seen.

'C'mere,' he said, tugging at Theo's hand.

Theo tipped his head towards the bowl. 'Not until you eat some more of your soup.'

Jake narrowed his eyes. 'I'll have some more of the soup if you come here.'

They reached a compromise, whereby Theo got onto the bed and wrapped an arm around Jake, but Jake continued to eat until most of the soup was gone. He put the bowl aside, then sat up and turned to straddle Theo's lap. Theo put his hands on Jake's hips.

'So, to recap,' Jake said, his smile shifting into a grin. 'You *like* me.'

Theo tightened his grip on Jake's hips. 'I'm not thirteen years old.'

'I get it,' Jake said, his hands settling on Theo's shoulders. 'I'm pretty great.'

'You're insufferable,' Theo told him.

It was hard to sound convincing with Jake in his lap, smiling at him like that. Jake tucked his cheek against Theo's shoulder and sighed.

'You're just going to leave me hanging?' Theo said against his hair.

'Don't worry.' Jake's breath was warm against Theo's neck. 'I'll be your boyfriend if you ask nicely.'

'I don't know if you can agree to that with a concussion,' Theo said. Jake's lips brushed the side of his throat and he tried not to shiver. 'Don't do that.'

'Can't I kiss my boyfriend?' Jake pressed a kiss under Theo's ear. He wriggled in his lap, and Theo decided that the situation needed to be controlled before it got out of hand.

'No,' he said, firmly, rolling Jake carefully off his lap and onto the pillows. 'You have a concussion. You need to rest.'

Jake pouted up at him. 'I'm not sleepy, and I'm bored.'

'Life is hard.'

'I want my phone.'

'No.'

Xen had initially taken possession of Jake's phone – he'd called Debbie to let her know Jake was alright – and then he'd delivered it into Theo's custody.

'I can read to you?'

Theo half expected Jake to scoff, but instead Jake just blinked at him. 'Read what?'

'A book.'

Jake looked mulish. 'No shit. What book?'

Theo had expected instant rejection of the idea. Jake didn't have any books in his room, so Theo went out to the living room to search for something appropriate.

Xen was on the couch with headphones on. He looked up when Theo came in. 'He good?'

'Yeah. Do you have something I could read to him?'

Xen smiled. For a moment, Theo thought he looked a bit wistful. 'Sure, what do you want?'

'Something soothing?'

'Well, Paddy has a lot of thrillers and books about music, so probably not those. There's some random stuff out here.' Xen waved at the bookcase next to the TV. It was mainly full of things that weren't books, but there were a few shoved onto one of the top shelves.

Theo made a selection and returned to Jake's bedroom. Jake was in the process of making a nest out of the covers. After some careful manoeuvring, and a lot of grumbling from Jake, they ended up with Jake settled back on the pillows and Theo arranged with the book in one hand and the other hand free to stroke Jake's hair.

'What's the book?' Jake asked.

'Never you mind, just listen.' Theo cleared his throat. 'Emma Woodhouse, handsome, clever, and rich, with a comfortable home and happy disposition, seemed to unite some of the best blessings of existence; and had lived nearly twenty-one years in the world with very little to distress or vex her.'

'Are you trying to make a point?' Jake murmured. But he didn't tell Theo to stop.

Jake was falling asleep by the end of the first chapter. Theo put the book aside and settled in next to him. Jake immediately turned and tucked his face into Theo's chest.

'We're not going to sleep like this,' Theo warned. He'd never been able to sleep while someone else used him as a pillow. Spooning – as the big spoon – was where he drew the line.

'Speak for yourself.' Jake nestled closer.

Theo sighed.

'You have to be nice to me,' Jake said. 'I'm your *boyfriend*. And I'm *injured*.'

'Is that how it works?' Theo realised he was not helping his argument by continuing to stroke Jake's hair.

'Yeah.'

'I guess I wouldn't know. I've never had a boyfriend before.'

'I've never had one like you before,' Jake said, so softly that Theo wasn't sure he'd meant for Theo to hear.

Theo didn't say anything in reply, just kept stroking Jake's hair until his breathing evened out. If it turned out he *could* fall asleep like this after all, at least Jake wouldn't be awake to be smug about it.

Chapter Twenty-Three

'Who's it even for?' Tenders grumbled. 'No offence,' he said to Gabby.

It's for me, Jake wanted to say, like he'd wanted to say a thousand times before. Or *at least, for the kid I was when I was thirteen.*

'Come on, Tenders,' Yelks said. 'We want to make sure everyone knows they're welcome.'

Both Falcons teams were gathered in the locker room, ready for open training. Jake had exited concussion protocols just in time to take part. He was, in theory, absolutely in favour of Pride open training. He was particularly in favour of the bet he had with Dex about who'd get the most shots on goal. But it got tiring, wondering which teammates had a problem with it. Wondering whether someone would actually come out and say something.

Paddy was sporting rainbow nails. He'd probably made Xen do them, because they were too neat for a DIY. Jake was going to stick with a rainbow armband and some rainbow socks. Stavs was kneeling down to put rainbow laces into his boots, but he was looking at them as though they might come to life and strangle him.

Yelks ran a tight ship when it came to inclusion. The only time Jake had ever seen him *really* lose it was when Collins had gone on a homophobic spray about an umpire. He'd been traded away soon after.

Nobody would be stupid enough to say anything shitty where Yelks might detect it. Or Raze. Once Raze had rainbow tape around one of his massive biceps, nobody was going to fuck around. Except sometimes Jake thought he'd rather hear it. At least when people said it out loud, you knew who thought that kind of shit. He hated not knowing who was thinking it and just not saying it.

'Yeah, but they obviously are, right?' Tenders jerked his head in a way that might have been intended to capture the AFLW team. 'The girls are playing, and some of them are, you know.' He shrugged, apparently unwilling to say *queer*. 'We can train together without all this rainbow PC shit.'

Jake saw Gabby's mouth tighten, saw her shaping a sensible, conciliatory answer.

'It's for me.' Jake heard the words as though somebody else was speaking. He felt like they'd just forced their way out of his mouth. He swallowed. 'I care about it. And other, uh, other queer people care about it.'

Gabby shifted, stepping in to flank him. She didn't say anything. Stavs was staring at him, still kneeling, his face unreadable, and *oh fuck*, they really should have talked about this first. But it was too late.

'I'm . . . I'm gay.' His voice sounded steady, which was weird, because he was pretty sure his heart was in the back of his throat. Was it possible to vomit up your own heart? 'It's . . . it's fucking sucked, sometimes. There was nothing like this when I was a kid. I guess I knew even then that I could either be out or I could play footy. I chose footy. But maybe when we do stuff like this, kids coming through now won't have to choose. And that *matters*. It fucking *matters*, okay?' He was getting choked up. He realised he was looking at Yelks. Looking for *something*. But Yelks didn't say anything. He was staring at Jake like he'd never seen him before.

'It's for me, too.'

For a second, Jake thought it must have been Stavs speaking, even though it didn't sound like him at all. But it was Raze who was stepping forward, wearing only his shorts, a rainbow armband around one bicep. 'I'm bi,' he said, in his soft, even voice.

'You're fucking kidding,' Tenders said. He was staring at them both.

'Yeah,' Raze said, voice flat. 'This is my idea of a joke.'

Tenders blinked.

'Do either of them look like they're fucking kidding?' Paddy asked. He stepped forward and wrapped one arm around Raze's shoulders, the other around Jake's. He was looking at Tenders like he'd throw down if he said something that pissed Paddy off even a little bit.

'I just —' Tenders started.

Raze held up a hand, and thank God, he was going to talk. Jake didn't want to do any more talking.

'I've never said anything because I didn't want anyone to look at me differently,' Raze said. 'I'm with Jake – it would have meant a lot to me to see rainbow tape and rainbow jumpers when I was growing up. And it's always meant something to me as a player. Made me feel more welcome, and safer, even though I wasn't out.' His voice got firmer as he spoke. 'If you don't get it, maybe you've never known what it's like not to know if you're welcome some-where. And I like doing this stuff, but it stresses me out, too. That it hasn't occurred to everyone that there could be someone queer in the room. Someone standing right next to them. That there's probably someone on every team – more than one person – who chose footy over being out.' He looked around, his eyes catching and lingering on Yelks. 'So, yeah. It's for me, too.'

Jake swallowed hard. Raze was looking at him like it was Jake's turn to say something. *Someone* definitely had to say something. Stavs had come to his feet. He took a step back and sat down, hard, still looking at Jake.

'I love this team,' Jake managed. 'I love this game. I figured it'd be worth staying kinda closeted in order to play it.' He crossed his arms over his chest. 'And now I reckon I've proved I can play footy. Maybe someone here needs to hear that I'm queer, and it makes me feel shitty to think my teammates won't even put on some rainbow fucking socks.'

He didn't know who to look at. Not Stavs – he didn't think he could do that. Raze stepped forward and pulled him into a hug before he had to decide. Someone whistled, and then several people started to clap. Jake let himself slump a bit into Raze's arms. Wished they were Stavs' arms.

'Thanks,' he said, softly enough that only Raze would be able to hear it.

'Thank *you*.' Raze's arms squeezed him tighter for a moment.

'Give him to me,' someone said, and then Jake was being hugged by Drips and Dex at the same time. That gave him the courage to look up, to see what was happening.

The noise gradually settled. Tenders was staring at both Jake and Raze.

He looked . . . not horrified. Just stunned.

'Is there a fucking problem?' Paddy asked.

Maybe it was the whipcord tension between Tenders and Paddy that snapped Yelks out of his surprise. 'Right,' he said, in the kind of tone that made everyone stand up a little straighter. He looked *shook*. Jake didn't blame him. *Jake* was shook.

'Jaze, Raze. Thank you for telling us. It was brave of you. I'm sorry you didn't feel like you could say something to the team until now. Or that . . .' He paused, and for a second he just looked *sad*.

'That you felt like you couldn't say anything to me.' He looked around the room, his gaze intent. 'That's on me, and that's on us – the men's team. We talk about being family, being brothers, but what's the point of family if you can't be yourself? So we're going to go out there and we're going to show that this is a club for everyone, and we've got even more reason to do that now than we did ten minutes ago.'

Yelks paused, and Gabby stepped forward. 'And in case it doesn't go without saying,' she said, 'nobody says anything to anyone about this unless the boys say it's alright.'

'Too right,' Yelks said. 'Now, let's play some fucking footy.' Gabby whooped, and the room broke out into shouts again.

Jake exhaled fully for the first time in what felt like hours. Yelks might have dropped the bundle for a minute or so, but he was a good captain. He *cared*, and that was enough for Jake.

Dex came over and elbowed Jake in the ribs. 'Always need the limelight,' they teased.

'Yeah, I was worried you might show me up on the field. Had to get in first.'

Jake looked around for Stavs, but he was nowhere to be found.

Maybe he'd already run out with Xen and Paddy.

'You good?' Dex asked. They were almost the last people still in the rooms.

'Yeah,' he said, although something felt wrong in his chest. 'Yeah, let's go.'

Theo was sure he'd felt worse at some point in his life. He just couldn't remember when. He wasn't sure how he'd made it through open training, how he'd smiled for selfies and signed posters and run drills like nothing was wrong, like he wasn't choking on nausea and listening to the thud of his own heart.

Like he wasn't hearing *coward, coward, coward* with every step he took. He'd avoided Jake, which he'd known was a shitty thing to do – an *awful* thing to do – but he'd also known that if he'd spoken to Jake, *touched* Jake, he wouldn't have been able to keep it together.

Xen had said, 'You good?' and Theo had said, 'No,' because lying was too hard. And maybe Xen had understood, because after that he'd run interference, sticking close to Theo and keeping them both away from Paddy and Jake.

Theo had known, even as he grabbed his stuff and bolted once training was finished, that he was being a dick, that Jake would want to talk to him, that he needed to talk to Jake. But he'd felt the panic creeping up from the tips of his fingers and he'd run, got himself into the car and driven home even as he struggled to breathe, knowing he should pull over. Not pulling over. He'd managed to park the car and get inside and into his bedroom before he lost his breath completely, before he had to sit on the floor and put his head between his knees.

The one thing he could have done. The moment when he could have been brave. When Jake was waiting for him to be brave. Had *needed* him.

He knew he should get up, should eat something, should make a cup of sweet tea. Should tell Eva something was wrong. Should call Priya. Should look at the texts he knew he'd have from Jake.

He didn't do any of those things. He curled up instead, closed his eyes as though that could shut everything out. Listened to his own shallow breathing, the scratching at the corners of his mind.

He wasn't sure how long he'd been sitting there on the ground when there was a tap at the door.

'Yeah?' His voice sounded wrong.

'Theo?' It was Eva.

He made himself get up and take the five steps to open the door. Eva was in the hallway, looking back towards the stairs.

'Jake's here to see you. He said he texted.' She looked at Theo and her eyes widened. 'Are you alright?'

'Fine,' he said.

Her hand twitched, as though she wanted to reach out to him. 'If you . . .' She hesitated. 'If you don't want to see him,' she said, a little cautiously, 'I can tell him you're not well.'

He almost said yes. He wanted to shut the bedroom door and let her deal with it. But he wasn't going to be *that* much of a coward.

'No,' he said. 'No, we have some stuff to talk about.'

'Okay,' she said. She was looking at him like she'd put two and two together. 'I'm going to be in a conference in the study. I'll be in there for a while.'

'Sure,' Theo said. He'd deal with the knowledge and sympathy in her dark eyes later.

He took his time, as though delaying the inevitable was going to achieve anything. Jake was standing in the living room, his hands shoved into his pockets. He was wearing trackies and an oversized hoodie, his hair messy. When Theo came in, Jake's whole body swayed, like he wanted to step forward and had to hold himself back.

'Hey,' Theo said.

'You lose your phone?' It was a Jake kind of question, but he didn't sound like himself. His eyes were wide and blue and raw.

'Sorry.' Theo stopped a couple of paces away from him.

Jake's gaze dropped to his feet. 'Are you pissed?' he asked.

'What?'

'Me coming out like that. Without talking to you about it. I should've . . . I know I should've talked to you about it, but it just kinda *happened*, and then I'd said it and I couldn't take it back.'

'No! No —' Theo heard his voice crack. 'No, I . . .' *I'm a coward. I'm pathetic. I couldn't say it. I wasn't there when you needed me.*

'Hey.' Jake's voice was soft. 'Stavs . . . Theo . . . what's going on?'

'I . . .' Theo was not going to cry.

'Can we talk about this in your room? Like, I wanna talk about it, but . . .' He gestured to the living room. His voice was gentle. It made it worse. Jake shouldn't have to be gentle. Jake shouldn't be comforting *him*.

'Yeah.' Theo led the way up the stairs, Jake padding behind him. He wanted to reach for Jake's hand. He didn't.

Theo realised, opening the bedroom door, that he was still wearing his training singlet and compression tights. Jake reached over to flick the light on.

'C'mere?' Jake asked, and Theo's body moved before he could think about it. Jake's arms went around him and then he could breathe again: breathe in the smell of Jake's shampoo, his body wash, the lemongrass fabric softener Xen liked. Jake ducked his head to press his cheek against Theo's shoulder.

'I'm sorry,' Theo managed. 'I'm so fucking sorry, Jake.'

Jake took a step back so he could look up into Theo's face. 'Theo, what the fuck are you talking about?'

'I should have said something. I didn't back you up.' He swallowed, made himself keep going, even though he felt like he might choke on the words. 'And even if Raze hadn't said anything . . . I don't think I would have. I'm so sorry.' He watched Jake's face, waiting for . . . contempt, maybe. Disappointment.

Jake reached up and cradled his face in both hands. 'You're a fucking idiot,' he said.

'What?'

'It'd be pretty fucking hypocritical of me to be pissed because you didn't come out. I would've felt guilty as fuck if you'd done it just because I had.'

'But —'

'But nothing. It's fine that you weren't ready,' Jake said. He was closer, their lips a breath apart. 'It's fine, Theo.'

Theo's mouth found Jake's and they were kissing, one of Jake's hands still on Theo's cheek, the other sliding up to tangle in Theo's hair. Theo wasn't sure what he needed. To be close to Jake. To be touching Jake. He didn't want sex, not now, not when he already felt ripped down the seams, and maybe Jake sensed that, because he kept the kisses gentle, guiding Theo back towards the bed. Theo sat when his calves hit the mattress and Jake followed him down, pushing him back and then stretching out beside him.

Jake kissed him again.

'I'm sorry,' Theo said against Jake's mouth. 'I'm —'

Jake broke the kiss. 'Stop saying that.'

Theo exhaled shakily. 'Okay.'

They kissed for a long time. Gently, not building towards anything, until all the tension in Theo's body had drained away and he felt warm and safe and absolutely exhausted.

'Are you okay?' Theo asked, belatedly.

Jake rolled over onto his back, one arm behind his head. 'Yeah,' he said, finally. 'Yeah, it's . . . fucking weird. But I feel kinda good about it. Guess I can stop thinking about whether to do it, now I've done it. Gotta deal with some shit tomorrow, but it's fine.'

'Like what?'

'Oh, just talk to Davo, talk to HR, that sort of stuff. I guess they wanna know if I'm gonna make an Instagram reel about liking dick.'

Theo twined their legs together. 'Still thinking about coming out publicly?'

Jake sighed. 'Yeah. Like, not right now, but maybe. Not necessarily making a post or something, but I guess . . . not hiding it. But also' – he tipped his head to look at Theo – 'it might make people ask questions about us. So kinda depends where you're at.'

'I have no idea where I'm at,' Theo admitted.

Jake leaned in to kiss him again, just a brush of his lips against Theo's. 'It's cool,' he said, pressing another kiss to Theo's shoulder. 'We can talk about it later. I reckon you need to sleep.'

'Probably.' Theo hesitated. 'Stay?'

'Yeah, 'course. Though your sister . . .'

'I'm going to tell her. If that's okay with you. I think she's guessed, anyway.'

'Fine by me. You might wanna shower first, though. I'm not complaining, but . . .'

Theo stayed under the shower for a while, resting his head against the glass shower wall and letting hot water run down his back. He got out, eventually, and dug out a spare toothbrush for Jake. The study door was still closed, and he decided he'd talk to Eva in the morning.

Jake went to brush his teeth then got back into bed, nudging Theo onto his side and then pressing himself up against Theo's back. Theo wouldn't normally have allowed it, but he was willing to concede that it did feel nice. Comforting. Jake's arm over his chest, Jake's chin against his shoulder.

'Hey,' Jake said against his ear as Theo was drifting off to sleep. 'At least now, if we want a threesome, we know who we can ask other than Paddy. Good to have options.'

Theo elbowed him, but not very hard.

Theo woke up pressed against Jake's back, with one of his arms wrapped around Jake's chest. Jake took hold of his forearm and murmured discontentedly when Theo tried to move it. Theo managed to extract himself, with some effort, and took a moment to look down at Jake, asleep in his bed. He looked good there.

Theo could hear the blender going in the kitchen and knew Eva would be up; she'd probably already gone for a run. Sure enough, she was sitting at the dining table scrolling on her phone, a half-finished green smoothie at her elbow.

Theo paused in the doorway. 'Hey, can we chat?'

Eva looked up. She looked tired. She always looked tired these days, and Theo realised with a furl of guilt that, for all he'd wished she'd ask more about what was going on with him, he hadn't asked about what was going on with *her*. Had just accepted when she left early, and came home late, and worked weekends, because that was what their siblings did and what their parents had always done.

'Of course. There's coffee in the pot.'

He poured himself a cup and took it over to the table. It was one of those silver winter mornings, the weak sunlight stretching tendrils across the floorboards. He sat down and Eva raised an eyebrow.

'Just so we're clear, Jake is your mystery boy, right?'

'Yes.'

'I see the break-up didn't stick.'

'No.'

She nodded. 'I'm glad. You're serious about him.' It wasn't really a question.

Theo shrugged. He knew he was smiling. Knew he was giving himself away. 'It's still kind of new. But maybe.'

She beamed at him. 'I haven't seen you smile like that in a long time.'

'He's . . . he's pretty great.'

He saw the moment she switched into lawyer mode. 'Are you going to tell the team?'

'We haven't talked about that yet. Maybe.'

She nodded, and he could tell she was making an active effort to keep from giving him useful advice. 'Are you going to tell Ommi and Abi?'

Theo sighed. 'Again, maybe. If we're still together in the off-season.'

Eva took a sip of her smoothie, grimaced and set it aside. It was *very* green. She was thinking hard about what she wanted to say. She'd never been one to rush words.

'You know,' she said finally, 'I always admired the fact that you did what you wanted. I get that it must be hard, but I'm proud of you. If that's allowed.'

Theo swallowed. 'It's allowed.'

She hesitated. 'Maybe I could talk to them? Sometimes I think you've all been frustrated by this for so long that none of you listen anymore.'

Theo bit back a retort and let her keep speaking. She was usually right about this sort of stuff. Unfortunately.

'I know what they're like,' she continued. 'And they definitely need to listen to you. But I think that, because they didn't get it, you gave up trying to explain it. That's on them. But you might have to give a little, too. If you do want them on board. You seem to be doing pretty well, no matter what they think.'

Theo thought about that day on the beach months ago; thought about Jake saying, 'Would that convince them?' He thought about Paddy, and Xen, and Yelks, and every game he'd played this year. Thought about being sprawled on the couch with Jake tucked up next to him, the way it felt to walk into training, the roar of the crowd as he walked up the race on game day.

'I don't need them to get it,' he said, and was surprised to find it was true. 'No matter what happens next, I'm glad I did this. But I'd like it if they made an effort.' He sighed. Let something go.

'Paddy's parents flew out from Ireland to see his first game, you know? They've never even come to one of mine. I'll try to meet them in the middle, but I just . . . I'm not holding my breath.'

'That's fair,' she said. 'I'll talk to them. And while we're on the subject of annoying our parents, I've been meaning to tell you: I'm going to quit my job.'

'What?'

'I've had enough of being a lawyer. I'm sick of the hours, I'm sick of the work, I'm sick of the people.'

'What are you going to do?'

She smiled. 'Retrain as a teacher. I love the idea of teaching, and I've really enjoyed the bit of uni tutoring I've done, but it just never felt like an option. There's a program set up for people who want to switch to teaching, and I'm going to do that. I know it won't be easy, but I want to do it.' She grinned. 'Maybe someone inspired me to think about what I really want.'

Theo reached across the table to take her hand. She'd been biting her nails. 'I'm proud of you, too. If that's allowed.'

'It's allowed.'

'Hey.' They both looked around. Jake was standing in the doorway. He'd stolen one of Theo's hoodies and was wearing it over his boxers. It was big on Theo, so it came halfway down Jake's thighs. He looked sleepy and soft, his feet bare on the tiles. Theo wanted to grab him and drag him straight back into bed.

'Good morning,' Eva said. 'There's coffee in the pot if you want some.'

'Thanks.' Jake ambled over to the counter and poured a cup. He hesitated for a second behind Theo's chair, as though he'd been thinking about leaning down to kiss him and changed his mind. He took the chair next to Theo, nursing the coffee between his hands.

'Now,' Eva said, putting her glasses on. 'I hear you want to date my little brother.'

Theo groaned and buried his head in his hands. 'No, Eva.'

Jake grinned. 'Yeah, I was hoping I could take him to the school disco. I'll have him home by nine.'

'I can probably allow it,' she said. 'Maybe even nine thirty. You seem like a nice young man.'

Theo snorted. He couldn't help it. He raised his head in time to see Jake looking at him, mock-wounded.

Eva shook her head at Theo. 'Don't be rude to your date, Theodore.'

'Yeah, *Theodore*,' Jake said.

'You know what?' Eva pushed her smoothie aside. 'I think this calls for pancakes. What do you think?'

'Agreed,' Jake said. 'I'll help.'

Theo watched them cross to the kitchen, feeling a bit dazed. Jake had Eva laughing almost immediately as she fished ingredients out of the fridge and dug out the whisk. He looked across at Theo, grinning, and Theo smiled back.

Chapter Twenty-Four

Theo wasn't panicking. He was just considering all of the possibilities and choosing to focus on the ones in the box labelled 'catastrophes'. There were several possibilities in there, and he was taking them out individually and examining them.

He'll hate it. It's too much.

Everyone else will hate it.

This is the worst idea imaginable and everyone was too polite to tell you.

Intellectually, he knew it wasn't the *worst* idea. Xen would have told him if it had been. And if not Xen, then Paddy, because Paddy was also quite perceptive but, unlike Xen, he didn't adjust his comments to avoid hurting people's feelings.

But nevertheless, here Theo was, sweaty-palmed and knocking on Jake's door, feeling like he was picking up his date for the school formal. All he needed was a wilting corsage.

It had been a big couple of weeks. The two of them had told Paddy and Xen that they were together, and endured the ensuing hail of jokes. He'd told Jenny he was bisexual, though not about Jake. She didn't give much away, but the smile she'd given him when she'd said, 'Thank you for telling me,' had felt very real. He'd recruited Eva and hit send on the email he'd drafted to his parents. They'd called him the following day, and they had the best chat they'd had in quite a while. Theo suspected he had Eva's intervention to thank for that, but he'd take it. He'd also been able to report to them that he'd earned a Distinction in Property Law, which had probably helped.

He exhaled. This was a good idea. This was going to be fine.

Jake opened the door, grinning. He'd followed Theo's instructions and was wearing jeans and sneakers with one of his nicer hoodies. Theo was almost one hundred per cent sure that Jake was going to love this idea. He'd made sure to run everything past Jake – subtly. Checked that Jake was cool if Theo organised something for his birthday, checked that he was okay with Gabby, Dex and Drips knowing they were together, ascertained if Jake had a violent aversion to laser tag or Italian food.

'Hey.' Jake pulled him into a kiss as soon as he was through the door.

'Happy birthday,' Theo said against Jake's mouth.

'Thanks.' Jake's hands were roaming, sliding down Theo's back to his ass, and Theo grabbed his wrists.

'We don't have time,' he said.

Jake looked up at him, all mischievous blue eyes. 'Are you sure? It is my birthday.'

'Yes,' Theo said firmly.

Jake sighed. 'Fine. You gonna tell me what we're going?'

Theo looked nervous. That wasn't new, but Jake wasn't sure what he was nervous about. Jake still had both his hands on the small of Theo's back. He thought that if he was really persuasive, he might get them down the front of Theo's pants before they had to go.

'So what are we doing?' he asked, crowding Theo against the wall.

Theo exhaled. He couldn't meet Jake's eyes. 'I wanted to take you on a date,' he said, speaking faster than usual. 'And I know we can't just go on a date in public, but I can take you on a date with some cover, so we're going go to laser tag, and then we're going to go to dinner, and I've sorted it so a few other people are coming. But they're all people you know, so we can also be on a date.'

He looked like he actually thought there was a possibility Jake wouldn't love this idea.

'You're taking me on a *date*?' Jake took his hands off Theo's back, but only so he could hook them behind Theo's neck and pull him down for a kiss.

'Yeah,' Theo said, when they broke apart.

'Are you doing this because I said I'd never been on a date?'

Theo looked a bit sheepish. 'I want to take you on a date. And you should get to go on dates. You'd like dating.'

'Why?'

Theo pressed a kiss to Jake's jaw. 'You like people.' Another just under his ear. 'And you *love* attention.'

Jake shoved Theo away, then tugged him back in for a proper kiss. 'Don't be mean to me on my birthday,' Jake told him, once he needed to breathe.

'You like the idea?'

'Fuck yeah,' Jake said. 'Best birthday ever.'

He pulled Theo down for another kiss and tried to show his enthusiasm for the idea with his mouth. Theo spun them so Jake was pressed against the wall, and Jake was pretty committed to being late for laser tag when Theo broke the kiss.

'We shouldn't be late,' Theo said, re-tucking his shirt. 'Xen and Paddy are meeting us there, and we don't want to give them ammunition to pay us out.'

'It's my birthday. The party starts when I get there.'

'But our laser-tag booking starts at six.'

Jake pouted, but allowed himself to be led out the door.

He hadn't played laser tag since he was at school, and it turned out that playing with a group of professional athletes was quite different. Theo was the most competitive player imaginable, and the sort of person who *strategised*. Theo and Gabby formed an unholy alliance for a while, and because it was Jake's birthday everyone was making it their personal mission to fuck him up. It was a good thing he was quick on his feet.

Theo was so focused on actually winning at laser tag that Jake had to shoot him several times before he'd allow himself to be pulled behind some fake debris to be kissed. Jake had just managed to distract him very thoroughly from the game when Paddy – fucking Paddy, fucking *again* – managed to fall over them, and then Dex barrelled in to end Paddy's life and Jake was glad for the low lighting.

It was absolute chaos. Jake wasn't sure he'd ever seen Theo laugh so much. They were all going to have a lot of bruises for people playing a game that was, theoretically, non-contact. Lucky it wasn't paintball, or somebody might have died.

Theo won, because he shot Gabby in the back (figuratively, literally) at a crucial moment, and his smug little smile made Jake want to do unspeakable things to him. They piled out, sweaty and laughing, and Jake hoped wherever they were going wasn't posh, because none of them looked ready for anything with tiny plates or weird edible foam.

In fact, dinner was at a low-key Italian place in Collingwood. Jake had heard of it but had never been. The waiter led them into a small room at the back, separated from the rest of the restaurant by a floor-to-ceiling wine rack. There was a round table set up for five, and then a two-person table complete with flowers and a candle. Jake blinked at it. It definitely said *date*, but it also . . . wasn't exactly subtle.

'Jaze and Stavsy lost at laser tag,' Dex told the waiter, who'd clearly recognised the group. 'So they're on a date now.' They gestured at the table. Dex lowered their voice theatrically. 'Jake was hoping it would be Drips.'

Jake looked at Theo. It was brilliant. Not that Jake really thought anyone would give a shit, but if the staff were footy fans and recognised them, it was perfect cover. Exactly the sort of joke they'd expect.

'Is this okay?' Theo asked. He held the chair for Jake. *Held the chair.* Jake heard someone snort behind them and gave them the finger behind his back. He was on a date, and he was going to take all the fucking chivalry Theo wanted to give him while they were here, and then he was going to take anything else Theo wanted to give him later. Say *please* and *thank you*, too.

'It's perfect,' he told Theo.

Theo sat down across from him. 'I mean, don't call it yet.'

Jake knew he was grinning like a dumbass. He reached across the table and brushed his fingers over the back of Theo's hand. 'Thanks.'

'You're welcome.'

It turned out that being on a sort of double date with a group of footballers was not the most intimate dinner imaginable, but it was definitely *funny*. The rest of the group managed to get through the entree and half of the main course before they started actively commentating the date. Dex could do eerily accurate impersonations of a lot of football personalities. Jake half expected Theo to be embarrassed about it, but he clearly thought they were hilarious. Jake was realising that Theo actually could be pretty chill – when he was around people he trusted.

'Want to try one of these?' Theo said, pointing to what Jake now knew were zucchini flowers. Who knew that zucchinis had *flowers*?

'Sure.'

Theo speared one with his fork and then, instead of putting it on Jake's plate, held his fork up to Jake's mouth. Jake blinked at him. Okay, if he wanted to play it like that. Jake leaned forward, holding eye contact, and opened his mouth, wrapping his lips around the fork and pulling back slowly. Something shifted in Theo's gaze.

Someone, probably Paddy, wolf-whistled.

'Urgh, gross,' Dex said, breaking their commentator impression. 'Make it stop.'

Theo started to laugh, and then there was almost a full-scale incident, because that set Jake off laughing too and his mouth was still full of cheese and zucchini flower.

They managed to eat dessert without too much input from anyone else, because Paddy and Gabby had become so outrageous in trying to one-up each other that they'd drawn the attention away from the date. Jake and Theo were able to share some sort of chocolate-and-caramel thing and make heated eye contact without anyone making vomiting noises.

'So, what do you think of dating?' Theo asked, quietly.

Jake glanced towards the other table. 'Next time, let's see if we can lose the entourage.'

Theo smiled. 'Agreed.'

'But I would've been stressed if we'd just gone out on a date. Like, maybe it would've been fine, but also maybe someone would have snapped a pic and put it on Big Footy or something.'

They wrapped up dinner when the volume reached an uncontrollable level. Xen was making noises about bedtime while the others were in an argument about where to go next.

Jake looked at Theo. He was also in favour of bedtime.

'I got us an Airbnb,' Theo said. 'It's a ten-minute walk.'

Jake felt a grin spread over his face. 'You did, huh?'

'I did.'

Theo looked pretty pleased with himself. Jake was pretty pleased with him too.

Jake stepped a little closer. Not so close that it would be *obvious*, but close enough that he could look up at Theo through his lashes and see the way it made Theo's eyes darken. 'Why? You planning to be loud?'

Theo brushed his fingers over the inside of Jake's wrist, the barest touch. '*I'm* not the one who's loud.'

'Yeah, you hold back. Weak.'

'Because you have *housemates*.'

'You wanna know how many people I've heard Paddy fuck?'

'Absolutely not.'

'We're gonna go,' Jake announced to the group, over their spirited discussion about nearby pubs. 'It's been great, thanks.'

He got some more 'happy birthdays' and about twenty per cent less ribbing than he'd expected. He wanted to reach out and take Theo's hand. Maybe he'd be able to one day.

'Come on,' he said. 'I wanna see how loud you get.'

'I'm going to jump in the shower, can you keep yourself amused?' Theo asked.

Jake had learned early that Theo was not a *showering together* person. He said he liked to be able to think in the shower, and Jake supposed he could understand that. Although these days when he was in the shower he mainly just thought about Theo.

The Airbnb was *nice*. It was a loft in a warehouse conversion, all exposed brick and heavy beams, but it had been furnished in a way that made it feel cosy: heavy Turkish rugs on the floor, a forest of houseplants, a king-sized bed covered in pillows and the types of blankets that even Jake could tell were expensive.

There was also a bottle of champagne on ice on the kitchen counter, and some chocolate-coated strawberries. Jake had never fed anyone a chocolate-coated strawberry, but he was keen to give it a go. He tested one while Theo was out of the room and they were *tasty*. There were two bathrobes on the bed, so Jake stripped and put one on. It felt like wearing clouds. He put on a playlist using the apartment's speaker and decided to assess how sturdy the bed was.

Theo came out of the shower ten minutes later looking . . . nervous? He towelled off and wrapped himself in the other bathrobe. Jake had expelled a number of throw pillows from the bed, but the doona was very snuggly and the blankets were cosy. Theo was looking at him in his nest, not quite smiling, and something turned over under Jake's ribs.

'It's been a really great night,' Jake said. 'Thank you.'

Theo crossed the room and leaned over the bed to find Jake's mouth with his own. 'I haven't even given you a present yet,' he said when he broke the kiss.

Jake wriggled back and propped himself up on the pillows. 'Oh yeah? You gonna?'

'Guess you'll find out.'

Jake pulled Theo in for another kiss, then all the way down onto the bed, Theo's thigh settling between Jake's legs. Theo slid his hands under Jake's unfastened robe and Jake sighed, let himself be touched, ran his own hands over Theo's familiar body. It felt different, somehow. They were alone plenty, but it was always in Jake's room. It never felt *really* private. Not like this.

The kiss started slow and sweet, stayed slow but turned filthy, Theo's tongue in Jake's mouth, his hands on Jake's sides. Jake was trying to touch all of Theo at once, needing to be closer. He wrapped one leg around Theo's hips, arching up so their dicks brushed together. They both groaned. Theo had two hands buried in Jake's hair, his mouth hot on Jake's neck, then his jaw, then his mouth again.

Theo broke the kiss after what might have been hours, panting, and Jake reached up to trace a thumb over Theo's mouth. Theo was looking down at him, eyes dark, mouth determined. 'I want you to fuck me,' he said. 'If you want to.'

Jake closed his eyes for a second. 'Are you giving me your ass for my birthday?' he asked, instead of saying other, dumber things. Like *I think I might be in love with you.*

That made Theo laugh. 'It's more of a loan.'

Jake pouted. 'It's rude to take back a gift.' He ran his hands down Theo's back, then over his ass, and Theo shifted, restless, pushing closer. 'Are you . . . it's not . . .' Jake tried to find the right way to say it. 'I wanna do this, but not if you're only suggesting it for my sake. I don't want it to be, like, a sacrifice.'

Theo stroked a hand down Jake's chest, teased his thumb over one of Jake's nipples, then the other. Jake inhaled.

'It's not because of that,' Theo said. He bent his head to follow his thumb with his mouth, then looked up at Jake, and, *eyelashes.* 'I want to try it. I don't know if I'll like it, but I want to try it. I've been thinking about it. It's just at your place it felt a bit complicated with the, uh, prep and stuff. Do you want to try it?'

It wasn't like Jake was going to run screaming from a bit of mess, but now wasn't the time to bring that up. 'Hell yeah,' he said, wriggling out of his robe. 'Get naked. Come here.'

'You're such a romantic.' Theo shrugged out of his robe and tossed it onto the bed. Jake let himself just *look* for a moment. Theo was fucking hot all the time, but there was something about him here and now, smiling in a way that made Jake feel stupid and soft.

'I'll fucking romance you alright,' Jake said. 'See if I don't.'

They kissed for a while, slow and hot, Theo's dick hard against Jake's thigh.

'Roll over,' Jake said, finally. Theo shifted onto his stomach and Jake brushed his fingers over the nape of Theo's neck, then put his mouth on the same spot. Theo sighed. He wasn't *bossy* in bed, but he liked to let Jake know who was in charge. Now he lay still, turning his head to smile over his shoulder at Jake.

Jake let himself take all the time he wanted, stroking his fingers over the muscles of Theo's back, the dip of his spine, the slight curve of his waist. He wasn't usually patient, but it felt as though time had gone sticky around him, as though there was nothing in the world but Theo's warm skin under the pads of his fingers, Theo's breathing, the way Theo started to shift under his hands, needy but too stubborn to say anything.

Jake pressed a kiss to the base of Theo's spine and Theo shivered under him.

'Your ass is mine tonight, right?' he asked, sliding his palms over the ass in question. It was a really good ass. Jake had been thinking about that ass in some pretty specific ways for a while.

'Mm,' Theo murmured. He sounded a bit dazed.

Jake traced a finger down Theo's spine just to watch him shudder. 'Does that mean I can lick it?'

Theo stilled for a second, then exhaled a laugh. 'I think the saying is: if I lick it, it's mine.'

'Yeah, whatever, but can I?'

Theo wriggled a little. 'You want to . . .' He hesitated.

Jake did want to. He *really* wanted to. 'Eat you out? Fuck yeah. But only if you're into it.'

Theo looked back over his shoulder again and Jake shifted to lie next to him, stroking one hand down Theo's back. Theo's expression was some combination of turned on and apprehensive. 'I've never . . . I don't know if I'd be into it. Would *you* be into it?'

'Duh.'

'I'm just worried you'll think it's gross?'

'Hands are gross, and you shove your fingers in my mouth all the time,' Jake pointed out.

'Well, maybe not anymore,' Theo said, wincing.

Jake grabbed his hand and pressed a kiss to his palm. 'I like it. Also, you literally just showered,' Jake said. 'Pretty sure my mouthguard is way dirtier by half-time. But it's all good if you don't want to.' He stroked a hand over the curve of Theo's ass again and Theo shivered.

'I'd like to try.'

'You sure?'

Theo exhaled. 'Yeah,' he said, and Jake felt like his heart was going to pound out of his chest. He actually hadn't done this very often. Kyle hadn't liked it, and it wasn't something he was necessarily going to chuck on the table with some random. He didn't find it gross, but that didn't mean he was going to put his mouth on every asshole going around.

He kissed his way down Theo's spine – started at the nape of his neck and explored every inch of his back, so much warm skin and glorious muscle – until Theo was shifting under him, his hands twisted in the sheets. Then he spent some time kissing around the crease of Theo's ass, feeling the way it made Theo tense and relax all at once.

'Hand and knees, baby,' he said, because it would be easier that way. 'Or elbows and knees.'

Theo went easily, propping himself up, his head bowed. But Jake knew this *wasn't* easy for him. He stroked his hands over Theo's ribs and said, 'Yeah, that's right.'

He felt Theo sigh under his palms. He kissed the hollow at the base of Theo's spine again, moved down, then just let Theo feel his breath against that sensitive skin. It felt intimate in a way

Jake hadn't expected. In a way that it hadn't when he'd done this before. Knowing that Theo trusted him, knowing that Theo wasn't sure about this but was letting him try.

He lifted his head. 'You're so fucking hot,' he said, then got back to it.

He just used his lips at first, until Theo relaxed under him. Theo jumped a little at the first touch of his tongue and Jake pulled back. 'We good?'

'Yeah,' Theo said, shifting a little. 'Yeah, it feels . . . it's good. I'll tell you if I want to stop.'

Theo did not tell him to stop. He didn't say anything coherent at all while Jake teased him with his tongue, then pressed it deeper, ate him out until Theo was just gasping, 'Oh fuck, oh fuck,' into a pillow and Jake had to pause to tug the pillow away and throw it off the bed. He was *earning* those sounds. He wasn't sure how long it had been, but he was pretty sure he could do this for hours, sinking into the sensation of Theo's body opening under his mouth, the way Theo was squirming, trying to find friction against the bed, the way he sounded, strung out and desperate, like he'd beg if Jake threatened to stop.

Jake did stop, eventually, because the situation with his own dick was getting fucking critical. Theo looked back at Jake over his shoulder and that was almost the end right then and there. His hair was falling into his eyes, tangled and sweaty. 'Fuck, Jake, you gotta . . .' His eyes dark and wild. 'Please, I need . . .' He stopped.

'What do you need?' Jake wanted to hear him say it.

'More . . . something . . . come on, please.'

'My tongue again or my fingers?'

'Fingers, fuck, please,' Theo said, all hesitation gone, and some primal part of Jake purred with satisfaction. He loved this: getting Theo to the point where he stopped thinking, stopped *worrying*, stopped biting back the sounds he wanted to make. Jake reached for the lube on the bedside table and realised his hands were shaking.

Theo tensed a little when he slid the first finger in. Jake remembered his first time, too, the oddness of the feeling, and the vulnerability of it.

'Yeah, that's it,' he said as Theo shifted. 'It's gonna feel so good, I promise.'

He took his time. By the time he pressed another finger in alongside the first, Theo was rocking back against him.

'Good?' Jake asked. He was pretty sure it *was* good, but Theo wasn't saying anything, just panting and pushing back against Jake's hand, sweat sheening his back.

'Yeah,' Theo said. 'Yeah, Jake.' And then, 'please,' like he didn't quite know what he was asking for but needed it badly. Jake kept it slow, wanted it to be good for Theo, *needed* it to be good for Theo.

'If you don't stop doing that I'm going to come,' Theo gasped, finally, when Jake had three fingers inside him.

'Okay, okay.' Theo made a soft sound of protest when Jake pulled his fingers free. 'Condom?'

'Not unless you want to,' Theo said.

Jake grabbed the base of his dick to get himself under control. It would be a *tragedy* if he came before he was inside Theo. Although the thought of painting Theo's back and ass was . . . not something he was going to think about now.

'Clean-up can be a bit messy without one,' he pointed out. Because as much as he wanted to feel Theo's body around him with nothing in between them, he didn't want Theo to be uncomfortable. Personally, Jake liked the messiness, but that was not a universal feeling.

'I don't mind,' Theo told him. 'I want to feel it.'

Jake made an inadvertent noise and reached for the lube again. He slicked himself up, used too much, probably, and then dragged the head of his dick down Theo's ass. Theo groaned, pushing back, but Jake saw the way his shoulders tensed when Jake's dick pressed against him.

Jake stilled. 'Hey, breathe out for me,' he said.

Theo did, exhaling with a sigh and settling under Jake's hands.

'Tell me if it hurts,' Jake said. He had one hand on his dick, holding himself steady, the other on Theo's waist, tracing soothing circles on his hipbone with his thumb.

'I will,' Theo said.

Jake pushed in slowly and Theo breathed out while he did it. Theo's body around him was everything: hot and tight and slick.

'Okay?' Jake asked, and realised that he sounded a bit insane.

He *felt* a bit insane.

'It's . . . yes. I just . . . it's a lot.'

It was. Jake kept still, letting Theo adjust, feeling the sweat popping out on his brow. Theo pushed back against him and it ripped a moan out of the back of Jake's throat.

Theo looked back over his shoulder. 'You good?' he asked. There was a mischievous edge to his smile, and Jake grinned back.

'I'd be better if I was moving,' he said. He was trembling a little with the effort of holding himself still.

'Go slow,' Theo said.

Jake did go slow, so slow he thought he might die, letting Theo get used to the feel of it. He knew when he got the angle right, because Theo made a sound like he'd been winded and shoved back against Jake. Jake did it again; he couldn't tear his eyes from Theo under him, the stretch of his back, the sweaty tangle of his dark hair, the flex of his arms and shoulders.

He took it slow until Theo cracked and said, 'harder,' until Theo was losing it a bit under him, pressing back against him, finding a rhythm that worked for him. Jake grabbed his hips, knowing his fingers would leave bruises, and fucked Theo in earnest, needing to hear every punched-out gasp, the way it sounded when Theo lost all his words.

He got a hand under Theo's body and around Theo's dick. Theo groaned Jake's name, louder than he'd ever been in bed before, and Jake stroked him, felt Theo's body tense, felt how close he was. Jake was close, too, holding off the orgasm through sheer force of will, needing Theo to come first, needing to feel it.

'Wanna see you come,' Jake said. 'Come on. Let me feel it.'

He wanted to remember this forever. The way Theo sounded, too desperate to hold back. The way he felt under Jake's hands, the way he felt *around* Jake. The way he was shaking, caught on the edge.

Theo shuddered and came, hot and wet against Jake's hand, his whole body jerking, and that was the end for Jake as well. Theo made a soft, startled noise when Jake came, shivered under him, and Jake lost his balance and slumped forward against Theo's sweaty back. He felt like he'd shot his brain out of his dick. He tried to catch his breath, tried to think of something to say.

'Alright?' he managed. He wasn't quite sure if it was a welfare check or a request for feedback.

'Mm,' Theo said, sounding fucked-out and happy. 'I am worried about this blanket, though. It looks like it might be handwash only.'

Jake was too sex-drunk to be worried about anything. He leaned forward and pressed a kiss to Theo's shoulder. 'I'll be back.' He pulled out slowly and made his way to the bathroom on wobbly legs. He cleaned himself up quickly, then got a warm flannel and a towel. Theo was sprawled on his back by the time he got back and, yeah, it was probably curtains for the blanket. 'You good?' Jake asked.

'Mm,' Theo said, opening one eye.

Jake snorted and began cleaning Theo up gently with the flannel. Couldn't resist stroking his thumb down the crease of Theo's ass to feel him shiver a little. He threw the cloth off the bed once he was done and pulled the blanket over them both.

'You wanna sleep?'

Theo blinked at him. 'Why, you want to go another round?' He sounded smug. Like he knew that the sex had knocked Jake on his ass.

'Up for it if you are,' Jake said.

Theo huffed out a laugh. 'Sure.'

It *almost* sounded like a challenge. 'Oh yeah?'

'You tired or something?' Theo rolled so he was straddling Jake's thighs, then leaned down to kiss him. Jake threaded his fingers into Theo's hair and kissed him back.

As it turned out, neither of them was *that* tired.

SEPTEMBER

FINALS

Chapter Twenty-Five

People had said that finals were different in Melbourne, but Theo hadn't really *gotten it* until he was in it. The whole city was suddenly permeated with buzzing energy, an undercurrent of anticipation. Everywhere Theo went there were footy caps, footy scarves; he'd bought Eva a Falcons beanie and she was actually wearing it. He'd get a morning coffee and the barista would be chatting with the regulars about injuries and ins and outs. Dogs were wearing footy jackets and footy bandanas. If a player left training early or took a moment too long to get up, it was on the evening news. The Falcons had finished unexpectedly high on the ladder after some upsets.

Theo wasn't getting much attention in the media, because he'd been playing well and wasn't nursing a niggling injury, whereas Yelks' shoulder alone was probably paying a journalist's salary. Everyone knew it wasn't right, and Theo suspected Yelks was playing through serious pain. But losing him would be so much more than losing their best defender: half of what Yelks did on the field was coaching, setting things up, marshalling the troops, pulling someone aside for a quick word at a stoppage. So he was still playing every week, even though there were shadows under his eyes like bruises and he moved like he was in pain when he thought nobody was watching.

Brayden Hunter had written a whole opinion piece about how Yelks should bow out, how he wasn't up to it, and Theo – who'd never had particularly strong feelings about any of his captains – would have happily broken Hunter's laptop over his head.

Theo knew his place in the team for the finals was secure, absent some disaster; Rigger was still in the middle, and there was nobody else really pushing for Theo's spot. It felt strange to go to training without the spectre of being dropped hanging over him. It could still happen – could happen to anyone – but it didn't feel like a present threat. Just a reality of the game.

Sometimes in the evenings, when he was wiped out, or in the early morning when he woke up before his alarm, the anxiety got louder. He remembered last year, that last kick, his shaking hands, the roar of the crowd. But it wasn't last year. It was different. And it was hard to be stressed about finals when he could roll over and bury his face in Jake's hair. When Jake was there in the morning to make him laugh. When Jake was so obviously delighted to be playing finals, and so endlessly confident that they could win.

They'd decided they'd tell the team they were together once finals were done. It was probably pushing it a bit, but there wasn't anything in their contracts that said they *had* to disclose a romantic relationship (Eva had checked). Kat knew, and if something happened that meant someone else needed to know before the end of the season, then Jake and Theo would tell them.

The Falcons had finished third, meaning they'd get a second chance even if they lost the qualifying final. Theo knew there was a lot of water to clear between the end of the regular season and a flag, but it didn't feel impossible. And if they didn't make it, well, there was always next year.

'What are you thinking about?' Jake asked, plonking himself down next to Theo's locker. They'd had a light training session, and Jake had grass stains all down one side from a tackle.

'Finals,' Theo said.

Jake grinned. 'I love finals.'

'We've never played real finals,' Paddy pointed out.

'Finals footy is different,' Tenders agreed.

'You'll love it,' Yelks said.

Theo had never heard anything as loud as the crowd during the semi-final. He could barely hear the whistle; he had no chance of hearing what anyone was yelling. The qualifying final the previous week had been loud, but not like this. Tonight a loss would mean their season was over, and the fans were backing them accordingly. The crowd was evenly split between the teams. Whenever anything happened, the nearest pocket of the crowd would erupt, their reaction rippling around the stadium in both directions, half exaltation and half abuse.

Theo managed a couple of deep breaths, watching the stoppage. They were four points down with probably two minutes to go. He'd played a solid game. Set up a couple of good goals. But they'd lost Yelks in the second quarter with a dislocated shoulder, and Tommy had limped off ten minutes later. Raze had definitely broken some ribs in a smother, but he'd had them strapped and was still on the field, pale under his tan. It was a brutal, grinding game that felt like a war of attrition. Theo wasn't sure he'd ever run harder. It was only determination and pickle juice keeping his legs from cramping.

Tenders had been right. Finals footy was different. Faster, harder, more brutal. Everything ratcheted up a few notches, and the umpires were ready to let a bit more go. The Falcons had missed their chance in the qualifying final by two goals. Missed the chance of a week off and a home preliminary final. They'd come back swinging in this game, but the Currawongs were a good team, and without Yelks the back line had been battling to keep their two key forwards contained.

Theo stayed on the move, holding his space. The umpire balled it up almost dead in the middle of the ground. The tap went the Falcons' way and Raze grabbed it, bursting out of the centre. He got it on his boot just in time to get crunched, and Theo couldn't even look back to check if he was okay. He probably wasn't. The ball pinged into the forward line, got knocked loose, and Theo was on the edge of the arc, locking it in. Paddy picked it up and immediately got sandwiched by two Currawongs players. The whistle blew and Paddy tossed the ball to the umpire.

Theo could almost *feel* the crowd underneath his sternum. It was like the buzz of bass when you got too close to a speaker. The sign on the bench said forty-five seconds.

The ball went up and the Currawongs' ruck thumped it towards the arc. Jake was there, running through, scooping the ball up. His back was to the goals and he didn't have time to get around. Theo led hard, screaming for it, and got a couple of metres on his direct opponent. It should have been impossible for Jake to hear him over the roar of the crowd, but maybe he did hear, or maybe he saw Theo in his peripheral vision, or maybe he just kicked it and hoped, but he got the ball on his boot and it smacked neatly into Theo's chest. The siren blared and the crowd was howling.

Theo sucked in a breath. For a second, he was a year in the past, the ball in his clammy hands, knowing that this was *it*, this was *the* moment.

Then there was a hand on his shoulder, and a familiar voice in his ear.

'You've fucking got this,' Jake said. Theo looked into his eyes, blue and certain. 'You've fucking *got this. Breathe.*'

Theo glanced across at the bench as he walked back. Kat and Xen were on the edge of the boundary, both shouting. Kat caught his eye and held up two hands to say *steady*. Theo could hear Paddy's accent, though he didn't know what he was saying. Could see Raze shouting encouragement, one hand pressed against his side, almost doubled over with pain.

He took out his mouthguard and tucked it into his sock. Took a breath, then another. Spun the ball in his hands. The man on the mark was shouting, but Theo didn't hear it. Didn't hear anything except Jake's voice in his head. *You've fucking got this.* He could see Jake out of the corner of his eye, exchanging compliments with a Currawongs player, grinning like Theo had already kicked the goal.

Theo exhaled. Thought about Kat. Thought about Yelks. Thought about lying on the beach on a summer's day and the way something had shifted these past few months, clicked into place. He let everything wash away in the tide until all he could feel was the ball in his hands, familiar. He looked up at the goals, at the mass of colour and movement behind them.

He inhaled. Exhaled. Started to move.

The moment the ball hit his boot he knew he'd done it.

He struck it perfectly – maybe better than he'd ever struck a ball before. Smashed it through the centre of the posts, the ball clearing the outstretched fingers of the Currawongs fullback by a couple of metres.

He couldn't hear anything. He was frozen, numb, but it was the opposite of the last time he'd felt the world go still around him. Then the crowd erupted, a tsunami of sound, like someone had turned the volume back up. The elation hit him like a punch and he grabbed the front of his jumper, pulling it away from his chest. Paddy got to him first, actually picked him up and spun him around, and then there were other hands on his back, on his hair, a mess of voices and shouting, a blur of colour and sound.

He looked up. Saw Jake. Couldn't see anything else. Jake laughing, grinning. Jake in his arms, his legs wrapped around

Theo's waist. His hands were on Theo's face, and he was leaning close.

'I wanna kiss you so fucking badly,' Jake said.

'Do it, then.' Theo felt giddy. Felt like time had stopped.

'What?'

'Kiss me. If you want to.'

Jake stared down at him, his eyes impossibly blue. Whatever he saw in Theo's face must have convinced him, because then his mouth was on Theo's, his hands in Theo's hair, and they were kissing, hard and hot. It was not the sort of kiss that anyone was going to write off as *teammates share a brotherly embrace*. Theo wasn't sure he'd ever been as happy as he was in that moment.

They broke apart after what might have been twenty seconds, might have been twenty minutes. Theo put Jake down but kept hold of his hand.

'Jesus fucking Christ,' Paddy said, wrapping an arm around each of them. 'You don't do anything by halves, do you?'

There were various people running towards them, Kat in the lead, closely followed by Gabby. Kat grabbed Jake in a fierce hug as Gabby threw her arms around Theo.

'Fuck yes,' Gabby said into Theo's shoulder. 'You boys. You're going to make me cry.'

Theo looked up. The kiss was being replayed on the big screens and, well, it was some kiss. It dawned on him, somewhat belatedly, that they were all about to find out how a crowd of ninety thousand people felt about two football players making out. Someone with a microphone had bailed Raze up and was gesturing at the screen. Raze looked like he was about to pass out, but that was probably his ribs.

'I'm gonna go help out with that,' Paddy said and jogged in Raze's direction.

Kat had let Jake go and pulled Theo into a hug. 'I'm so fucking proud of you,' she said. She was definitely crying. '*So proud of you.*'

'Sorry, I think we might have caused some drama after all,' Theo said. They were replaying the kiss *again* while the team song started up for a second time. It wasn't stopping anyone from singing along.

Kat smiled. A bit like a shark. 'I love queer drama,' she said.

'Stavs, Jaze.' Yelks had his shoulder strapped, and they'd obviously stuck him full of painkillers. He was sheet white and sweaty. 'Let's go see the fans.'

He put his good arm over Jake's shoulder and they walked over to the goals to see the cheer squad. Theo had time for a moment of trepidation, but if anyone had a problem with queer footballers it was swallowed up in the ecstasy of the win. Fans reached for him and he gave out high fives, signed things, watched Jake do the same.

A woman grabbed his arm as he passed. She was crying, her arm around the woman beside her, a pride scarf draped around both of them.

'Thank you,' she said. '*Thank you.* Both of you.' Theo leaned over the fence to hug her. Jake pressed up next to him and then they were all hugging, and maybe Theo was crying a bit as well.

Jake wasn't sure how long it took them to get down to the rooms. Yelks had given them more time than usual to spend with the fans. Jake was desperate to get down the race to see his mum – she'd come down for the game with Lydia and Keeley – but he also wanted to stay with the fans, to soak up the atmosphere, to spend a few more minutes here before he had to go and face the consequences of his actions.

He didn't regret it. It felt right, down to his bones, but a small part of him wondered whether Theo would regret it. It had been a very *Jake* thing to do. But Theo had looked at him like he was sure, and Jake hadn't second-guessed it.

'Hey,' he said, as Theo handed a football back to a fan and started to make his way towards the players gathered at the top of the race.

'Hey,' Theo said, reaching for Jake's hand. His smile told Jake everything he needed to know. 'You good?'

'Yeah.'

Theo met his eyes. 'I don't regret it,' he said. 'And I'm not going to.'

Jake smiled and stood on tiptoes to kiss him. 'Me neither.'

Davo was big on letting family and friends into the rooms after the game. Jake let himself be pulled into the circle by Yelks for the song, but all he could see was his mum, grinning from ear to ear over Tenders' shoulder. He got her in a hug as soon as he could, Lydia and Keeley throwing their arms around them both. Then they all had to grab Theo as well.

Eva was there, hanging back a little, so Jake introduced her to Keeley. She gave Theo a hug and then looked at Jake like she wasn't sure if she was allowed to hug him. He hugged her, and then introduced her to his mum and Lydia.

It felt weird. This thing that had hung over him for a decade had been cut loose and had floated away. He knew there would be shit to deal with, knew it wouldn't be easy, but he'd done it. Knew he could make it work. Maybe he wasn't the best role model, but he knew how he would have felt if, as a kid, he'd seen two players kiss on the MCG.

Yelks couldn't keep the reporters away forever, and of course it was Brayden Hunter who found Jake first, smiling his oily smile.

'Hi, Hunter,' Jake said. In this mood, he could even find a real smile for his least favourite reporter.

'Cunningham,' Hunter said. 'You surprised some people today.'

'Probably,' he agreed.

'Pretty unexpected,' Hunter prompted.

'Was it?' Jake caught Theo's eye over Hunter's head.

Theo tilted his head like, *Need rescue?* and Jake shook his head. Hunter leaned closer, raising his voice to be heard over the noise in the rooms. 'Had you planned that celebration in advance?'

Jake inhaled, focusing his attention on not saying any of the things he was thinking. 'Nah, I don't think I would've guessed that was how the game would go.'

'Are you worried this will distract from the victory?'

'Mate, I just wanted to kiss my boyfriend. You're the reporter. If you wanna get distracted, that's on you.'

'Your boyfriend,' Hunter repeated. Like he'd never heard the word before.

'My boyfriend,' Jake confirmed.

'His boyfriend,' Theo said, appearing at Jake's shoulder. He smiled his most charming smile at Hunter. 'Sorry, I've got to steal him away, they want a clip of him with his mum.'

Jake didn't wait around to see what Hunter had to say about that.

Theo twined their fingers together as he towed Jake across the room.

brunswickfalcons Here at the falcons we want everyone to be able to be themselves.

falconfortnightly ok ok emergency episode coming out tonight. did anyone see that coming? we did not see that coming.

  falconfortnightly to be clear, we are excited, this is exciting.

falconsaflw love to see falcons making history

katlloyd proud to be part of the @brunswickfalcons today.

dexxx33 y'all are acting like you've never seen a queer footballer before. congrats @jcjk9 and stavsy. 🌈

gabriellada14 guess im gonna have to follow mens sport now.

rainonme @dexxx33 @gabriellada14 they come work out with us in the gym a few times and now . . .

aflthirst wtffffffffff congratulations @jcjk9 and theo bestavros!!! 🌈

  itsgayfl I KNEW IT.

  itsgayfl SINCE VALENTINE'S DAY.

  itsgayfl I KNEW THOSE WERE NOT HETEROSEXUALS.

  falconsfangirl!!! 🤩

  flyhighfalcons I have watched that clip so many times omg.

  itsgayfl that kiss was 1000/10

Five best pieces of commentary on *that* kiss

Unless you've been living under a rock, you'll know that Brunswick Falcons players Jake Cunningham and Theo Bestavros shared a pretty spectacular on-field kiss after their win on Saturday. Cunningham confirmed in the locker room after the game that he and Bestavros are a couple. We're not going to add to the hot takes (except to say congratulations), but here are our favourite radio and TV commentary moments.

Five – Channel 6
'What a kick! What a win! What a . . . what a . . . what a . . .'
'That's a kiss, Henry. They're kissing.'
'What a . . .'
'They're still kissing.'

Four – 4BM Radio
'Well, that's certainly one way to celebrate a win.'

Three – Ferret Footy
'Bestavros and Cunningham sharing a brotherly . . .'
'Yeah, I don't know about that.'

Two – Australian National Radio
'Bestavros! Bestavros! What a goal. He's in the midst of a flock of Falcons players. He's . . .' [the sound of someone falling off a chair]

One – AFL Federation Radio
'Bestavros is going to be remembered for – oh my God. Oh my GOD.'
'Wow.'
'We are witnessing HISTORY. THIS IS HISTORY.'
'We are also witnessing a lot of tongue.'
'HISTORY.'

Chapter Twenty-Six

Theo sat up and slid the slice of cucumber off his right eye. Priya had arrived two days after his on-field kiss with Jake, and she'd wasted no time in booking them in for an afternoon at the kind of day spa that didn't list their prices anywhere you could see them. They'd had to put their phones in a box, and now they were lying on very comfortable massage tables in soft linen robes. Kiara, their 'wellness guide', had left them with a platter of sliced fruit, a pot of green tea, and an instruction to 'let go of all your worries and spend some quality time together'. (Priya had booked them a couples package in order to get the bonus mud wrap. Theo's protests that he spent enough time covered in mud had been ignored.)

Jake had been a little disappointed that he wasn't invited, but Theo had explained that it was mainly Priya's stratagem for getting him away from Eva, his visiting parents, and his phone. Jake had accepted his lot, but had demanded that Theo bring him back 'some bougie skin stuff'.

Theo exhaled. The spa was ridiculous, but he had to admit it was quite soothing. The room had a fountain on one wall, and the soft sound of running water mingled with the sort of gentle music Theo associated with yoga classes. It *was* nice to be in a space where he couldn't reach for his phone every thirty seconds.

He didn't regret what he and Jake had done, but there was a lot to deal with. The Falcons had been able to keep things pretty locked down, taking a firm line that they weren't going to say anything about anything until the season was done. But there had been articles, and opinion pieces, and talk-back radio callers. He and Jake had a dozen invitations each to be interviewed or appear on podcasts. The team, taking their lead from Yelks, had been supportive, but Theo still felt a bit like he was white-water rafting towards the preliminary final, hoping his boat wasn't going to smash into a boulder.

He peeled off the other cucumber slice and set them both down next to the tray of fruit. Hopefully he'd remember not to eat them. '"Wellness guide"?' he asked. He supposed it could have been worse. He'd have drawn the line at *wellness guru* or *wellness sherpa*.

Priya sat up and removed her own cucumber slices. 'I feel very effectively guided towards wellness.' The face mask she'd chosen was a vibrant green. He'd gone for a lavender one.

'Sure, Elphaba.'

She picked up an apple slice and munched on it thoughtfully. 'So, where should we start? I feel like we need a meeting agenda.'

'I'm surprised you didn't prepare one.'

'Trust me, I was tempted. But seriously, are you okay?'

Theo thought about it. 'I mean, it's a lot. But I'm okay.' He'd had a bit of a moment the day after the semi-final, but he'd been able to go and see Jenny, and they'd talked things through and come up with a plan. A lot of the plan was about writing things down and setting them aside to deal with after the prelim.

'Not to get all sappy, but it was a pretty awesome thing to do.' Priya hadn't been watching the game, but a mutual friend had called her and got her to switch on the TV in the minutes afterwards. 'A lot of the coverage has been great.' Priya had banned Theo from any googling, but she was collating an album of material he could look at once the finals were done. She took a dainty bite out of a strawberry. 'Things with your parents seem more relaxed.'

Theo nodded and poured tea for them both. Genmaicha, from the nutty smell. 'I think it's been good that Eva had a heart-to-heart with them as well. They're definitely trying to be supportive with both of us. And to at least ask questions to see where we're coming from, rather than just making pronouncements. I think it's going to take a while, but at least they're making an effort. And maybe I was projecting some of my own insecurities and anxieties on to them.'

Priya nodded. 'And they like Jake?'

'I think so.' It was hard to tell, with his parents. Jake was nothing like either of his previous girlfriends. 'I don't think they really know what to make of him. But, again – it's a start.'

'Please invite me to the Cunningham and Bestavros family introduction when it happens. I want to see it, and I also want to meet Keeley properly.' Priya and Keeley had joined Jake and Theo for a very lively FaceTime call; she and Keeley had immediately devised a social-media strategy for Jake, and had created a collaborative document to shortlist social media and marketing managers Jake could employ.

Theo snorted. 'Let's not get ahead of ourselves.'

'Come on. You two are so revoltingly in love that I'm already planning my best-man speech. It's going to be the highlight of your wedding.'

Anything Theo said in response to that was going to be either a lie or deeply incriminating. 'Do *you* like him?' he asked instead.

Priya took a sip of her tea. 'Yeah, more than I thought I might, to be honest. I like the two of you together. He makes you smile, and he won't let you take yourself too seriously. I wasn't sure I'd be able to get beyond the socks-and-Crocs aesthetic, but I'm making an effort, just for you.'

'That's very generous of you.'

'I know.' Priya stretched. 'I can't wait for the massages – my lower back hates me.'

'Whereas I'm all about the mud wrap, as you know.' He put his cup down. 'Thanks for coming to visit. Having you around makes everything feel more manageable. You know it means a lot.'

'Let's not get emotional,' she said. 'I don't want my face mask to run.'

'That face mask looks like concrete, I think it could survive anything.'

'I don't want Kiara to think we're fighting.'

That made Theo laugh. 'Still, thanks.'

'There's nowhere else I'd rather be,' she told him. 'More tea?'

'Yes please.'

It was Priya, in the end, who accidentally ate one of the cucumber slices. Kiara walked in just as she threw the other one at Theo's head.

Jake had thought he'd known what it was like to be the centre of attention. It turned out that there was attention and then there was *we are the first two out queer men's footy players and we're dating one another*. Jake was getting so many messages on social media that he was letting Keeley manage them. Theo and Jake been photographed getting out of Jake's car together in the club car park like Jake was a fucking Kardashian.

Some of the coverage had been . . . not great. Jake had expected that, of course. Tried to keep away from it. But it was hard to be online at all and not catch glimpses of it. There had, in fact, been a *Full Forward* skit. He hadn't watched it. Paddy *had* watched it, making a sound the whole time like a kettle on the boil.

A small, scared part of him had wondered if Theo would end up regretting it, even though after the game he'd said he didn't. But Theo seemed like a weight had come off his shoulders, too. He laughed more easily, and he'd started to touch Jake casually in public; linking their fingers together or slipping a hand into Jake's back pocket.

Jake was never wearing pants without back pockets again.

One downside was they'd had to attend a lot of meetings. Apparently the idea that two players might *date* was a real shock to management. And to Greg.

Greg had been very supportive, in a confused kind of way, and was working on a media release from the club. Jake had heard on the grapevine that the club was hiring a consultant to help manage the social media. That seemed wise. Greg couldn't even keep track of what all the letters in LGBTQIA+ stood for.

Theo's parents had tickets to the prelim final. Jake had met them during the week, briefly, for dinner, and had done his best to make a good impression. He'd worn a shirt with buttons and everything. Jake thought it had gone pretty well, all things considered. Coming out was one thing. Snogging your boyfriend on national TV was another.

Theo had obviously been nervous, but he'd given Jake an unimpressed look when Jake had joked that he wasn't model-boyfriend material for serious, academic parents. *All they should care about is that you make me happy,* he'd said. And then they'd nearly been late for dinner.

They'd all had drinks together in the courtyard of Eva's terrace. Eva had pulled Jake into the kitchen to help with the salad to give Theo some time alone with his parents. By the time they'd come back, Theo was laughing at something his mum was saying. His dad had asked Jake some questions about football, and Jake thought he'd done a pretty good job overall. It had been a bit awkward, but Jake didn't know if meeting someone's parents was ever not a bit awkward. They'd been nicer than Kyle's parents had ever been.

(Jake hadn't been allowed to *actually* help with the salad. Not after Eva had seen him chop the first tomato.)

Jake sighed and shifted on the foam roller. They had an hour or so before they needed to be warmed up. It was going to be a rough game. You never knew your luck in the big city, but they'd lost Yelks, Tommy and Raze, and they were playing the Crocodiles, who were on a hot streak and almost untouched by injury. Still, it was footy. Anything could happen, and if Jake had his way they'd be going to the granny.

'Hey,' Theo said, settling down beside him. 'All good?'

'All good.'

They'd driven in together, but Theo had gone off to lie on the grass and do whatever mindfulness stuff he did before games.

It had been fine in the locker room during the week. The main problem seemed to be everyone trying to work out how much shit they could dish out before it became homophobic. Paddy was leading the charge to find out.

Jake was assisting Theo with a hamstring stretch when Tenders walked in.

'Jesus, at least save it until after the game,' he said. But it was good natured. He came over to stretch with them. Tenders hadn't *said* anything about any of it, but he'd taken to putting himself in their proximity, as though he could signal support with his physical presence.

The energy was high before the game, even if they were the underdogs by a country mile. Nobody had thought they'd go deep into the finals this year, so it all felt like a bonus. Yelks gave them a good gee-up before warm-ups, and then Jake put his headphones on and jogged an easy lap of the MCG, Theo running beside him.

The crowd was already filtering in and Jake stopped a couple of times to sign things. He had a bet with Gabby about the reappearance of the snowflake signs, but there was no evidence of them yet.

He took shots on goal for a while, mucking around with Paddy like he always did. It felt absolutely normal, but also absolutely new. His first game as an out player.

He went back down the race a little earlier than usual, before the crowd had really filled up.

By the time they were ready to go, Jake was rocking back and forth on the balls of his feet, itching to be out there. His favourite sound in the world was the roar of the crowd growing louder as he walked up the race. The way that, as he got closer, he could hear individual voices, individual shouts. The way people dangled scarves down like banners. The blur of faces, shouting encouragement.

With Yelks and Raze benched, Sheds led them up as acting captain. Jake exchanged his game-day fist bump with Xen and his game-day chest bump with Paddy. Theo found a spot beside him. Jake knew he still got stressed about games – fuck, *Jake* was stressed about this one – but he was smiling all the same.

They set off up the race together, and Jake reached for Theo's hand. They walked out into a wall of sound and Jake heard people yelling his name, yelling Theo's name. The air was thick from the smoke machine, and there was the pop of fireworks as Sheds led them towards the banner.

They stepped out onto the grass together, and Jake froze. The stands were always a sea of colour on game days. This time, it was a sea of rainbows. There were rainbow flags everywhere: behind the Falcons' goals, behind the Crocodiles' goals, throughout the MCC. People in both teams' jumpers waving flags and scarves and rainbow cut-outs. Kids being held up with rainbow face paint on. The volume increased, and Jake realised he and Theo were up on the screen, both looking stunned. It wasn't *everyone*, but it was enough. More than enough.

The camera started to cut between people in the crowd: queer couples waving, queer families holding up their kids, someone with a rainbow mohawk, a group of friends in rainbow wings and glittery eyeshadow. The Falcons mascot in a pride scarf. A group of fans each holding a rainbow letter to spell 'Falcons'.

'Wow,' Theo said, softly. Like he was in a library, or in church.

'Yeah.'

Jake realised he could do this. *They* could do this. He blew a kiss to the crowd, then stood on his tiptoes to kiss Theo on the cheek. That got him another roar of approval.

'You boys ready?' Tenders asked, coming up behind them to nudge them towards the banner. 'Or are you going to smooch?'

'Play now, smooch later,' Jake confirmed.

They jogged forward to join the rest of the team, still holding hands, stepping into the smoke and sparks. They ran through, together, between Xen and Paddy. Jake looked up at the rippling strands of the banner as it disintegrated around the team, at the blue sky, at the swirl of rainbow all around the MCG.

'I love you,' he said to Theo, leaning close so Theo could hear him over the crowd. He wasn't sure why he needed to say it *now*.

Theo grinned at him. 'I get it. I'm pretty great.'

Jake grinned back. 'Asshole.'

'I love you too.'

'Let's play some footy?'

Theo nodded. 'Let's play some footy.'

Acknowledgements

I love reading Acknowledgements. They remind me that my favourite books by my favourite authors didn't appear fully formed on the shelf. It is deeply weird, and deeply lovely, to be sitting down to write an Acknowledgements section of my own. There are quite a few people I need to thank. You have been warned.

I should start with my Australian agent, Rochelle Fernandez, for her support, enthusiasm, and sage advice. Thanks also to my wonderful US agent, Kate McKean, for being willing to embrace the alien sport of AFL.

Next comes the team of wonderful people at Penguin Random House – especially Chris Ebbs, who really *got* this book from the very beginning, and Johannes Jakob, who made it a much better book. I knew from the moment I met both of you that I could trust you with this story. Massive thanks also to Phoebe McKenzie, Grace Howe and Chi Chi Zhu. I'm also indebted to Bobuq Sayed for their thoughtful comments.

Before I get to anyone else, I want to acknowledge my wonderful wife. Thank you for your unflagging love and belief, and your encyclopaedic AFL knowledge. I'll dedicate the next one to you, I promise.

After The Siren had a strange pathway to publication, and I want to thank the team of people who did incredible work on it when I planned to take the indie-publishing path: Steph Preston at The Preston Edit, Duncan Blachford at Typography Studio, and Alaina Gougoulis. The fact that Jess Cruickshank's wonderful cover has made it onto this version of the book is a delight to me. I can't imagine it with a different one.

Anna Cowan is basically a literary fairy godmother, and none of this would have happened without her.

Charlotte Ivey has been working with me on marketing and design plans since I first decided I wanted to launch this book into the world, and I can't imagine doing any of this without her. Will Cox gave me some excellent advice (I even followed some of it).

Deanne, you have been a staunch supporter of my writing for so long. You made this book better. Bridget, Tom – thanks for being my first readers, and for loving these two boys. Radhika, I can't imagine the last ten years of my life without you in them. Em, I'm so glad we met when we did.

There are many other people who have supported me and this book. To avoid the trap of trying to list everyone and inevitably forgetting someone important, I'm going to leave it there. I do have to say a big thank you to the owners and staff of John Gorilla (now O.X. Cafe). You've kept me going on some bad days.

Okay, okay, I'm nearly done. A final thank you to everyone who encouraged me to write – my family, good teachers, comment-ers on LiveJournal and AO3.

Gran, I know you always thought I'd write a book. You probably wouldn't have expected it to be this one, but – I did it. I love you.

Powered by Penguin

Looking for more great reads, exclusive content and book giveaways?

Subscribe to our weekly newsletter.

Scan the QR code or visit penguin.com.au/signup